I must be near the camp now! he thought desperately, his paws skidding on the loose leaves.

Pain pierced his tail as the fox cub snapped at it with thorn-sharp teeth. Jaykit dug his claws into the ground, running faster and faster, until, without warning, the ground disappeared from beneath his paws.

With a jolt of horror, Jaykit felt himself plunging into empty air.

I've fallen into the hollow!

WARRIORS

Book One: Into the Wild

Book Two: Fire and Ice

Book Three: Forest of Secrets

Book Four: Rising Storm

Book Five: A Dangerous Path

Book Six: The Darkest Hour

WARRIORS: THE NEW PROPHECY

Book One: Midnight

Book Two: Moonrise

Book Three: Dawn

Book Four: Starlight

Book Five: Twilight

Book Six: Sunset

WARRIORS: POWER OF THREE

Book One: The Sight

Book Two: Dark River

WARRIORS MANGA

The Lost Warrior

Warrior's Refuge

WARRIORS SUPER EDITION: *Firestar's Quest*

WARRIORS FIELD GUIDE: *Secrets of the Clans*

POWER OF THREE

WARRIORS

THE SIGHT

ERIN HUNTER

HarperTrophy®
An Imprint of HarperCollinsPublishers

Harper Trophy® is a registered trademark of HarperCollins Publishers.

The Sight
Copyright © 2007 by Working Partners Limited
Series created by Working Partners Limited

Library of Congress Cataloging-in-Publication Data
Hunter, Erin.
  The Sight / Erin Hunter — 1st ed.
      p.   cm. (Warriors, power of three ; bk. 1)
  Summary: In a troubled time for the Clans, three young cats,
grandchildren of the legendary Firestar, begin their training as warriors
and, in the course of many adventures, discover their true destiny.
  ISBN 978-0-06-089204-3
  [1. Cats—Juvenile fiction. 2. Brothers and sisters—Juvenile fiction.
3. Adventure and adventurers—Juvenile fiction. 4. Cats—Fiction.
5. Brothers and sisters—Fiction. 6. Adventure and adventurers—Fiction.
7. Fantasy.] I. Title.
PZ7.H916625 Sig 2007   2007011860
[Fic]—dc22   CIP
                                                              AC

Typography by Rob Hult
❖
First Harper Trophy edition, 2008
12 13 LP/BR 20 19 18 17 16 15 14

With special thanks to
Kate Cary

ALLEGIANCES

THUNDERCLAN

LEADER

FIRESTAR—ginger tom with a flame-colored pelt

DEPUTY

BRAMBLECLAW—dark brown tabby tom with amber eyes
APPRENTICE, BERRYPAW

MEDICINE CAT

LEAFPOOL—light brown tabby she-cat with amber eyes

WARRIORS

(toms, and she-cats without kits)

DUSTPELT—dark brown tabby tom
APPRENTICE, HAZELPAW

SANDSTORM—pale ginger she-cat
APPRENTICE, HONEYPAW

CLOUDTAIL—long-haired white tom
APPRENTICE, CINDERPAW

BRACKENFUR—golden brown tabby tom

THORNCLAW—golden brown tabby tom
APPRENTICE, POPPYPAW

BRIGHTHEART—white she-cat with ginger patches

ASHFUR—pale gray (with darker flecks) tom, dark blue eyes

SORRELTAIL—tortoiseshell and white she-cat with amber eyes

SPIDERLEG—long-limbed black tom with brown underbelly and amber eyes
APPRENTICE, MOUSEPAW

BROOK WHERE SMALL FISH SWIM

(BROOK)—brown tabby she-cat with gray eyes, formerly of the Tribe of Rushing Water

STORMFUR—dark gray tom with amber eyes, formerly of RiverClan

WHITEWING—white she-cat with green eyes

BIRCHFALL—light brown tabby tom

APPRENTICES   (more than six moons old, in training to become warriors)

BERRYPAW—cream-colored tom

HAZELPAW—small gray and white she-cat

MOUSEPAW—gray and white tom

CINDERPAW—gray tabby she-cat

HONEYPAW—light brown tabby she-cat

POPPYPAW—tortoiseshell she-cat

QUEENS   (she-cats expecting or nursing kits)

FERNCLOUD—pale gray (with darker flecks) she-cat, green eyes, mother of Dustpelt's kits: Icekit and Foxkit

DAISY—cream long-furred cat from the horseplace

SQUIRRELFLIGHT—dark ginger she-cat with green eyes, mother of Brambleclaw's kits: Lionkit, Hollykit, and Jaykit

ELDERS   (former warriors and queens, now retired)

LONGTAIL—pale tabby tom with dark black stripes, retired early due to failing sight

MOUSEFUR—small dusky brown she-cat

SHADOWCLAN

LEADER   **BLACKSTAR**—large white tom with huge jet-black paws

DEPUTY   **RUSSETFUR**—dark ginger she-cat

MEDICINE CAT   **LITTLECLOUD**—very small tabby tom

WARRIORS   **OAKFUR**—small brown tom

ROWANCLAW—ginger tom
APPRENTICE, IVYPAW

SMOKEFOOT—black tom
APPRENTICE, OWLPAW

SNOWBIRD—pure white she-cat

QUEENS   **TAWNYPELT**—tortoiseshell she-cat with green eyes

ELDERS   **CEDARHEART**—dark gray tom

TALLPOPPY—long-legged light brown tabby she-cat

WINDCLAN

LEADER   **ONESTAR**—brown tabby tom

DEPUTY   **ASHFOOT**—gray she-cat

MEDICINE CAT   **BARKFACE**—short-tailed brown tom
APPRENTICE, KESTRELPAW

WARRIORS   **TORNEAR**—tabby tom
APPRENTICE, HAREPAW

CROWFEATHER—dark gray tom
APPRENTICE, HEATHERPAW

OWLWHISKER—light brown tabby tom

WHITETAIL—small white she-cat
APPRENTICE, BREEZEPAW

NIGHTCLOUD—black she-cat

WEASELFUR—ginger tom with white paws

ELDERS

MORNINGFLOWER—very old tortoiseshell queen

WEBFOOT—dark gray tabby tom

RIVERCLAN

LEADER

LEOPARDSTAR—unusually spotted golden tabby she-cat

DEPUTY

MISTYFOOT—gray she-cat with blue eyes
APPRENTICE, DAPPLEPAW

MEDICINE CAT

MOTHWING—dappled golden she-cat
APPRENTICE, WILLOWPAW

WARRIORS

BLACKCLAW—smoky black tom

VOLETOOTH—small brown tabby tom
APPRENTICE, MINNOWPAW

REEDWHISKER—black tom
APPRENTICE, POUNCEPAW

MOSSPELT—tortoiseshell she-cat with blue eyes
APPRENTICE, PEBBLEPAW

BEECHFUR—light brown tom

RIPPLETAIL—dark gray tabby tom

QUEENS

DAWNFLOWER—pale gray she-cat

ELDERS

HEAVYSTEP—thickset tabby tom

SWALLOWTAIL—dark tabby she-cat

STONESTREAM—gray tom

CATS OUTSIDE CLANS

GRAYSTRIPE—long-haired gray tom

MILLIE—small silver tabby kittypet

POWER OF THREE

WARRIORS

THE SIGHT

Hareview Campsite
Sanctuary Cottage
Sadler Woods
Littlepine Road
Littlepine Sailing Center
Littlepine Island
River Alba
Whitchurch Road

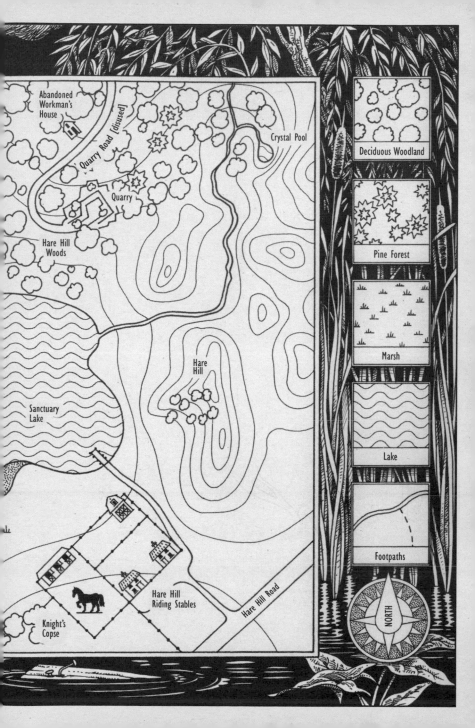

Abandoned
Workman's
House

Quarry Road [disused]

Crystal Pool

Quarry

Hare Hill
Woods

Sanctuary
Lake

Hare
Hill

Hare Hill
Riding Stables

Hare Hill Road

Knight's
Copse

Deciduous Woodland

Pine Forest

Marsh

Lake

Footpaths

NORTH

PROLOGUE

❧

Muddied tree roots shaped a small opening. In the shadows beyond, the knotted tendrils cradled the smooth soil floor of a cave, hollowed out by moons of wind and water.

A cat padded up the steep path toward the opening, narrowing his eyes as he neared. His flame-colored pelt glowed in the moonlight. His ears twitched, and the bristling of his fur gave away his unease as he sat down at the mouth of the cave and curled his tail across his paws. "You asked me to come."

From the shadows, a pair of eyes blinked at him—eyes as blue as water reflecting the summer sky. A gray tom, scarred by time and battle, was waiting in the entrance.

"Firestar." The warrior stepped forward and brushed the ThunderClan leader's cheek with his white-flecked muzzle. "I have to thank you." His mew was hoarse with age. "You have rebuilt the lost Clan. No cat could have done better."

"There's no need for thanks." Firestar dipped his head. "I did only what I had to."

The old warrior nodded, blinking thoughtfully. "Do you think you have been a good leader for ThunderClan?"

Firestar tensed. "I don't know," he mewed. "It hasn't been easy, but I've always tried to do what is right for my Clan."

"No cat would doubt your loyalty," the old cat rasped. "But how far would it go?"

Firestar's eyes glittered uncertainly as he searched for the words to answer.

"There are difficult times ahead," the warrior went on before Firestar could reply. "And your loyalty will be tested to the utmost. Sometimes the destiny of one cat is not the destiny of the whole Clan."

Suddenly the old cat rose stiffly to his paws and stared past Firestar. It seemed he no longer saw the ThunderClan leader but gazed far beyond, to something Firestar could not see.

When he spoke again, the ancient rasp was smoothed from his voice, as though some other cat used his tongue.

"*There will be three, kin of your kin, who hold the power of the stars in their paws.*"

"I don't understand," Firestar meowed. "Kin of my kin? Why are you telling me this?"

The old warrior blinked, his gaze fixed once more on Firestar.

"You must tell me more!" Firestar demanded. "How can I decide what I ought to do if you don't explain?"

The old cat took a deep breath, but when he spoke it was only to say, "Farewell, Firestar. In seasons to come, remember me."

★ ★ ★

Firestar jerked awake, his belly tight with fear. He blinked with relief when he saw the familiar stone walls of his den in the hollow by the lake. Morning sunlight streamed through the split in the rock. The warmth on his fur soothed him.

He heaved himself to his paws and shook his head, trying to dislodge the dream. But this was no ordinary dream, for he remembered being in that cave as clearly as if it had happened a moon ago, rather than the many, many seasons he had lived since then. When the old warrior cast his strange prophecy, Firestar's daughters had not been born and the four Clans had still lived in the forest. The prophecy had followed him on the Great Journey over the mountains and settled with him in his new home by the lake; and every full moon, the memory of it returned to fill his dreams. Even Sandstorm, who slept beside him, knew nothing of the words he had shared with the ancient cat.

He gazed out from his den at the waking camp below. His deputy, Brambleclaw, was stretching in the center of the clearing, flexing his powerful shoulders as he clawed at the ground. Squirrelflight padded toward her mate, greeting him with a purr.

I pray that I am wrong, Firestar thought. And yet his heart felt hollow; he feared the prophecy was about to reveal itself.

The three have come. . . .

CHAPTER 1

✢

Leaves brushed Jaykit's pelt like falling snow. More crackled under-paw, stiff with frost and so deep that he struggled with every step. An icy wind pierced his fur—still nursery soft—and made him shiver.

"Wait for me!" he wailed. He could hear his mother's voice ahead, her warm body always a few steps out of reach.

"You'll never catch it!"

A high-pitched mew sliced into his dream, and Jaykit woke with a start. He pricked his ears, listening to the famil-iar sounds of the bramble nursery. His sister and brother scrabbling in play. Ferncloud lapping her dozing kits. There was no snow now; he was in the camp, safe and warm. He could smell his mother's nest, empty but still fresh with her scent.

"Oof!" He let out a gasp of surprise as his sister, Hollykit, landed heavily on top of him. "Watch out!"

"You're awake at last!" She rolled off him and pushed her hind paws into his flank. With a leap, she twisted away and grasped for something just out of reach.

Mouse! Jaykit could smell it. His brother and sister must

be playing catch with fresh-kill newly brought into camp. He sprang to his paws and gave a quick stretch that sent a shiver through his small body.

"Catch this, Jaykit!" Hollykit mewed. The mouse whistled past his ear.

"Slow slug!" she teased as he turned too late to grab it.

"I've got it!" Lionkit called. He pounced on the fresh-kill, his paws thudding on the nursery's packed earth floor.

Jaykit wasn't going to let his brother steal the prize from him so easily. He might be the smallest in the litter, but he was fast. He leaped toward Lionkit, knocking him out of the way and stretching his forepaw to reach for the mouse.

He landed in a clumsy skid and rolled over, feeling a jolt of alarm as he realized it wasn't moss underneath him, but the squirming warmth of Ferncloud's two tiny kits. Ferncloud gave him a shove, pushing him away with her hind paws.

Jaykit gasped. "Have I hurt them?"

"Of course not," Ferncloud snapped. "You're too small to squash a flea!" Foxkit and Icekit mewled as she tucked them closer into her belly. "But you three are getting too rough for the nursery!"

"Sorry, Ferncloud," Hollykit mewed.

"Sorry," Jaykit echoed, apologetic even though Ferncloud's comment on his size had stung him. At least the queen's anger would not last. She would easily forgive kits she had suckled—when Squirrelflight's milk had not come, it was Ferncloud who had fed Jaykit, Hollykit, and Lionkit in the moons before Foxkit and Icekit were born.

"It's about time Firestar made you apprentices and moved you to the apprentice den," Ferncloud meowed.

"If only." Lionkit sighed.

"It won't be long," Hollykit pointed out. "We're almost six moons old."

Jaykit felt the familiar surge of excitement as he imagined becoming an apprentice warrior. He couldn't wait to begin his training. But without even seeing Ferncloud's face, he could sense the flicker of doubt that prickled through the queen's pelt and knew that she was looking at him with pity in her eyes. His fur bristled with frustration—he was just as ready to become an apprentice as Hollykit and Lionkit!

Ferncloud answered Hollykit, unaware that Jaykit had sensed her moment of unease. "Well, you're not six moons yet! And until you are, you can do your playing outside!" she ordered.

"Yes, Ferncloud," Lionkit replied meekly.

"Come on, Jaykit," Hollykit called. "Bring the mouse with you." The branches of the bramble bush rustled as she slid out through the nursery entrance.

Jaykit picked up the mouse delicately in his teeth. It was newly killed and soft, and he didn't want to make it bleed—they could have a good, clean game with it yet. With Lionkit close behind him, he scrabbled out after his sister. The barbs of the entrance tunnel clawed satisfyingly at his fur, sharp enough to tug at his pelt but not so sharp that they hurt.

Outside, the air smelled crisp and frosty. Firestar was sharing tongues with Sandstorm below Highledge. Dustpelt sat with them.

"We should be thinking about expanding the warriors' den," the dark tabby advised his leader. "It's crowded already, and Daisy and Sorreltail's kits won't be apprentices forever."

Nor will we! thought Jaykit.

Brightheart and Cloudtail were grooming each other in a pool of sunlight on the other side of the clearing. Jaykit could hear the steady lapping of their tongues like water dripping from a rain-soaked leaf. Like all the ThunderClan cats, their pelts were leaf-bare thick, but the muscles beneath had grown lean with scarce prey and hard hunting.

Hunger was not the only hardship leaf-bare had brought. Molepaw, one of Sorreltail's kits, had died of a cough that had not responded to Leafpool's herbs, and Rainwhisker had been killed during a storm, struck by a falling branch.

Brightheart paused from her washing. "How are you today, Jaykit?"

Jaykit placed the mouse between his paws, safe from Hollykit's grasp. "I'm fine, of course," he meowed. Why did Brightheart have to make such a fuss over him? He'd only been sleeping in the nursery, not out raiding ShadowClan territory! It was like she was always keeping her one good eye on him. Eager to prove he was just as strong as his brother and sister, Jaykit flung the mouse high over Hollykit's head.

As Lionkit thundered past him and grappled with Hollykit to be the first to catch it, Squirrelflight's voice sounded from the side of the nursery. "You should show more respect for your prey!" Their mother was busy pressing leaves into gaps in the prickly walls that surrounded the queens' den.

Daisy was helping her. "Kits will be kits," the white she-cat purred indulgently.

Jaykit's nostrils flared at Daisy's strange scent. It was different from the Clanborn cats', and some of the warriors still referred to her as a kittypet because she had once lived in the horseplace and eaten Twoleg food. Daisy wasn't a warrior, because she showed no sign that she ever wished to leave the nursery, but her kits Mousepaw, Hazelpaw, and Berrypaw were apprentices, and it seemed to Jaykit that they were as Clanborn as any of his Clanmates.

"They won't be kits much longer," Squirrelflight told Daisy, sweeping more leaves to her side with her long tail. The brittle rustling noise reminded Jaykit of his dream.

"All the more reason to let them enjoy themselves now," Daisy replied.

Jaykit felt a wave of affection for the milky white she-cat. Though Squirrelflight was his mother, it had been Daisy who had warmed and washed him alongside Ferncloud when Clan duties had kept his mother away from the nursery. Squirrelflight had returned to her warrior duties soon after her kits had been born. Though she still had a nest in the nursery, she used it less and less, preferring to sleep in the warriors' den, where she wouldn't disturb the kits and nursing queens when she left on early patrols.

"Can you feel the draft now, Ferncloud?" Squirrelflight called through the nursery wall.

"No." Ferncloud's voice drifted out through the tangle of branches. "We're warm as fox cubs in here."

"Good," Squirrelflight meowed. "Can you clear up here, Daisy? I promised Brambleclaw I'd help him check for loose rocks around the hollow."

"Loose rocks?" Daisy gasped.

"It's good to have such solid defenses." Squirrelflight's voice echoed a little as she gazed at the sheer stone cliffs that enclosed the camp on almost every side. "But the frost might have loosened stones, and we don't want them falling into the camp."

Jaykit's attention was distracted by the bitter stench of mouse bile that came from the elders' den. Leafpool must be removing a tick from Longtail or Mousefur. A much nicer odor heralded the return of two of Daisy's kits—Mousepaw and Hazelpaw were bringing fresh-kill back from a hunting expedition. They hurried excitedly into the camp, Mousepaw carrying two mice and Hazelpaw with a large thrush in her jaws. They dropped them at the fresh-kill pile.

Dustpelt padded over to greet them. "Looks like you did well, Hazelpaw!" he praised his apprentice. "You both did." The apprentices purred, and Jaykit noticed how much they sounded like their mother, as though their purrs were muffled by their thick, soft pelts.

A sudden rush of wind and fur knocked Jaykit off his paws.

"Are you playing with us or not?" Hollykit demanded.

Jaykit leaped up, shaking himself. "Of course I am!"

"Well, Lionkit's got the mouse, and he won't let me have it!" Hollykit complained.

"Let's get him then!" Jaykit hared across the clearing

toward his brother. He bundled into Lionkit and pressed him to the frosty earth while Hollykit dragged the mouse from Lionkit's claws.

"Unfair!" Lionkit protested.

"We don't have to be fair," Hollykit squeaked triumphantly. "We're not in StarClan yet!"

"And you never *will* be if you keep playing with food that way!" Stormfur had paused beside them on his way to the warriors' den. His words were stern, though his voice was warm. "It's leaf-bare. We should thank StarClan for every morsel."

Lionkit wriggled out from underneath Jaykit. "We're just practicing our hunting skills!"

"We have to practice," Jaykit added, sitting up. "We'll be apprentices soon."

Stormfur was silent for a moment; then he stretched forward and gave Jaykit a quick lick between the ears. "Of course," he murmured. "I was forgetting."

Frustration flared in Jaykit's belly. Why did the whole Clan treat him like a newborn kit when he was nearly six moons old? He shook his head crossly. Stormfur wasn't even a proper ThunderClan cat! His father, Graystripe, had once been ThunderClan's deputy, but Stormfur had grown up with his mother's Clanmates in RiverClan, and his mate, Brook, had come from far away in the mountains. What right did he have to act superior?

Hollykit's belly rumbled. "How about we eat this mouse instead of playing with it?"

"You two share it," Lionkit offered. "I'll get something from the fresh-kill pile."

Jaykit turned toward the heap of prey caught by the warriors that morning. A faint odor disturbed him. He took in a deeper breath, opening his jaws to draw the scents into his mouth: he could smell Hazelpaw's freshly killed thrush and Mousepaw's mice, their blood still warm. But below there was a sour smell that made his tongue curl. He padded past his brother, his tail held stiffly behind him.

"What are you doing?" Lionkit asked.

Jaykit didn't answer. He nosed his way in among the small dead bodies, caught hold of a wren, and pulled it free. "Look!" he mewed, rolling the bird over with his paw. The creature's belly was alive with maggots.

"Ugh!" Hollykit squealed.

Leafpool emerged from the elders' den, a wad of moss in her jaws. Jaykit could smell the mouse bile on it even over the stench of the rotten wren. She paused by the three kits. "Well spotted," she praised them, dropping the bile-soaked moss at her paws. "I know prey is scarce at the moment, but better to eat nothing than to eat something that will hurt your belly."

"Jaykit found it," Hollykit told her.

"Well, he's saved me a patient," Leafpool meowed. "I'm busy enough as it is. Brackenfur and Birchfall have white-cough."

"Do you want help gathering herbs?" Jaykit offered. He had never been out of the camp, and he was desperate to explore the forest. He wanted to smell the boundary markers;

up till now he had tasted only the weak scents of ShadowClan and WindClan carried from the borders on the pelts of ThunderClan patrols. He wanted to feel the breeze fresh off the lake, untainted by the scents of the forest. He wanted to learn where the markers were along each boundary so that he could defend every pawstep of his Clan's territory.

"You could gather far more herbs with us to carry them back to camp!" Lionkit put in.

"You know you're not meant to leave the camp until you're apprentices," Leafpool reminded them.

"But you'll need help if there are sick cats . . . ," Jaykit insisted.

Leafpool silenced him by flicking the tip of her tail over his mouth. "I'm sorry, Jaykit," she meowed. "It won't be long until Firestar gives you your apprentice names. But until then, you'll have to wait like any other kits."

Jaykit understood her meaning. Their father was the Clan deputy, and their mother was Firestar's daughter; Leafpool was reminding them yet again that it did not entitle them to special treatment. His tail twitched crossly. Sometimes it felt like the rest of the Clan went out of their way to make sure he and his littermates *never* got special treatment. It wasn't fair!

"I'm sorry," Leafpool meowed. "But that's just the way it is." She picked up the foul-smelling moss and padded back to the medicine den.

"Nice try," Lionkit whispered in Jaykit's ear. "But it looks like we're stuck in the camp for a while longer."

"Leafpool always thinks she can win us over just because she brings wool for our nests from the moorland," Jaykit hissed. "Or pieces of honeycomb to lick. Why can't she just give us what we really want—a chance to explore outside the camp?"

Hollykit swished her tail over the frozen ground. Jaykit knew she wanted to explore beyond the camp walls as much as he and Lionkit did. "But she's right," she mewed grudgingly. "We must stick to the warrior code."

They ate, sharing the mouse and a vole between them. As Jaykit washed his face afterward, drawing his paws over his ears to give them a thorough cleaning, he noticed Brook emerging from the warriors' den to join Cloudtail and Brightheart in the sun. She carried a different scent from the other warriors, the scent of mountains and tumbling water. It seemed to make her the strangest of all the cats who were not Clanborn. Was it just her scent, Jaykit wondered, or was it something more he sensed in the mountain she-cat—some wariness that had never left her? He could not quite put his whisker on it, but he was sure that Brook felt out of place here in the forest.

A rustle in the thorn barrier that protected the entrance to the camp signaled Berrypaw's return. Daisy's third kit charged over to the fresh-kill pile and threw down his catch—a plump wood pigeon.

"Where's Brambleclaw?" Berrypaw called out to the kits. Brambleclaw was Berrypaw's mentor, and Jaykit could not help but feel a small pang of jealousy that Berrypaw spent so much time training with Brambleclaw when his own paws ached to hunt in the forest with his father.

"He's with Squirrelflight," Jaykit replied. "They're checking for loose stones." He pricked his ears, listening for the sound of his mother's and father's voices. He could not hear them, but the breeze blowing down from the cliff behind the medicine den carried their scent.

"Up there," he told Berrypaw, lifting his nose toward them.

"You're sharp today, Jaykit!" Berrypaw meowed. "I wanted to show him my pigeon and ask him if we were doing battle training after sunhigh."

Jealousy gnawed harder in Jaykit's belly. *Why can't I be an apprentice now?*

"You must be really good at hunting." Lionkit sighed, clearly thinking the same thing.

"It's just practice," Berrypaw told them. "Look." He crouched down. "This is how you begin."

Lionkit's belly swished against the ground as he tried to copy Berrypaw.

"Get your tail down!" Berrypaw ordered. "It's sticking up like a bluebell!"

Lionkit's tail slapped against the frozen earth.

"Now pull yourself forward, smooth as a snake," Berrypaw commanded.

"You look like you've got wind!" Hollykit crowed.

Lionkit gave a playful hiss and leaped at her, rolling her onto the ground. She fought back, purring with amusement while Lionkit pummeled her belly with his hind paws.

They were so busy in their play fight that they did not notice the sudden noise outside the camp.

But Jaykit did.

Cats' paws were pounding toward the camp entrance. Jaykit recognized the scents of Spiderleg and Thornclaw. The patrol was returning. But something was wrong. The warriors' paws drummed the forest floor in a panicked rush, their scents bitter with fear.

Jaykit's fur stood on end as Spiderleg and Thornclaw burst through the entrance.

Firestar and Sandstorm were on their paws in an instant.

"What is it?" Firestar meowed.

Spiderleg drew in a deep breath, then announced, "There's a dead fox on our territory!"

CHAPTER 2

"Where?" Firestar's meow was tense.

"By the Sky Oak," Thornclaw mewed, panting. "It was killed by a trap."

Jaykit heard loose pebbles clattering down the wall of the hollow. Brambleclaw was scrambling down into the camp, followed by Squirrelflight.

"What's happening?" he called.

"Thornclaw and Spiderleg have found a dead fox," Firestar explained. "Killed by a trap."

"Male or female?"

"Female," Spiderleg told her.

"Then there may be cubs," Brambleclaw growled.

Jaykit was puzzled. "What harm can a couple of fox cubs do?" he whispered to Hollykit.

"Cubs grow up into foxes, mouse-brain!" she hissed back. "An adult fox can kill a cat."

"The fox had the scent of milk on her," Thornclaw reported.

"So there are definitely cubs," Firestar concluded.

The warriors' den rattled as Ashfur scrambled out.

"Where was this trap?" Brambleclaw asked. Was that anxiety Jaykit heard in his voice? Surely his father knew enough about the Twolegs' traps not to be scared by them? No, Jaykit decided, it wasn't anxiety, but something else, some darker emotion Jaykit did not recognize.

Thornclaw's answer broke into his thoughts. "The trap is lakeside of the camp, not far from the Sky Oak."

"The cubs must be near," Brambleclaw guessed. "Their mother will not have wandered far from them."

"What should we do?" Ferncloud had emerged from the nursery. "We can't let the forest be overrun by foxes! What about my kits?"

"We must find the den," Brambleclaw replied without hesitation.

"If the cubs are very young, they'll starve without their mother," Firestar meowed. "It would be best to kill them quickly."

There was nothing malicious in the ThunderClan leader's voice; Firestar had to do what was best for the Clan.

"What if they're old enough to survive alone?" Hollykit asked curiously.

"Then they must be driven out," Firestar told her. "They can't be allowed to settle in our territory."

"The cubs will be hungry by now," Ashfur pointed out. "What if they've ventured out of their den already?"

"They might find the camp!" Ferncloud gasped.

"The camp will remain well guarded," Firestar promised. "I'll take Sandstorm and check the old Thunderpath up to the empty Twoleg nest. Brambleclaw, you sort out the other patrols." The ThunderClan leader and his mate raced away through the prickly thorn barrier that shielded the camp from the forest.

"Stormfur, Brook!" Brambleclaw called. "Patrol outside the hollow! Ashfur, guard the entrance."

Brightheart and Cloudtail paced in front of him. "What do you want us to do?"

"Head toward the ShadowClan border," Brambleclaw told them. "The earth is sandy there, ideal for a den. Squirrelflight will lead you. Do whatever she tells you. There may be more traps, and Squirrelflight is the best at springing them. Take Cinderpaw, but keep her close to you."

Cloudtail called his apprentice's name, but the young gray tabby was already charging across the clearing.

Squirrelflight headed toward the entrance. Jaykit felt her warm pelt brush past him.

Brambleclaw called to Thornclaw and Spiderleg, "Go back to where you found the fox. See if you can trace its scent back to her den."

Sorreltail's kit Poppypaw and Mousepaw were waiting expectantly, hardly able to stand still.

"Can we go with them?" Poppypaw called.

"Yes, but do everything your mentors tell you," Brambleclaw warned.

Jaykit felt their excitement crackle in the air like lightning as they headed out of the camp after Spiderleg and Thornclaw. His paws itched with frustration. Nearly all the apprentices were out hunting down the fox cubs. It wasn't fair! He might be small, but he could still fight a cub.

"We're not going to be left behind!" Lionkit announced, echoing Jaykit's thoughts. "Brambleclaw!"

"What?" Brambleclaw's voice was impatient.

"Can't we do something to help?" Lionkit begged. "We're nearly apprentices."

"*Nearly* isn't good enough," Brambleclaw replied. He must have seen a look of disappointment on Lionkit's face, because his voice softened as he added, "You, Hollykit, and Jaykit can help guard the camp. I'm taking Dustpelt and Hazelpaw to search the lakeshore. We need brave cats to make sure those fox cubs don't come into the hollow. If you scent or see anything strange, send Leafpool to fetch me at once."

"Okay," Lionkit mewed eagerly.

He hurried back to his brother and sister. "We've got to guard the camp," he told them. "In case the fox cubs try to get in."

"You don't think the fox cubs would really get this far, do you?" Jaykit mewed grumpily. "There must be a Thunder-Clan apprentice behind every tree out there. Brambleclaw's just trying to keep us busy."

Lionkit sat down with a bump, like a leaf that had been dropped by the breeze. "I thought he really wanted us to help."

"You never know," Hollykit mewed. "The fox cubs might head this way, and if they do I bet we could smell them first— especially with Jaykit helping."

A surge of anger pulsed in Jaykit's paws. "You're just as bad as Brambleclaw," he snapped. "Stop trying to pretend we're important to the Clan when we're not."

Hollykit kneaded the ground with her forepaws. "We will be important one day," she vowed.

Lionkit suddenly stood up and turned in an excited circle, his tail fluffing out. "We'll be important today!" he declared. "We're going to chase those fox cubs off ThunderClan territory ourselves!"

Hollykit gasped. "But if we leave the camp without permission, we'll be breaking the warrior code!"

"We'll be doing it for the good of the Clan," Lionkit argued. "How can that be against the warrior code?"

Jaykit thought of something else. "We're not warriors yet—we're not even apprentices! So why do we have to obey the warrior code?"

A purr rose in Hollykit's throat. "If we did chase off those fox cubs, Icekit and Foxkit would be safe," she mewed.

"Exactly." Lionkit turned and padded to a shady part of the thorn barrier that cut the camp off from the forest. Jaykit knew where he was heading. There was a small tunnel there that led to the place where the cats made their dirt. No one would question them using that way out. He doubted if anyone would even notice them slipping away. The clearing was deserted as the warriors and their apprentices went about their guarding and patrolling duties. The elders, Mousefur and Longtail, were tucked away in their den, and Ferncloud was hiding with Daisy in the nursery. Leafpool was busy with the two whitecough patients in her den.

His heart pounding, Jaykit followed Lionkit through the narrow tunnel.

"No one saw us," Hollykit whispered, close behind him.

He smelled the dirt place and veered away from it, following Lionkit up the sloping bank away from the camp. Ashfur's pawsteps rustled the leaves outside the thorn barrier, where he was keeping guard.

"Can he see us?" Jaykit hissed.

"Not from where he is," Hollykit reassured him. "The barrier's blocking his view."

"And the other patrols won't see us if we stay off the main paths," Lionkit meowed.

"But we don't know where the main paths are," Jaykit pointed out. The ground beneath his paws felt strange, littered with leaves and twigs, unlike the smooth, clear ground inside the hollow.

"We can guess where they are by where the scents are strongest," Hollykit mewed. "There's hardly any scent coming from up ahead. The slope is steep, and there aren't any tracks through the bracken."

"Let's go that way, then," Lionkit meowed.

"What do you think?" Hollykit asked Jaykit.

"Thornclaw said they'd found the fox lakeside of the camp, which is over there." He flicked the tip of his tail away from the slope.

"How do you know which way the lake is?" Hollykit mewed, sounding puzzled.

"I can smell the wind from the water," Jaykit explained. "It tastes fresher than the wind from the hills or the forest."

The three kits ran back down the slope and began to climb a thickly wooded rise. The ground here felt damper underpaw, and Jaykit guessed it had less sunshine than the other slope. He shivered.

"Not scared, are you?" Hollykit teased.

"Of course not," he mewed. "It's just cold out of the sun."

They carried on up the slope until they reached the crest where the trees thinned out. Jaykit felt the warmth of dappled sunlight flickering through the branches.

His nose flared in alarm. "Stop!" he warned. He stretched to sniff a bracken frond, trying to distinguish the many ThunderClan warrior scents. "The warriors come this way a lot."

"I can't see anyone," Hollykit mewed.

"We'd better be careful, though," Jaykit urged. "What if we bump into a patrol?"

"If only it were greenleaf!" Lionkit spat. "Then there'd be loads more undergrowth to hide in."

"What about over there?" Hollykit mewed. "The trees are thicker . . ."

". . . and there are brambles!" Lionkit finished.

He darted forward with Hollykit and Jaykit following, away from the strong-scented bracken and into the trees beyond. The air was clearer here, less laden with ThunderClan scents. The muscles in Jaykit's shoulders began to relax. And then he heard a familiar sound—Stormfur's rumbling yowl.

"Brook?" The gray warrior was calling to his mate.

"Get down!" Jaykit hissed.

Instantly the kits crouched. Jaykit pressed his belly to the cold earth, aware of his heart thudding against the leaf mulch.

The ground vibrated with approaching pawsteps.

"They're coming this way," he whispered. How would they explain being this far from camp?

"Let's hide under that holly bush," Hollykit suggested.

Lionkit was already padding toward it, and Jaykit felt Hollykit nudge him from behind, urging him forward. He hissed crossly and shot forward after Lionkit. Prickly leaves scratched his nose and ears as Hollykit shoved him under its low branches.

"They won't see us in here," she whispered.

Stormfur's call sounded again. "Let's head to the ShadowClan border." The warrior's voice sounded frighteningly close.

Brook answered him, her low mew only tail-lengths away. "Do you think they might be using the old fox den?"

"Probably not," Stormfur meowed. "It still reeks of that she-badger Squirrelflight chased off. But it's worth checking."

"If only Stormfur and Brook smelled like ThunderClan cats, it would've been easier to detect them!" Lionkit complained.

"We'd never have smelled them whatever their scent," Jaykit pointed out. "The wind was blowing the wrong way."

"Sh!" Hollykit warned.

The warriors' pawsteps were heading straight toward the

holly bush. The branches quivered as Stormfur's pelt brushed against them. Jaykit flattened himself against the ground and closed his eyes.

"Come on; let's be quick!" Stormfur urged his mate. "Then we can head back and patrol the top of the hollow." The warriors' pawsteps faded away.

"Let's get out of here," Jaykit whispered.

"Which way?" Lionkit asked.

Jaykit smelled the air, once more tasting the fresh wind from the lake. "Over there," he mewed, pointing with his tail.

The kits set off again, keeping low. Lionkit led them along a winding route through swathes of bracken and tangled undergrowth. "Through here," he urged.

Jaykit squeezed after him into a clump of bracken, its stems so knotted that he could only just manage to haul himself through the narrow gaps. "I bet no warrior's ever gotten through here," he boasted.

"They should take us out on patrols all the time!" Lionkit mewed.

"We could explore places they'd never get close to," Hollykit agreed.

They scrabbled under the arching roots of a sycamore, tunneling a path through the leaf litter bunched beneath it.

Jaykit stopped. He could scent the fresh mark of Spiderleg. "Wait!" he ordered. "Thornclaw's patrol has just passed this way."

Immediately the kits scrambled back into the shadowy hole they had burrowed beneath the sycamore's roots.

"We must be heading in the right direction," Hollykit whispered.

"That must be the Sky Oak over there," Lionkit mewed. "It's the tallest tree in the woods by a long way."

"Where's the patrol?" Jaykit asked.

"Listen!" Hollykit commanded.

Jaykit could hear the patrol thrashing around in the bracken several fox-lengths away. Then his fur bristled. He tasted the air, recoiling at the stench that bathed his tongue. It was a smell he'd never met before, but it sent a shiver down his spine.

"Can you smell that?" he asked Lionkit and Hollykit.

"Ugh!" Lionkit wrinkled his nose.

"It must be the dead fox!" Hollykit guessed. "We're near the trap."

"Can you see it?" Jaykit asked.

Hollykit wriggled away from him. "I can see over the root!" she whispered from just above his head. "The dead fox is lying under the oak. The patrol is beyond it, searching the bracken."

"They're looking in the wrong place," Jaykit mewed. He suddenly realized that despite the scents of the patrol and the dead fox, he could smell a far subtler and sweeter smell— milk. It was right here beneath the sycamore. "The fox came past this tree," he told the others. "I can smell her milk-scent."

"We've found her trail!" Hollykit mewed.

Lionkit scrabbled out from under the root. "Let's follow it!

It'll lead us to her cubs!"

Jaykit turned away from where Thornclaw, Spiderleg, Poppypaw, and Mousepaw were plunging through the frost-blackened undergrowth. Heading out from the sycamore roots, he padded along the scent of the milk-trail.

"Watch out!" Lionkit warned. "There are brambles ahead."

His senses trained only on the milk-scent, Jaykit had not noticed the spiky bush.

"I'll find a way through!" Hollykit offered. She pushed into the lead and wriggled into the branches.

"But the trail leads around it," Jaykit objected.

"We can't afford to stay in the open," Lionkit told him. "We can pick up the scent on the other side, once there are brambles between us and Thornclaw's patrol."

Reluctantly Jaykit followed Lionkit as their sister found a narrow tunnel through the tangle of branches. He was relieved when he picked up the fox's scent quickly on the other side.

The trees were more widely spaced here. Jaykit could feel the wind in his fur, and sunlight reached down to the forest floor, mottling his pelt with warmth. The fox's milky scent grew stronger and as they neared a clump of bracken that shielded a small lump in the ground, Jaykit scented a new smell. The cubs?

"Wait here!" Hollykit ordered.

"Why?" Lionkit objected.

"Just wait while I take a look behind this bracken!"

"I'm coming too," Lionkit insisted.

"We don't want the cubs to know we're here," Hollykit mewed. "If all three of us go blundering in, they'll know something's up and we'll lose the element of surprise."

"My golden pelt will blend in better against the bracken than your black fur," Lionkit pointed out.

"What about me?" Jaykit mewed.

"We won't attack the den without you," Hollykit promised. "But first, you and I will wait here while Lionkit finds the way in."

Jaykit felt a twinge of frustration, but he knew Hollykit's plan was sensible. "Come back as soon as you find it," he called in a whisper as Lionkit disappeared into the bracken. For the first time he wondered if taking on the fox cubs was a wise idea. But how else was he going to persuade the Clan that there was no need to treat him like a helpless kit?

He strained his ears for the sound of Lionkit returning. It seemed an age before his brother finally pushed his way out of the bracken.

"The main entrance to the den is right behind this clump," Lionkit whispered, shaking leaves from his pelt. "But there's a smaller entrance on the other side of the lump of earth— probably an escape route—that leads into the back."

"Are the cubs inside?" Jaykit asked.

"I didn't go in, but I could hear them crying for food."

"They must still be young, then," Hollykit guessed. "Otherwise they'd have come out by now."

"It'll be easier to flush them out if we go down the escape passage," Lionkit proposed. "If we rush them, the surprise will be enough to get them out of the den, and then we can chase them toward the border."

"Which way is the border?" Hollykit asked.

Lionkit snorted impatiently. "There'll be a border whichever way we drive them!" he snapped. "ThunderClan territory doesn't go on forever. Let's get on with it, before Thornclaw finds them and takes all the glory."

He surged away into the bracken before either Jaykit or Hollykit could reply. He led them up the slope, out of the bracken, and over the top of the leaf-strewn mound of earth.

"The escape route is here," he announced, skidding to a halt.

"It's no bigger than a rabbit hole!" Hollykit mewed in surprise.

"Perhaps that's what it used to be," Lionkit answered. "Who cares, so long as we can fit down it?"

Thornclaw's meow sounded in the trees not far away. The warrior patrol must have given up searching the bracken near the dead fox and were heading toward the mound of earth.

"Hurry!" Lionkit hissed. "Or Thornclaw will find the cubs first!"

Taking a deep breath, Jaykit plunged into the hole. Its earthen sides pressed against his pelt as he scrabbled down it. He didn't mind that there would be no light down here; he trusted his nose to lead him to the den. He could feel Lionkit pressing behind him and pushed onward until he exploded into the foxes' den.

The air was warm and stank of fox—more than one. Jaykit

let out a threatening hiss. Lionkit, at his side in an instant, spat ferociously, and Hollykit gave a vicious yowl.

Jaykit could not see the foxes, but as soon as he heard them scramble to their paws, he realized that they were far bigger than they had expected. Fear shot through him as the cubs let out a shrieking cry.

"They're huge!" wailed Lionkit.

"Let's get out of here!" Jaykit screeched.

He turned and shot back up the escape tunnel. The hot breath of a fox cub blasted his tail fur. Were Hollykit and Lionkit trapped in the den? He could not stop and turn to find out. The fox cub's jaws were snapping at his heels as it pursued him out of the hole.

Wild with terror, Jaykit hurtled down the bank and through the bracken. "Thornclaw!" he yowled.

The warrior did not answer, and Jaykit fled toward the bramble thicket. He hoped the thorns would stop the fox, but it chased him into the bush. Thorns tore at Jaykit's nose and ears, but the fox plunged through them as though racing through grass. He floundered on, tearing free of the brambles and running for the camp. He could smell the familiar scents of the hollow and headed straight for them. The fox cub was still at his heels, growling and snapping.

I must be near the camp now! he thought desperately, his paws skidding on the loose leaves.

Pain pierced his tail as the fox cub snapped at it with thorn-sharp teeth. Jaykit dug his claws into the ground, running faster and faster, until, without warning, the ground disappeared from beneath his paws.

With a jolt of horror, Jaykit felt himself plunging into empty air.

I've fallen into the hollow!

CHAPTER 3

❧

Jaykit tried to move, but pain shot through his limbs and gripped his chest like claws.

Panic flooded him. *I'm broken!*

He tried to mew for help.

"Hush, little one." Warm breath stirred his fur, and a soft nose nuzzled his flank.

He figured it must be Leafpool, though she sounded strange. Perhaps the throbbing in his head was confusing him. Jaykit knew he was in the cleft in the wall of the hollow that formed Leafpool's den. Moss softened the ground beneath him. Cold air flowed down the smooth rock walls, soft as water. Tendrils of bramble shielded the entrance. The scent of herbs filled the air; instinctively Jaykit tried to distinguish one from another. He identified juniper easily—Leafpool had fed it to Lionkit for bellyache after he had eaten too much fresh-kill. Borage he remembered from when Ferncloud had a fever after Icekit and Foxkit were born.

Where were Hollykit and Lionkit?

He couldn't smell them anywhere.

He writhed in his nest, trying to find them.

"Lie still, little one."

Jaykit opened his eyes and saw a she-cat crouched beside him. He realized he must be dreaming. She wasn't a cat he recognized, but she had ThunderClan scent. Her image was hazy, a jumble of shapes, but he could make out the beautiful orange and brown markings on her lithe body as she sniffed along his pelt.

Her eyes were large and pale, one rimmed with darker fur than the other, and her mottled face narrowed to a soft white muzzle. "Don't look so frightened," she told him. "You are safe."

"What about Hollykit and Lionkit?"

"They are safe too."

Jaykit let his head rest back into the moss as the she-cat continued to nuzzle his fur, gently touching every aching spot on his body. The parts she touched seemed to flood with heat until he felt warm all over.

"Drink now, precious," she urged. She dragged a leaf to his mouth. It held a tiny pool of water. It was cool and sweet and made him feel sleepy. He closed his eyes.

When Jaykit awoke the she-cat was gone. His body still ached, but not as much as before.

"You're awake." Leafpool's voice surprised him.

"Where is the other cat?" he asked groggily.

"What other cat?"

"The one that brought me water to drink." He recalled the distinctive mottled markings on her body. "She was a tortoiseshell, with a white muzzle."

"Tortoiseshell with a white muzzle?" Leafpool's mew sharpened with interest.

Jaykit couldn't understand why Leafpool was just repeating everything he said. He tried lifting his head, but his neck felt too stiff and he winced in pain.

"You'll be sore for a while," Leafpool warned him. "But you were lucky that no bones were broken." She rolled a ball of water-soaked moss to his muzzle. "Here, you should drink something."

"I'm not thirsty," Jaykit mewed. "I told you, that other cat brought me some water."

Leafpool pawed the moss away from his mouth. "Tell me about her," she prompted gently.

Jaykit started to feel uneasy, as if he might have done something wrong. He was puzzled by the tension in Leafpool's shoulders, and the way the tip of her tail stirred the moss-covered ground. "I'd never seen her before, but she smelled of ThunderClan and she was here in your den, so I guessed it was okay to drink the water she gave me."

There was a long pause, then: "It was Spottedleaf," Leafpool meowed. "One of our warrior ancestors."

"Like in StarClan? I . . . I'm not dead, am I?"

"No, of course not. It must have been a dream."

"But why would I dream of a cat I've never met?"

"StarClan works in its own way. Spottedleaf chose to come to you for a reason," Leafpool murmured. She turned away to tidy a wrap of herbs. "Thank StarClan your ancestors took pity on you," she told him briskly. "You could have died falling over the cliff. You were lucky you weren't badly hurt!"

"I feel hurt enough," Jaykit complained.

"You have no one to blame but yourself. You should never have gone hunting foxes. You're mouse-brains, the three of you! And you most of all. What were you thinking of, leaving the camp like that?"

Her irritation sparked anger in Jaykit. Ignoring his aching stiffness, he scrabbled to his paws and glared at her. "It's not fair!" he snapped. "I should be allowed to do the same things as any cat!"

"None of you should have been outside the hollow," Leafpool pointed out. "Hollykit and Lionkit have been in serious trouble with Firestar and Squirrelflight." Jaykit opened his mouth to defend himself, but she went on. "Thank StarClan that Thornclaw was close enough to save Hollykit and Lionkit from that den. Those fox cubs were old enough to have torn them to pieces."

Jaykit lifted his chin defiantly. "We were trying to protect the Clan."

"One day you will," Leafpool promised. "But first you need to learn as much as you can, which includes learning not to go off by yourself!"

"Do you think Firestar will delay my apprenticeship because of this?" he mewed, suddenly anxious.

Leafpool drew the tip of her tail gently around his ears and said nothing.

"You do, don't you!" Jaykit wailed. "Has Firestar said anything? Tell me!"

"Dear Jaykit." Leafpool sighed. "You must know that you can never become an ordinary apprentice like Hollykit or Lionkit." She ran her tail along his back.

Jaykit shrugged it away. It was as though a gale had swept him up and he could hear nothing but the rushing of wind in his ears. He began to walk to the entrance of the den, but each pawstep made him wince with pain.

Leafpool called to him, sounding unhappy. "Jaykit, wait. I thought you understood. . . ."

"Understood what?" Jaykit whipped around to face her. "That I'm not good enough to fight for my Clan?"

"This has nothing to do with not being good enough," Leafpool meowed. "There are other ways to serve your Clan."

But Jaykit hardly heard her. "It's not fair!" he raged. He started to push his way out through the brambles.

"Jaykit!" Leafpool's voice was firm. "Come back!"

Instinctively Jaykit paused.

"You described Spottedleaf to me perfectly. Have you always been able to see like that in your dreams?"

Jaykit tipped his head to one side. "I guess," he mewed.

"What do you see?"

"It depends what I'm dreaming about." Jaykit was growing impatient. How could his dreams help him become a ThunderClan warrior? The hazy images he saw while he slept were pale in comparison to the rich world his senses brought him while he was awake.

"Now tell me which herbs I used to treat you."

Curious now, Jaykit padded back to his nest, focusing on

the pungent scents that lingered on his pelt, scents left by the herbs Leafpool had massaged into his wounds. "Dock on my scratches and comfrey where my body is stiff."

"You have a good memory for plants. There are other ways to serve your Clan than being a warrior. You'd make a good medicine cat, for example."

"A medicine cat!" Jaykit echoed in disbelief. Always stinking of mouse bile and cleaning up bad-smelling wounds?

"You could be my apprentice," Leafpool urged.

"I don't want to make do with being a medicine cat!" Jaykit hissed. "I don't want to live half a life, separated from my Clanmates like you are. I want to be a warrior like Brambleclaw and Firestar."

He turned away from Leafpool, bristling with fury. "I hate being blind. I wish I had never been born!"

CHAPTER 4

Hollykit waited in the center of the clearing, where Brambleclaw had left her. The sun was sinking behind the trees, pulling a shadow across the camp. Lionkit sat beside her, his pelt golden in the fading sunshine. Cold air drifted down into the hollow, and Lionkit shivered.

Suddenly the brambles at the entrance of the medicine den trembled, and Hollykit saw the gray-striped head of Jaykit poke out. She nudged Lionkit. "Look!"

"He's okay!" he mewed in relief.

"Thank StarClan!"

Jaykit turned around and went back into the den.

"Leafpool must be keeping him a bit longer," Hollykit observed. She dug her claws into the ground to stop her paws from trembling. At least she knew her brother was all right. But they still had to face Firestar. How was he going to punish them this time?

She glanced around, hoping no cat was staring at them. Mousefur was leaning against halfrock, a smooth low stone that stuck out of the ground near the entrance to the elders' den. It would still be warm from the sun. Dustpelt was sharing tongues with Whitewing beside the thornbush that formed the warriors' den. His apprentice, Hazelpaw, nodded to him before picking up a mouse from the fresh-kill pile and carrying it over to the apprentices' den. Her littermates, Mousepaw and Berrypaw, were there already, eating.

Hollykit caught Mousepaw's eye. The young gray-and-white tom blinked sympathetically at her before looking away. Hollykit lifted her chin a little higher. She wasn't going to let any cat see how scared she was. She would take her punishment like a true warrior.

She watched Sorreltail carry fresh-kill to her mate, Brackenfur. The dark ginger tom was resting beneath Highledge, his breath hoarse after his bout of whitecough. Sorreltail skirted the clearing, avoiding the kits, and dropped a mouse at his paws.

"How are you?" she asked him.

"Better," he croaked. "I'll be fine in a couple of days. Birchfall's recovered already, thanks to Leafpool."

"Well, at least you're not in the medicine den anymore," Sorreltail meowed gratefully.

"Leafpool needed room for Jaykit," Brackenfur reminded her.

"Poor mite," Sorreltail meowed. "Do you think he'll be okay?"

Hollykit felt a surge of irritation. Jaykit had been as keen to chase off the fox cubs as she and Lionkit, but he was being fussed over in Leafpool's den, while she and Lionkit had to sit here for the whole Clan to stare at.

She gave a small snort of anger.

"Have you got a tick in your ear?" Lionkit whispered.

"No, but it's just not fair!" she hissed back. "We wouldn't be in so much trouble if Jaykit hadn't fallen over the edge! Why does he have to act like he can do anything and then be so *helpless?*"

"We shouldn't have taken him with us," Lionkit murmured.

"Can you imagine the fuss he would have made if we hadn't?" Hollykit spat. But then she pictured her brother keeping up with them, finding the milk-scent that led to the den they had been looking for, and guilt swept over her.

He could have died.

The thought pierced her heart like a thorn. The three of them always did everything together. Losing Jaykit would be like losing her tail.

She sighed ruefully. "None of us should have gone."

"I wish you had realized that earlier!"

Firestar's meow took Hollykit by surprise. Tiny stones were still tumbling into the clearing where he had leaped down the rockfall that led from his den.

Brambleclaw and Squirrelflight followed him down and stood a little behind the ThunderClan leader. Hollykit's heart sank when she saw anger in her father's eyes and disappointment in her mother's. She stared down at her paws, remembering the disastrous ending to their assault on the fox's den. Thornclaw's patrol had arrived just in time to see her and Lionkit flee the den with two fox cubs at their heels.

Thornclaw had yowled in surprise as she sped into the trees, but she dared not stop, fearing the snapping jaws behind her, till she hurtled into Brambleclaw's patrol on its way back from the lakeshore.

"What's happening?" Brambleclaw demanded. He had grasped her by the scruff as she tried to race past. "What are you doing out here?"

Hollykit had tried to explain, but she'd been panting too hard, her heart thudding like a woodpecker on a hollow tree.

Spiderleg caught up with her. "The kits found the fox cubs," the black warrior told Brambleclaw. "It seems they decided to organize a patrol of their own."

Hollykit did not dare catch her father's eye.

"Where are Lionkit and Jaykit?" Brambleclaw growled.

"Lionkit's with Poppypaw," Spiderleg reported. "He's okay. We haven't found Jaykit yet, but the fox cubs have scattered. It's going to take a while to hunt them out."

Brambleclaw had glanced up at the sky and muttered under his breath, then escorted Hollykit and Lionkit unceremoniously back to the ThunderClan camp.

But that had not been the worst part.

When they'd reached the camp, Whitewing and Leafpool were crouching at the edge of the clearing, their fur spiked in horror. Ferncloud trembled beside them, moaning a low, mournful yowl.

Between them, Jaykit lay on the ground like a scrap of gray fur. Brambleclaw darted forward and crouched beside his son. He nudged Jaykit gently, as though he was trying to wake him from sleep, but his eyes were frantic with fear.

"He's still breathing, and his heartbeat is steady," Leafpool told him.

Brambleclaw stared desperately at Leafpool, then sat up. "Fetch Firestar and Squirrelflight," he ordered Whitewing.

After that he had told Lionkit and Hollykit to wait in the clearing and carried Jaykit to the medicine den. Firestar had returned with Squirrelflight, and the three warriors had disappeared, faces grim, into Firestar's den, not even glancing at Hollykit and Lionkit.

Hollykit leaned against Lionkit as Firestar, Squirrelflight, and Brambleclaw lined up in front of them once more. She was glad she didn't have to face them alone.

"Jaykit's going to be okay," Firestar told them.

"I know," Hollykit answered. "We saw him—"

Firestar silenced her with a glare and went on. "But Thornclaw's patrol has not returned. Which means they are still hunting the fox cubs."

"What possessed you to leave the hollow?" Brambleclaw demanded.

Firestar narrowed his eyes. "I know they are your kits, Brambleclaw," he meowed, "but I'll deal with this."

Squirrelflight's tail flicked. Hollykit guessed there were a few sharp words she wanted to share with her kits, but she held her tongue as Firestar spoke.

"We only wanted to help the Clan!" Hollykit protested.

"Then do as you are told!" Firestar growled. "What if Jaykit had died? Would that have helped the Clan?" His fierce gaze flicked from Lionkit to Hollykit, and they shook their heads.

Firestar pressed on. "You almost led the foxes right into the camp—as it is, you have given them a scent trail they're not likely to forget!"

"We're sorry," Hollykit whispered.

"We thought if we could find the foxes—" Lionkit began.

"If you'd thought at *all* you would have let our warriors deal with the foxes and the Clan would be safe now!" Firestar lashed his tail. "Instead we have one badly injured kit and three hungry foxes who know where our camp is!"

Hollykit glanced guiltily at the nursery.

Squirrelflight pawed the ground in small, frustrated steps. Firestar nodded for her to speak.

"I'm so disappointed in you both!" she burst out.

"What about Jaykit?" Lionkit objected. "We didn't force him to go with us!"

"We will speak to Jaykit when he's recovered," Brambleclaw answered. "Right now, it's you two that concern us. You seem to have no more sense than hatchling chicks!"

"Are you going to stop us from becoming apprentices?" Lionkit asked in a small voice.

Hollykit's breath caught in her throat. Would their father really do that? She looked pleadingly up at him.

"If it were up to me," Brambleclaw meowed, "I would make you wait another moon. But it is Firestar's decision."

The Clan leader narrowed his eyes. "I'm not going to decide right now," he told them. "Go back to the nursery.

Ferncloud and Daisy will keep an eye on you, and it is up to you to make sure one of them knows where you are at all times. If you're not where you are supposed to be, then you're clearly not ready for the responsibilities of apprenticeship."

"We won't wander off again," Lionkit promised.

"Hollykit?" Firestar prompted.

"I won't do anything that might stop me from becoming an apprentice," she vowed, meaning every word.

"Very well," Firestar meowed. "I just hope you have learned something today. True warriors think of the Clan's safety before anything else." He turned away, padding to where Brackenfur was sharing tongues with Sorreltail.

His parting words seared Hollykit's fur. She had let her Clan down. She glanced nervously at Brambleclaw and Squirrelflight. "We're sorry," she ventured.

"I should hope so." Squirrelflight sighed.

"You should be setting an example," Brambleclaw added.

Squirrelflight's gaze softened a little. She bent down and licked Hollykit and Lionkit each between their ears. "I know you thought you were doing the right thing," she sympathized.

"We just wanted to help the Clan," Hollykit insisted.

"Your chance will come," Brambleclaw promised.

"Will Jaykit have to stay in the nursery, too?" Lionkit asked.

"He'll stay with Leafpool until he's recovered," Squirrelflight told him. "Then he can rejoin you."

"Will he be well enough in time for the naming ceremony?" Hollykit mewed.

"If there *is* a naming ceremony," Lionkit added.

Squirrelflight drew her tail over her son's flank. "You know your brother can't become a full apprentice."

Hollykit stared at her mother. "What do you mean?"

"Well, it would be impossible to have a blind warrior—" Brambleclaw began but Hollykit turned on him, her paws pricking with fury.

"No, it wouldn't!" she spat. "Jaykit can smell and hear and sense everything that happens in the camp!" She glanced at Lionkit for support. "It's like he *can* see things, but with his nose and ears instead of his eyes!"

She glared at her father, waiting for him to say something, but he only glanced at Squirrelflight, exchanging a look of sadness that made Hollykit tremble with indignation.

Suddenly she heard pawsteps pounding toward the camp. A voice called from beyond the barrier. It was Thornclaw. The golden brown tabby hurried through the thorns with Spiderleg, Poppypaw, and Mousepaw close behind.

Firestar left Brackenfur and Sorreltail and padded over to meet them. Brambleclaw joined him. "Any luck finding them?" the deputy asked.

"Poppypaw and Mousepaw chased one of the cubs over the border into ShadowClan territory," Thornclaw reported. "But there's no sign of the other two."

Hollykit's ears burned with shame.

"The cubs are old enough to look after themselves," Thornclaw went on. "They could cause a lot of trouble in the future."

Ferncloud pushed her way out of the nursery. "Are the fox cubs nearby?" she fretted.

"No." Thornclaw shook his head. "We made sure of that. There's no fresh scent this side of the Sky Oak."

Ferncloud looked a little comforted, but her ears still twitched nervously, and she hurried back to her kits, who were mewling in the nursery.

Hollykit caught Squirrelflight's eye. Her mother blinked at her sympathetically. "Don't be too hard on yourself," she murmured. "Every cat makes mistakes. You just have to learn from them."

"I will make it up to the Clan," Hollykit promised.

"I know you will," Squirrelflight assured her. "Why don't you go and visit Jaykit? I'm sure he'd love some company."

"Can I go too?" Lionkit begged.

"I don't know if he's well enough for both of you," Squirrelflight meowed. "You can go later. But don't forget to tell Daisy or Ferncloud before you leave the nursery. That's what Firestar said, remember?"

Lionkit lashed his short tail but didn't answer. Instead he stalked toward the nursery.

"I'll tell Jaykit you said hi!" Hollykit called after him.

"Whatever," Lionkit grumbled, not looking back.

Hollykit nosed her way through the brambles into the shadows of Leafpool's den. Jaykit was lying by the pool at one side of the den. He turned his jay-feather blue eyes on her as she entered.

"Hi, Hollykit." His mew sounded tired. His pelt was slicked flat with poultices, making him look as small as a newborn kit. Hollykit felt a stab of pain. He had nearly died.

Jaykit flicked his tail. "There's no need to feel so sorry for me," he mewed.

Hollykit blinked. How was it that her brother always knew exactly what she was feeling? Sometimes it could be so annoying to have him sniffing out her private thoughts like an inquisitive mouse.

"I'm not going to die," he went on.

"I never thought you would," she lied. She padded to Jaykit's side and smoothed the fur between his ears with her tongue.

"What did Firestar say?" Jaykit asked.

"We've got to stay in the nursery until he decides if we can become apprentices," Hollykit told him.

"*If?*" Jaykit echoed.

"If we do as we're told and stay in camp, then I think we'll be okay," Hollykit assured him. She hoped it was true. She had never seen Firestar so angry.

"It *has* to be okay!" Jaykit struggled to his paws, then winced with pain.

"Are you all right?" Hollykit mewed in alarm.

Leafpool was mixing herbs in the far corner of her den. "He's just sore," she meowed. "But he's healing well." Leaving her work, she joined the two kits. "I've been giving him comfrey to chew on."

"Is that what you were mixing there?" Hollykit asked.

"I like to mix in a few heather flowers when I have them," Leafpool explained. "The nectar sweetens the mixture and makes it easier to swallow."

"How did you learn all that?" Hollykit mewed, genuinely curious.

"Cinderpelt taught me," Leafpool answered. There was sadness in her voice as she spoke about her mentor, but Hollykit was more interested in Leafpool's skill. Having so much knowledge must make her feel very powerful—no other cat in the Clan knew herbs like she did. She had cured Brackenfur and Birchfall and now Jaykit. *Imagine being that important to the Clan.*

"Leafpool?" Brightheart called from the den entrance. "Brackenfur's coughing again."

"I'll give you some honey to take to him," Leafpool replied. "Can you see to Jaykit for me, Hollykit? A wash will help his stiffness. Just avoid the poultice patches."

"Okay." Hollykit wrinkled her nose at the thought of putting her tongue near the tangy-smelling goo plastered over her brother's pelt. But she began to wash him anyway as Leafpool fetched a leaf wrap of honey from the back of the den and gave it to Brightheart.

"Not so roughly!" Jaykit complained. "I'm sore all over."

"Sorry," Hollykit apologized, lapping Jaykit's pelt with softer strokes.

"You're not as gentle as Spottedleaf," Jaykit moaned.

Hollykit stopped licking. "Who?"

"Spottedleaf," Jaykit repeated. "Leafpool says she's one of

our warrior ancestors. She came to me in a dream and poked me all over with her nose."

"How can you dream about a cat if you've never met her?" Hollykit asked, puzzled.

Leafpool padded back from the den entrance and sat down. "Are you telling Hollykit about Spottedleaf?"

Jaykit nodded.

"Who is she?" Hollykit mewed.

"She was the ThunderClan medicine cat when Firestar first joined the Clan," Leafpool explained. "She died before I was born, but she comes to my dreams just like she did with Jaykit." Hollykit noticed that the medicine cat's eyes were glittering with excitement. "Spottedleaf was very wise. She's never stopped looking after her Clan. I guess that's why she came to see Jaykit, and why she still visits my dreams."

"Does Cinderpelt visit you too?" Hollykit asked.

Leafpool shook her head. "Just Spottedleaf. She helps me find the answers to questions that are worrying me, and she warns me if something threatens the Clan."

Hollykit was surprised to hear Leafpool talk so warmly about a cat she'd never met in real life. "You talk about Spottedleaf like she's a friend."

"Our warrior ancestors can be our friends."

Jaykit let out a moan. "I hurt."

"I'll fetch more comfrey," Hollykit offered. She bounded over to the pile of herbs and carried a mouthful back to Leafpool.

"Thank you," Leafpool meowed. "Can you fetch some

poppy seeds, too? You'll see them at the back. They're tiny, round black seeds."

"Okay." Hollykit hurried to the back of the den and searched among the piles of herbs until she found the poppy seeds. "How many?" she called.

"Five," Leafpool answered. "Pick them up by wetting your paw and dabbing the pile."

Hollykit followed her instructions, shaking the extra seeds from her pad, and hopped back to where Jaykit lay. He licked them from her paw, his eyes growing sleepy.

"Is he all right?" she asked, worried.

"He will be," Leafpool reassured her. "But we should let him rest."

Hollykit did not want to leave the medicine den. Excitement was buzzing in her paws. Leafpool could cure sick cats, and share tongues with her ancestors, and warn the Clan leader of troubles ahead. If Hollykit wanted to be important to her Clan, perhaps becoming a medicine cat was the way to achieve it. After the disastrous adventure with the foxes, maybe she wasn't cut out to be a warrior at all.

She padded away from Jaykit but lingered at the bramble-covered entrance. "Leafpool," she called quietly.

"Yes?" Leafpool padded to her side.

"When do medicine cats take on an apprentice? Is it only when they get old?"

Leafpool looked seriously at her. "I can take an apprentice anytime."

"But would your apprentice have to stay an apprentice

until you . . ." *Died?* Hollykit could not bring herself to say the word out loud.

Leafpool's whiskers twitched with amusement as she guessed what Hollykit was trying to ask. "No," she purred. "Once a medicine cat apprentice has learned enough, he can take his proper name and assume full responsibilities, even with his mentor still alive."

Hollykit wondered why Leafpool had said *he.* "Do you have someone in mind already?"

Leafpool flicked the tip of her tail. "I've not decided anything yet."

Before Hollykit could say anything else, she heard Ferncloud calling her from the nursery.

"You'd better go," Leafpool meowed. "You've been in enough trouble for one day."

Her pelt prickling with frustration, Hollykit pushed her way through the brambles and raced back to the nursery. She had just discovered how she wanted to serve her Clan, how to make sure that what she did really mattered. She wanted to be the next ThunderClan medicine cat!

CHAPTER 5

❧

Lionkit woke in his nest. A draft ruffled his golden pelt.

Where's Jaykit?

Jaykit usually slept beside him, but there was an empty space there now.

Then he remembered.

Lionkit felt sickness surge in his belly as he pictured Jaykit lying limp at the side of the clearing. *He's going to be okay,* he reminded himself.

But in the clearing, watching Leafpool and Brambleclaw crouch by his body, Lionkit had thought that his brother was dead. A shiver ran down his tail. He nudged Hollykit, who was still sleeping beside him, her black pelt almost making her invisible in the darkness. "It's cold without Jaykit."

"He'll be back soon," she murmured, not opening her eyes.

"But it's weird when he's not here."

"He's only on the other side of the clearing, and he'll be back in a day or two." Hollykit rolled over. "Go back to sleep." Within moments her breathing deepened and she was asleep again.

Lionkit still felt a tug of sadness. Jaykit should be with them, just like always.

He closed his eyes but the image of his brother lying in the clearing filled his mind again. *It was my idea to leave the camp.* Jaykit could be dead, or the fox cubs could have chased them into the hollow. What a mess!

Lionkit got to his paws. He needed fresh air to clear his head.

He peered through the shadows to where Daisy slept. Her long, creamy fur blended into Ferncloud's dark gray pelt. Ferncloud's whiskers were twitching as she dreamed, her two kits snuggled against her flank. Neither queen would be pleased at being woken just so he could ask permission to leave the den; besides, he'd be back before they woke.

With a flick of his tail, he picked his way past Hollykit and squeezed through the prickly entrance.

Cold night air stung his nose, and the frosty ground made his paws ache as he padded around the edge of the camp. Prey scents drifted from the forest. A bird chattered an alarm call far away. He glanced up at Silverpelt, spread across the inky sky. He was glad StarClan had let Jaykit stay down here with his Clanmates. Perhaps he could look in on his brother. Leafpool would be asleep by now.

Lionkit kept to the shadows, painfully aware that he was not supposed to be outside the nursery without permission. As he crept along the stretch of thornbush that sealed the camp, his heart seemed to pound in his chest loud enough to wake his Clanmates. When he scanned the clearing, Lionkit realized with a start that he was not the only cat awake so late. A shape was stirring on the other side of the clearing. The lithe outline of a cat peeled away from the shadows, followed by another.

Lionkit ducked under a branch, relieved to find a small space inside the prickly barrier where he could hide. He peered through the twigs at the emerging shapes: Dustpelt and Spiderleg were padding side by side into the pool of moonlight that lit the center of the camp.

"They're nearly here," the long-limbed warrior told Dustpelt.

"Good," Dustpelt meowed.

Lionkit strained his ears, listening. Frozen leaves crackled beyond the camp wall. He felt the thorn barrier tremble as Stormfur and Brackenfur pushed their way through the entrance tunnel into the camp. The moonhigh patrol had returned.

Dustpelt hurried toward them. "Anything to report?"

"All quiet," Stormfur replied.

Lionkit pressed himself further into the thorns. He could always say he had slipped out only to make dirt, but he was not ready yet to be sent back into the nursery.

Brackenfur held a mouse between his teeth. He dropped it. "It's good to be out hunting again," the golden tabby purred.

"Did you patrol the new border at the edge of the clearing?" Spiderleg asked.

Brackenfur nodded. "ShadowClan have marked it well," he meowed. "But there's no sign they strayed onto Thunder-Clan territory."

Dustpelt narrowed his eyes. "They'd better not. It's bad enough Firestar gave them that piece of land in the first place. If I catch any ShadowClan cat on the wrong side of the border I'll rip his fur off!"

"They wouldn't dare!" Brackenfur growled.

"They dared before Firestar gave them the territory," Spiderleg pointed out. He glanced at the scar on Brackenfur's flank, a reminder of one of the vicious quarrels the two Clans had fought over the stretch of open ground on either side of the stream running down from the Twoleg clearing. ShadowClan had always laid claim to the territory, and Firestar had finally granted it to them at the last Gathering to save further blood being spilled over a stretch of land that was too bare to offer good hunting.

"It wasn't worth fighting over," Stormfur commented. "Firestar was right to give it up."

Dustpelt snorted. "ThunderClan has never given up territory before!"

"No," agreed Brackenfur.

Spiderleg turned in an agitated circle, tail lashing, but Brackenfur went on. "However, the land was too exposed, and the Twolegs will be there soon, once it's greenleaf."

"And ThunderClan are more used to hunting in the forest," Stormfur added.

"Firestar still shouldn't have given it up so easily," Spiderleg insisted.

Lionkit watched nervously from his hiding place as

Spiderleg glared at Stormfur. The long-limbed black warrior was more hotheaded than his father, Dustpelt. But Stormfur refused to be intimidated.

"We gave up nothing but a piece of barren land that was too close to Twoleg territory!" he hissed.

"You sound like Brambleclaw." Dustpelt curled his lip. "He only agreed with Firestar's decision because any cat knows he'd rather face a pack of dogs than a Twoleg!"

Lionkit's fur bristled with anger. His father wasn't scared of anything!

"Brambleclaw sided with Firestar because it was a wise decision, not because he was scared of Twolegs!" Stormfur retorted.

"Was it wise to stand before all the Clans and announce that ThunderClan can no longer defend its boundaries?" Spiderleg meowed hotly. "ShadowClan have no right to set one mangy paw on ThunderClan land!"

"Well, it's ShadowClan land now," Stormfur concluded.

Spiderleg glared at him. "Of course, you don't care how much territory we give up," he snarled. "You're not a ThunderClan cat!"

Lionkit flinched. Stormfur had fought off the invading ShadowClan warriors as fiercely as any cat. He watched closely, waiting to see how the gray warrior would react. But Stormfur only stared back at Spiderleg, his eyes wide with shock.

Brackenfur stepped between them, his eyes glinting

anxiously in the moonlight. "It doesn't matter if we disagree," he meowed. "The decision has been made."

"But now ShadowClan will think they can take whatever they want from us!" Spiderleg objected.

"Firestar made it clear that he was doing ShadowClan a favor when he let them take the land," Brackenfur reminded him. "He left no cat in any doubt that he was acting out of wisdom rather than weakness."

"Then why did Onestar and Leopardstar look so interested?" Dustpelt snapped. "It was obvious they thought ThunderClan couldn't defend their territory."

"What if WindClan decide they want a piece of the forest on the other side?" Spiderleg chipped in. "Onestar hasn't exactly been a friend of ours since he became leader."

"He's been okay since he helped us with the badger attack," Brackenfur pointed out.

"But he's still going to be looking out for his Clan," Dustpelt argued. "If he thinks we're weak he might see a chance to expand his territory."

"Can you imagine Firestar giving up any prey-rich part of our territory?" Stormfur asked.

Dustpelt glared at him for a moment, then dipped his head. "No," he conceded.

"And we don't have to worry about RiverClan," Brackenfur pressed. "We share no boundaries with them, and Leopardstar's been pretty quiet since Hawkfrost died on our territory."

"Does any cat really know what happened to Hawkfrost?" Stormfur asked.

"Only that Firestar found his body while he was on patrol with Brambleclaw and Ashfur," Spiderleg meowed.

Lionkit did not fully understand. He had heard Daisy and Ferncloud talking about Hawkfrost, the RiverClan deputy who had died on ThunderClan territory, impaled on a wooden spike from a fox trap. No one was sure what the RiverClan warrior had been doing there. Lionkit had tried to ask his father once about Hawkfrost—after all, Hawkfrost was Brambleclaw's half brother and therefore Lionkit's kin— but Brambleclaw had been reluctant to answer. The only information he would give was that Brambleclaw and Squirrelflight had carried the dead RiverClan warrior back to his camp as they would have done with any fallen warrior, and that he had been mourned by his Clanmates.

As Lionkit strained to hear whether the warriors' conversation would reveal anything new, he felt the thorn barrier rustle around him. He realized with a jolt that he was right beside the small entrance that led to where the cats made their dirt—the same entrance that he, Jaykit, and Hollykit had sneaked out of in search of the fox cubs. Alarmed, Lionkit sniffed the air. Mousepaw was squeezing his way back through less than a tail-length away.

He shrank further back into the shadows, but he could not escape Mousepaw's sharp nose.

"Lionkit?" Mousepaw hissed into the darkness.

Lionkit wondered for a moment whether to bury himself deeper in the barrier, but he didn't like the look of the thorns, and besides, his pride would not let him. "I'm in here," he confessed.

As he spoke, Dustpelt's amber gaze flashed toward them. "Mousepaw?" he called.

Lionkit held his breath. Would the apprentice give him away? They had been denmates for a while in the nursery, but Mousepaw might side with the warriors now.

"I'm just on my way back to the den," Mousepaw told Dustpelt. A moment later he squeezed into Lionkit's hiding place. "Aren't you supposed to be in the nursery?" he whispered.

Lionkit flicked his tail crossly. He was grateful that Mousepaw hadn't given him away, but he hated being treated like a feeble kit. "I couldn't sleep," he grumbled. "I'm used to having Jaykit around."

"Why were Dustpelt and Stormfur arguing?"

"They were talking about Firestar's decision to give ShadowClan the bit of land by the river," Lionkit explained. "Dustpelt accused Stormfur of not being a real ThunderClan warrior."

Mousepaw flattened his ears, shocked. "I'm surprised that Stormfur didn't shred him!"

"But Stormfur's *not* a real ThunderClan warrior, is he?" Lionkit pointed out, puzzled.

"You'd better not say that to his face!" Mousepaw warned.

"But he was born in RiverClan and lived with the Tribe."

"Mousepaw!" Dustpelt's voice sounded from the clearing.

Mousepaw shoved Lionkit further back into the bush. He stifled a squeak of pain as thorns dug into his pelt, and Mousepaw squeezed out from under the branches.

"Shouldn't you be back in the apprentices' den?" Dustpelt queried.

"I thought I smelled a mouse," Mousepaw lied.

"Straying into the camp would be stupid even for a mouse," Dustpelt muttered. "Go to your den. I'm sure Spiderleg won't be pleased if you're too tired for training in the morning."

"Yes, Dustpelt." Mousepaw dipped his head and padded quickly away.

Lionkit waited, thorns poking him, until Dustpelt and the other warriors headed to their den. It seemed foolish to risk going to the medicine cat's den now. As soon as he was sure that no cat stirred, Lionkit dragged himself out from under the thorn barrier and crept back to the nursery.

Several thorns from the barrier had caught in his fur and were tangled in his pelt. They pricked him as he curled gingerly back into his nest. He closed his eyes and waited for sleep, but his conversation with Mousepaw echoed in his mind. It hadn't occurred to him before how important it was to the warriors whether a cat was truly ThunderClan or not. His own place in the Clan had always been something he had taken for granted. He supposed that not every cat was lucky enough to be born in the forest, with the Clan deputy and Clan leader as kin. But he still didn't understand why Mousepaw had taken the quarrel between the warriors so seriously. So long as Stormfur and Brook were loyal to ThunderClan, what else mattered?

CHAPTER 6

❧

Hollykit was dreaming that the nursery was filled with hedgehogs. They filed in through the entrance, rudely brushing Ferncloud and her kits aside and settling into the mossy nest around her. Their sharp prickles spiked her back. She fidgeted to move away from her uncomfortable new denmates.

"What are you doing here?" she muttered. "Go away!" But the prickles still dug into her. Opening her eyes, she twisted around and saw Lionkit curled up asleep beside her. He looked like he'd fallen out of a tree, his golden pelt ruffled and studded with black thorns.

She jabbed him with her forepaw. "Hey!" she whispered. "Where did you pick up these thorns? They're ripping me to shreds."

Lionkit opened his amber eyes. "What?" he murmured, his mouth stretching into a yawn.

"You're covered in thorns!" Hollykit guessed he'd been out of the den. "What have you been up to?" she demanded.

"I couldn't sleep," Lionkit confessed. "I went for a walk in the clearing."

Hollykit stared at him in dismay. "Aren't we in enough

trouble? Do you want to stop us from being made appren-tices?"

"It's okay," Lionkit soothed. "No one saw me." He sat up and wiped a paw over his face. "Except Mousepaw, and he won't tell. It was Mousepaw who pushed me into the thorns so Dustpelt wouldn't spot me."

Hollykit hissed softly. *Why doesn't he think before he acts?* "We'd better get those thorns out of you before anyone else sees them."

"They really sting," Lionkit complained, twisting around to tug one from his flank with his teeth.

"I'd better go to the medicine den and get something to treat them with," Hollykit told him. "We don't want your scratches getting infected."

"What will you tell Leafpool?"

"Don't worry. I'll tell her there was a thorn in your bed-ding and you rolled on it." She climbed out of her nest and headed toward the entrance. "You start pulling out all the thorns you can reach," she instructed. "I'll get the rest when I come back." Before she began to nose her way out of the den, another thought struck her. "And don't leave them lying around. If Icekit or Foxkit spike themselves on one, Ferncloud will pluck your whiskers till you're bald as a bird!"

She ran across the clearing, relieved to find it empty. The sun was rising behind the trees that topped the cliffs, but the camp, still in shadow, was cold. Hollykit guessed that the dawn patrol must have left already and the other cats were making the most of their snug dens until the sun had reached into the hollow and warmed the camp.

She reached the medicine den unnoticed and pushed through the brambles that concealed its entrance. Leafpool was nowhere to be seen, and her scent was stale. She hurried to Jaykit's nest.

"Are you feeling better?"

Jaykit was curled up tight in the moss, a bundle of striped gray fur. His head shot up at the sound of Hollykit's voice, and he gazed at her with his sightless blue stare.

"What are you doing here? Aren't you confined to the nursery?"

"Lionkit's got a thorn stuck in him," Hollykit explained. "I wanted something to keep the scratch from getting infected."

Jaykit nodded sleepily to the back of the den. "Leafpool used dock on my scratches," he mewed. "You'll have to find it yourself. Leafpool's out collecting stinging nettles."

"Okay," Hollykit mewed, hurrying over to the supply store. "Can you remember what it smelled like?"

"It's got a sort of tangy scent." Jaykit lifted his nose and breathed in. "It's one of the piles near the front," he told her.

Hollykit stared at the array of leaves and seeds. At the front there were two piles, one darker green than the other. She sniffed the darkest first. "This smells kind of icky," she mewed back to Jaykit.

"Dock doesn't have a bad smell," Jaykit told her. "Just sharp."

Hollykit sniffed the other pile and screwed up her eyes. It was definitely tangy. She grabbed a mouthful and carried it over to Jaykit.

"That's the right one," he mewed.

The brambles rustled at the den entrance, and Hollykit jumped.

It was Leafpool, holding a bunch of nettles carefully by their stems. The dew still glistened on their jagged leaves. She dropped them and looked at Hollykit. "You're up early." She noticed the pile of dock leaves beside Hollykit. "Your brother's healing well," she meowed. "He doesn't need any more treatment. He only needs rest."

"I'm not treating Jaykit," Hollykit explained. "Lionkit's been scratched by a thorn in his bedding."

Leafpool opened her eyes wide in surprise. "How did you know to use dock?"

Hollykit stared uncertainly at the medicine cat. *Jaykit told me.*

"She remembered the smell from when you used it to treat me," Jaykit mewed.

Hollykit ran her tail across his flank so he knew she was grateful. It wasn't that she wanted Leafpool to think she was more clever than Jaykit; she just wanted her to see that she would make a great medicine cat.

"Well done, Hollykit!" Leafpool meowed. Hollykit felt warm to the tip of her tail. She told herself that one day she *would* know which herb was which and wouldn't have to pretend.

"Let me show you how to apply it," Leafpool offered. She crouched over the pile of dock, taking a single leaf in her mouth and chewing it. Once it was well chewed she held out her paw and licked the juice from the dock into her fur. Then she spat out the remainder of the leaf. "Make sure you lick it in firmly so that it seeps right into the wound," she advised. "It may sting, but it will save a lot more pain later if you do it properly."

Hollykit watched carefully.

"Do you want to try it before you go?" Leafpool asked.

"I think I should get back to Lionkit," Hollykit mewed, wanting to return to the nursery before Daisy and Ferncloud realized she was missing. "He was pretty sore."

"I could come too," Leafpool offered.

Hollykit was about to say yes when she hesitated. If Leafpool saw how many thorns were tangled in Lionkit's pelt, both kits would be in trouble. "Thanks, but you must have things to do," she mewed. "I'll come and get you if I need help."

"Very well." Leafpool nodded. Was that a knowing glint Hollykit saw in her amber gaze? Had she guessed that Hollykit was not telling her the whole truth about Lionkit's injuries?

Not eager to find out, Hollykit picked up the dock leaves in her jaws and trotted out of the medicine den. Her heart sank when she saw that the camp was growing busy. Daisy had come out of the nursery and was warming herself in a spot where the sun's weak rays were just beginning to reach. Her kits huddled together outside the apprentices' den, blinking sleep from their eyes. They looked like a single soft cloud, Berrypaw's creamy fur merging with the gray and white of

Hazelpaw and Mousepaw. Cinderpaw, Honeypaw, and Poppypaw were sharing tongues by the halfrock. Their slender dappled bodies reminded Hollykit of their mother, Sorreltail, who was nosing through the remains of yesterday's fresh-kill pile with Thornclaw and Spiderleg.

There's no reason they should think I don't have permission to be here, Hollykit told herself. She stalked across the clearing, nodding to the apprentices as casually as she could manage. She avoided looking at Thornclaw and Spiderleg. Her paws burned with every step, but she kept her tail high and tried not to look hurried as she approached the nursery.

She reached the entrance unchallenged and scrabbled through with the dock leaves clamped tightly between her jaws.

Ferncloud's voice startled her. "Where have you been?"

Hollykit dropped the dock leaves and glanced at Lionkit. She was relieved to see that he'd gotten most of the thorns out of his pelt and smoothed down his fur enough to look as though he'd spent the whole night in his nest.

"I told Ferncloud about the thorn in my bedding," Lionkit put in hastily.

"I've brought some dock leaves for Lionkit's scratch," Hollykit explained to Ferncloud. "Sorry I didn't ask first, but I didn't want to wake you."

"You should have waited until I was awake and asked permission. But I suppose you were only thinking of your littermate, and I can't disapprove of that." Ferncloud sighed. "Though StarClan knows how thorns got into the nursery in the first place!" She glanced at her two kits wriggling at her belly. "You must be careful not to carry anything in on your pelts when there are small kits in the nursery."

"We'll be extra careful in the future," Hollykit promised. She hurried over to Lionkit with the leaves. "Did you get all the thorns out?" she whispered.

"All except one behind my ear," Lionkit whispered back.

Hollykit licked the back of Lionkit's ear and felt the thorn. Gripping it with her teeth she tugged it out.

"I put the rest under the brambles at the edge of the den." He flicked his tail to the den wall near his nest. Hollykit went and spat out the thorn with the others.

"We can reach under from outside and drag them out later," she mewed. "Now, where are the worst scratches?" She began to chew up a dock leaf while Lionkit twisted and pointed with his nose to a sore spot on his flank.

The dock leaf tasted foul. "Yuck!" Hollykit screwed up her nose as she chewed. She leaned down and licked the juice into Lionkit's scratch, just as Leafpool had shown her. As she dragged her tongue firmly across the wound, Lionkit flinched and let out a squeak of pain.

Hollykit leaped back in alarm.

"Are you two fighting?" Ferncloud asked, not looking up from her kits.

"No," Lionkit meowed. "The dock juice hurts; that's all."

Hollykit felt her tail tremble. She couldn't do this! Seeing Lionkit's pain made her feel queasy. But she couldn't let any of his scratches get infected, and if she was going to become a medicine cat, she would have to get used to treating patients.

She chewed another horrible-tasting leaf and set to work licking the juice into another scratch. Lionkit only winced this time, but it was enough to send Hollykit leaping away again.

"Sorry!" she squeaked. Then she remembered Leafpool's advice. *It may sting, but it will save a lot more pain later if you do it properly.* Focusing on Leafpool's words, she carried on, forcing herself to ignore Lionkit's squeaks of pain and the sickening taste of the dock.

"That feels much better," Lionkit breathed as she tended to his last wound. Hollykit sat back with relief.

Ferncloud looked up. "Why don't you two go to the fresh-kill pile and have something to eat? Daisy's in the clearing. I'm sure she'll keep an eye on you and make sure you don't get into any mischief."

Happy to be able to leave the nursery without breaking any rules, Hollykit hurried out into the clearing, Lionkit on her heels. But the taste of dock had ruined her appetite, and she followed Lionkit to the fresh-kill pile without enthusiasm.

Mousepaw, Hazelpaw, and Berrypaw still sat in the flattened grass patch in front of their den. Mousepaw could hardly keep still. "Brambleclaw told me that our assessment would begin after sunhigh," he mewed excitedly.

Hollykit pricked her ears. Daisy's kits had been training for nearly four moons. It wouldn't be long before they would be made warriors.

"Who's assessing us?" Berrypaw asked anxiously.

"Brambleclaw wouldn't tell me," Mousepaw replied.

"Do you think it'll be Firestar himself?" Hazelpaw's tail twitched with excitement.

"Don't say that!" Berrypaw breathed. "I won't remember any of my training if I think *he's* watching!"

"Can we hunt together?" Hazelpaw asked.

"Spiderleg said it was up to us," Mousepaw reported.

Ashfur and Whitewing were sharing tongues nearby. Ashfur's whiskers twitched with amusement as he overheard the apprentices talking. "You'd be wiser splitting up!" he called over. "On your own, you might just manage to surprise your prey, but the three of you clumping through the forest will scare everything from here to sun-drown-place!"

Whitewing poked him with her snowy paw. "Don't tease them, Ashfur!" she scolded. "You were an apprentice once. You must remember how tense you were about your first assessment."

Brook trotted through the entrance carrying three mice by their tails. Hollykit watched as the Tribe cat dropped her catch on the fresh-kill pile.

Lionkit helped himself to one and began to eat hungrily. "Thanks, Brook," he mewed with his mouth full.

Brook eyed him with her soft gray gaze. "You should eat more slowly," she advised. "In the mountains we say that prey eaten slowly feeds us longer."

Lionkit looked at her in surprise. "Okay." He nodded and began to chew more carefully.

Hollykit watched as the mountain cat twisted to smooth down her brown tabby pelt. She had always liked the sound of Brook's mew—it was low and strange compared with the forest cats'.

A yowl sounded outside the camp entrance, followed by a threatening hiss. Hollykit recognized Honeypaw's voice.

Honeypaw's mentor, Sandstorm, raced toward the entrance tunnel. "Honeypaw?" she called. "What is it?"

Hollykit held her breath. Was the camp being attacked?

Then she heard a friendly yowl of greeting. Sandstorm returned through the thorn tunnel, leading Mothwing, the RiverClan medicine cat, and her apprentice, Willowpaw. Honeypaw padded after them, her tail bristling with embarrassment.

"I'm sorry," she mewed. "I didn't realize who it was. I just smelled RiverClan."

Sandstorm reassured her apprentice with an old nursery saying: "It's better to scare off a mouse than welcome a badger."

Hollykit's heart leaped like a fish at the sight of Willowpaw. She had met the medicine cat apprentice once before, when Mothwing had brought precious supplies of catmint from the clump that grew in a sheltered part of RiverClan territory. Leafpool had welcomed the gift, since the patch that grew near the abandoned Twoleg nest in ThunderClan territory had been killed by frost. Hollykit had spoken to Willowpaw then because she wanted to find out what it was like to belong to a different Clan. But this time she wanted to find out something else: how to become a medicine cat's apprentice.

While Sandstorm went to find Leafpool, Hollykit scampered across the clearing toward Willowpaw. "Hello!" she mewed shyly.

Willowpaw, who had been looking troubled, brightened up. "Hello, Hollykit!" she purred. "Or is it Hollypaw now?"

"Not yet," Hollykit told her. "Why are you here?" The RiverClan cats weren't carrying anything. Perhaps they had come to ask for supplies in return for the catmint.

Willowpaw's whiskers twitched. "I had a dream," she mewed. "I want Leafpool to help me interpret it."

"Can't Mothwing do that?" Hollykit asked, confused.

Willowpaw glanced at her paws. "Mothwing suggested we get Leafpool's opinion."

"What was it about?"

Willowpaw looked solemn. "I can't tell you until I've shared it with Leafpool."

"Mothwing, Willowpaw!" Leafpool stood at the entrance to the medicine den. "Welcome! Come in!" She waited, holding back the trailing brambles, while Mothwing and Willowpaw weaved past her into the shadows beyond. Hollykit stared wistfully after them as the leaves swished back into place. She felt a nudge in her flank and turned to see Lionkit butting her gently with his head.

"Why are you staring at them like a dumb rabbit?" he

mewed. "Mothwing and Willowpaw have visited the camp before."

Hollykit was unable to keep her wish to herself a moment longer. "I want to be a medicine cat!" she blurted out.

CHAPTER 7

"A medicine cat?" Lionkit stared at Hollykit, bewildered. "Why?"

"There are other ways to serve your Clan apart from being a warrior," Hollykit snapped.

"But you'll be stuck in the camp with all the sick and injured cats instead of out in the forest hunting or fighting." There was no criticism in Lionkit's tone, only disbelief.

Hollykit did not want to hear about what she would be missing. "But think how much I'll *know*," she pointed out. "I'll learn all about healing herbs, and I'll be able to share dreams with StarClan." She stared at him, willing him to understand. "What could be more exciting than that?"

"Fighting ShadowClan?"

"But I want to have dreams just like Leafpool and Willowpaw!" Hollykit insisted.

"You already do," Lionkit purred, his eyes glinting with amusement. "Dreams about hedgehogs!"

"You cheeky kit!" Hollykit squeaked in mock anger. With a small leap, she pushed Lionkit to the ground and began to tussle with him.

"What are you two doing?" Squirrelflight's stern meow made Hollykit freeze. Lionkit struggled from her grasp, and the two kits sat up and faced their mother. "If you've got nothing better to do than make the fresh-kill pile dusty with your fighting, you may as well go back to the nursery."

"But I haven't eaten yet!" Hollykit protested.

"Then take something with you," Squirrelflight answered. "And take something for Ferncloud, too."

Hollykit hated eating in the nursery. Prey always tasted better eaten in the fresh air. But she didn't protest. She saw that Squirrelflight had already turned to look at Thornclaw, who was resting beneath Highledge.

"I hope Thornclaw's remembered that he's leading the sunhigh patrol," the flame-colored she-cat meowed, half to herself.

"You'd better go and remind him, seeing as you seem to be keeping an eye on everyone around here," Hollykit muttered.

"What was that?" Squirrelflight's thoughtful gaze remained on Thornclaw.

"Nothing," Hollykit mewed guiltily.

"Don't forget Ferncloud," Squirrelflight reminded her, padding away.

Hollykit stared after her mother, feeling a surge of rebellious anger. "It wouldn't be so bad if she even noticed she was spoiling our fun!"

"She's just busy," Lionkit mewed. "You know what she's like."

"I suppose." Hollykit sighed. She knew she wasn't being fair. How could she criticize her mother when, in truth, she wanted to be just like her, brave and loyal and respected by her Clanmates? "Let's go back to the nursery."

Hollykit dragged one of Brook's mice from the fresh-kill pile. Lionkit pulled off a thrush more than half his size and began hauling it toward the nursery. Hollykit guessed that Ferncloud wouldn't be able to eat such a large piece of prey, but her brother never changed his mind once it was made up.

Back in the nursery she ate the mouse, giving thanks to StarClan for the food before she tucked in. When she had finished she gave her paws and muzzle a quick lick and then lay flat on her belly to peep out under the brambles at the clearing. Lionkit had fallen asleep beside her, and Ferncloud was trying to persuade Foxkit and Icekit to try a piece of the thrush that she'd softened with her teeth. Hollykit narrowed her eyes and stared at the entrance to the medicine den, watching for any movement. She wanted to speak to Willowpaw again.

At last the brambles twitched and Leafpool led Mothwing and Willowpaw out into the clearing. Hollykit glanced back at Lionkit, still sleeping, and Ferncloud, busy with her kits. As quietly as possible she slithered out under the bramble wall of the den, dislodging a wad of leaves that Squirrelflight had pressed into place the day before. *I'll fix it later,* Hollykit vowed as she scooted across the clearing.

"Hello!" she mewed to Willowpaw.

Willowpaw's ears twitched. She blinked at Hollykit, and the faraway look cleared from her gaze. "Hi," she mewed.

"Did Leafpool help you?"

Willowpaw nodded. "I can tell you about the dream now, if you still want to know."

Hollykit flicked her tail excitedly. "Yes, please."

"Well," Willowpaw began, "I dreamed that clouds were streaming across the sky, flowing and tumbling across the blue. And then they stopped and the sun scorched down onto the RiverClan camp, shriveling the plants and drying up the nests until there was no shelter from the burning heat."

Hollykit shuddered. "What did it mean?"

"Leafpool thought it could be a warning of trouble with our water supply. But there's been plenty of rain this leaf-bare, so it probably doesn't mean a drought. She advised me to tell Leopardstar to check all the streams near the camp and make sure they are safe."

Hollykit leaned forward. "How did you become Mothwing's apprentice?" she asked.

"I helped her with some of her patients when there was an outbreak of illness," Willowpaw told her. "I enjoyed the tasks she gave me, so I just kept going back to the medicine den and helping out until Mothwing suggested I should become her apprentice."

"Did you always want to be a medicine cat?"

"I didn't really think about it," Willowpaw admitted. "It just sort of happened, and then I couldn't imagine doing anything else. Being a medicine cat is great!"

Hollykit opened her mouth to agree, but before she could speak, Mothwing called her apprentice away. "Willowpaw, we're leaving."

Mothwing brushed muzzles with Leafpool and headed for the thorn tunnel. Willowpaw bounded after her. "Bye, Hollykit!" she called over her shoulder.

Hollykit watched the two cats disappear through the tunnel. Willowpaw had made her even more determined to be Leafpool's apprentice. Forgetting that she was not meant to be out of the nursery, she hurried after Leafpool, following her into her den.

Jaykit was sprawled in his nest, the soft gray fur of his belly showing. He was clearly sleeping more comfortably than last time Hollykit had visited.

Leafpool turned as Hollykit followed her in. "Do you need more herbs for Lionkit?"

Hollykit shook her head. A question fizzed on the tip of her tongue, but she was struggling for the right words.

"Is something wrong?"

Jaykit flipped over and lifted his head. "What do you want, Hollykit?" he asked, his ears pricking as though he sensed that something important was happening.

Leafpool glanced at him. "Go back to the nursery, Jaykit," she meowed softly.

"Am I well enough?" Jaykit mewed, sitting up.

"As long as you don't start play fighting the moment you

get back," Leafpool warned him. "But you might as well sleep in your own nest now."

Jaykit got to his paws. His first steps out of his nest were a little unsteady, but he soon found his balance and padded toward the bramble-covered entrance. "Thanks, Leafpool," he mewed. His sightless gaze flicked toward Hollykit, taking her by surprise. Sometimes it was almost as if he were looking straight at her, though she knew he couldn't see her.

"I'll come and check on you at sundown," Leafpool promised him.

As soon as Jaykit had disappeared through the brambles, Leafpool sat down. "Now," she meowed, gazing at Hollykit, "tell me what's troubling you."

"Nothing's *troubling* me," Hollykit answered at once. "But I have something important to ask you."

A look close to alarm flashed momentarily across Leafpool's gaze. "What?"

Hollykit took a deep breath. "I want to be your apprentice!" She tensed as she waited for the reply. What if Leafpool refused to take her on?

Leafpool looked stunned. "I never would have thought—" She stopped midsentence, then meowed gently, "Being a medicine cat is a big commitment. You will rarely fight in battles or go on patrol. You won't be able to take a mate, or have kits." Hollykit saw her eyes darken with sadness. Was that regret she saw in their amber depths? There was no time to wonder. "What has made you want to be a medicine cat?"

"I want to be able to help the Clan," Hollykit told her. "If

I were a medicine cat, I could heal my Clanmates when they were sick, and I could share dreams with StarClan." Leafpool was still gazing at her questioningly, so she went on. "As a warrior I could feed the Clan and defend it—I would *die* to protect the Clan if I had to—but as a warrior I would be limited to fighting with tooth and claw. As a medicine cat I could fight with all the knowledge and power of StarClan. What better way could there be to serve ThunderClan?" She stopped, breathless, and stared hopefully up at Leafpool.

Leafpool's tail twitched. "Those are all good reasons," she agreed.

Hollykit's heart soared. Was she going to say yes?

"But," Leafpool went on, "before I can make a decision, I must talk with Firestar."

Hollykit blinked, feeling a flash of doubt. But she pushed the doubt away. *She hasn't said no.* "Thanks, Leafpool!" she mewed. She turned and trotted from the den. Of course Leafpool would have to talk to the Clan leader before making such an important decision, she thought as she bounced back across the clearing.

She wriggled into the nursery and found Ferncloud asleep, her kits quiet for once. Lionkit was plucking the feathers from the remains of the thrush. They would make a good nest lining.

Jaykit looked up from his nest as she squeezed through the entrance. "What was so secret that I had to leave the medicine den?"

"I'm going to be her apprentice," Hollykit announced.

"Whose apprentice?"

"Leafpool's, of course."

Lionkit looked up from the thrush, delighted. "Did she say yes?"

"Well, she's got to talk to Firestar first, of course."

"You want to be a medicine cat?" Jaykit mewed, putting his head to one side.

"Why shouldn't I?" Hollykit demanded.

"I'd hate to be stuck in the medicine den, worrying about sick cats and sorting out piles of old herbs." Jaykit sank his claws into the moss that lined his nest. "I'd much rather be a warrior, patrolling and hunting and fighting in Clan battles!"

Hollykit looked at her brother, fierce and proud. Firestar had to let him become a warrior!

Hollykit awoke before dawn. The nursery was dark and cozy, warmed by her sleeping denmates. She lay in her nest and listened to an owl calling from the trees lakeside of the camp. She was too excited to go back to sleep. Brambleclaw had told her last night that Firestar would be going ahead with the naming ceremony after all.

"You've behaved well and not left the nursery without permission," he meowed as she took prey from the fresh-kill pile.

Hollykit glanced over to her brothers, who were already eating by the half-buried rock. "What about Jaykit?"

"Don't worry," Brambleclaw had reassured her. "Firestar hasn't forgotten about Jaykit."

Hollykit rolled over in her nest and stretched. By sunhigh she would know if she was to become Leafpool's apprentice. She pictured herself working in the medicine den, soothing bellyaches with herbs, rubbing salves onto bruises, going out into the forest with Leafpool to gather herbs—herbs that she'd know the names of, what they smelled like, how to prepare them. Her pelt bristled at the thought of all the knowledge that would be inside her head. She closed her eyes and tried to imagine how StarClan would appear in her dreams, but instead she saw only herself, a full-fledged medicine cat, leading her own apprentice through the wood, showing one plant after another, demonstrating all the skills and techniques Leafpool had taught her, wandering farther and farther into the darkening forest. . . .

Hollykit blinked open her eyes. Dawn was creeping through the knotted bramble walls. Lionkit and Jaykit were still asleep beside her. Squirrelflight's nest smelled stale and cold. She must have returned late from patrol again and chosen to sleep in the warriors' den.

Hollykit sat up and stretched.

"Awake already?" Ferncloud meowed. The queen was feeding her kits, her pale gray pelt glowing softly in the half-light.

"I'm too excited to sleep!" Hollykit mewed.

"You may go outside if you like," Ferncloud allowed. "The dawn patrol will be back before long. They might bring warm prey."

Icekit wriggled around and stared at Hollykit with round blue eyes. "You won't be sleeping in the nursery tonight," she mewed.

Hollykit blinked at her. "No. Hopefully I'll be in Leafpool's den."

Foxkit pushed away from his mother. "I'd rather be in the apprentices' den with Lionkit!"

"You will be soon," Hollykit promised.

"Not soon enough!" Foxkit mewed. He reached out and caught Icekit's twitching tail between his auburn paws. "I can't wait to be a warrior."

Icekit flicked her tail away from him. "Will you come back and tell us what it's like being an apprentice?"

"Of course," Hollykit purred. She dipped her head to their mother. "Bye, Ferncloud."

Foxkit and Icekit scrambled out of Ferncloud's nest.

"Bye, Hollykit," Icekit mewed, reaching up to push her white muzzle against Hollykit's cheek.

"Bye, Icekit." Hollykit bent down and licked Foxkit between the ears. "Don't get into trouble."

With a twinge of sadness she turned and squeezed out of the nursery.

The clearing sparkled with dew. Mist clouded in the bushes and clefts that ringed the base of the enclosing rock wall. Hollykit stretched, first her forepaws, then her hind, arching her back and enjoying the fresh scents of the forest.

"Good morning!" Squirrelflight called. She was sitting in

front of the warriors' den, a paw raised, ready to wash behind her ears. Brambleclaw sat next to her.

"Hi!" Hollykit mewed, trotting over to greet them.

Brambleclaw purred loudly. "It's your big day!" He touched Hollykit's head with his muzzle.

"It sure is," Hollykit agreed, trying not to think how close she had come to ruining her chance of being made an apprentice.

The thorn barrier trembled; the dawn patrol was returning. Cloudtail emerged from the entrance with his apprentice, Cinderpaw, and Stormfur trotting behind. They each carried prey in their jaws.

Brambleclaw padded away to meet them as they dropped their catch, his dark tabby pelt glistening where it had brushed dew from the branches overhanging the warriors' den. "All clear?"

"No cat has crossed the boundaries," Cloudtail reported. "Although WindClan and ShadowClan are keeping their markers fresh."

Hollykit noticed Squirrelflight's ears prick warily.

"Do you think that's a problem?" Brambleclaw asked.

Cloudtail looked thoughtful. "No, but it feels as if they're both making an effort to remind us that they're there."

"You think they're showing signs of aggression?"

"Not aggression," Cloudtail corrected. "But they never used to be so thorough about marking their boundaries."

"Should we be stepping up patrols?" Ashfur slid out of the

warriors' den, making Hollykit jump. He padded toward Cloudtail and Brambleclaw, and Squirrelflight followed him, leaving Hollykit alone.

"We'll ignore it for now," Brambleclaw decided.

"Isn't that a decision for Firestar to make?" Ashfur meowed.

Brambleclaw looked sharply at the gray warrior, but Ashfur's eyes showed no disrespect, only concern.

Brambleclaw nodded. "I'll speak to him about it, of course," he meowed. "But there's no point overreacting if ShadowClan and WindClan are just trying to provoke us."

Squirrelflight looked at Cloudtail. "Did you refresh our boundary markers?"

Cloudtail nodded.

Hollykit felt another pelt brush her side. Lionkit had joined her, and Jaykit was scrambling out of the nursery after him.

"What's going on?" Lionkit mewed.

"The dawn patrol's reporting back," Hollykit told him. The idea that ShadowClan and WindClan were pressing on their borders worried her. But if she was going to be a medicine cat, she must learn not to be so bothered by warrior concerns and concentrate instead on the needs of her Clanmates.

She glanced around the clearing. Whitewing, Spiderleg, and Thornclaw shared a pigeon beside the halfrock. Honeypaw and Poppypaw were play fighting on the grass patch outside their den. As she watched, the apprentices stopped and looked up at Highledge. Hollykit followed their gaze, her paws pricking with anticipation.

Firestar was leaping down the tumble of rocks that led from his den. Sandstorm nimbly picked her way after him. Hollykit's heart felt as if it flipped right over when Firestar called to the Clan: "Let all cats old enough to catch their own prey gather here beneath the Highledge. It is time to fulfill a promise I made to three of our kits."

Hollykit glanced at her brothers. This was it! The moment when they would begin serving their Clan!

Brambleclaw and Squirrelflight hurried toward them. Squirrelflight quickly smoothed the fur between Lionkit's ears.

"Are you ready?" Brambleclaw's eyes were shining.

"Totally!" Hollykit mewed.

"Good." Brambleclaw padded away and sat beside Birchfall.

Does that mean Birchfall's going to be a mentor? Hollykit wondered.

Squirrelflight licked Jaykit's cheek. "Good luck, all of you." She went to join Brambleclaw.

Mousefur emerged stiffly from the elders' den, guiding her blind denmate, Longtail, with her tail. Honeypaw, Poppypaw, and Berrypaw clustered together, whispering. Whitewing, Spiderleg, and Thornclaw padded over from the halfrock, leaving the remains of their meal behind. Within moments, the whole Clan stood gazing at Firestar. For the first time that morning, Hollykit's excitement felt closer to anxiety. The expectations of Brambleclaw and Squirrelflight, of Firestar, of the whole Clan, pressed down on her shoulders like a badger's paws.

She felt a soft muzzle nudging her from behind. She turned to see Leafpool ushering her toward the circle. She searched Leafpool's eyes, but they gave no clue about what would happen next, only encouraged her forward with a gentle blink.

Hollykit pushed her way between Ferncloud and Daisy and halted. Lionkit and Jaykit squirmed into place beside her, and she felt herself trembling against Daisy's flank. The cream-colored queen glanced fondly at her and ran a smoothing tail over her black pelt.

"I gather you all for one of my favorite duties," Firestar announced. "Hollykit, Lionkit, and Jaykit have reached their sixth moon."

So Jaykit was going to be included in the apprentice-naming ceremony after all.

"They have had an adventurous kithood," Firestar went on with a hint of amusement in his voice, "but I hope they have learned valuable lessons, and I believe they are ready to become apprentices."

The Clan meowed in approval. Firestar waited for the noise to die away before going on. "Lionkit!"

The golden brown tabby kit bounced forward, quivering with excitement.

"From this day until you receive your warrior name, you will be Lionpaw."

Berrypaw called his name and the other apprentices joined in. Firestar looked at the cloud-darkened sky. "I ask StarClan to watch over you and guide you until you find in your paws the strength and courage of a warrior."

Lionpaw's eyes sparkled as he gazed up at his leader.

"Ashfur," Firestar called.

The pale gray tom lifted his head. His eyes brightened, and excitement showed in the tiny twitch of his tail as he stepped forward.

"You mentored Birchfall, and he is a credit to his Clan," Firestar meowed. "Now ThunderClan asks you to prove yourself once more a great mentor."

Ashfur dipped his head as the Clan leader went on. "I trust you to pass on all you have learned to Lionpaw and help him become a warrior the Clan can be proud of."

"I won't let ThunderClan down," Ashfur promised.

Lionpaw hurried forward and raised his muzzle to touch noses with his new mentor.

"Hollykit," Firestar announced.

Hollykit suddenly forgot to be nervous, and she raced to the center of the clearing, skidding to a halt beside Firestar.

His whiskers twitched. "From this day until you receive your warrior name, you will be Hollypaw."

"Hollypaw! Hollypaw!" Cinderpaw led the chant this time.

Hollypaw stared at the apprentices as they called her new

name. Berrypaw and Hazelpaw seemed so big and strong. In the nursery she had been older than Icekit and Foxkit. Now she would be one of the youngest of her denmates. Her heart drummed like paws racing over the forest floor. Then she remembered: *I might not be sleeping in the apprentices' den!*

"Leafpool," Firestar called.

Yes! Hollypaw felt so light on her paws she was afraid the breeze would carry her away over the trees. She was going to be a medicine cat apprentice!

Leafpool padded forward and stopped beside Hollypaw.

"I know that I am putting Hollypaw in safe paws," Firestar meowed. "I pray that StarClan gives your apprentice all the strength and wisdom she will need."

"I will teach her everything I know," Leafpool promised. She touched Hollypaw's muzzle with hers, but she didn't meet Hollypaw's eyes; instead, she looked past her, her expression clouded.

Surprised, Hollypaw turned and saw that Leafpool was staring at Squirrelflight. She wondered why there was sadness in both cats' eyes.

Jaykit marched into the clearing and stood in front of Firestar. "What about me?"

"Surely he can't become an apprentice?" Whitewing's whispered comment hung in the still, damp air.

"Longtail moved to the elders' den when he went blind," Thornclaw murmured, as if he agreed that blind cats couldn't be warriors.

"He wouldn't be safe out in the forest," Spiderleg put in.

"Poor mite," breathed Sorreltail.

Hollypaw's pelt bristled. Why shouldn't her brother be given a chance like any other cat?

"I want to be an apprentice like Lionpaw and Hollypaw," Jaykit spat defiantly.

"Of course you do," Firestar agreed. "And your mentor will be Brightheart."

CHAPTER 8

❧

Brightheart?

Jaykit felt a rush of anger so strong it almost knocked him off his paws. Why had Firestar chosen one-eyed Brightheart when there were so many other warriors to choose from? As if he couldn't guess!

He dug his claws into the earth, refusing to step forward to greet his mentor. He ignored her embarrassment, although he could sense it like holly leaves pricking his pelt. He ignored the encouraging murmurs of the other apprentices. He ignored Spiderleg's angry, "Sshh!" which quieted them. And then he felt a muzzle gently but firmly pushing him forward.

Leafpool's voice murmured in his ear. "Go on."

Gritting his teeth, he padded toward Brightheart and Firestar.

"I know it must be hard for you," Brightheart greeted him sympathetically. "But I promise I will teach you how to protect your Clan even without sight."

She pitied him! He could hear it in her voice. His anger swelled up again, sending blood pounding through his ears.

"Why bother if you think I'm so useless? Why don't you just send me off to the elders' den with Longtail?" he hissed.

Brightheart stiffened. "No cat has said that you're useless. And Longtail won't thank you for being rude about him!" She stepped back from Jaypaw and lifted her chin. "I've asked him to help with some of your training."

Jaykit lashed his tail. *Oh, great*, he thought. *Let's lump all the useless cats together and hope a tree falls on them!*

Firestar stepped between Jaykit and Brightheart. "From this day until you receive your warrior name, you will be Jaypaw."

"Jaypaw! Jaypaw! Jaypaw!" Mousepaw's and Berrypaw's call rang around the hollow, and the other apprentices joined in loudly.

Jaypaw clawed the ground. *You don't have to try so hard! You're only doing it because you feel sorry for me!*

"Brightheart," Firestar meowed, "you have never let what happened to you prevent you from being a fine warrior. I can think of no one better than you to teach Jaypaw how best to serve his Clan."

"I will share with him all I have learned," Brightheart vowed.

Big deal, Jaypaw thought.

Reluctantly, he forced himself to touch muzzles with Brightheart, accepting her as his mentor. His whiskers brushed the side of her face that had been ravaged when she had been attacked by the dog pack. It felt strange to sense space where other cats had fur and flesh, and he had to suppress a shudder.

The whole Clan raised their voices to cheer the new

apprentices. *Not me*, Jaypaw thought bitterly. *There's not a cat here that thinks I'll become a great warrior.*

When the calls died away Firestar spoke again. "Thunder-Clan is lucky to have so many apprentices. I hope they will train hard and serve their Clan well."

"We will!" Lionpaw mewed.

"When can we start training?" Hollypaw asked.

"That's up to your mentors," Firestar told her.

"Come on, Lionpaw," Ashfur meowed. "Let's find you a nest in the apprentices' den; then I'll show you the forest."

"Right now?" Lionpaw mewed excitedly.

"Why not?"

Hollypaw's paws pattered on the ground around Leafpool. "Can we go with Lionpaw when Ashfur shows him our territory?"

"It's a nice idea, Hollypaw," Leafpool meowed. "But I need to show you the best herb-gathering places, and I'm sure Ashfur will want to show Lionpaw the boundary markers and the best places for hunting."

"Oh." Hollypaw sounded disappointed.

"But first, let's look at the herb store," Leafpool suggested, "so you get to know some of the leaves we'll be looking at in the forest."

"Okay," Hollypaw mewed, sounding more cheerful.

As Lionpaw and Hollypaw padded after their mentors, Jaypaw sat down crossly. *How come they get real mentors?* He felt Brightheart's tail touch his shoulder. "Come with me," she meowed.

Sullenly he followed her to a clump of wilting grass that overflowed from a quiet alcove in the rocky camp wall.

"I think it's best if we start . . ." Brightheart began.

Jaypaw did not listen to the rest. Instead he let his attention slip until her voice had blended with the sound of the wind swishing through the branches above the hollow. He could hear Lionpaw hurrying after Ashfur, eagerly following his mentor out of the camp and into the forest. Hollypaw's scent was clear beyond the bramble-draped entrance to the medicine den; Jaypaw could taste the tang of the comfrey she was tearing and laying out to dry.

At least I'm not a medicine cat apprentice. He felt a flicker of gratitude that Hollypaw had taken that role.

He went on scanning the camp. With the sureness he had possessed since his first memory, he knew that Daisy was circling in her nest, preparing for a nap. Mousefur was guiding Longtail back to the elders' den. He sensed the old she-cat's longing to be out in the forest; she was in a hunting mood, though her movements were stiff with age. Longtail padded quietly beside her, his limbs still as supple as a warrior's.

It's not fair he should live in the elders' den, Jaypaw thought. *He's not old yet.*

Then, like a storm cloud shadowing the hollow, he sensed a darkness sweep over the camp. He pricked his ears, and heard claws scraping the rocky ledge outside Firestar's den. He knew by the scent that it was not Firestar who sat up there, flexing his paws. It was Brambleclaw.

Jaypaw knew his father sat up there often, a good deputy

keeping watch over his Clan. But now he could sense something cold and uncomfortable, like a murky fog, in Brambleclaw's mind. He struggled to understand it, groping for the right word.

Suspicion!

Brambleclaw was suspicious of his Clanmates! He was not watching over them, but searching for a cat he feared might betray him. Jaypaw shivered, the fur on his spine lifting. Why would any cat betray Brambleclaw? He was a great deputy.

He blinked, and his thoughts jerked back to Brightheart. She had jumped to her paws and was obviously waiting for him to say something. He flicked his tail, wondering how he could cover up the fact that he hadn't been paying attention. But she had already guessed that he had not been listening to a word.

She snorted impatiently. "We're going to see Longtail, remember?"

Jaypaw's heart sank. More pointless advice from a second-rate warrior. "Okay," he mewed unenthusiastically.

Brightheart sighed. "Come on."

Dragging his paws, he followed her across the clearing.

At the entrance to the elders' den, Brightheart called through the spindly branches that brushed the ground around its edge, "It's Brightheart and Jaypaw!"

"Come in, come in," Longtail meowed.

Brightheart ducked down under the low branch entrance and padded into the space that ringed the trunk of the honeysuckle bush. Jaypaw followed, keeping his head low, uncertain for once about his surroundings. He had not been in this den before, but he knew by the scent that Longtail was alone. Mousefur must have gone out into the forest after all.

"Congratulations, Jaypaw!" Longtail purred. "You've been given a great mentor."

"Thank you, Longtail." Jaypaw heard shyness and pride in Brightheart's mew.

"Firestar has set you quite a challenge for your first apprentice, Brightheart," Longtail remarked.

"Just because I'm blind doesn't mean—" Jaypaw began hotly.

"I wasn't referring to your blindness," Longtail interrupted. "I meant your attitude."

"What's wrong with my attitude?"

"It's not many cats who'd try foxhunting before they were even out of the nursery." There was humor in Longtail's mew.

Jaypaw bristled. *I was only trying to help my Clan!* But before he could point this out, Brightheart was issuing orders.

"First I want you to clean out the moss, get rid of any dusty or dirty pieces," she instructed. "I'll fetch some fresh for now, because you don't know the best place to gather it."

Cleaning out bedding! Jaypaw knew it was a routine apprentice task—he had heard Berrypaw and Hazelpaw complain about it often enough—but knowing that Lionpaw was already exploring the territory made him want to snarl.

"Then," Brightheart went on, "check Longtail for fleas and ticks, and Mousefur too, if she's back by then. While you're busy, Longtail can tell you about using other senses rather than sight."

Jaypaw wanted to wail with frustration. He and Longtail were totally different. Longtail had lost his sight *after* he had been a warrior. Blindness must have been devastating after relying on his sight for his whole life. But Jaypaw had never seen the world with any other senses apart from sound, scent, and touch. Being blind was totally natural for him. How could Longtail know what that was like? He could probably give Longtail more advice than the blind cat could give him—how to pick the freshest prey from the pile, how to tell where your denmates had been by the scents on their pelts. . . .

"You might as well make a start, Jaypaw," Brightheart suggested. Was that impatience he heard in her mew? *You'll be feeling more than impatience if you keep giving me rubbish tasks like this!* he predicted mutinously.

As Brightheart nosed her way out of the den, he began sorting through the moss, feeling with his paws for pieces that had grown dry and scratchy and sniffing for pieces that were beginning to smell stale. "This apprenticeship is going to be so dull," he hissed under his breath.

"What was that?" Mousefur had padded into the den, her pelt smelling of the forest. Her pawsteps were uneven, and she breathed in sharply as she sat down. "You've missed a bit over here," she pointed out.

"He's only just started," Longtail defended him.

Mousefur snorted. "Does that mean we'll have him scrabbling around the den until sunhigh? I was hoping to get some sleep."

"It's not my fault you're stiff!" Jaypaw snapped. "You're the one that went out into the forest when it's damp."

He felt Mousefur look closely at him. "How did you know I was stiff?"

"I could tell when you sat down," Jaypaw replied, hooking out a wad of dry moss and flinging it toward the den entrance. "You moved slowly and made that noise."

"What noise?"

"A sort of gasp, like it hurt."

A purr of amusement suddenly rumbled in the old she-cat's throat. "I see Brightheart is going to have her paws full," she meowed.

Jaypaw felt a glimmer of hope. *Perhaps they'll stop underestimating me quite so much once they realize it doesn't matter that I can't see.* He finished sorting through the moss, then padded over to Longtail and began nosing through his fur.

"I bet you can't wait to start training in the forest," Longtail meowed. "I remember my first time out like it was last moon." A wistful edge entered his mew. "Of course, I wasn't blind then. Everything seemed so green and fresh. But you'll still love it, even though you're blind. There are so many scents out there."

I'd kind of noticed. Jaypaw felt the hard body of a flea in the warrior's pelt.

"That's the one thing I've noticed about being blind," Longtail went on. "Scents become so much sharper and more important."

Thanks for the information. Jaypaw cracked the flea between his teeth.

"And sounds, of course," Longtail added. "I can sometimes hear the mice moving at the top of the hollow. I never would have noticed that before. You should make sure you listen really well, all the time."

Jaypaw began to check the fur around Longtail's scruff. A tick was lodged behind the warrior's ear.

"When it comes to hunting, it'll help to have sharp hearing and smell. Prey is always hard to *see*, but smelling it is easy. Even when I could see, it was usually the scent or sound of prey that told me where it was hiding."

You'll be telling me that a fresh mouse tastes juicier than a stale one next, Jaypaw thought, tugging at the tick harder than he needed to.

"Ow!" Longtail complained.

"How's it going in here?" Brightheart's voice sounded at the den entrance. "Have you finished?"

"I think so." Jaypaw looked hopefully toward Mousefur. "You don't have any ticks, do you?"

"Only one in my side, but I can reach it myself," she replied.

Jaypaw turned to his mentor. "I've finished, then."

Brightheart began bundling pawfuls of fresh moss into the den. "Good. Spread this out and then come with me," she meowed. "I'm going to show you the territory around the camp."

At last! Hollypaw and Lionpaw had been out for ages.

"Good luck!" Longtail called as Jaypaw followed Brightheart out of the den.

She led him out of the camp and up the steep slope that

led lakeward. "This trail leads to the top of the ridge," Brightheart explained. "It's steep."

"Okay." Jaypaw decided not to tell her that he could already feel the slope beneath his paws. He followed his mentor as she weaved through the trees, feeling the damp leaves slippery underpaw.

"Watch out!" Brightheart called, but Jaypaw could smell the bark ahead of him and swerved just in time to avoid the tree, his whiskers grazing the trunk.

"The trees are thick here, but there's not too much undergrowth."

"Oh." Jaypaw breathed in the scent of a mouse trail as the ground began to flatten out.

"We're at the top of the ridge now," Brightheart told him. "Follow my scent and I'll lead you along the crest."

"Right." He could tell by the slope of the land that the forest fell away on either side; it felt as though they were climbing the spine of a great cat.

"If we go up this trail, we'll be out of the trees soon."

Jaypaw was beginning to feel out of breath, so he didn't reply. He listened to the flies buzzing around him and shook his head when they tickled his ears.

"We're out of the trees now, so don't worry about bumping into anything," Brightheart meowed. Jaypaw knew they had left the cover of the forest. A light, damp wind brushed his face.

"Stop here," Brightheart meowed. But Jaypaw had already halted, feeling the land drop steeply away at his pawtips.

Scents flooded him—distant, strange smells he didn't know yet—and he could hear water lapping far below. He knew that they were looking out over the forest and lake.

"We've followed the ridge out of the forest and right up to the end," Brightheart explained. "The land slopes down steeply from here to the lake. RiverClan territory is across the water. Over where the sun sets is ShadowClan territory. And if you look back toward where the sun rises you'll be able to see—" She broke off abruptly.

For the first time that day, Jaypaw felt sorry for his mentor. She must have hoped that her first apprentice would be a healthy kit she wouldn't have to make special allowances for. If only she realized that he didn't want any special allowances, that he didn't *need* them.

"I might not be able to see what you see," he told her, "but I can tell a lot from what I can hear and smell and feel." He lifted his nose. "I know ShadowClan is over there, not just because the stench of them is strong enough to scare a rabbit, but because the tang of the pines tells me there can't be much undergrowth, so the cats who hunt there must be cunning and good at stalking." He turned his head. "And over there I can smell the moorland. The wind comes in a great unbroken sweep, undisturbed by trees. The WindClan cats who live there must be fast and small to hunt in such open country." Then he gazed at the lake in front of them. "I know RiverClan live across the lake, though I can't smell their scent. It's hidden by the scents from the lake, which are stronger today because of the wind. But I know that

RiverClan will feel the coming rain first because the wind is driving the waves this way—I can hear them slapping against the shore."

"You can tell all that without seeing it?"

"Yes, of course."

Suddenly Brightheart stiffened. She was listening intently, ears pricked. "A patrol is coming," she announced.

Jaypaw had heard it already. A ThunderClan patrol was climbing the ridge toward them, rustling though the bracken and heather. He knew from the scents that it was Dustpelt, Hazelpaw, Thornclaw, and Poppypaw, but he didn't say so out loud. He was pleased he had impressed Brightheart with his description of what was around them, but he didn't want her to think he was showing off.

"Hi!" Poppypaw bounded out from the bracken first. Thornclaw followed with Dustpelt and Hazelpaw close on his heels. "You're out of the camp at last!" Poppypaw mewed.

"Isn't it great being an apprentice?" Hazelpaw added. "I still remember my first day. I was so excited!"

I bet your first day as an apprentice was more exciting than this.

"We've just done a border patrol," Hazelpaw went on.

"And now we're going to do battle training in the mossy clearing!" Poppypaw finished.

"Great," Jaypaw muttered.

"You can come with us!" Poppypaw suggested suddenly. She turned to her mentor, Thornclaw. "He can come, can't he?"

"Perhaps another day," Brightheart meowed.

"We haven't finished exploring our territory," she

explained, addressing Jaypaw as much as Poppypaw.

"Oh, okay," Poppypaw mewed.

"Where are you heading now?" Thornclaw asked Bright-heart.

"I'm going to show Jaypaw the old Thunderpath."

Thornclaw paused. "You'll be careful?" he cautioned. "Don't stray over the ShadowClan border."

Jaypaw bristled. They might have only one eye between them, but they weren't idiots! As he prepared to snarl a reply, Brightheart mewed sharply, "I know a border marker when I smell it!"

Jaypaw sensed a flash of reproach shoot from Dustpelt. "Firestar trusted Brightheart with Jaypaw," he reminded Thornclaw quietly.

Thornclaw's paws rustled on the leafy forest floor. "Of course," he acknowledged. "Sorry, Brightheart."

Brightheart met his apology with stony silence, and Jaypaw felt a prick of satisfaction that he wasn't the only one who felt patronized by the other warriors.

"There's a steep slope ahead of us," Brightheart warned as they set off.

You don't say! Jaypaw bit back the sharp reply, feeling the curve of the ground under his paws.

"Can you manage it?"

"Of course I can." Angrily Jaypaw stepped forward. To his surprise, the ground dropped away much more steeply than he expected, and he half fell, half skidded down the muddy slope, scrabbling to slow his descent until a clump of heather slowed it for him.

"Are you okay?" Brightheart panted, catching up with him.

Jaypaw struggled out of the heather, then gave his chest a couple of brisk licks. "I'm fine," he mewed.

"That was quite a tumble. We can rest if you want," Brightheart offered.

"I told you, I'm fine," Jaypaw hissed. He shook the last scraps of heather from his pelt. "Which way now?"

He could feel Brightheart looking closely at him, but she didn't say anything else about his fall. "Come on," she meowed. "We can head around to the old Thunderpath from here."

Jaypaw padded after her, furious with himself for losing his footing so easily just when Brightheart seemed to be treating him like a normal apprentice.

The wind had picked up by the time they reached the old Thunderpath. Jaypaw smelled rain on its way.

"We'll head back to the camp from here," Brightheart told him when they reached the gap in the trees where Twolegs had once cut a path, now overgrown and deserted.

"But there must be more ThunderClan territory than this!" Jaypaw objected.

"Too much to explore today," Brightheart meowed.

Crossly Jaypaw turned away from the Thunderpath and followed Brightheart back into the trees. He didn't believe that they couldn't circle the whole territory in one day.

Brightheart obviously thought he wouldn't be able to cope with a long day out of the camp.

They padded through the trees. Rain was beginning to fall, spattering on the leaves above them. Jaypaw looked up just as a raindrop found its way through the canopy and splashed onto his nose. He shivered and shook off the wetness. Perhaps it was not so bad that they were going back to the hollow. The rain was cold, and the wind that carried it over the lake even colder. He heard Brightheart's step quicken and guessed she must be feeling the same way.

Then he stiffened.

There was another scent on the breeze, sharper than the rain and the leaves. Memories flooded him of his terrifying dash through the forest. Fox! Another sniff showed it was the same fox that had chased him over the edge of the hollow, with the scent of earth and bracken in its pelt. And it was close. Jaypaw dropped into a defensive crouch and opened his mouth to warn Brightheart, but her fear-scent told him that she had smelled the creature already.

"We must find Thornclaw's patrol!" she hissed.

Jaypaw sniffed the air, searching for a scent-trace of the patrol. It would tell them which way to run. With relief, he picked up a faint smell of Thornclaw, but it was too late. The bracken up ahead rustled, and the fox hurled itself out and charged toward them. Jaypaw's heart almost burst with fear. The fox cub's paws pounded on the forest floor; its stench was stronger and its snarl was deeper than he remembered. The fox had grown since their last encounter.

"Run!" Brightheart ordered, throwing herself between the fox and Jaypaw.

"I won't leave you!" Jaypaw yowled. "I can fight!"

He heard the clack of teeth as the fox snapped at Brightheart. She hissed, her paws skidding as she dodged. The fox's pained screech told Jaypaw that she had caught it with a claw as it had lunged past.

A rush of air tugged his fur as the fox darted past him. He twisted, claws unsheathed, and prepared to lunge forward. The fox was scrabbling to turn on the slippery leaves for another attack. Jaypaw leaped, spitting, but something tugged him back. His tail was caught in a bramble bush! He collapsed on the ground, dragged back by the thorns. A heavy paw landed on his back, knocking the wind from him. The fox had thundered straight over him, heading once more for Brightheart.

The one-eyed warrior screeched, anger and fear combined, and Jaypaw froze with terror.

Then he heard Thornclaw's yowl only rabbit-lengths away. The patrol had come!

The air filled with the battle cries as warriors and apprentices streamed into the clearing, ears flattened and claws unsheathed. The fox let out an angry yelp and raced into the trees, with Dustpelt and Hazelpaw pounding after it.

Jaypaw struggled to his paws, yanking his tail to unsnag it from the bramble bush.

"Jaypaw!" Poppypaw was at his side. "Are you okay?"

He wrenched his tail free with the sound of ripping fur. "I'm fine!" he snapped.

"Did the fox hurt you?" Brightheart called.

Jaypaw was relieved to hear his mentor. He smelled no blood on her, and her voice was strong. The fox had not wounded her.

"Don't tell me you tried to fight the fox?" Thornclaw demanded. "You should have run for help!"

"I couldn't leave Brightheart alone with it," Jaypaw objected.

"I thought you would have learned by now that you're no match for a fox!" Thornclaw growled. Jaypaw curled his lip but said nothing.

"Is your tail okay?" Poppypaw asked sympathetically.

Jaypaw lashed it over the leaf-covered ground, ignoring the pain of the thorns still stuck in it. "It's fine," he muttered. The whole patrol must have seen him struggling like a helpless kit, defeated by a bramble bush. A hot wave of embarrassment washed over him from nose to tail.

"Will Dustpelt and Hazelpaw be all right?" he asked.

"They'll chase the fox away from the camp," Thornclaw told him. "I don't think it'll turn on them. Not after the fright we gave it."

"We should get Brightheart and Jaypaw back to camp and send a patrol after them," Poppypaw suggested.

"Good idea," Thornclaw agreed.

The rain eased as dusk began to chill the air. Jaypaw lay pressed into the same sheltered clump of grass where Brightheart had taken him that morning. He had wanted to be alone, and the thorny wall of the warriors' den hid him from the rest of the camp. But now Lionpaw had returned with Ashfur; he could hear them in the center of the clearing.

"Where's Jaypaw?" Lionpaw sounded worried.

Hollypaw answered from outside the medicine cat's den. "I haven't seen him, but Brightheart's back. He must be in the camp."

"Shall we ask her where he is?"

Jaypaw didn't want Brightheart to tell them what an idiot he had made of himself today. He slipped out and headed Hollypaw and Lionpaw off at the fresh-kill pile.

"There you are!" Hollypaw called.

"Hi," Jaypaw muttered. He padded past them and pulled a mouse from the top of the pile.

Hollypaw followed him and picked up a sparrow. She dropped it on the ground next to Jaypaw while Lionpaw rooted among the prey until he found the fresh-smelling body of a vole. "I caught this myself!" he announced proudly, tossing it onto the ground beside Hollypaw.

"You caught prey on your first day?" Hollypaw sounded impressed.

"Well," Lionpaw admitted, "Ashfur spotted it and showed me how to stalk it."

"He probably held it down for you to finish off," Jaypaw growled.

There was a moment's silence; then Hollypaw brushed her tail over Jaypaw's pelt. "I heard you ran into trouble," she mewed. "It could have happened to any cat."

Jaypaw shrugged away her tail. "But it happened to me," he growled.

"It's only your first day," Lionpaw reminded him.

Yes, and you caught a vole on your first day, didn't you?

Hollypaw sniffed at the thorns in Jaypaw's tail and plucked at one with her teeth.

"I can do that myself," Jaypaw hissed, flicking his tail away from her.

"Do you want some herbs?" she offered. "I know which ones will soothe the pain and stop infection." There was pride in her mew.

"No need." Jaypaw took a bite of mouse, but it felt dry and tasteless. He nudged the mouse over to Lionpaw with his muzzle. "Here, you finish it. I'm not hungry."

"Wait . . ." Lionpaw began. But Jaypaw padded gloomily away.

He headed toward the apprentices' den, which was underneath a bushy yew tree growing close to the wall of the hollow. It took him a moment to figure out where the entrance was, and when he had, he nosed his way in cautiously. The unfamiliar scents confused him—moss rich with the smell of different apprentices, the strong tang of yew sap. He had no idea what lay around him or where he should lie down.

"Hey, Jaypaw." Hazelpaw's mew came from the far side of the den. "There's no one here but me. Just head toward my voice. There's some clean moss next to my nest where you can sleep."

Jaypaw was too tired and miserable to make a fuss about

being helped. Gratefully, he padded toward Hazelpaw's nest, and as he did, the scents around him began to fall into place, like a flight of birds settling one by one into a tree. He smelled Poppypaw's scent, so stale that she had clearly not been in here since sunrise; Berrypaw's nest had been slept in more recently, and Honeypaw's smelled warm as though she'd just left it. Jaypaw weaved cautiously among the little patches of scent until he found the clean moss beside Hazelpaw.

"Thanks," he murmured, settling down.

"No problem," she answered sleepily.

He was glad she sounded too tired to talk. Right now, all he wanted to do was to tuck his nose under his paw and sleep.

CHAPTER 9

❧

Silverpelt glittered overhead as Jaypaw followed the narrow valley upward. He glanced up at the jagged rocks that lined his path, sharp as fox teeth. Ahead, a stream danced down the mountainside, sparkling in the moonlight. A cold breeze whisked down from the gray peaks and set his fur rippling like water. It felt as though he had been following this stony path for days, and still he had to follow the stream upward, into the mountains.

A paw jabbed his side, catching him painfully between the ribs. Jaypaw flinched. He blinked open his eyes and saw only darkness.

He had been dreaming.

The paw jabbed him again.

"Watch out!" he complained.

"Sorry!" Lionpaw apologized.

"Why are you so fidgety this morning?" Jaypaw lifted his muzzle. He could smell dew on the leaves and guessed that it was hardly dawn. Only Lionpaw and Berrypaw were stirring.

"We're going on border patrol with Ashfur and Brambleclaw," Lionpaw explained excitedly.

"Big deal," Jaypaw muttered. "Brambleclaw's only taking you because nothing happens on the borders these days."

"What about ShadowClan and WindClan leaving extra scent markers?"

"Are you scared of smells?" Jaypaw snapped back.

Lionpaw flinched away from him.

"I'm sorry," Jaypaw murmured. "I'm sure it'll be great."

"Yeah," Lionpaw agreed quietly. "I'll see you later." Without another word he padded out of the den, followed by Berrypaw.

Jaypaw wriggled deeper into his nest, cold now Lionpaw had gone. He tried to go back to his dream but sleep would not come again.

The fresh scent of dawn was filtering slowly into the den when Mousepaw and Hazelpaw began to yawn and stretch.

Hazelpaw nudged Jaypaw. "Stop pretending to be asleep," she mewed.

Jaypaw lifted his head reluctantly.

"Has Berrypaw gone already?" she asked him.

"Yes."

"Oh, well." Hazelpaw sounded disappointed at missing her brother. "I'll see him at battle training later."

"Hazelpaw!" Dustpelt's deep growl sounded through the den entrance. "The fresh-kill pile is empty. Bring Mousepaw. We're going hunting."

Hazelpaw's tail fluffed up. "Great," she mewed. "I thought I was going to have to spend the morning cleaning out the elders' den!"

Why would they ask you to do that when they've got me? Jaypaw thought as she disappeared from the den with Mousepaw. *Daisy's kits have more important duties than me, and they're not even Clanborn!*

"Hi, Jaypaw!" Poppypaw called. "How was your first night in the apprentices' den?"

"Fine," Jaypaw mewed halfheartedly.

Cinderpaw was stirring too. "What are you doing today?" she asked.

"Well, I'm *not* patrolling and I'm *not* hunting," Jaypaw informed her.

"Perhaps Brightheart has planned battle training for you," Poppypaw suggested.

"I hope so!" Cinderpaw put in. "We're training in the clearing this morning. It'd be great if you could come too."

Jaypaw did not answer.

"I hope we see you there," Poppypaw called over her shoulder as she headed out of the den.

And rabbits might fly, Jaypaw muttered to himself.

Only Honeypaw remained in the den, and she was fast asleep. Jaypaw wasn't going to wait for her to wake up and start chirping like a fledgling about what duties she was looking forward to. Instead he crept from his nest and ducked out of the den.

The frosty ground beneath his paws told him that the skies were clear today. The camp was already busy, even though the sun had not yet begun to warm the hollow. Firestar stood with Brackenfur and Spiderleg, organizing hunting parties and border patrols. Leafpool was heading for the nursery, and Squirrelflight was sharing tongues with Stormfur and Brook.

There was no sign of Brightheart. She had probably forgotten Jaypaw and gone on the dawn patrol without him. Resentment rose like bile in his throat. *I'll show her I'm not useless!*

He hurried across the clearing to the tunnel leading to where the cats made dirt. As he emerged, he scented Sandstorm heading into the camp. There was no time to go back. Instead he dived forward and plunged behind a clump of bracken. Sandstorm's pawsteps halted, and Jaypaw could hear her sniffing the air. He held his breath, praying to StarClan she wouldn't see him. She paused a moment more and then carried on back through the tunnel and into the camp.

Jaypaw let out a sigh of relief and scrambled out of the bracken, shaking a scrap of dried leaf from his ear. He quickly found the path that he and Brightheart had taken yesterday. If Brightheart wasn't going to show him the whole of ThunderClan territory, he would explore it by himself. He would start by going farther toward the lake. He had never been that far, and the fresh scents of wind and water excited him.

It was easy enough climbing the slope and following the ridge again, and when he came to the end of it, he was prepared this time for the steepness of the slope. He scrabbled down it, using his claws to slow his descent, and when he reached the heather bush that had stopped him last time he headed away from the Thunderpath, in the opposite direction from the one they had taken yesterday.

Jaypaw followed the side of the ridge down through the trees. Weaving his way through the undergrowth was easy; he just followed his whiskers, padding confidently over the leaf-strewn forest floor. But gradually the trees and undergrowth began to thin out and the slope flattened. The ground became soft, no longer covered with leaves, but springy with moss. Heather brushed his pelt.

He tasted the air, wondering how far from the lake he was. Yesterday the wind had flowed in over the water, and he had smelled it quite clearly. But today the wind blew from ThunderClan territory, giving no clue about the land ahead. He listened for the slapping of water on the shore, but it sounded very distant, and it was hard to tell where it was coming from.

Suddenly his forepaw slipped into a dip in the ground. He had stumbled into a rabbit hole. His paw twisted beneath him and pain shot up his leg. Wincing, he scrambled out of the hole and licked his paw. It was not badly hurt, but it was several moments before he dared test it on the ground.

This isn't like the woodland at all. For the first time he wondered if exploring on his own had been a good idea. But he was determined to reach the lake by himself. Gingerly he lowered his paw, relieved when it was able to take his weight.

He padded forward cautiously, shivering as water from the boggy ground seeped up and soaked the fur between his claws. Suddenly his forepaws sank deep into the peaty earth.

Freezing mud soaked his legs up to his chest. *StarClan, help me!* He scrabbled backward, his hind claws gripping desperately onto the solid ground behind. With a frantic heave he freed his forepaws from the sucking mud and twisted his whole body, grabbing for the nearest clump of heather. He scrambled in among its bristly branches, and stood trembling on its sturdy web of roots.

I must test the ground before I step forward, he warned himself, his heart pounding so loud that it drowned out the noise of the waves and the wind. He reached out a tentative paw and poked the ground on the other side of the heather. It felt springy with moss but firm, and he slipped out from the heather and warily padded forward.

Concentrating hard, he felt his way forward, one slow pawstep at a time, always staying within reach of heather— something to cling to if he lost his footing again. Little by little the ground underpaw grew firmer and drier. The land was sloping up again, and he sensed space opening before him. Surer now, he began to relax. He sniffed the air. The wind still blew from behind him, carrying the familiar scent of home. He wondered for a moment if he should go back, but he pushed the thought away. *I won't give up!*

He tried to build an image of the landscape in his mind, storing it so that the next time he was here he could travel more confidently. The springy moss was turning to smooth grass underpaw. He could hear the rustling of the forest far behind him. The sound of the lake rippling in the wind was louder now, making his paws prick with excitement. He quickened his step, beginning to enjoy the freedom of the open space—the sun warm on his face, the wind tugging his fur.

Happily he sniffed the air again.

WindClan!

Alarm gripped him. The scent of WindClan cats was so strong here that it covered his own. And yet he hadn't heard any movement around him. He was sure there were no cats nearby. Had he strayed across the border without realizing it?

Confused, he twisted around, hunting for the scent of home. He stepped backward, frightened—and without warning the land disappeared. He thrashed with his paws, trying to grasp some branch or rock, but there was nothing but a sheer, empty drop beneath him.

Then he hit water.

The shock of the cold water knocked the breath from him, so that he found himself flailing beneath the waves, his lungs screaming for air while he struggled to work out which way was up. Jaypaw tried to wail out loud, but water filled his mouth and his eyes and his ears.

I'm going to drown!

Suddenly a sharp tug on his scruff dragged him backward. Something was heaving him through the water. Instinctively he stopped struggling and fell limp like a kit in its mother's jaws. He let himself be wrenched upward until, his chest bursting, he broke the surface.

In his first gulp of air he swallowed a mouthful of water which made him cough and splutter until he thought he was going to be sick.

"Keep still!" a voice hissed through clenched teeth.

Jaypaw felt himself being tugged awkwardly through the rippling waves. His paws churned in the water as he felt for the bottom.

"Stop wriggling!" the voice hissed again, and Jaypaw suddenly felt pebbles scrape against his pelt as his rescuer hauled him out of the water and onto a stony beach.

He collapsed, retching and gasping. Paws began to work on his chest, pumping the water from him.

"Will he be okay?" The anxious mew of a young cat sounded close by.

Jaypaw was too shocked to make sense of the scents around him. "Who's there? Are you warriors?" he rasped.

"What do you mean?" The voice sounded puzzled, then shocked. "He can't see!"

"What in the name of StarClan is he doing out here by himself?" Jaypaw heard a deeper voice and recognized the angry hiss of his rescuer.

A rough tongue began to lick him, massaging his cold body. Another tongue joined it, and he closed his eyes again and lay helpless, weak with shock, letting the rhythmic strokes soothe and warm him.

As his mind cleared, he realized that the cats were Wind-Clan. Their scent was the same one that had been blown to him across the moorland the day before. And there were four of them, two older, two younger—warriors and their apprentices?

"Will he be okay, Whitetail?" one of the apprentices

mewed. She crept forward and crouched beside Jaypaw. He could feel her pelt trembling against his.

"He'll be fine, Heatherpaw." Not his rescuer, but a gentler voice, the mew of a female warrior. "Can you hear me?"

Jaypaw nodded. Clumsily he dragged himself into a sitting position. His ears were full of water, and he shook his head to clear them. Pebbles crackled as the WindClan cats leaped away from the droplets that sprayed from his waterlogged fur.

"Typical that a ThunderClan cat should thank us by trying to drown us!" Jaypaw had not heard this mew before. He guessed it belonged to the other apprentice—a tom, by the sound of it.

The older tom growled a stern reply. "Stop making a fuss, Breezepaw! It's only a few drops of water." Jaypaw felt warm breath on his cheek as the warrior leaned in close. "What were you doing so far from your camp?" he demanded. "Is there anyone with you?"

"Be gentle, Crowfeather," Whitetail pleaded. "He's had a bad shock." Jaypaw felt a soft tongue lick his ear. "You're safe now, little one."

Jaypaw relaxed against her, sheltering from the wind in her warm, dry fur.

"I'm Whitetail," the she-warrior went on. "This is Crowfeather, and these are our apprentices, Heatherpaw and Breezepaw. We won't hurt you."

"I think he might have guessed that by the way we just saved his life!" Breezepaw muttered.

"I wish you'd teach your son some manners, Crowfeather!"

Whitetail meowed sharply. She turned her attention back to Jaypaw. "What were you doing out here alone? Did you know you were heading for WindClan territory? Are you in trouble?"

"I will be," Jaypaw mewed under his breath.

"I should hope so," Crowfeather snapped. "What was your Clan thinking, letting you wander off like that?"

Heatherpaw leaned closer in, brushing Jaypaw's pelt with her whiskers. "Can you see anything at all?" she asked curiously.

Breezepaw snorted. "If he can, he must be stupid, walking off the edge of a cliff!"

"I didn't walk off the edge!" Jaypaw hissed.

"It looked like it from where we were standing." Breezepaw sniffed.

"Be quiet, Breezepaw!" Crowfeather scolded.

Breezepaw fell silent, but Jaypaw could hear his tail twitching crossly over the pebbles.

"I suppose I'd better take him back to ThunderClan," Crowfeather meowed. "Are you well enough to travel?" he asked Jaypaw.

Jaypaw nodded. His legs still felt shaky, but he wasn't going to give Breezepaw the satisfaction of mocking a Thunder-Clan cat again. He stood up. "Thank you for rescuing me, but I can find my own way home," he mewed politely.

"There's no way I'm letting you wander off by yourself again," Crowfeather insisted. "Whitetail, you take Heather-paw and Breezepaw back to camp." He laid his tail firmly on Jaypaw's shoulder and began to guide him up the beach.

"See your medicine cat as soon as you get home!" White-tail called after him.

Crowfeather hardly spoke as they trekked back into ThunderClan territory and headed toward the camp. He only meowed curt warnings when they came across rabbit holes or roots that might trip the ThunderClan apprentice. Jaypaw was content with the silence. The ground was unfamiliar, and he was too furious to concentrate on anything but Crowfeather's occasional instructions. He resented Crowfeather's tail resting lightly on his shoulder, but he did not complain. He was in far too much trouble already. Once again his attempt to prove he was as good as any other cat had ended in disaster.

I know this place, he thought suddenly. The sloping earth beneath his paws was strewn with twigs. Trees rustled overhead. They were nearing the top of the hollow. Jaypaw's heart sank. How was he going to explain why he wasn't with Brightheart? What would his father say? He scented a ThunderClan patrol and realized that Squirrelflight, Stormfur, and Brook were heading straight for them. He tensed his shoulders.

"Crowfeather?" Stormfur's surprised mew sounded from the bracken ahead.

Paws raced toward them. "Jaypaw!" Squirrelflight's mew was shrill with relief and anger as she pressed her muzzle into his damp fur. "What in StarClan happened to you?" She licked him ferociously between the ears. "Where did you find him?" she asked Crowfeather.

"He'd wandered into WindClan territory," Crowfeather explained gruffly. "I had to fish him out of the lake."

Jaypaw bowed his head, his pelt burning with embarrassment. To make it worse, he could tell Squirrelflight was feeling an awkwardness that strengthened as Crowfeather went on. "Do your kits always go out by themselves?"

"I'm not a kit; I'm an apprentice!" Jaypaw snapped. He felt his mother's tail brush his muzzle, silencing him.

"Crowfeather," she meowed coolly, "I believe WindClan once had cats who went wandering farther than they should." Her mew was laced with a meaning that Jaypaw didn't understand. But Crowfeather clearly did. The WindClan warrior flicked his tail away from Jaypaw's shoulders and snorted.

"You should get him back to camp," he meowed. "He almost drowned, and the water was freezing."

"Yes, I should," Squirrelflight agreed. She nudged Jaypaw down the slope that led to the thorn barrier.

To Jaypaw's surprise, Crowfeather accompanied them back to the hollow. Squirrelflight did not question it, and Jaypaw sensed positive joy in Stormfur's step as he padded alongside the WindClan warrior.

Brook fell into step beside Jaypaw. "Do not be ashamed," she purred in his ear. "I got up to far worse when I was still training." She pressed her warm flank against his cold, wet pelt. He knew the mountain cat was trying to make him feel better, but it didn't help.

Suddenly he heard the thorn barrier rustle, and Mousepaw rushed out of the camp entrance. "You found him!" the apprentice called, delighted.

Squirrelflight sighed. "Yes, we found him."

"Go and find Brightheart's patrol and tell her to stop searching," Stormfur told Mousepaw. "Ask Cloudtail if you can take Cinderpaw with you."

"Yes, Stormfur," Mousepaw mewed, dashing back into the camp.

Squirrelflight led the way through the tunnel. Jaypaw clenched his claws and followed her into camp.

"Go straight to Leafpool," Stormfur advised him softly.

"I'll come and see you once I've spoken to Brambleclaw," Squirrelflight mewed. "He'll want to know you're safe."

Feeling lower than a worm's belly, Jaypaw slunk toward the medicine cat's den. Crowfeather padded after him. Jaypaw blinked in confusion. Was the WindClan warrior determined to follow him wherever he went? Surely Crowfeather had no business with ThunderClan's medicine cat? But he wasn't going to challenge the warrior. Instead he tried to sense what Crowfeather was feeling, but it was like trying to reach into a bramble bush—he could sense nothing but prickles.

Leafpool spun around as Jaypaw padded through the entrance to her den. She hurried to his side, and he felt her relief like a blast of air. "You're safe."

She tensed suddenly, jerking her head to stare at Crowfeather as he pushed his way through the brambles. Jaypaw's fur pricked as tension set the air crackling like lightning in greenleaf.

"Hello, Crowfeather," Leafpool meowed. She sounded as though she had a burr caught in her throat.

"Leafpool." Crowfeather's greeting was curt, but for the first time Jaypaw sensed some feeling other than irritation stir beneath the WindClan warrior's pelt. "I was out with Breezepaw and his mentor when we found him."

Leafpool stiffened. "Your son's an apprentice already?" Her mew was brittle.

"He is," Crowfeather replied, his voice strangely flat.

"Jaypaw!" Hollypaw rushed up and rubbed her muzzle against his cheek. "You look half-drowned!"

Tiredness suddenly swept through Jaypaw, and he let himself sink down to the ground.

"Fetch some thyme, Hollypaw," Leafpool ordered.

Hollypaw darted away to the back of the den and returned a moment later, breathless and flustered, her jaws full of leaves. Jaypaw recognized the scent of feverfew, not thyme.

"He hardly needs cooling down," Leafpool meowed impatiently. She hurried to the herb piles herself and grabbed a mouthful of thyme.

Crowfeather stood and watched silently.

"And why am I giving him thyme?" Leafpool prompted Hollypaw, dropping the leaves beside Jaypaw.

"To make him warm?" Hollypaw ventured.

Leafpool shook her head. "You can warm him by lying next to him," she meowed.

Hollypaw crouched down and pressed her body against Jaypaw's.

Leafpool nosed the thyme leaves toward Jaypaw. "The thyme will calm him and help with the shock," she explained. She licked Jaypaw's cheek. "Eat them all," she encouraged. "They don't taste too bad, and I'll send Hollypaw for a nice fresh mouse to wash the taste away once you've begun to warm up."

Jaypaw swallowed the leaves without complaint. He felt too cold and tired to object to anything. He let his eyes close and felt the warmth of his sister's body seep into his. He was still vaguely aware of the piercing emotion that raced between Crowfeather and Leafpool, but even that slid away as he slipped into the comforting stillness of sleep.

CHAPTER 10

❧

Lionpaw glanced up at the moon shining full and bright into the hollow. *Clouds aren't going to stop this Gathering.*

Dustpelt, Spiderleg, and Ashfur were already waiting by the camp entrance. Firestar stood beneath Highledge with Sandstorm and Brambleclaw, talking quietly to them.

"Why are we hanging about?" Hollypaw fussed, tearing the grass with her thorn-sharp claws.

"It can't be much longer," Lionpaw mewed. He felt every bit as excited as his sister. This was their first Gathering, their first chance to meet apprentices from rival Clans, to swap stories and compare training—knowing that the next time they met might be in battle, with claws unsheathed and teeth bared.

"It looks like Firestar's waiting for Leafpool," Hazelpaw put in.

"Why's it taking her so long?" Hollypaw complained. "She's only sorting through the new herbs we gathered before sunhigh."

"She might sort them quicker if she had her apprentice

helping," Berrypaw pointed out.

"I tried helping!" Hollypaw protested. "But Leafpool said it would be quicker if she did it herself."

Mousepaw's whiskers twitched. "Are you sure you're cut out to be a medicine cat?"

"Of course I am," Hollypaw snapped. "One day you'll be waiting for *me* to come out of the medicine den!"

"They're only teasing you," Lionpaw soothed her. He thought it was odd that Daisy's kits were all going to the Gathering, while the Clanborn kits, Cinderpaw, Honeypaw, and Poppypaw, were staying behind. *I guess it's only fair*, he decided. *Three Clanborn apprentices and three non-Clan.* He sighed. *At least, it* would *have been three, if only . . .*

He looked at Jaypaw, crouching in the entrance of their den, and sighed. He had been sitting there since sundown, forbidden to go to the Gathering as punishment for the adventure that had ended with his half drowning in the lake. Now he glowered angrily out of the shadows, his sightless blue gaze fixed on his brother and sister joking with Daisy's kits as they waited to leave.

Why did he have to be so reckless? It was harder now that they were apprentices—Lionpaw's duties kept him so busy that he could not keep an eye on Jaypaw, as he used to when they were kits. He felt a flash of guilt but pushed it quickly away. His first responsibility was to the Clan now. Jaypaw would have to learn to be more sensible.

He padded over to his brother and smoothed the fur

between his ears with his tongue. "I wish you were coming," he mewed.

"You're the only one who does," Jaypaw grumbled.

"You know that's not true," Lionpaw argued. "It's your own fault you've been confined to camp."

"Perhaps Firestar just doesn't want a blind cat at the Gathering."

"What do you mean?"

"I mean it doesn't look good having an apprentice like me in the Clan," Jaypaw growled.

Was that true? Before Lionpaw could say anything, he heard Firestar's call.

"I have to go," he told Jaypaw. "But I'll tell you all about it when we get back."

He ran after the other apprentices, who were already racing toward the entrance. Firestar padded to the head of the party and, with a sharp nod, bounded away through the tunnel. Lionpaw charged after his Clanmates, his heart soaring as their paws drummed the forest floor. He felt Hollypaw's pelt brushing his, rippling with excitement. A moment later they burst out of the tunnel and charged up the slope.

They raced past Sky Oak and down to the lake. The pebbles on the shore clattered beneath their paws. The stones grazed Lionpaw's pads but he didn't care; he could already see the island on the far side, rising from the water, crowded with trees. Their slender leafless branches reached up to the

star-pricked sky, trembling like whiskers, and Lionpaw
flicked his tail excitedly.

As the cats began the long trek through WindClan territory, Firestar steadied the pace. They passed the horseplace,
where Daisy used to live, and crossed into RiverClan territory, always keeping within five tail-lengths of the waterline,
as agreed by all the Clans. The ground became muddier as
they neared the island. Lionpaw slowed down after he nearly
slipped. He didn't want to arrive covered in mud. He could
make out dark shapes streaming over the fallen tree that
bridged the gap between shore and island. The scent of
WindClan mingled with the scents of ShadowClan and
RiverClan; the other Clans were arriving.

"Will you mention the border markers?" Lionpaw heard
his father meow. He peered past Mousepaw and Spiderleg
and saw Brambleclaw keeping pace with Firestar.

"Do you mean the fact that ShadowClan and WindClan
have marked every tree and blade of grass on our borders?"
Firestar asked.

"Yes," Brambleclaw replied.

"I can't dictate what the other Clans do in their territory,"
Firestar reminded him.

"But it's an open show of hostility!" Brambleclaw growled.

"We're not going to react," Firestar told him. "Yet."

"Firestar's right." Ashfur hurried to catch up with them. "It
would be better to send out more frequent border patrols
than give the other Clans the satisfaction of knowing they've
got us worried."

"It takes more than the stench of ShadowClan to worry us!" Firestar declared. He broke into a run, bounding the last few tail-lengths to the fallen tree, and skidded to a halt by the withered roots.

Lionpaw stared up at the trunk that bridged the water between the shore and the island. The air was filled with the scents of WindClan, ShadowClan, and RiverClan. "We must be the last to arrive!" he whispered to Hollypaw. Suddenly he felt shy about facing all three Clans at once. "Do you suppose Ferncloud's nursery stories about ShadowClan are true?"

"You don't actually believe they let their elders starve, do you?" Hollypaw mewed scornfully.

"Well, no," Lionpaw murmured. "But what if all the other apprentices are bigger than us?"

"We've been apprentices for only a quarter moon," Hollypaw pointed out. "There're bound to be some apprentices bigger than us."

Firestar leaped up onto the fallen trunk, picked his way carefully across to the far shore, and jumped down. The pebbles swished beneath his paws as he turned to watch his Clanmates cross. Brambleclaw followed him, then Dustpelt, and before he knew it, Lionpaw was watching Hollypaw leap up ahead of him onto the tree. The smooth, black water flowed beneath her, lapping gently at the dead branches that held the tree fast in the lakebed. She weaved her way through the stubby twigs and knots until she reached the other end. Then she jumped down and turned to watch Lionpaw cross.

Trembling with excitement, he scrambled up onto the

branch. The bark was surprisingly slippery and his paws slithered in all directions. He felt the tree jerk and looked back to see that Ashfur had leaped up behind him. Ahead of him was a jutting shard of bark where a smaller branch had once sprouted. He curved his body around it, keeping his eyes fixed firmly on the far end of the tree.

Suddenly his forepaw slipped and his paw shot off the trunk. He felt himself begin to fall and stared in horror at the water shining cold and dark beneath him.

A gray pelt flashed behind him, and Lionpaw felt the nudge of a muzzle against his flank. It pushed him up, supporting him until he regained his balance. His mentor had saved him from a humiliating start to his first Gathering.

"Thanks!" Lionpaw gasped.

"It's always tricky the first time," Ashfur meowed.

Lionpaw unsheathed his claws and gripped the trunk like a squirrel the rest of the way. He jumped down onto the beach, happy to be on solid ground once more. The pebbles felt good on his tingling pads.

"Thought you were fish food for a moment there," Hollypaw welcomed him.

"Me too!" Lionpaw purred.

He longed to race into the trees, impatient to see what was there, but he forced himself to wait while the others crossed. Hazelpaw weaved her way among the jutting twigs; Berrypaw pushed his way through with his powerful shoulders, while Spiderleg slipped around them like a snake, clearly accus-

tomed to the crossing. Lionpaw felt very small and inexperi-
enced, but he lifted his chin and forced his fur to lie flat.

Finally, all the ThunderClan cats stood on the beach.
Firestar swept his gaze over them, then, with a single nod,
turned and padded into the trees. *At last!* Lionpaw raced
between the shadowy trunks, bracken scraping his pelt. His
ears twitched with anticipation as the trees thinned and a
clearing opened ahead.

There were cats everywhere. Lionpaw had never seen so
many different shades of pelts. Some were lithe, some broad-
shouldered. Most seemed much bigger than him. There were
more cats here than Lionpaw had imagined could live around
the lake, and these were just a few from each Clan! At the far
edge of the clearing, with the lake behind it sparkling dis-
tantly through the leaf-bare forest, he saw the Great Oak, the
center of every Gathering.

"Is it what you expected?" Hollypaw whispered.

"I didn't realize there would be so many cats." Lionpaw
stared at a RiverClan tom, his pelt so sleek that it shone in
the moonlight as he flexed his well-muscled shoulders.
"Imagine meeting him in battle! I'm going to train twice as
hard from now on."

"How can you be thinking about fighting?" Hollypaw
scolded. "There's a truce tonight. You should be trying to
work out whether he thinks like a ThunderClan warrior."
Her eyes narrowed. "If you know how your enemy thinks,
then you have already won half the battle."

Lionpaw glanced sideways at his sister. Where did she come up with this stuff? Here he was, wondering if he could match any of these cats in a fight, and she was already working out battle strategies like she was a Clan leader.

Mousepaw's eyes twinkled. "Why not go and ask him?"

Hollypaw gasped. "Can we really just go up and talk to any cat?"

"Well," Mousepaw cautioned, "you'd be better off talking to the apprentices." He dipped his head toward a group of smaller RiverClan cats. "The warriors from the other Clans aren't dangerous or anything, but they won't be pleased to have some young apprentice pestering them."

"What if *they* talk to *us*?" Lionpaw asked.

"Just be polite and don't give too much information away," Hazelpaw warned. "Some of the warriors might use your inexperience to find out what's happening in ThunderClan."

"Did *you* spill any secrets at your first Gathering, Mousepaw?" Hollypaw asked.

"Of course not!" Mousepaw sniffed.

"Yeah, right!" Berrypaw interjected sarcastically. "If I hadn't clamped my tail over your mouth you would have told Russetfur that Firestar was about to give up the land by the river before Firestar had a chance to announce it himself."

"But she's the ShadowClan deputy!" Mousepaw argued. "I couldn't just ignore her."

"You didn't have to tell her your Clan's whole history either," Berrypaw mewed, his whiskers twitching.

"Well," Hollypaw mewed suddenly, "I'm going to see what everyone else is talking about."

She began to head toward the group of wide-eyed RiverClan apprentices when a small, pale tabby came hurtling toward her across the clearing.

"Hollypaw!" It was the RiverClan medicine cat apprentice, her bright green eyes flashing in the moonlight.

"Hi, Willowpaw!" Hollypaw stopped to greet her.

Willowpaw skidded to a halt and stared at her in delight. "Mothwing told me that you're Leafpool's apprentice now."

Hollypaw dipped her head. "That's right."

"Great!" Willowpaw mewed. "Have you had your first dream from StarClan yet?"

"No, not yet."

"I bet you do soon," Willowpaw assured her. "Come on!" She swept her tail around Hollypaw. "I'll introduce you to the other medicine cats."

Willowpaw led Hollypaw toward where Leafpool was sharing tongues with a group of cats. Lionpaw felt a flash of envy. As a medicine cat apprentice, his sister would have a special connection with all the Clans. He shuffled his paws nervously as he gazed at the strange faces around him. Then he remembered that the truce lasted for only one night. These cats were his enemies. There was no point making friends. His duty was to get to know them so that he knew their strengths—and their weaknesses—when he met them in battle.

"I'm going to talk to Harepaw," Berrypaw announced.

"I'm coming too," Hazelpaw mewed.

Lionpaw, alone now with Mousepaw, glanced around the clearing. He spotted a tightly clustered group of cats watching from the foot of the Great Oak. The shadows disguised the color of their pelts, and something about the way their eyes shone in the gloom made him shudder.

"Are they ShadowClan?" he whispered to Mousepaw.

Mousepaw nodded. "Don't let them scare you. They like to look like they're enemies with all the world. But once you start talking to them, they're okay."

"Are you sure?" Lionpaw wasn't entirely convinced.

But Mousepaw didn't hear him. "Minnowpaw!" he mewed. He was staring at a young gray-and-white RiverClan she-cat whose pelt looked as downy as kit fur.

"She looks barely out of the nursery," Lionpaw remarked.

Mousepaw's ears twitched. "She's a whole moon older than me," he corrected. "Come and talk to her," he went on. "You'll see she's not as soft as she looks."

Lionpaw followed Mousepaw over to where Minnowpaw sat with two more RiverClan apprentices, one gray and one brown tabby. His nose twitched as he scented them. He knew the stench of ShadowClan and WindClan from their border markers, but RiverClan's fresh, fish-tinged scent smelled strange.

Minnowpaw nodded to them in welcome. Though she was slighter and softer in looks than her Clanmates, her amber eyes were sharp and intelligent. "Who's your friend?" she asked Mousepaw.

Mousepaw was staring at her with a wistful look in his eyes. "This is Lionpaw."

"Hello, Lionpaw," mewed Minnowpaw. "This is Pouncepaw"—she nodded toward the brown tabby she-cat beside her—"and Pebblepaw." She flicked her tail toward the gray tom.

"What do you think of the island?" Pouncepaw asked.

"It's great," Lionpaw replied.

"We can show you around, if you like," Minnowpaw offered.

Mousepaw's eyes lit up. Clearly he liked the idea of a star-lit stroll with the pretty apprentice. But Lionpaw would rather explore the place for himself, especially if Mousepaw was going to be round-eyed and moony over Minnowpaw the whole time.

"Thanks for the offer," he mewed. "But Mousepaw's promised to introduce me to some of the other cats."

Mousepaw gazed at him blankly. "Huh? Have I?"

"Come on!" Lionpaw prompted before Mousepaw could object. He padded away from the group and Mousepaw sighed, but followed him across the clearing.

Suddenly a soft voice sounded in his ear. "Are you Jaypaw's brother?"

He swung around to find a light brown tabby she-cat gazing at him with eyes the color of a late-afternoon sky.

"Y-yes," he stammered. "How did you know?"

"Berrypaw told me. I'm Heatherpaw, by the way."

Because your eyes are the color of heather . . .

"Jaypaw might have mentioned me," Heatherpaw went on. "I was there when Crowfeather saved him from drowning. Has he recovered?"

Lionpaw forced himself to stop gaping like a startled rabbit. "Jaypaw?" he echoed. "Oh, he's fine now."

"Is he here?" Heatherpaw inquired.

Lionpaw was having trouble remembering where any of his littermates were right now.

"Not this time," Mousepaw answered for him, sounding impatient.

"I still can't believe he was out alone when he's blind," Heatherpaw breathed. "He must be so brave!"

Lionpaw felt a twinge of envy. "Most of the time he's just grumpy," he told her. "Especially now that he's been confined to the camp for a quarter moon."

"Poor Jaypaw," Heatherpaw sympathized. "I'd be miserable if I were stuck in camp."

"Me too," Lionpaw agreed.

"How long have you been an apprentice?" Heatherpaw asked.

"Since quarter moon. What about you?"

"For a moon and a half now," she replied. "This is my second Gathering."

"Have you met Mousepaw before?" Lionpaw asked, sensing that his Clanmate was growing restless and casting longing glances back to the RiverClan apprentices.

"We've never spoken," Heatherpaw confessed. "But I saw him last time talking to Russetfur." She looked at Mousepaw. "Did Russetfur get any information out of you? She tried to from me, but fortunately Crowfeather had warned me not to give anything away."

Before Mousepaw could answer, a black tom with amber eyes trotted up to them. "We ought to join our Clan," he told Heatherpaw gruffly, ignoring the ThunderClan apprentices. "The meeting's about to begin."

"This is Breezepaw," Heatherpaw told Mousepaw and Lionpaw. "He's our newest apprentice." Her whiskers twitched. "Though you couldn't tell it from his manner. He's been trying to boss the other apprentices from the moment he went from a 'kit to a 'paw."

Breezepaw stared furiously at her, and the tip of his tail flicked from side to side.

"Don't worry, Breezepaw," Heatherpaw went on. "You'll be a warrior before you know it, and then you can boss all the apprentices around."

Breezepaw narrowed his eyes, clearly unsure whether she was being serious or not.

Heatherpaw glanced at Lionpaw, then whispered loud enough for Breezepaw to hear, "He thinks that I have to do what he says because his father, Crowfeather, is my mentor."

"You know Crowfeather would never—" Breezepaw started to object.

"Oh, come on, Breezepaw!" Heatherpaw pleaded. "Lighten up!" She gave his flank a nudge with her muzzle, then turned back to Lionpaw. "It's hard to believe, but Breezepaw can be great fun on a good day."

A commanding meow sounded from the Great Oak. "We meet beneath Silverpelt—"

"That's Onestar calling for the meeting to start!" Heatherpaw gasped.

Lionpaw swung around and saw the four Clan leaders sitting like owls in the lowest branch of the tree. Onestar, the lithe brown tabby who led WindClan, was speaking.

". . . commanded by the truce of the full moon."

Breezepaw flashed Heatherpaw a look that said, *I told you so,* and hurried away to join the rest of his Clan. Heatherpaw rolled her eyes at Lionpaw, then followed her Clanmate.

Feeling more confident now, Lionpaw joined the cats gathering around the base of the oak. He weaved among his Clanmates till he found a space between Hollypaw and Spiderleg.

Firestar sat beside Onestar on the branch. A sleek, spotted tabby she-cat sat next to him. Lionpaw guessed that was Leopardstar of RiverClan. Beyond her was a huge white tom with jet-black paws—ShadowClan's leader, Blackstar.

"WindClan has one new apprentice this moon," Onestar announced. "Breezepaw." The black-pelted apprentice lifted his chin, apparently quite undaunted by having cats from all four Clans turning to stare at him. Lionpaw's heart began to race. He hoped he could act so coolly when it was his turn to be named.

"Leaf-bare has been kind to us this last moon," Onestar went on. "The rabbits are running, but not too fast to catch, and the windy weather has made hunting hard for the buzzards and hawks, which leaves more prey for us."

An alarming thought struck Lionpaw. Would Onestar mention Jaypaw's intrusion into WindClan territory? He leaned forward, ears pricked.

"Other than that," Onestar went on, "WindClan has nothing important to report."

Lionpaw glanced, relieved, at Hollypaw. She leaned against him. "Thank StarClan he didn't say anything about Jaypaw," she whispered.

Onestar turned to Blackstar, nodding for him to speak next.

"ShadowClan has one new apprentice too," Blackstar began. He looked down at a wiry brown she-cat sitting among the ShadowClan warriors. "Ivypaw."

Ivypaw nodded, her eyes narrowed. She didn't look pleased or proud to be announced as a new apprentice, as Breezepaw had.

Do ShadowClan cats ever show their feelings? Lionpaw wondered. He felt Hollypaw fidgeting beside him. Her eyes were shining with excitement. "Our turn next!" she breathed.

But Blackstar had not finished. "Hunting has been good for ShadowClan since we enlarged our territory."

Lionpaw stiffened as he heard a gasp from the Thunder-Clan warriors around him. Was Blackstar really going to make out that they had seized the land by the river from ThunderClan?

"Our new stretch of territory is a great source of prey," Blackstar meowed.

Liar!

Spiderleg muttered under his breath, "Firestar would never have given it up if it were!"

"ShadowClan would like to thank Firestar for his generos-ity in granting it to us," Blackstar finished with poisonous gratitude.

Firestar stared levelly at him. "I am pleased to hear that you are getting so much out of a piece of land prey-poor by ThunderClan standards," he meowed.

"Yes!" Hollypaw hissed. A subdued ripple of approval passed through the ThunderClan cats.

Then Firestar turned his green gaze on the crowd. "ThunderClan are fortunate to have more than *one*"—he lin-gered over the word—"new apprentice this moon."

Lionpaw's ears twitched. Pride and anxiety churned in his belly.

"Jaypaw couldn't come tonight." Murmurs of surprise rose from the other Clans, but the ThunderClan leader carried on. "But Hollypaw is here." Hollypaw's green eyes shone like stars, her black pelt almost invisible in the gloom. Then Firestar's gaze flicked to Lionpaw. "And Lionpaw."

Lionpaw could hardly hear anything for the blood rushing

in his ears. He puffed his chest out and held up his chin, feeling his pelt burn under the stares from the other cats. In a moment that was at once too short and too long, it was over, and Firestar was carrying on with his report.

"We have been lucky this leaf-bare," he meowed. "There has been frost but little snow, and the prey has continued to run."

Lionpaw's pelt prickled. There was a new scent in the air, something he hadn't smelled before. Some of the other cats clearly scented it too—he could see their heads turning, searching the edge of the clearing.

There was a rustle in the bracken close to where the WindClan cats were gathered and in the shadows Lionpaw saw movement.

Firestar fell silent and watched with the other cats as two lithe shapes emerged from the undergrowth.

"Intruders!" The alert spread through the Clans like wildfire. All around Lionpaw felt pelts bristling in alarm and battle-hungry muscles tensing, ready to spring.

The WindClan warriors who were nearest lunged at the strangers. Yowling and hissing, they wrestled the trespassers to the ground.

Are they going to kill them? Lionpaw turned back to the Great Oak, wondering what the leaders would do.

Firestar's fur was standing on end. His tail was stiff with shock, and his ears were pricked as he sniffed the air and sniffed again.

"Stop!"

The WindClan cats froze and drew back, leaving the two strangers standing alone on the edge of the Clans. Lionpaw strained to see over the heads of the other cats.

In a voice that was taut with shock and disbelief, Firestar called a name Lionpaw had only ever heard mentioned in nursery stories.

"Graystripe!"

CHAPTER 11

❧

Hollypaw stared in amazement. Graystripe?

"But he's dead!" she hissed to Lionpaw.

Her brother did not reply. He was too busy trying to balance on his hind legs to get a better view.

Hollypaw ducked down and weaved among the legs of the Clan cats until she reached the edge and peeped out between the pelts of Crowfeather and Breezepaw.

A gray tom with a stripe of darker fur along his spine stood in front of the bracken. His pelt clung to bone and wasted muscle, the fur matted and dull. His left ear was torn, and there were whiskers missing from his scratched and filthy muzzle. Beside him shivered a light gray tabby she-cat. Her short fur stuck out in clumps, and her tail hung limp and bedraggled.

But Graystripe's dead!

"You're alive!" Firestar burst out from between Onestar and Tornear. He faced Graystripe round-eyed, his fur on end.

Graystripe stared back. His companion flattened her ears and lifted her front paw defensively. She was trembling, her eyes bright with fear as she tried to look at all the cats at once.

"Easy now, Millie," Graystripe cautioned.

Firestar stretched his muzzle forward, sniffing tentatively, as though he could hardly believe what he saw. "The Twolegs didn't kill you. . . ." He lifted his face to the moon. "Thank StarClan," he whispered.

Startled mews erupted among the watching cats.

"Graystripe's come back!"

"He must have escaped from the Twolegs!"

"How did he survive?"

"What about Brambleclaw?"

What about Brambleclaw? Hollypaw looked at her father. Firestar had held a vigil for Graystripe as he would for any dead Clanmate, and made Brambleclaw his deputy instead. But Graystripe was alive, and now he had come back. . . .

The ThunderClan deputy was staring at Graystripe. "I can hardly believe that you found us." His voice was filled with admiration, but his gaze glittered uneasily as he stepped forward and brushed muzzles with the gray warrior.

Firestar flicked his tail. "Where did they take you?"

Graystripe didn't answer. He was staring at Firestar. "So you didn't wait for me."

Pain flashed in Firestar's eyes. "I couldn't."

Graystripe dipped his head. "You could not risk the Clan by keeping them in the forest."

Firestar leaned forward. "If it had been only *my* life at stake"—he glanced around the Clans, then lowered his voice—"I would have waited."

Hollypaw felt a rustling behind her. The other Thunder-Clan warriors were pushing their way forward to greet their old denmate.

"Graystripe!" Dustpelt dashed over. "You're alive!"

Berrypaw, Hazelpaw, Ashfur, and Spiderleg crowded excitedly around, sniffing his fur, poking him with their muzzles.

Graystripe flinched away.

"Give him some space," Leafpool warned. "He's exhausted."

"But he's a legend!" Hazelpaw complained as Leafpool shooed her and the others away with her tail.

Squirrelflight was staring at Graystripe's companion. "Who are *you*?"

"This is Millie," Graystripe meowed. "I met her in Twoleg-place."

Squirrelflight gasped. "A *kittypet* made the journey with you?"

"I couldn't have managed it alone," Graystripe meowed.

Brambleclaw narrowed his eyes. "Did you follow our trail?"

"No," Graystripe told him. "We found our own way."

"We searched for Graystripe's home first," Millie explained. Her voice had a hard edge that surprised Holly-paw. She thought all kittypets would speak with the same soft mew as Daisy.

Graystripe's ragged pelt bristled. "The whole forest was devastated when we got there. No cats, no prey, nothing but torn-up trees and monsters."

"How did you know which way we had gone?" Leafpool asked.

"We saw Ravenpaw."

Firestar's eyes glowed. "How is he?"

"He's well, but concerned for you all." Graystripe stopped for breath before going on. "He said he'd seen you pass and that you were heading toward the setting sun. So we carried on over Highstones—" He broke off, his tail quivering.

Leafpool darted forward. "Are you okay?"

"Just tired."

Leopardstar shouldered her way through the Thunder-Clan cats. A loud purr was rumbling in her throat. "It's good to see you again, Graystripe."

As she spoke the warriors from every Clan raised their voices.

"Welcome back, Graystripe!"

"How did he find us?"

"StarClan must have been watching over him!"

Cats from all four Clans surged around Graystripe until he was almost lost in a forest of pelts, brown, white, ginger, and tabby. Purrs blended, rumbling like thunder, louder than the sound of the wind in the branches.

Hollypaw watched in disbelief. She knew there was a truce at the Gathering, but this was not how it was supposed to be. There were meant to be four Clans, yet the warriors were acting like they belonged to the same one. She wriggled through the crush of pelts to where Lionpaw was watching with round eyes.

"It's not natural," she whispered in his ear. "Graystripe is ThunderClan. Why are the other Clans making such a fuss over him?"

"I don't know," Lionpaw admitted. "I thought that being a warrior meant protecting your Clan. Shouldn't the other Clans be worried that ThunderClan has an extra warrior now?"

Hazelpaw nosed in beside them. "They sound like they're in one of Squirrelflight's stories about how the Clans came together to make the Great Journey."

"The Great Journey's over," Hollypaw pointed out.

But Hazelpaw wasn't listening. She was gazing at Graystripe. "How did he know we were on the island?"

"Do you think StarClan guided him?" Lionpaw wondered.

"How did you know we were here?" called a sleek gray RiverClan she-cat.

Graystripe lifted his muzzle toward her. "Mistyfoot, it's good to see you again. We met a rogue who told us there were cats living by this lake," he explained. "When we reached the top of the ridge, the full moon was shining on the water and I could see shapes moving on the island."

"After that, we just followed the freshest scents," Millie explained. "They led us down to the shore and over the fallen tree."

Hollypaw heard a stifled hiss of disgust. Blackstar was staring at Millie with open malice. The gray she-cat glanced at him, then lifted her chin and returned his stare, and, even though her tail was trembling, she held the ShadowClan leader's gaze until he looked away. Hollypaw was impressed.

Graystripe saw what was happening and bristled, the muscles flexing on his broad shoulders.

"Let's not forget the truce!" Leopardstar warned.

"The truce is for *warriors*," Blackstar snarled.

"The *Gathering* is for warriors!" Onestar called.

A murmur rippled through the WindClan cats and spread through ShadowClan.

"Is ThunderClan going to allow another kittypet to join its ranks?" muttered a disbelieving voice.

"I have trained Millie as a warrior!" Graystripe hissed. "A kittypet would never have survived such a long journey." His voice cracked into a cough, and Hollypaw saw that the gray warrior was trembling from his ears to the tip of his tail.

Firestar must have seen it too. He padded over to Graystripe and pressed against him. "Let us take you back to camp."

Graystripe glanced at Millie. "Do you think you can travel a little farther tonight?"

"I'll keep going as long as you need me to," she assured him.

"Very well," Firestar meowed. He looked at the other Clan leaders. "Was there any other news to be shared at the Gathering?"

"Not from RiverClan," Leopardstar answered.

"WindClan is satisfied," Onestar told him.

Blackstar shook his head.

"Then let us return," Firestar called to ThunderClan, "and show Graystripe and Millie their new home."

"Does this mean ThunderClan has two deputies now?" Breezepaw called boldly.

Hollypaw pricked her ears and, as she did so, she noticed Ashfur lean forward, whiskers twitching.

Sandstorm stepped up to Firestar's side. "Graystripe and Millie are tired," she reminded him quietly. "We should get them home as soon as possible."

"Yes." Firestar flicked his tail toward Brambleclaw. "Lead the way," he ordered.

Brambleclaw instantly headed away through the wood toward the fallen tree.

Sandstorm wove around Millie. "Stay close to me," she advised. "We'll have you in a warm, dry den before the moon is much farther across the sky."

Millie nodded and padded, limping slightly, alongside the pale ginger she-cat. Hazelpaw hurried to join them, clearly excited to be helping guide the stranger back to camp.

Hollypaw fell in beside her brother and they trailed after the others. She was acutely aware of the other Clans watching them leave. One WindClan apprentice dipped her head to Lionpaw as they passed.

"Do you know her?" Hollypaw asked, surprised.

"That's Heatherpaw," Lionpaw replied. "I met her tonight."

Hollypaw looked back over her shoulder at the WindClan apprentice. Heatherpaw was whispering in her companion's ear, her eyes fixed firmly on Graystripe as he disappeared into the trees.

Then Hollypaw heard a voice above the murmuring of the lake.

"Surely Firestar will restore Graystripe to deputy!"

Hollypaw glared at the RiverClan warrior who had fur the color of stone.

Another voice whispered, "The vigil to Graystripe was false!"

Rage flared in Hollypaw, but not enough to sweep away the foreboding that pricked her pelt. Had Brambleclaw been made deputy *by mistake*? She pushed the thought away, closing her ears to the gossip from the other Clans.

The tree-bridge loomed ahead, and she scrambled up through the dead branches to pick her way along the slippery trunk. Lionpaw waited at the other end. His eyes sparkled with excitement, and as she landed he mewed, "I hope all the Gatherings are as exciting as that one! Imagine Graystripe finding us!"

Hollypaw hurried after him, irritated. "Aren't you worried?"

"What about?"

"About Graystripe coming back, of course!" Hollypaw flicked her tail. "How can StarClan approve of Brambleclaw being deputy when Graystripe is still alive?"

"StarClan didn't tell us he was still alive," Lionpaw reminded her. "If it meant so much to them, they should have sent a sign or something."

Mousepaw slowed and fell into step beside them. "I think Brambleclaw is a great deputy, and Firestar can't ignore that," he mewed.

"Exactly," Lionpaw agreed.

"But what about the warrior code?" Hollypaw protested.

"Does the code say anything about warriors coming back from the dead?" Lionpaw demanded.

Hollypaw shook her head. No cat had mentioned the warrior code at the Gathering. And yet she could not shake the feeling that some rule had been broken by appointing a new deputy when the old one wasn't dead.

"Graystripe was deputy first," she argued, half to herself.

"Do you *want* him to replace Brambleclaw?" Lionpaw asked, surprised.

"Of course not," Hollypaw snapped.

"And the Clan is fine as it is," Mousepaw pointed out. "So why bother changing anything?"

Hollypaw looked up ahead at Sandstorm and Millie. The two she-cats were padding along the lakeshore beside Firestar and Graystripe. Around her, the rest of the Clan murmured in hushed whispers, and Hollypaw guessed that they were as uncertain as she was about what would happen now that Graystripe had returned to ThunderClan.

CHAPTER 12

♣

A line as pale as spilled milk gleamed on the horizon as Hollypaw followed her Clanmates back into the hollow. The excited whispering, which had buzzed along with them like a swarm of bees during the long trek home, ceased as they padded through the thorn tunnel. Moonlight bathed the clearing, but the edges of the camp lay in shadow. Hollypaw's pelt pricked with anticipation as she saw two small shapes hurrying from the apprentice's den.

"How was the Gathering?" Cinderpaw called.

Firestar halted, Graystripe beside him. "You should be asleep," he meowed to the apprentice. "You will be too tired for your training in the morning."

"Sorry, Firestar," Cinderpaw apologized. "But we couldn't sleep until we'd heard about the Gathering."

Graystripe's whiskers twitched with amusement. "We would have done the same when we were apprentices," he reminded Firestar.

"Who are you?" Cinderpaw's eyes grew round as she stared at the gray warrior.

"He was ThunderClan's deputy before you were born," Firestar told her.

"Graystripe?" Cinderpaw guessed, tipping her head to one side.

"Graystripe!" Poppypaw echoed excitedly.

Cinderpaw ran in an excited circle. "Can I tell Cloudtail? Oh, please?" Without waiting for an answer, she charged toward the warriors' den, calling her mentor's name.

Cloudtail appeared at the den entrance, his sleep-ruffled pelt glowing in the moonlight. "What's the matter, Cinderpaw?" he complained.

"Graystripe is back!"

Brackenfur pushed past Cloudtail and stood outside the den. "Graystripe?" He stared, blinking, across the clearing, then raced toward his old friend.

"Graystripe's back!" Cloudtail yowled. As he bounded over to greet his Clanmate, Stormfur and Whitewing burst from the den, mewing excitedly.

"I thought I'd never see you again," Brackenfur murmured, touching muzzles with Graystripe.

"Firestar was right!" Stormfur added, pushing past Brackenfur. "He told us you'd find your way back!"

Graystripe stared at Stormfur—his son—in astonishment. "Do you live with ThunderClan now?"

"What's all this noise?" Mousefur's grumpy mew sounded as the old she-cat squeezed stiffly out through the tangled entrance of the elders' den.

Longtail appeared behind her, his blind eyes staring blankly ahead. He sniffed the air. Even in the dim light of the moon, Hollypaw saw the fur prick along his spine. "I smell Graystripe," he meowed.

"Graystripe?" Mousefur scoffed. "You're dreaming."

"He's not dreaming," Firestar promised.

Graystripe pushed his way out through the knot of warriors in the center of the clearing. "It really is me," he meowed.

"Great StarClan!" Mousefur raced over to Graystripe and ran her tail along his flank. "How in Silverpelt did you find us?"

Sandstorm stepped forward. "It's a long story that can wait till morning," she meowed softly. "Graystripe and Millie are exhausted."

"Millie?" Mousefur glanced at the stranger standing beside Graystripe.

"Millie helped me make the journey here," Graystripe explained. "She is my mate now."

Mousefur narrowed her eyes, and Hollypaw's belly tightened with anxiety. How would the crotchety elder react? Warriors were not supposed to find mates outside their Clan, and certainly not kittypet mates.

But Mousefur only dipped her head to Millie. "Still breaking the rules, I see, Graystripe," she mewed.

Hollypaw flicked the tip of her tail uneasily. The Clan seemed ready to accept Millie, but what did StarClan think about it? She glanced at Firestar. Perhaps having a leader with kittypet roots meant it was okay. The most important thing was that Millie had proved herself a warrior by helping Graystripe find his way back to the Clan. They had both survived, and that must mean StarClan approved of her.

A shadow by the warriors' den caught her eye. Brook had woken up. The mountain cat padded over to Stormfur and murmured in his ear.

Jaypaw emerged from the apprentices' den, his nose twitching. "What's going on?"

Lionpaw bounded over to him. "Graystripe's back!"

Jaypaw turned his sightless gaze toward Graystripe and Millie. "Who's with him?"

"His new mate," Cinderpaw explained. "From Twolegplace."

Jaypaw wrinkled his nose. "Well, tell Leafpool she's got an infected wound. I can smell it from here."

"Brambleclaw!" Firestar called to his deputy. "Find nests for Graystripe and Millie in the warriors' den."

Brambleclaw padded away with a nod.

Hollypaw was aware of a growing murmuring among the cats.

"Graystripe's not as big as I imagined," Cinderpaw whispered. "He looks small next to Brambleclaw."

"He smells of crow-food," Jaypaw mewed.

"He must have been eating like a loner for moons," Lionpaw pointed out. "Once he starts eating like a warrior again, he won't seem so small."

Whitewing looked uneasily at Squirrelflight. "What will happen now? Who is our deputy?"

Squirrelflight's gaze flicked anxiously from Graystripe to the warriors' den entrance, where Brambleclaw had disappeared. "I don't know."

Firestar gazed steadily at his Clanmates. "Nothing is going to change right now. We should just be grateful that Graystripe has returned to his Clan."

"There's no room in the den for two new nests," Brambleclaw informed Firestar, returning. "One, maybe, but that's all."

"It doesn't matter where we sleep, but I want to stay with Millie," Graystripe mewed wearily.

"You shall," Firestar promised. "We were going to expand the den anyway."

"We'd rather sleep separate from the others at first," Graystripe told him. "Just till we get used to being around so many cats again."

"There's an alcove behind the warriors' den," Brightheart suggested. "The ground is grassy there, so it's soft."

"And there are plenty of brambles left from when we cleared the entrance to the medicine den," Leafpool put in. "If we arranged them in front, the alcove would be sheltered."

Firestar looked at Graystripe. "You'd prefer this?"

The gray warrior nodded.

Hollypaw jumped to her paws. As a medicine cat apprentice she knew that she must take care of the new arrivals. Their bedding would need to be warm and comfortable, and they should have herbs to help them recover from their long journey.

"Brackenfur, Cloudtail, and Brambleclaw," Firestar called,

"start moving the brambles."

"Yes, Firestar." Brambleclaw hurried away to the browned and brittle brambles pushed into the shadows beside the medicine den. Brackenfur and Cloudtail followed.

"Can I help?" Cinderpaw begged.

Brackenfur stopped and turned, ready to answer, but Cinderpaw was already hurtling toward him. She careened into him, and fell backward, tumbling tail over whiskers.

"Sorry, Brackenfur!" she mewed, scrambling to her feet, her eyes filled with dismay.

Brackenfur purred at his daughter. "You're always a tail-length ahead of yourself, Cinderpaw," he meowed. "You remind me of my sister when she was an apprentice."

"Come on, Cinderpaw!" Cloudtail called. "Help me drag this bramble over to the alcove."

"Sorry," Cinderpaw mewed again, and raced over to help her mentor.

By the time dawn broke over the camp, spilling pinks and oranges over the cloud-dappled sky, the den was finished. With a sleepy nod of thanks, Graystripe and Millie padded inside.

On the other side of the clearing, Sandstorm and Spiderleg were leading Honeypaw and Mousepaw out of the camp on the dawn patrol. Brambleclaw and Cloudtail headed to their den to sleep. Hollypaw stayed with Leafpool outside the makeshift den and admired their work.

"That moss you collected will keep them warm," she mewed. Leafpool had gathered a little from each of the dens, and Hollypaw had helped her shape it into a comfortable nest for Graystripe and Millie. Graystripe might be ThunderClan's rightful deputy; Hollypaw wanted to make his nest as cozy as possible.

"Should I fetch them some herbs?" Hollypaw offered. "Jaypaw said that Millie's got an infected wound."

"How did he know?" Leafpool looked at her in surprise.

Hollypaw shrugged. "He smelled it." She was groping for the name of some leaf or seed that might help, but after all the excitement of building the den, her mind felt too fuzzy.

"We'll make sure we see to it come sunhigh," Leafpool told her. "Right now, Graystripe and Millie need rest more than anything else."

Hollypaw stifled a yawn.

Leafpool gazed down at her. "You must be tired too," she observed.

"A little," Hollypaw admitted. In fact, she was almost numb with exhaustion.

"Let's get some sleep," Leafpool suggested. She got to her paws and padded toward the medicine den. Gratefully, Hollypaw followed her. She was looking forward to curling up in her nest and closing her eyes.

When Hollypaw awoke, weak sunlight was flowing through the brambles, rippling like water on the sandy earth. Immediately she thought of Graystripe. Firestar had told them nothing would change *right now*. Did this mean that he planned to replace Brambleclaw with his old friend eventually? Would StarClan expect him to?

She padded from the warm moss, scenting the chilly air. Her belly rumbled.

Leafpool lay in her nest, eyes closed. But as Hollypaw stirred, she lifted her nose. "Awake already?" She got to her paws and stretched, curling her tail till it shivered. "You had a busy night. I thought you'd sleep longer."

"I'm hungry," Hollypaw confessed.

"There's fresh-kill on the pile," Leafpool told her, scenting the air.

Hollypaw fetched a mouse for her mentor and a vole for herself. She ate ravenously, swallowing it in a few mouthfuls before licking her paws and washing her face. "Shall we check on Graystripe now?" she asked eagerly.

"Is it sunhigh?"

"Not yet."

"Then let them sleep a little longer," Leafpool decided. She padded over to the piles of herbs at the back of the den and began sifting through them. "I need you to fetch some borage," she meowed. "We're running low, and Graystripe or Millie might have a fever. There's some lakeward, over the ridge."

Alarm pricked at Hollypaw's claws. "You won't wake them before I return?" There might be a lot to learn from the Clan's newest patients. She hadn't had a sick cat to treat since she became a medicine cat. She had tried to learn the names of herbs and what they were used for, but she was looking forward to actually using some. It might help her memorize them a little more easily.

"So long as you don't dawdle," Leafpool warned.

"I won't," Hollypaw promised.

Leafpool turned back to her herbs, spreading poppy seeds under her paw to count them.

Hollypaw turned to leave, then paused. "The Clan sat vigil for Graystripe, didn't it?"

"Yes, we did." Leafpool didn't look up from sifting through a pile of feverfew leaves.

"Does that mean he's officially dead? In the eyes of StarClan, I mean?"

"I think StarClan will have noticed that Graystripe's with us and not them," Leafpool meowed dryly.

"But what about the warrior code? Is he officially dead according to the warrior code?"

"Did he look like he was dead last night?" Leafpool meowed.

"But if he's not dead, then surely he's still dep—"

"We are here to heal." Leafpool looked directly at her. "Firestar's problems are not ours, unless StarClan wishes them to be. Now, are you going?"

"Going?" Hollypaw echoed.

"To fetch the borage." Leafpool sighed. "If you're not back before sunhigh I shall wake them without you."

"I'm going!" Hollypaw promised, spinning around and pushing her way out of the den.

* * *

Up on the ridge, a cold, fresh breeze was blowing through the trees from across the lake. Hollypaw thought she could detect the scent of RiverClan on it.

Her paws itched to go exploring, but she wanted to get back before Graystripe and Millie woke up. She ducked her head and began to sniff the ground, hoping to find a scent trail that might lead her to borage. She desperately tried to remember what it smelled like in the medicine den, but her nose was too full of the scents of water and wind.

She padded down the steep slope, heading for where the trees thinned. The sun sparkled on the lake. What a great day for hunting! She pushed the thought away. She *was* hunting. Hunting for borage. Sniffing the ground once more, she picked up a tangy scent that seemed familiar. She followed it carefully, clambering over the low boulders that dimpled the ground, and tracked the scent into some long grass, where she spotted green, jagged leaves growing in a clump on long, thin stems. They carried the scent she had been following. It was stronger up close and more bitter. Was this borage? She had seen this before, she was sure.

She glanced up at the sun. It shone high above her. Leafpool would be waking Graystripe and Millie soon. Quickly she nipped a few stems, breaking them at the base, careful not to swallow any of the bitter sap. She pitied the cat who had to eat such a foul-tasting herb as she picked up the fallen stems in her jaws and hurried back to the camp.

* * *

"This isn't borage." Leafpool stared in dismay at the stems Hollypaw had placed in front of her. "This is yarrow. This makes cats sick."

Hollypaw closed her eyes, ashamed and angry. Why couldn't she remember anything Leafpool taught her?

"Don't be hard on yourself," Leafpool encouraged. "There's a lot to learn."

Hollypaw couldn't meet her eyes. *Don't make excuses for me. I should be doing better than this by now!*

"Come on," Leafpool meowed briskly. "We can do without borage. Fetch some marigold leaves and we'll go and wake Graystripe."

Marigold leaves! Hollypaw knew what they looked like. She bounded to the back of the cave and picked up a mouthful, then followed Leafpool across the clearing to Graystripe and Millie's makeshift den.

Firestar stood outside with Sandstorm and Honeypaw. Dustpelt, Thornclaw, Poppypaw, and Hazelpaw milled around eagerly. Graystripe and Millie, still ruffled from sleep, sat among them. Millie was staring from face to face, her ears twitching. Even Graystripe looked uncomfortable, like he had forgotten what it was like to have so many cats around him.

"Have you been awake long?" Leafpool asked, weaving through the others to reach Graystripe. She glanced sternly at the cats clustered around the gray warrior and his mate. "I hope no cat woke you."

"No." Graystripe drew his paws closer in and tucked his

tail tighter around him. "The sun woke us."

"You can catch up with everyone later." Leafpool twitched her tail, making it clear she wanted the other cats to leave.

"Let me know how they are when you've finished," Firestar requested before he led his Clanmates away.

Graystripe's shoulders loosened as they left. Millie looked relieved too.

"Any scratches?" Leafpool asked.

"Millie has a cut on one of her pads."

"Let's have a look."

Gingerly Millie held up her forepaw. "There's a thorn in there," Leafpool meowed. "Jaypaw was right; it's infected." She flicked her tail at Hollypaw. "My apprentice will pull it out while I prepare some leaves to heal the infection."

Hollypaw gulped and inhaled a fragment of marigold leaf from the bunch she still held in her jaws. She coughed, spitting the leaves out onto the ground, and glanced anxiously at Millie, who gazed equally anxiously back. Hollypaw knew she couldn't refuse. This was what she had wanted, a chance to practice instead of simply learning. She peered closely at Millie's paw. Sure enough, a thorn was buried deep in the pad. To Hollypaw's dismay she could see blood and pus oozing around it.

"That must be sore," she breathed. Did she really have to pull it out with her teeth?

Leafpool narrowed her eyes. "Perhaps I'd better do it."

Self-consciously, Hollypaw backed away and let Leafpool take her place. "Shall I chew the marigold leaves into a poultice?" she offered, her fur prickling with guilt.

"Yes." Leafpool was concentrating on Millie's paw with a detached intensity that Hollypaw wished she could copy. Why was it all so difficult?

Graystripe began to wash his face. "It's so good to see the Clan again," he meowed between licks. "I always hoped I would find you, but I guess I never knew for sure. . . ."

"How did you know where we were?" Hollypaw asked.

"Ravenpaw told us to head toward the setting sun. We were lucky, and StarClan watched over us."

"Were you angry at Firestar when you found he'd left without you?" Hollypaw meowed boldly.

Graystripe twitched the tip of his tail. "Yes, I was disappointed, but I can understand why he did it. The forest was in ruins. No cat could have survived there."

"Ow!" Millie leaped backward and began to lick her paw.

Leafpool was holding the thorn between her teeth. She spat it out. "Press the marigold into the wound with your paw," she told Hollypaw.

Millie held out her sore paw, which was bleeding and swollen where the thorn had been stuck. Hollypaw shuddered and rubbed her paw in the marigold pulp. She began to smear the juice gingerly onto Millie's swollen pad. Millie stayed very still, even though it must have hurt.

"Cinderpelt would be proud of you both," Graystripe meowed.

I wish that were true, Hollypaw thought, forcing herself to hold back the bile rising in her throat. *But if Cinderpelt is really watching me right now, she'll know that I can't do anything right for Leafpool.*

"We'll do some battle training this afternoon," Leafpool announced after they had finished treating Graystripe and Millie. "Even medicine cats need to know how to defend their Clan in battle."

Hollypaw's heart soared. No pus, no bitter-tasting herbs, no cats wincing in pain—this was going to be fun! They climbed the slope outside the camp, heading away from the lake, and followed the track that led down to the mossy hollow that the apprentices used for battle training. As they padded through the trees, Hollypaw heard energetic mews up ahead. She sniffed the air. Cinderpaw and Cloudtail were already there.

She raced ahead of Leafpool, wanting to know what real warrior training was like. Through the trees she glimpsed the small gray tabby rushing toward Cloudtail. The white warrior twisted faster than a leaf caught in a breeze, and Cinderpaw hurtled past, missing him entirely.

"No, no!" Cloudtail meowed. "Didn't you hear what I told you? Aim for where you think I'm going to be, not where I am!"

"Sorry!" Cinderpaw panted. "Can I try it one more time?"

Hollypaw padded down the bank and into the clearing. "Hello," she mewed.

"Are you collecting herbs?" Cloudtail asked.

"No. Leafpool's going to teach me some fighting moves."

"Great!" Cinderpaw mewed. "We can train together."

Leafpool padded to Hollypaw's side. "Maybe another time," she meowed. "I think it's better if I show Hollypaw some basic moves before she joins in with warrior apprentices."

Hollypaw scowled and scuffed the earth with her paw.

Cinderpaw looked back at Cloudtail. "Can we try that move again?"

Cloudtail nodded. "Just remember—" But Cinderpaw was already hurtling toward him. He whipped around in a circle once more, and once more dodged neatly out of her path.

"Come on," Leafpool meowed to Hollypaw. "We'll use that space over there." She pointed with her nose to the far side of the mossy green clearing. Hollypaw noticed how smooth and soft it looked. Perfect for fighting on. No roots to trip over, no leaves to skid on.

"We'll start with a defensive move, I think." Leafpool turned her back on Hollypaw and meowed over her shoulder, "I want you to watch me and then copy what I do." She dipped her head, twisted around, and rolled onto her back before springing back up onto her paws. The whole move was over in a heartbeat. "Do you want to have a go?"

Hollypaw nodded. "I think I've got it." She ducked her head, twisted around, and rolled over, leaping to her paws again in an instant.

Cloudtail called across the clearing, "Was that your first go?"

"Yes," Hollypaw answered. "Did I do it right?" She glanced anxiously at Leafpool.

"You did it brilliantly," Leafpool told her. "Let's try something else."

Leafpool demonstrated a few more moves, and Hollypaw copied each one with the same fierce intensity. Although Cloudtail made no more comments, she knew he was keeping one eye on her.

"We could try some combat now," Leafpool suggested after a while. "Run at me and try to get past me."

"How?" Hollypaw asked.

"Any way you can," Leafpool told her. "We'll discuss tactics afterward."

Hollypaw crouched down and stared at Leafpool. Her gaze flitted to a sapling at the edge of the clearing behind the medicine cat. That was where she would aim. Leafpool was merely an obstacle to avoid. She darted forward, aware that Leafpool was rearing onto her hind legs, ready to bring her weight down on Hollypaw the moment she tried to slip past. Hollypaw saw that the medicine cat was leaning back a little and guessed that her weight was mostly balanced on one side. With lightning speed, she swerved the other way. Leafpool didn't have a chance to rebalance herself, and she slammed down a mouse-length away from where Hollypaw flashed by.

Hollypaw felt a rush of triumph as she reached the sapling and spun to see Leafpool blinking with surprise. Then a prick of guilt jabbed her. Was she meant to be faster than her mentor?

"That was very good!" Leafpool panted.

"Yes, it was!" Cloudtail was padding over from the other

side of the clearing, Cinderpaw on his heels.

"You were so fast!" Cinderpaw complimented her.

"Thanks!" Hollypaw trotted back to Leafpool's side.

Cloudtail dipped his head toward Leafpool. "Tell me if I'm butting in," he began, "but I think Cinderpaw and Hollypaw should try training together. Cinderpaw has more energy than a well-fed rabbit, and she has more experience than Hollypaw. But Hollypaw knows how to watch and listen, and she clearly has an instinct for judging her opponent."

Hollypaw was almost too excited to speak. A real warrior was offering to help with her battle training!

"I don't see why not," Leafpool meowed.

Cloudtail flicked his tail. "Cinderpaw, why don't you show Hollypaw that fighting move we've been practicing?"

Cinderpaw led Hollypaw into the center of the clearing. The sunshine flooding through the branches overhead dappled her smoky pelt. "You come at me, and I'm going to try to unbalance you."

Hollypaw took a quick breath, then threw herself at Cinderpaw. Before she knew what was happening, Cinderpaw had knocked one of her forelegs from under her with a powerful front paw, then tipped her over with a rolling shove from her hind legs.

Hollypaw scrambled to her feet and shook herself. "Wow!" she mewed, impressed. "Can I try?" She wanted to try the move in a slightly different way. As soon as Cinderpaw rushed her, she ducked her head, knocking Cinderpaw's forepaw from under her with her muzzle. She was so low to the ground that it was easy to roll onto her side from there and thrust her hind legs in a powerful kick that sent Cinderpaw flying.

Cinderpaw scrambled to her paws. "I love the way you used your muzzle instead of your paw! It made your rollover much smoother. Can I try it that way on you?"

"Sure!"

Cinderpaw lunged for Hollypaw, this time using her muzzle to unbalance her, just as Hollypaw had done. She finished the move with a hind kick so much quicker that it sent Hollypaw skidding backward across the clearing.

Hollypaw sat up, panting.

"That was great, you two," Cloudtail praised them.

Cinderpaw licked her paw and drew it over her ear to wipe off some moss that had caught on it. As she went to lick it again her paw twitched as though she were flicking dirt from between her claws. Hollypaw's whiskers twitched with amusement; Cinderpaw's little paw flick was something none of the other cats did.

"What did you think?" Hollypaw asked, turning to Leafpool. But Leafpool did not answer. She was staring at Cinderpaw with a look of startled disbelief. Hollypaw wondered if the apprentice had suddenly changed into a badger, but Cinderpaw was still sitting quietly, washing her ears.

"Leafpool?" Hollypaw mewed again.

Leafpool dragged her gaze from Cinderpaw, her eyes still

round with shock. "Y-yes?"

"Are you okay?"

Leafpool shook her head as though to clear it. "Yes, of course. It's just that Cinderpelt used to flick her paw just like that." She glanced uneasily back at Cinderpaw, who had finished washing and was circling Cloudtail.

"Will you teach me how to do a back kick?" the gray apprentice begged.

"It'll be dusk soon," Cloudtail observed. "I think we should head back to camp."

Leafpool nodded. "I want to check Millie's paw while there's still light."

The sky was darkening above the trees, and the air was growing chillier. Even so, Hollypaw was sorry to leave the mossy clearing. Her body felt bruised and tired, but her mind was buzzing as she tried to work out how to make the moves she had learned even better.

As she followed Cloudtail and Cinderpaw up the bank and into the trees, Leafpool fell into step beside her. "You fought well. I was really impressed."

For a moment Hollypaw was thrilled. Joy surged through her paws, making them light as dandelion floss. Then her heart plummeted. *She's never praised me like this for being a medicine cat apprentice.* Why wasn't she as good at remembering herbs as she was at remembering fighting moves?

It will happen! Hollypaw told herself firmly. One day her

mind would be as sharp in the medicine den as it was in the mossy clearing. It was just a matter of time. She had chosen to become a medicine cat, and she was not about to let herself or her Clan down.

CHAPTER 13

❧

Jaypaw dawdled over his meal, taking minuscule bites from the mouse he had plucked from the fresh-kill pile.

Brook padded past with Stormfur. "No appetite today?"

"Not much," Jaypaw muttered.

He went back to nibbling at his meal as the two warriors took fresh-kill from the pile and settled at the edge of the clearing. He was in no hurry to begin his apprentice duties. Still confined to camp—*days* after Crowfeather had brought him home—he was bored with clearing out dens and running errands. This morning he was supposed to clean out Graystripe and Millie's den. The new arrivals had recovered enough to eat in the clearing with the rest of the Clan.

"Nice catch, Dustpelt!" Graystripe called out from below Highledge, where he was sharing a rabbit with Millie.

"Thanks," Dustpelt meowed back.

Jaypaw liked Graystripe. He was easygoing and good-humored, though still guarded when there were lots of cats around. Millie was all right too, for a kittypet. Still, he wasn't looking forward to clearing the soiled moss from their den while they went out on their first patrol. It wasn't fair; they

would be out exploring the forest while he would be scrabbling through their stinky bedding.

He took another tiny bite from his mouse. He could sense
Brightheart watching him from where she sat by the halfrock.
She was sharing tongues with Dustpelt, but her gaze kept
flicking back to him. He could feel her frustration like thorns
in his pelt. What did she expect of him? Was he supposed to
be happy about cleaning out dens instead of learning how to
hunt and fight? Even though he was confined to camp, there
was enough space in the clearing for her to teach him some
battle moves. But she seemed interested only in making him
run around looking after his Clanmates. Was that all she
thought he was good for?

"Hurry up, Jaypaw," Brightheart called. "Once you finish
Graystripe's den, I promised Ferncloud that you'd play with
her kits while she went hunting. She hasn't been out of the
camp for two moons."

Jaypaw lashed his tail. "And when am I going to get to
hunt?"

"Once you've learned to serve your Clan without complaining," Brightheart told him mildly.

Jaypaw heard an amused purr rumble in Dustpelt's throat.
"You'll have to take him out eventually, Brightheart," he
meowed. "Before he drives us all crazy."

"It was Firestar who confined him to camp," Brightheart
pointed out.

"I'm sure you could persuade Firestar that Jaypaw needs to
be out training," Dustpelt argued.

Jaypaw's heart skipped with hope.

"There's more to being a warrior than hunting and fighting," Brightheart replied.

The thorn barrier rattled. The dawn patrol had returned. Whitewing, Ashfur, Lionpaw, Spiderleg, and Mousepaw carried the scent of the forest temptingly into the clearing. And yet Jaypaw could sense anxiety among them; Ashfur was lashing his tail while Whitewing padded in agitated circles.

Brambleclaw swished out through the entrance of the warriors' den, followed by Squirrelflight. "Anything to report?"

"ShadowClan are marking every tree along the border," Ashfur replied, his mew sharp with anger.

Jaypaw felt an explosion of energy as Graystripe leaped to his paws. "Are ShadowClan up to their old tricks already?" the warrior spat. "If any of them set paw on ThunderClan territory while I'm on patrol, I'll claw their ears off."

"They haven't crossed the new border yet," Brambleclaw informed him. "So we've decided to ignore them."

Graystripe snorted. "Ignore ShadowClan? You may as well try to ignore the wind and the rain—it won't stop you from getting cold and wet!"

"That may be how it was in the forest," Brambleclaw meowed. "But it's not necessarily the best thing to do here."

"Things are different since the Great Journey," Squirrelflight added.

"Not so different that we should trust ShadowClan!" Ashfur growled. "Some cats will always try to take what another cat has."

Jaypaw sensed his mother flinch, as though stung. What did Ashfur mean, exactly?

"ShadowClan will always push for more than is rightfully theirs!" Dustpelt agreed.

Jaypaw's whiskers quivered. He knew there had been dark mutterings about Firestar's decision to give up territory to ShadowClan, but now the warriors were openly agreeing with Graystripe. Shouldn't they be loyal to their leader first?

"Firestar has decided to ignore ShadowClan for now." Brambleclaw kept his voice steady, but Jaypaw could tell he was watching and listening for the slightest sign of rebellion among his Clanmates.

Pebbles clattered from Highledge as Firestar leaped down into the clearing. "What's going on?" he asked.

"Graystripe feels that we shouldn't ignore ShadowClan," Brambleclaw replied.

"I think Graystripe's right," Firestar meowed.

Jaypaw waited for his father to object, but Brambleclaw remained silent.

"Graystripe may not have been in our new home for long," Firestar went on. "But he knows ShadowClan of old. I agree with him—ShadowClan will keep pressing on our borders unless we make a stand."

"That's not what you said before the Gathering," Brambleclaw meowed quietly.

"But at the Gathering, ShadowClan were obviously look-ing for trouble," Firestar reminded him. "I didn't want to overreact before, but now I think we need to do something to show them we are ready to defend our borders."

Why didn't you tell me this before? Jaypaw felt the question burning in his father's mind.

"Are we going to fight them?" Ashfur asked.

"Not unless we have to," Firestar replied.

"But we must increase patrols along the border," Dustpelt put in.

Firestar nodded. "And we'll start matching ShadowClan's markers, tree for tree. If they think they can intimidate us into giving up more territory, they are wrong."

"Very well, Firestar," Brambleclaw meowed. "Stormfur and Brook can mark the trees along the ShadowClan border while Squirrelflight leads the hunting patrol as planned."

Dustpelt shifted uneasily. "Surely it would be better to let Squirrelflight's patrol mark the ShadowClan border? Their scent markers are pure ThunderClan and will send a stronger message to ShadowClan."

Jaypaw felt resentment flash from Stormfur; he half expected the gray warrior to lunge at Dustpelt and rake his flank with thorn-sharp claws. But Brook got to her paws before Stormfur could react.

"There is truth in Dustpelt's words," she conceded.

"But ShadowClan must know by now that you and Stormfur are ThunderClan," Whitewing argued.

"In a battle over boundaries, it is better to make things as clear as possible," Ashfur meowed.

An uncomfortable silence hung in the hollow until Firestar decided, "Squirrelflight will lead her patrol to mark the ShadowClan border. Stormfur and Brook can hunt."

As the patrols assembled, Jaypaw gulped down the rest of his meal and got to his paws. He didn't want to watch his Clanmates head out into the forest, while he wished he could go with them. He might as well get Graystripe's den cleaned. He scanned the camp for Brightheart and found her with Leafpool outside the medicine cat's den.

"Where shall I get clean moss if I can't leave the camp?" he demanded, interrupting them. He turned to Leafpool. "Have you got any to spare?" He knew she kept clean bedding in case of injured cats.

"There's some inside my den," Leafpool told him. "Help yourself. Hollypaw's out looking for borage. She can fetch more moss when she gets back."

Brightheart's pelt bristled as he brushed past her, and he heard her whisper to Leafpool, "I don't think I'm making him very happy so far. I don't know how to get through to him."

How about realizing that having one eye doesn't make you so much better than me?

The clean moss was easy to sniff out, piled at one side of the cave. Jaypaw picked up a large wad in his jaws. The fresh, grassy taste reminded him of his adventure into WindClan territory. He may have ended up in the lake, but at least for one morning he had been free.

Before he reached the trailing brambles at the entrance to Leafpool's den, he heard Firestar's hushed mew outside. Brightheart had gone, and Firestar was talking to Leafpool. Jaypaw dropped his moss and pricked his ears.

"I need you to share tongues with StarClan," Firestar meowed softly to the medicine cat.

"You are worried about Graystripe," Leafpool guessed.

"I have to know who ThunderClan's rightful deputy is," Firestar explained. "Vigil or no vigil, Graystripe was still alive when I appointed Brambleclaw."

Leafpool paused. "Are you prepared for any answer they give?"

"Graystripe's my friend. I owe him so much. But Brambleclaw is a brave and loyal warrior." Firestar sighed. "Whatever StarClan say, a decision must be made."

"What if StarClan have no answer for you?"

"Then I will do what I think is best for the Clan."

"I'll visit the Moonpool," Leafpool promised.

Jaypaw's whiskers twitched with curiosity. He had heard about the Moonpool. It had always sounded so mysterious—a place where only medicine cats visited to share tongues with StarClan. Would Hollypaw get to go with Leafpool tonight?

As Firestar headed away, Jaypaw recognized Hollypaw's quick step hurrying toward the medicine den. She halted beside Leafpool. "Are these the right leaves?"

Jaypaw smelled the familiar tang of borage.

"Yes," Leafpool purred. "Well done, Hollypaw."

"I knew I'd get it right in the end," Hollypaw mewed happily.

Jaypaw picked up his wad of moss and nosed his way out through the brambles.

"You took your time," Leafpool commented. Did she suspect that he had overheard his conversation with Firestar? If she did, she gave no sign. "Hollypaw," she mewed, turning to her apprentice, "you'll have to sort these leaves yourself. Make sure you store only the undamaged ones. Damaged leaves will rot before they dry."

"Won't you be here to help?" Hollypaw asked.

"I have to go to the Moonpool," Leafpool explained.

"But you don't have to leave now. It's not even sunhigh."

"Moonhigh is early this season," Leafpool explained. "I want to make sure I'm there in good time."

"What if a cat needs treatment?' Hollypaw mewed anxiously.

"You'll be fine. Brightheart knows a lot of the herbs and berries," Leafpool soothed. "Ask her if you need help."

"Could you show me which herb is which one more time?" Hollypaw pleaded.

"Okay," Leafpool agreed. "But then I must go."

The two cats disappeared inside the medicine den, leaving Jaypaw by himself. His mind was buzzing. He wasn't going to stay in the camp cleaning out bedding all morning. If Leafpool was going to the Moonpool, he was going to follow her.

He carried the moss across the clearing and deposited it outside Graystripe's den. Then he headed back toward Leafpool's den, as if he were going to fetch some more, except this time he hurried straight past the entrance and slipped into the clump of brambles beside it. This was a corner of the hollow too overgrown to be used for sleeping or storing fresh-kill, and Jaypaw knew that the rock wall behind had crumbled enough to make it possible to climb to the top. This was the fast route down from the forest that Brambleclaw had used when the patrol had discovered the trapped fox. It was steep, but Jaypaw hoped he could use it to get out of the camp without any cat noticing.

His heart pounding, he plunged through the brambles until he reached the cliff. Sniffing and feeling with his paws, he reached up and dug his claws into a bush rooted a tail-length up the stone. He hauled himself free of the bramble bush, then sniffed for the next hold. Little by little, grasping tussocks of grass for pawholds, he fought his way up, praying that he didn't give himself away by sending loose stones clattering down into the camp. At last a fresh breeze ruffled his ears. He had reached the top of the hollow. Digging his claws into the soft grass, he dragged himself over the edge of the cliff.

Following the slope of the forest, he headed down the steep bank that led to the camp entrance. On familiar ground now, he stopped a fox-length from the bottom and wriggled backward into the bracken.

A moment later Leafpool came pattering over the forest floor. Jaypaw let her pass, then scampered after her, keeping to one side so that he was never directly behind her. The trees were a good shield, and he wove between them, following his instinct as much as his whiskers. The scent of WindClan soon began to taint the air. Leafpool was heading toward the hilly moorland. But she did not cross the border; instead she veered toward the sun and kept going until the land grew steeper and the trees began to thin.

Jaypaw heard a stream and followed Leafpool's scent trail as it turned off the soft grass and onto the jagged boulders that lined the tumbling water. He dropped back a little, shivering in the sharpening breeze. There was less vegetation here to shield him. He would have to depend on the camouflage of his striped pelt against the stony ground. At least the sound of water disguised his stumbling steps. The rocks beneath his paws rose and fell unevenly, and he had to slow down. Fortunately Leafpool's scent remained strong and steady.

Suddenly his paws started to recognize the path, and images from his dream flooded his mind. He was trekking through the same narrow valley he had visited in his sleep— which meant that he knew what it looked like. He pictured the rocks that lined his path, sharp as fox teeth. Ahead, he knew that a stream danced down the mountainside, sparkling in the sunlight. He was following Leafpool to its source, and, with a prickle of excitement, he realized that its source must be the Moonpool.

Stones rattled in front of him, and Jaypaw stopped. He guessed that Leafpool was climbing the steep rocks that led up to the ridge. He waited until the noise had ceased and he was sure she had disappeared over the top. Then he followed, scrabbling from rock to rock, grazing his pads on the sharp granite.

Out of breath, he stopped at the top. He shivered; the setting sun must be blocked by the surrounding rocks. He was at the brink of a hollow; Leafpool's scent drifted up, mingled with new smells of damp stone, dusty lichen, and water, fresh and sharp with the smell of the mountains. It trickled and splashed, echoing off encircling stone.

As he padded cautiously forward, he realized there were other cats brushing against him, first one side, then the other, unbalancing him.

Stop pushing! He shoved back, stumbling when he found only air around him.

Voices whispered around the hollow.

"They have come."

"We must hurry. The moon is rising."

Who else is here?

Jaypaw tasted the air, but he could scent only Leafpool. Steadying his trembling tail, he listened to figure out where she was. The enclosing rocks amplified her breath as it rippled the water beneath her muzzle. He knew from its soft rhythm that she was sleeping.

Carefully, he followed the slope down toward the pool. The smooth stone beneath his paws was polished and dimpled, worn into a pathway over endless moons by countless pawsteps. It led him on until water lapped at his paws with a cool tongue. Then he lay down a fox-length away from where Leafpool slept and closed his eyes.

As soon as his nose touched the Moonpool, stars filled his vision. It was as though great paws had swept him up into the inky sky and freed him among countless blue-white lights.

Far below he could see the starlit slopes of the hollow

curving down to the glittering Moonpool. He stared, his breath coming quicker. The hollow was no longer empty but crowded with cats. They lined every ridge, their pelts bathed in moonlight.

StarClan!

He stared harder until he could see every pelt and muzzle clearly. The cats were watching Leafpool, crouching at the water's edge. He could see himself too, curled up asleep.

I'm watching from outside my body.

Jaypaw scanned the hollow, suddenly aware of cold stone beneath his paws. He was at the top of the ridge now, not the sky.

Leafpool stood and began to greet StarClan like old friends, padding around the slope and stopping to brush muzzles here and there. Jaypaw recognized none of them. They had lived before he was born. Only their Clan scents were familiar. He shrank back into the shadows, where he was sure no cat could see him, and watched.

"Bluestar." Leafpool dipped her head to a she-cat, broad-faced and round-eyed, with long, pale fur.

"You are welcome, Leafpool," Bluestar murmured. "We thought you might come."

Beside her sat a pale tom whose eyes shone with warmth. "It is good to see you again," he meowed.

"You too, Lionheart," Leafpool replied.

Bluestar's eyes sparkled. "You come with good news."

"Yes, Graystripe is back," Leafpool purred.

Murmurs of joy rippled around the cats.

"But there is a problem," Leafpool went on. "Firestar doesn't know who should be ThunderClan's deputy. Graystripe and Brambleclaw were both appointed according to the warrior code."

A deep mew echoed from across the hollow. "Both cats have an equal claim."

Leafpool jerked her head around. Behind her, a tom with a pelt as dark as the sky flicked his long, thin tail. Jaypaw tasted the air. He was WindClan.

"If Firestar is wise," mewed the tom, "he will choose the warrior who knows the Clan best."

"That will be a hard choice, Tallstar," Bluestar warned the WindClan cat. "One that no leader has ever had to make before."

Lionheart flicked his tail. "If only we had known that Graystripe was still alive. We could have let Leafpool know."

"He was in a place too far beyond our seeing," Bluestar reminded him. "And ThunderClan needed a deputy."

"Is that why you sent me the vision of thorn-sharp brambles encircling the camp?" Leafpool asked.

"We had to let Firestar know that it was time to appoint one," Bluestar meowed.

Lionheart nodded. "When we showed you that vision, Brambleclaw was the best warrior to help Firestar protect the Clan."

Leafpool looked up sharply. "Is he still the best?"

Bluestar and Lionheart exchanged glances but did not answer.

"Do you wish you had not sent the sign?" Leafpool pressed.

"Brambleclaw has done well," Bluestar reassured her. "He was the right choice. Firestar would have been foolish to go on without a deputy when no cat knew if Graystripe would return."

"But who should be deputy now?"

"There is no true answer," Bluestar warned.

Leafpool blinked. "Then the decision is Firestar's to make?"

"Yes." She sighed. "But Tallstar is right when he says Firestar must choose the cat who knows the Clan best. He must use his head, not his heart, to reach his decision."

"Should I tell him this?"

"Tell him only that he must make his own choice."

Leafpool dipped her head. "I will share this with him," she promised. She turned away from StarClan and padded back down to the Moonpool.

Jaypaw stared round-eyed at the cats. A well-muscled tom was murmuring something to the she-cat beside him. Jaypaw guessed from his glossy pelt he was RiverClan. A group of thin, lithe cats whispered together in the shadow of a boulder. *WindClan?* Jaypaw searched the slope, tasting the air, wondering which of the cats were ThunderClan. Then he froze, his paws turning to ice.

A she-cat was staring straight at him. Her fur was long and pale, and her face was broad and lined with old battle scars. Jaypaw could not guess her Clan from her shape. Her eyes sparked with a fierce spirit, and he drew farther back into the shadows. Something told him he should not be spying here.

Leafpool hesitated at the edge of the pool. "Cinderpelt?"

she called hopefully, looking at the cats around the hollow, but there was no reply. She blinked, her eyes wistful, before lying down with her paws tucked neatly under her chest. Resting her muzzle beside the water once more, she closed her eyes.

"Jaypaw!" Leafpool's shocked mew woke him from where he lay on the cold stone. He scrambled to his paws. The pebbles scraped his pads and he stumbled. He was blind again.

Leafpool's anger flashed against his pelt. "What are you doing here?"

"I-I—"

"This is a place for medicine cats! I came here to share tongues with StarClan!"

"I know." Jaypaw gulped. "I saw you."

"You *saw* me with StarClan?"

"I was watching from the top of the ridge while you were talking to Bluestar and Lionheart."

Leafpool looked stunned. "You were *watching*? How?"

"When I closed my eyes, that's what I dreamed. That's all."

Leafpool narrowed her eyes. "What did they say?"

"Bluestar said that Firestar must make his own decision," Jaypaw mewed. "But he should use his head, not his heart, which I suppose means he should choose—"

"You understood!" Leafpool cut in. Her mew came in a shocked whisper.

Jaypaw was puzzled. Why wouldn't he understand? Was it because he wasn't a medicine cat? Or because he was *blind*?

"How did you find your way here?" Leafpool asked.

Jaypaw sensed wariness prick the medicine cat's pelt, as though she were afraid of his answer. "I followed you. . . ."

"You followed my scent, do you mean? All the way from the hollow?"

"Partly. But I'd dreamed of the journey before, so I knew how it looked."

Leafpool gasped.

"I can't help what I dream!" Jaypaw protested.

Leafpool turned away. "Something extraordinary has happened here." Her words were little more than a murmur, half spoken to herself, but they echoed off the water. "I just wish I knew what it meant."

"Why should it mean anything?" Jaypaw mewed. What was so odd about having a dream at the Moonpool? Wasn't that what it was there for?

"Come," Leafpool ordered. "We should return to camp." Briskness masked the confusion flooding from her. She padded up the path to the top of the ridge, and Jaypaw followed. He let her guide him down the rocky slope beyond, though he had a clear enough sense of it now to manage by himself.

"Are you going to tell Firestar everything StarClan said?" he mewed.

"I'll tell him he must make his own choice about who is deputy."

"And that's all?"

"What do you mean?"

"I think Tallstar and Bluestar hinted that Firestar should

choose Brambleclaw. He's the one who knows the Clan best now." Jaypaw's nose twitched. He could smell mouse.

"Are you saying that I should influence Firestar's decision?"

"You'd only be interpreting what they really meant." The mouse was close. "Isn't that your duty?"

Jaypaw felt Leafpool's startled gaze like sunlight on his pelt. "Is that what *you* would do?"

"I would do what was best for the Clan." A pebble moved just in front of his paws. He darted forward and slapped his forepaws down, only to find that the mouse had escaped into its burrow. He lifted his muzzle, disappointed.

Leafpool had stopped. Fear seemed to enfold her like a cloud. Had he done something wrong?

"What's up?"

"Nothing," she replied, and padded on.

Jaypaw hurried after her.

"You know, that was pretty amazing what you did back there," she meowed. Her light tone didn't hide the anxiety sparking from her—or was it excitement? Why was she so edgy?

Jaypaw shrugged. "Aren't you supposed to see stuff like that at the Moonpool?"

"But this wasn't any old dream. You actually entered my dream. You saw what I saw."

"So?"

"I have entered another cat's dream only once."

"When?" Jaypaw asked.

"Feathertail led me into Willowpaw's dream so that I could tell her where to find catmint," Leafpool explained. "But Feathertail was already with StarClan. She invited me in. You entered my dream on your own, without the permission or knowledge of StarClan."

With a shudder Jaypaw remembered the fierce stare of the broad-faced warrior. "Are you sure they didn't know?"

"They would have told me," Leafpool meowed.

"Why did you call Cinderpelt's name?" Jaypaw asked. "Was there something you wanted to ask her?"

"I just wanted to know if she was there," Leafpool mewed quietly.

"She didn't answer."

"No, she didn't."

"But she's dead, right? Where else could she be?"

Jaypaw heard Leafpool's pawsteps halt. She was expectant, anxious; he could feel it like rain in the air. "What did you feel when you saw StarClan?" she asked. "Were you scared?"

"Scared of a bunch of dead cats?"

"They are your warrior ancestors," she reminded him. "They have seen and heard more than you could ever imagine."

"Of course they've *seen* more—I'm blind, remember?"

"You're not blind in your dreams, Jaypaw. Tell me, apart from the journey to the Moonpool, have you ever dreamed of anything else that has come true?"

Jaypaw shrugged. "Not really. Dreams are just dreams, aren't they?"

"Not to every cat."

"Sometimes I dream about when I was very small, traveling through snow," he confessed. "Is that right? That wasn't the Great Journey, was it?"

Tension crackled through Leafpool's fur. "No, the Great Journey was long before you were born. But your . . . your mother did make a long journey with you through the snow when you were very small. You were born outside the hollow, and she had to wait until you were all strong enough to travel."

Jaypaw could feel Leafpool staring at him, turning something over in her mind, like a fish too huge to be hooked out of the water. "What is it?" he asked.

"I think that you were destined to be a medicine cat," she meowed.

"Don't be silly," Jaypaw retorted. "I'm going to be a warrior."

"But you entered my dream," Leafpool pointed out.

Jaypaw's tail shot up indignantly. "You think I want to be stuck in camp worrying over kits and elders?"

Leafpool bristled. "There's more to being a medicine cat than that!"

"If there is," Jaypaw snapped, "let it be some other cat's destiny! I want to be out in the forest, hunting and fighting for my Clan. You're just like Brightheart! Always treating me differently just because I'm blind!"

"I'm treating you differently because you can see StarClan in *my* dreams! I don't know of any medicine cat with visions as powerful as that."

But Jaypaw didn't want to listen anymore. He padded

angrily ahead. "I don't care about having stupid dreams," he called over his shoulder. "I'm going to be a warrior. Besides, you've already got Hollypaw, remember? You can't have *two* medicine cat apprentices!"

CHAPTER 14

"Let all cats old enough to catch their own prey gather below Highledge!"

Lionpaw jerked up his head. Firestar's call had woken him from his warm nest. It was dawn, and he could feel Berrypaw stirring beside him.

Jaypaw was already stretching, curling his tail back till the tip brushed his spine. "What does Firestar want so early?" he yawned.

"Clan meeting!" Lionpaw leaped to his paws. He hurried to be first out of the den, squeezing ahead of his denmates.

"Stop pushing," Berrypaw complained.

"The fastest hunter catches the most mice," Lionpaw mewed cheerfully.

The air outside the den hit him like the lash of a birch sapling. Frost glittered on the bushes around the edge of the camp, and the icy ground made Lionpaw's pads ache. Breath billowing, he trotted into the clearing, where the cats were already gathering, huddling close for warmth.

Firestar sat on Highledge flanked by Brambleclaw and

Graystripe. Brambleclaw's pelt shone, the muscles beneath it taut. Graystripe's pelt was well-groomed, the knots and tangles smoothed at last, but it was dull and his ribs still showed beneath.

"He must have decided who the deputy should be," Hollypaw mewed, hurrying over from the medicine den and sitting down next to Lionpaw. She wriggled closer to him, shivering.

Jaypaw padded to join them, sitting beside Hollypaw.

"Graystripe and Brambleclaw are on Highledge with Firestar," Hollypaw told him.

"I know," Jaypaw answered sleepily. Lionpaw wondered why he looked so worn-out when he had not been outside the hollow in days.

Firestar's pelt glowed like fire in the cold dawn light as he gazed over the Clan. Millie settled beside Ferncloud, her eyes round with curiosity. Sorreltail, Whitewing, and Cloudtail sat in front of her, Brackenfur and Thornclaw behind. The gray kittypet no longer seemed intimidated by the warriors hemming her in and stared calmly up at Firestar.

"I know you've all been wondering what will happen now that our previous deputy has returned," the Clan leader began.

Graystripe wrapped his bushy tail tighter over his front paws. One of Brambleclaw's ears twitched.

"When we left the forest, I thought I would never see Graystripe again," Firestar confessed. "There were many nights when I stared up at Silverpelt and tried to imagine him among our ancestors."

Lionpaw glanced at Hollypaw and wondered what it would be like to lose her. He didn't like the feeling that stabbed at his belly.

The ThunderClan leader went on. "Graystripe was my deputy and my friend. I trained with him and fought with him. I trusted him more than any cat. Having him back is like having one of my own lives restored."

"He's going to make Graystripe deputy again!" Hollypaw hissed under her breath.

"Wait," Jaypaw warned.

Lionpaw shot his brother a look. Why did he sound so certain?

"But Brambleclaw has helped me lead the Clan through some of its most terrifying challenges. I've never seen him waver in his loyalty to his Clanmates. The last thing ThunderClan needs now is more change." He paused and glanced at the two warriors. "So I've decided that Brambleclaw should remain deputy."

"But—" The gasp escaped Brackenfur before he could stop it. Sorreltail echoed it, and mews of surprise rippled around the Clan. Lionpaw searched Graystripe's face for some sign of regret, but he couldn't read the gray warrior's expression.

Squirrelflight raised her voice happily. "Brambleclaw!"

"Brambleclaw! Brambleclaw!" Ashfur quickly joined in.

Squirrelflight whipped her head around and stared at him.

Why does she look surprised? Lionpaw wondered.

Dustpelt and Thornclaw started calling Brambleclaw's name too. Graystripe got to his paws and joined in, and Brambleclaw dipped his head respectfully to the former ThunderClan deputy.

"Told you so," Jaypaw murmured.

Lionpaw glanced suspiciously at his brother. "How did you know?"

Jaypaw shrugged. "It was the wisest choice."

"Do you think Graystripe minds?" Hollypaw whispered.

"Does it matter?" Jaypaw asked.

"He must know the Clan has changed a lot," Lionpaw replied.

"But what about when he's fully recovered?" Hollypaw persisted. "Will he be happy just being a warrior?"

"I think Firestar made the right decision."

The meow made Lionpaw jump. He glanced up and saw Ashfur padding toward them.

"And you must be pleased that your father's still deputy," the warrior purred.

"Brambleclaw *should* be deputy," Lionpaw told him firmly. "Graystripe doesn't even know the territory yet. He'd be as lost as a WindClan kit in a ShadowClan nursery."

"True." Ashfur nodded.

"And Graystripe is going to take another moon to recover," Jaypaw put in. "He still smells of crow-food."

"He'll be strong soon," Hollypaw mewed defensively.

"Soon isn't good enough," Lionpaw argued. "We need a strong deputy *now*. Leaf-bare's clearly not finished with us, and ShadowClan is never going to make our life easy. We can't afford to wait for Graystripe to recover."

"But he was deputy first!" Hollypaw protested. "Has everyone forgotten? When Mistyfoot was taken by Twolegs, Hawkfrost replaced her only until she returned. Because according to the warrior code she *never stopped being* the deputy!"

"Your sister has a point," Ashfur commented.

"I know, but"—Lionpaw was surprised at Hollypaw's fierceness—"Firestar has to be practical."

"If we start ignoring the warrior code, then we are no longer warriors!" Hollypaw declared. The fur along her spine was bristling, and her eyes glittered with anxiety.

"What if StarClan *told* Firestar to choose Brambleclaw?" Jaypaw asked softly.

Brambleclaw was padding toward them, with Berrypaw beside him. "We're going hunting."

"Can we join you?" Ashfur asked.

"Of course. Brightheart and Jaypaw are coming too. But if you don't mind a crowd—"

"Of course not." Ashfur narrowed his eyes. "I just thought it might be fun for Lionpaw and Berrypaw to have a little competition."

Brambleclaw's eyes glittered. "Good idea."

Berrypaw clawed the ground excitedly. "Oh, yes!"

"Great!" Lionpaw mewed.

"Okay," Brambleclaw decided. "The first apprentice to catch three pieces of prey gets first pick from the fresh-kill pile tonight."

Lionpaw glanced at Berrypaw. His denmate was larger than he and more experienced. He would have to rely more on senses than speed if he was going to win.

Brightheart and Jaypaw joined them.

"Why do we need to go with them?" Jaypaw was complaining. "I'm perfectly capable of hunting on my own."

Pity flashed in Brightheart's eye, and Lionpaw winced. Jaypaw glared at his mentor as if he knew exactly what she was thinking.

"We'll go in a moment," Brambleclaw meowed. "First, I want to ask Dustpelt and Birchfall to patrol the ShadowClan border. I'll meet you at the entrance." Before he padded away, the ThunderClan deputy glanced at Hollypaw. "Shouldn't you be helping Leafpool?"

"Um, yes," Hollypaw mewed hastily. She turned and slunk away, the tip of her black tail dragging over the ice-white clearing.

"So you think you can beat me, do you?" Berrypaw hissed in Lionpaw's ear.

"I caught a vole on my first hunting expedition," Lionpaw reminded him.

"Good," Berrypaw mewed. "I'd hate to win *too* easily."

"You'll be lucky to win at all!" Lionpaw growled.

"How's a tiny scrap like you going to catch three bits of prey in one morning?"

Lionpaw wasn't going to let his denmate get away with that. He crouched into attack position, wriggling his hindquarters. "Say that again!" he challenged.

"You're hardly bigger than a mouse!" Berrypaw purred.

Lionpaw launched himself at the young tom, and the two apprentices bundled toward the thorn barrier. Berrypaw's weight took Lionpaw by surprise. He scrabbled to push the larger apprentice off, but Berrypaw heaved him toward the prickly spines of the thornbush. Thinking quickly, Lionpaw let himself go limp, becoming so slippery that it was easy to wriggle out of Berrypaw's grip. Quick as a flash, he sprang onto Berrypaw's back and nipped his friend's scruff with his teeth. Berrypaw tried to shake him off, but even with his claws sheathed, Lionpaw found that he had the strength to hold his grip on Berrypaw's broad shoulders.

"Lionpaw!"

He looked up to see his sister charging back toward them, and, in that instant, Berrypaw threw him off and pinned him to the ground.

"You're my first catch of the day," Berrypaw mewed triumphantly.

"Hollypaw put me off!" Lionpaw complained.

"A good warrior is never distracted," Ashfur meowed. The pale gray warrior had stopped to watch the two apprentices.

Lionpaw scrambled to his paws, prickling with embarrassment.

Hollypaw was trotting around them in circles. "Leafpool wants me to collect some tansy in case this cold weather brings whitecough," she panted excitedly. "She says there's a clump by the old Thunderpath, and she asked if I could join your patrol to fetch some." She looked around. "Where's Brambleclaw?"

"Giving orders to Dustpelt," Ashfur answered.

As he spoke, Brambleclaw bounded over from halfrock. Graystripe was with him.

"Mind if I join you?" the gray warrior asked Ashfur. "I want to get familiar with the territory and see how the prey runs here."

"That's fine with me," Ashfur agreed. He nodded at Hollypaw. "We've got an extra apprentice, too."

Lionpaw hadn't been out with both Hollypaw and Jaypaw since their attempt to track down the fox cubs. They quickly fell into their familiar grouping: Hollypaw a pawstep ahead, and Lionpaw letting his pelt brush against Jaypaw's just enough to help him through the trees.

They headed deep into the forest, picking up the clearest route along the old Thunderpath. Lionpaw had been along it before, when Ashfur had shown him around ThunderClan territory. But he had never followed it all the way past the abandoned Twoleg nest.

Hollypaw was scanning the undergrowth on either side of the track.

"It looks a lot like yarrow," Jaypaw whispered to her. "But it tastes more like grass than mouse bile."

"I know!" Hollypaw snapped.

Why was Jaypaw helping her? Lionpaw wondered. Hollypaw was the medicine cat apprentice, not him.

She flicked her tail toward a clump of long-stemmed plants with thin, spiky leaves. "That's it, isn't it?"

"Have you found some?" Brambleclaw halted in the middle of the path.

The cats waited as Hollypaw bit into a leaf. She narrowed her eyes thoughtfully, then swallowed.

"Not bitter at all," she reported. "It's tansy."

"You'd better collect some and take it back to camp," Brambleclaw meowed.

Hollypaw's eyes clouded with disappointment. "Leafpool doesn't need it right away."

"It might not be safe for her to go back to camp on her own," Lionpaw pointed out, guessing his sister wanted a chance to stay out for a while. "Not with the fox cubs about."

"And don't forget the competition," Ashfur meowed. "We don't want to waste time escorting her back."

"If you're sure Leafpool doesn't need it urgently . . . ?" Brambleclaw prompted Hollypaw.

Her eyes brightened. "It was only for the store."

"We'll collect some on our way back, then," Brambleclaw agreed. He leaped away, heading into the shadowy woods.

Lionpaw waited on the Thunderpath for Jaypaw and

Brightheart to disappear among the trees with the others before following them in. Even in leaf-bare, the undergrowth here was thick. But without their leafy covering the plants looked like tall, thin skeletons littering the forest floor.

Lionpaw's breath came in clouds as the patrol padded quietly over the frozen ground. Graystripe turned back to face them. "There's no scent of fox here," he meowed. "And not too much cover for prey. This looks like a good spot to start the hunt."

Ashfur looked from Berrypaw to Lionpaw. "Who wants to go first?"

"There's a mouse over there," Jaypaw announced casually. For the first time Lionpaw wondered if his brother felt left out of the hunting contest. But Jaypaw held his chin high and flicked his tail toward the base of an oak tree several fox-lengths away. Ashfur jerked his head around in surprise.

"It's dug under the frozen leaves into the ground," Jaypaw told them.

Lionpaw pricked his ears. Sure enough, he could hear the scrabble of tiny paws against cold earth, though very faintly. And there was the musty scent of freshly turned leaf litter in the air.

"Lionpaw," Brambleclaw hissed quietly. "You have a try."

One stealthy pawstep at a time, Lionpaw crept toward the scuffling noise. He let each pad sink slowly onto the hard ground, so that his steps made no sound. The scuffling carried on as Lionpaw drew close enough to drop into a hunting crouch. Squatting with his muzzle outstretched, he let his tail rest on the earth behind him. He could smell the mouse now, and saw a slight movement in the leaves.

"Brambleclaw!"

The mouse scuttled out of the leaves and disappeared among the roots of a tree. Hissing with anger, Lionpaw spun around to see who had ruined his catch.

Birchfall exploded from the undergrowth and skidded to a halt. "ShadowClan have moved the border! They've put a new line of scent marks inside ThunderClan territory!"

"Where?" Brambleclaw demanded.

"I'll show you." Without waiting, Birchfall headed away through the trees.

"Where's Dustpelt?" Brambleclaw called after him.

"Heading back to camp to warn Firestar," came the reply.

Brambleclaw turned to Brightheart. "You'd better come with us. I'm not risking leaving you while those fox cubs are still around."

Brightheart narrowed her eyes. "What about Jaypaw? Will he be able to keep up?"

"Don't let him out of your sight, and keep as close to us as you can," Brambleclaw ordered. He glanced at Ashfur. "Stay near them." Then he nodded to Graystripe. "Come with me."

Brambleclaw bounded after Birchfall, Graystripe following. Lionpaw pelted after them, the mouse forgotten. Hollypaw raced at his side. He could hear the pawsteps of Ashfur, Brightheart, and Jaypaw pounding behind. Glancing over his shoulder, he saw his brother weaving through the trees as easily as a sighted cat. *He must be guided by StarClan!* he thought in astonishment. He turned back to look ahead, his pelt bristling as he ran. Had ShadowClan really dared to move the border?

Birchfall led them back along the Thunderpath before veering into the forest and up the slope that led to the ShadowClan border. He skidded to a halt near the top. "Here!" he gasped, flicking his tail to indicate the line of birches that followed the ridge.

Lionpaw sniffed the nearest trunk and wrinkled his nose. It was true. ShadowClan had marked ThunderClan trees.

"Isn't this the original border?" Graystripe asked.

"No!" Brambleclaw hissed. "The border is there." He pointed his muzzle to the top of the rise where the trees gave way to the grassy clearing.

"Did they think we wouldn't notice?" Hollypaw spat.

Ashfur raced out of the bracken behind them, followed by Brightheart and Jaypaw.

Jaypaw's hackles rose. "ShadowClan warriors nearby!" he warned.

As he spoke, three ShadowClan cats stalked over the rise and stood staring down at the ThunderClan patrol.

"Oakfur!" Brambleclaw hissed, staring at the small brown tom who led the trio. Lionpaw recognized the two others from the Gathering—Owlpaw and his mentor, Smokefoot.

"A blind kit noticed us before the ThunderClan deputy knew we were here," Oakfur sneered. "How humiliating."

"Is ThunderClan so desperate for warriors that it needs to

train even its most worthless kit?" snarled Smokefoot.

Jaypaw rushed forward, spitting. Brightheart grabbed his tail in her teeth and hauled him backward.

"A blind kit saved by a one-eyed warrior," mocked Oakfur. "ThunderClan isn't what it used to be. Filled with kitty-pets and cripples and worn-out deputies." He glared at Graystripe.

"You've moved the border," Brambleclaw growled.

"We've taken what should be ours, and we will take more," Smokefoot told him.

"ThunderClan is hardly a real Clan anymore—it's half kit-typet," Oakfur put in. "I'm sure StarClan agrees that only true warriors are entitled to hunt on Clan territory."

"ThunderClan has nothing but true warriors!" Brambleclaw yowled. He flattened his ears and stepped over the new marker line until he was only a tail-length away from Oakfur. "If you want our territory, you'll have to fight for every step."

Lionpaw's fur stood on end. His first real battle! He sank his claws into the earth, imagining it was ShadowClan fur.

"Are you *sure* we won't win?" Oakfur's eyes glittered as more ShadowClan warriors began to appear over the rise, lining up like starlings on a branch. Lionpaw's heart flipped over. It looked as though every ShadowClan warrior had come to fight. Their muscles bulged under their pelts, their claws glinting as they flexed them against the hard ground.

Lionpaw felt fur brush his flank. Hollypaw and Jaypaw had joined him.

"We fight as one," Hollypaw vowed.

Lionpaw suddenly pictured the three of them—three half-grown apprentices, one of them blind, facing what looked like the whole of ShadowClan.

StarClan, help us!

CHAPTER 15

"Get back to camp and tell Firestar to bring help." Graystripe's hiss sounded in Lionpaw's ear. "Now!"

Lionpaw turned and pelted away into the trees. He hated leaving Jaypaw and Hollypaw, but without help the battle was already lost.

"Stop him!"

He heard Russetfur's yowl, and the rustle of paws upon leaves.

Lionpaw glanced over his shoulder. Two ShadowClan warriors streaked toward him. Then he saw a flash of gray fur. Graystripe had launched himself onto one of the cats. The ShadowClan warrior yowled and the air exploded as the two Clans charged screeching into battle.

Lionpaw forced himself to run faster till he thought his heart would burst. Paws pounded behind him. Only one set now, thanks to Graystripe. Lionpaw dodged through a thick bramble swath, hoping that his small size would let him escape the ShadowClan warrior. But as he slipped out of the other side and glanced backward, he saw a burly tom thrusting his way through the bush with terrifying strength.

Lionpaw hurtled down the steep slope to the training hollow and pelted across it. Just a short way through the trees and then a clear run to the camp entrance. The ShadowClan warrior's pawsteps thundered ever closer as Lionpaw caught sight of the thorn barrier ahead.

"Help!" he wailed.

Claws raked his tail. The ShadowClan cat was at his heels. Wild with terror, Lionpaw dug his claws in and propelled himself forward.

A fiery flash of fur streaked from the thorn tunnel and flew past Lionpaw.

"I'll stop him," Squirrelflight yowled, lunging for the ShadowClan warrior.

The tom let out an agonized shriek. Lionpaw slowed, his breath coming in great gulps. He turned and saw Squirrelflight chasing the ShadowClan warrior up the bank, snarling as if all the warriors of StarClan raced beside her.

Lionpaw hurtled into the camp. "ShadowClan have invaded!"

Firestar was in the clearing with Dustpelt. He bounded to Lionpaw's side as soon as he saw him. "Dustpelt told me they've moved the border," he meowed.

"Brambleclaw took our hunting patrol to investigate," Lionpaw puffed. "But we walked into an ambush."

Firestar's eyes widened with alarm. "Are they fighting now?"

Lionpaw nodded, his paws trembling as he thought of Jaypaw and Hollypaw battling experienced ShadowClan warriors.

"Sandstorm, Spiderleg, Whitewing, Stormfur, Brook!" Firestar called to the warriors who were already pacing around the edge of the clearing, lashing their tails. "Shadow-Clan have crossed the border. Brambleclaw is holding them off, but they need help."

"Should I bring Mousepaw?" Spiderleg asked.

"If he's battle-ready," Firestar answered.

Squirrelflight raced back through the entrance. "There's one less ShadowClan warrior to deal with," she announced. "He'll not want to fight again today."

"Good work. I want you to stay and guard the camp," Firestar told her.

Squirrelflight nodded. "Yes, Firestar."

Millie appeared from behind the warriors' den. "I'm coming with you."

Lionpaw stared at her in astonishment. She was a kittypet!

"Okay," Firestar agreed. "But don't take any risks."

Lionpaw was still trembling with terror and exhaustion. Firestar looked at him. "Are you fit to fight?"

Lionpaw nodded.

"Good," Firestar growled. "Your brother and sister need you." Then he swept out of the camp, his warriors following.

Lionpaw pelted after the patrol. *How dare ShadowClan invade our territory?* He would fight tooth and claw to drive those fox-hearted warriors out. His paws stopped shaking and began to itch for battle.

"Always keep an eye out behind you!" Whitewing fell in beside him to give him some breathless advice. "ShadowClan fight dirty. You're fast and strong, even though you're small. You'll be nimbler than some of their warriors. Use that to your advantage."

As they neared the border, he heard screeches and yowls.

"This way!" Firestar called. They plunged through the forest until Lionpaw could glimpse teeth and claws flashing in the gaps between the trees ahead.

ShadowClan warriors had surrounded Brambleclaw's patrol, but the ThunderClan cats were standing their ground, lashing out at every cat within reach.

"Attack!" Firestar cried, and the ThunderClan warriors spread out and launched themselves into the battle.

"Head over there!" Spiderleg called to Lionpaw. He flicked his tail to the edge of the fighting. "Look for Jaypaw first and do what you can to defend him."

Lionpaw raced forward, scanning the fray for Hollypaw and Jaypaw. He spotted Ashfur and Birchfall fighting side by side with Brightheart, fending off four ShadowClan warriors. Jaypaw crouched behind them, pelt bristling with rage, slashing and jabbing at any ShadowClan warrior who made it through their defensive line. He didn't seem to need any help.

Lionpaw's heart thudded as he searched for Hollypaw's black pelt. Had she been wounded? Relief glimmered for a moment when he saw her fighting beside Graystripe. The gray warrior, ears flattened, his lips drawn back into a vicious snarl, raked the flank of a dark ginger ShadowClan warrior as it lunged for Hollypaw.

Russetfur! Lionpaw recognized the ShadowClan deputy.

Hollypaw ducked under Graystripe and shot out from beneath him, nipping the ShadowClan deputy on her hind leg with such ferocity that the warrior whipped around, claws flashing, and lunged at Hollypaw. Lionpaw pelted to his sister's defense, hurling himself at Russetfur and slashing her nose. The ShadowClan deputy howled in pain as crimson blood welled beneath her eyes.

"Nice work!" Graystripe called.

As he spoke, two ShadowClan cats slammed into him, knocking him to the ground. The larger of the pair, a black tom, pressed him to the ground, while the smaller white she-cat reared on her hind legs, flexing her long claws, ready to crash down on Graystripe's head.

Orange fur blazed past Lionpaw as Firestar flew at the white warrior. He threw the ShadowClan warrior backward and slashed her cheek with a well-aimed blow.

Lionpaw leaped onto the black tom who was pinning Graystripe to the ground. He dug in his claws and bit hard into the tom's shoulder. The warrior let go of Graystripe and reared backward. At once Hollypaw darted behind him and knocked the tom's paws out from under him. Lionpaw leaped off as the warrior crashed down.

"Great move!" Lionpaw called to Hollypaw.

"He's not finished yet," she warned.

The black tom was already on his paws, hissing ferociously, but Lionpaw and Hollypaw faced him side by side, and, jabbing and slashing with their forepaws, they drove him back toward the border until he was panting and streaked with blood.

Suddenly Lionpaw spotted Oakfur slinking through the bracken toward Firestar, a fox-length away. The Thunder-Clan leader still had the white warrior pinned to the ground, unaware of Oakfur's stealthy approach. Before Lionpaw could warn him, Oakfur had leaped onto Firestar's back and grabbed the ThunderClan leader's neck in his jaws.

The white warrior struggled from Firestar's grip and nipped at his front paws until the ThunderClan leader fell to the ground. He vanished beneath the two snarling Shadow-Clan warriors.

"Can you manage by yourself?" Lionpaw screeched to Hollypaw.

"I'll help her," Graystripe growled, leaping in beside her.

Lionpaw threw himself at Oakfur, clamping his jaws around the ShadowClan warrior's tail. *This is for calling Jaypaw worthless!* he thought as he bit down with all his strength. Oakfur screeched and let go of Firestar. Firestar leaped to his paws and whipped around to grab Oakfur by the scruff. As he held Oakfur in his jaws, he kicked out with his powerful hind legs and sent the white warrior sprawling into the bracken. Then he flung Oakfur with all his might against a tree. Oakfur hit it with such force that the branches trembled and he fell to the ground, dazed.

Seeing that Firestar was safe, Lionpaw turned back to Hollypaw. He expected to see her still fighting beside Graystripe, but she stood alone in a space among the battling cats. Graystripe had left her undefended.

"Watch out!" Lionpaw gasped, his heart lurching as he saw

Smokefoot rushing up behind his sister. Graystripe was two tail-lengths away, pulling a ShadowClan warrior off Millie. The former kittypet leaped to her paws.

"Go back and help Hollypaw!" Millie yowled to Graystripe. "I can take care of myself!" She lashed out with her front claws at the ShadowClan warrior and sent him screeching away with a blow that sprayed his blood across the forest floor.

Smokefoot was on top of Hollypaw, raking his claws along her flank, but Graystripe wrestled him to the ground and pummeled his belly with his thorn-sharp hind claws. Lionpaw darted to Hollypaw's side as Smokefoot yowled in pain, and Graystripe let the tom flee across the border.

"Drive the rest into the brambles!" Graystripe ordered.

"What?" Spiderleg yowled in disbelief.

"That'll only make it harder to fight them!" Birchfall called.

"Harder for ShadowClan!" Hollypaw hissed in Lionpaw's ear. "They don't have brambles in the pine forest."

Firestar nodded grimly. "They're not used to fighting in undergrowth!" he called. "Do as Graystripe says!"

"Everyone, spread out behind me!" Brambleclaw's order split the air. He had spun around so that his back was to the ShadowClan border.

The ThunderClan cats drew away from their enemy long enough to reposition themselves around their deputy. Confused, the ShadowClan warriors stared about them. Suddenly they were trapped on the wrong side of their border. Then Brambleclaw charged forward, his warriors flanking him on either side, and they began to press the ShadowClan warriors deeper into ThunderClan territory, where a tangle of brambles covered the forest floor.

Lionpaw spotted Jaypaw lashing out at Owlpaw. The ShadowClan apprentice was playing with Jaypaw, ducking the blows and teasing him with jabs and taunts.

Lionpaw raced to his brother's side. "You're nothing but a coward," he growled at Owlpaw.

Owlpaw thrashed his tail. "I'll show you I'm not a coward!" He lashed out and caught Jaypaw's muzzle with his claw. Jaypaw gasped with pain, but he didn't recoil, flailing his unsheathed claws more fiercely than ever.

"He's ducking," Lionpaw hissed to his brother.

Jaypaw instantly aimed his blows downward and raked Owlpaw's ears. Jaypaw gave a yowl of satisfaction.

"He's trying to get behind you now," Lionpaw warned as Owlpaw scooted past Jaypaw and balanced himself, ready to leap at the tabby apprentice. Lionpaw spun around, every instinct crying out to take Owlpaw on himself. But he knew Jaypaw would never forgive him for fighting his battle for him, and besides, Jaypaw had already turned nimbly around and was pummeling Owlpaw with his forepaws. Owlpaw tried to duck, but Jaypaw had learned that trick, and the instant Owlpaw lowered his head, Jaypaw leaped on top of him and rolled the ShadowClan apprentice onto his back. He clung to his fur and raked his hind claws along Owlpaw's spine until the ShadowClan apprentice begged for mercy.

"Get off!" he shrieked, and Jaypaw let go.

Owlpaw scrambled to his feet and spat at Jaypaw, ready to attack again, but Lionpaw fixed him with a threatening stare, and Owlpaw, faced by the pair of them, backed away, snarling.

The ShadowClan warriors were beginning to trip on the brambles, struggling as much against the thorns that clawed their pelts as against the ThunderClan warriors who were forcing them farther and farther into the bush. Sandstorm's tail lashed triumphantly as a ShadowClan warrior cowered beneath her blows. Beside her, Whitewing nipped at a mottled apprentice as he tried to battle past her out of the clinging thorns. Brook and Stormfur worked together, jabbing at Smokefoot with merciless claws as he struggled farther into the brambles to escape them.

Russetfur stared in dismay at her warriors thrashing helplessly in the undergrowth. "Retreat!" she yowled.

The ShadowClan cats scrambled out of the brambles, leaving clumps of fur behind as they pelted past the ThunderClan warriors and fled back into their own territory.

Lionpaw scanned the battered ThunderClan cats. "Hollypaw!"

"I'm over here!" Hollypaw squirmed backward out of the undergrowth, her bushy tail pricked with thorns.

"Is everyone okay?" Firestar staggered out, his muzzle crimson with blood.

"Sandstorm's twisted her paw." Brambleclaw was standing beside the ginger-colored warrior as she licked at a forepaw.

"It's just a sprain," she reassured him.

"Stormfur?" Firestar looked at the gray warrior. "That looks like a bad cut on your shoulder."

"It'll heal," Stormfur replied.

"I've lost a chunk of fur from my tail," Spiderleg spat. "But it was worth it if ShadowClan thinks twice before trying to steal our territory again."

"We need to make sure they're all gone," Firestar meowed.

"I'll check," Brook offered.

"Are you injured?"

"Just a torn ear."

"Then take Spiderleg with you and search beyond the brambles," Firestar ordered. "Make sure no cat went farther into our territory."

Spiderleg and Brook hared away through the trees.

Ashfur flicked Lionpaw's shoulder with his tail. "Thank StarClan you got help so quickly."

"You held out well till we came," Firestar praised him.

"Hollypaw fought like a warrior!" Birchfall commented.

"And Jaypaw never gave ground," Brightheart added.

"We couldn't let ShadowClan drive us from our own territory!" Graystripe growled.

Brambleclaw gazed across the clearing where the ShadowClan cats had fled. "We're going to have to do something about ShadowClan before the next Gathering," he vowed.

"Let's start by remarking the correct boundary," Firestar ordered. "Brambleclaw, you stay here with Ashfur and Birchfall and mark every tree twice along the border."

Brambleclaw nodded.

"I'll take the rest back to camp."

"Can't I stay with Ashfur?" Lionpaw begged.

Ashfur shook his head. "Go back to camp and get some ointment on those scratches. I want you back in training as soon as possible."

Reluctantly, Lionpaw turned and followed his Clanmates. Sandstorm was limping, and Stormfur kept stopping to lick at the blood welling from the wound on his shoulder. Millie's pelt was missing clumps of fur along her flank, but she was buzzing with the excitement that came from winning a battle, her ears pricked and her tail twitching.

Lionpaw caught up with Jaypaw and Hollypaw. "Did you see me jump on Oakfur?" he mewed proudly.

"I wish I had!" Hollypaw sounded even more excited than he felt. "I was too busy seeing to that tabby warrior." Her eyes were glowing. "I used a move Cinderpaw taught me the other day. It was brilliant doing it for real!"

"And you showed Owlpaw that he's no match for a ThunderClan apprentice," Lionpaw mewed to Jaypaw. The mottled apprentice was padding along quietly, tail down.

"Yeah, right," he muttered.

"Hollypaw!" Leafpool had come out to meet the returning warriors. "Are there any serious injuries?"

Hollypaw blinked. "S-Stormfur has a scratch . . ." she stammered.

"Haven't you checked?" Leafpool asked anxiously.

"Everyone can still walk," Hollypaw offered.

"What about the tansy?" Leafpool pursued. "Did you find any?"

"Oh, yes," Hollypaw mewed.

Leafpool looked at her questioningly. "Where is it?"

Hollypaw looked crestfallen. "We were going to pick some on our way back from hunting, and then Birchfall arrived to warn us that ShadowClan had moved the border, and Brambleclaw ordered us to—"

"It's okay," Leafpool meowed. "I'm proud that you fought with your Clanmates. But keep a lookout for any healing herbs on the way back to camp. There'll be plenty of bites and scratches to treat when we get home. I'm going to check on the others."

Hollypaw gazed at the undergrowth. "Do you think that juniper would do?" she murmured as they passed a large bush dotted with dark berries.

"The horsetail growing next to it would be better," Jaypaw advised.

Hollypaw closed her eyes. "Horsetail—good for infections," she recited. Then she hurried over to the clump of spindly plants and tore one out by its roots.

Lionpaw could feel his scratches beginning to sting. His muscles ached from the battle, and when they reached the camp he padded to the halfrock and collapsed beside it. Jaypaw climbed onto the smooth, low rock and hung his head over the side, while Hollypaw dropped the horsetail she'd been dragging and flopped down beside them.

"I still can't believe we fought real warriors," she breathed.

Jaypaw just stared blankly at the ground.

"Why are you looking so miserable?" Lionpaw asked him. "You fought brilliantly."

"Only with *your* help," Jaypaw pointed out.

"Every warrior needs help—that's what being in a Clan is all about!" Hollypaw reminded him.

"We had to work together to drive off one of Shadow-Clan's warriors," Lionpaw added.

"I couldn't even manage an apprentice by myself," Jaypaw mewed, flicking the tip of his tail. "They called me a worthless kit. Perhaps they're right. Perhaps I'm just kidding myself, thinking I could ever be a real warrior."

"Hollypaw!" Leafpool called from the clearing where the rest of the patrol were licking their wounds. "I can't see to all the injured warriors by myself."

Hollypaw leaped to her paws. "Coming, Leafpool," she mewed. "Sorry!" She stripped a leaf from the horsetail and scampered over to where Millie and Graystripe lay.

Lionpaw longed to cheer Jaypaw up, but this was one battle his brother would have to fight by himself. However much he prayed to StarClan, there was nothing Lionpaw could do to help Jaypaw see.

At least Hollypaw had enjoyed the fight with Shadow-Clan. Lionpaw watched her, letting his weary paws rest, as she chewed up the horsetail leaf and began licking the juice into Millie's scratches. Every time Millie flinched, Hollypaw leaped away, screwing up her face. A small worry began to flutter like a trapped bird in Lionpaw's belly. Hollypaw seemed so ill at ease now, her awkward movements nothing like the fluid grace with which she fought. She'd raced into battle, her eyes glowing at the challenge, but here she was fumbling among her injured Clanmates, her gaze shadowed by uncertainty. A strange thought pricked Lionpaw like a thorn in his bedding: *Does Hollypaw really want to be a medicine cat?*

CHAPTER 16

❖

"*Squirrelflight, take Cloudtail, Cinderpaw, Thornclaw, and* Poppypaw and bring back as much fresh-kill as you can." Jaypaw lay on the halfrock and listened as Firestar gave the order. "Our warriors will be hungry tonight."

Jaypaw dangled his tired paws over the edge of the halfrock, feeling the cold stone soothe his aching body. The battle had left him battered and scratched, but he could tend to his own wounds.

Leafpool left a trail of marigold scent in her wake as she went to apply a salve to the scratches on Stormfur's shoulder. Hollypaw was busy treating Millie, though Jaypaw was confused when he detected revulsion rather than concern pulsing through his sister's paws as she applied the pungent horsetail balm. Something was upsetting her, but he was too busy with his own thoughts to probe Hollypaw's much further.

He kept wondering if he could have beaten Owlpaw without Lionpaw's help. Stubbornly he told himself that he could. He'd been able to pinpoint the ShadowClan's apprentice by scent and sound. But a nagging doubt gnawed at his belly.

The battle had been so fast, he just hadn't been able to keep up. The sound of Owlpaw's breath in one ear had not warned him of the fierce jab that had raked the other. The thud of the ShadowClan apprentice's paws on the leaves had been drowned by the cries of the other warriors, and Jaypaw had twisted and spun, only to find Owlpaw had darted around him already and was clawing him from behind.

He would never be a warrior.

It was the one thing he wanted above all. But he had to accept that he couldn't fight alone. Fury raged inside him like a badger cornered in its set.

I don't know of any medicine cat with visions as powerful as that. Leafpool's words echoed in his head. *I think that you were destined to be a medicine cat.*

All his life he had imagined growing up to be a warrior. Why would he feel that way if StarClan had planned another destiny for him?

"Brambleclaw!" Firestar welcomed his deputy back into camp. Jaypaw had been so lost in his own thoughts that he hadn't noticed his father's return.

"We've remarked the trees and covered the stench of ShadowClan," Brambleclaw reported.

Something was bothering him; Jaypaw could sense hesitation tripping his father's tongue.

"Oakfur claimed ShadowClan had a right to our territory because ThunderClan has so many cats who are not . . ." Brambleclaw paused awkwardly. "Who are not Clanborn."

"So ShadowClan still believe a cat must be Clanborn to

become a warrior," Firestar growled.

"I told him that every cat in ThunderClan is a warrior," Brambleclaw meowed.

"Good." Firestar raised his voice so that every cat in the clearing could hear him. "There is not a single cat in ThunderClan who does not deserve to be here!"

Anxiety flashed from Dustpelt. "But there is truth in what ShadowClan says." The tabby warrior's words cracked the air like a stone hitting ice. "ThunderClan has taken in more cats than any other. That alone leaves us open to criticism from other Clans."

Stormfur got to his paws. "Do we care what the other Clans think?" he snarled. "I was raised in RiverClan, but does any cat here doubt my loyalty to ThunderClan?"

"Your father was a ThunderClan warrior," Dustpelt pointed out. "You have ThunderClan blood."

"And what about those of us who don't?" Hazelpaw protested, her soft gray-and-white pelt bristling. "I was born in the horseplace with Berrypaw and Mousepaw. Does any cat think we are not worthy to train as warriors?"

"Of course not!" Graystripe called. "Belonging has nothing to do with blood! I was born pure ThunderClan, yet I am more of a stranger here now than any cat. Millie was a kittypet only moons ago, but she fought as hard as Firestar to drive off ShadowClan today—and so did Brook!" His eyes flashed toward the Tribe cat, who blinked her thanks.

Sorreltail mewed loudly in agreement. "Loyalty is proved by what we do, not where we came from!"

Jaypaw jerked his head up. He could sense doubt pulsing from Hollypaw, horsetail balm still fragrant on her paws. "But the warrior code tells us we should drive strangers from our territory," she mewed uncertainly.

"We have taken in any cat who has asked us for help," Firestar meowed. "Does the warrior code condemn us for showing mercy?"

"N-no," murmured Hollypaw.

"And every cat we have taken in has helped make ThunderClan stronger!" Firestar went on. Mews of agreement rose from the other cats.

"But," Firestar added, "Brambleclaw is right to tell me what ShadowClan has said."

"When have we let the other Clans tell us what to do?" Graystripe challenged.

"*Never*. At the next Gathering I will make it clear that ThunderClan's business is its own," Firestar promised. "We will defend our borders as we have always done and let no Clan interfere in our decisions."

A ripple of approval passed around the hollow, but Jaypaw still sensed tension. He knew from furtive worried whispers that he was not the only cat who wondered how ThunderClan's mixed blood might change the way the other Clans saw them, or even the way StarClan thought of them.

The other apprentices were asleep, the air sighing with their gentle breathing. But Jaypaw was wide awake. Leafpool's words still haunted him. He kept trying to persuade

himself that he could learn how to be a warrior, that his fighting skills would improve. But every time he thought it, the
hope became hollower.

He would go to the Moonpool. Perhaps there would be an
answer for him there. Quietly he slipped out of the den. An
icy wind stirred the bare branches of the trees; he would need
to move very quietly, because every sound would travel far.

Brackenfur was guarding the camp entrance. Jaypaw could
smell his scent. If the warrior turned him back then he would
find another way out of the camp.

"You're out late," Brackenfur observed.

"I can't sleep."

"It can be like that after a battle," Brackenfur meowed.

"I'm going into the forest." Jaypaw waited for surprise to
flash from Brackenfur, but the warrior did not flinch.

"Do you want me to go with you?" he offered. "Brook
won't mind starting her watch early."

"No, thanks."

"You need some time alone," Brackenfur guessed.

Jaypaw nodded, and Brackenfur went on, "At least it's quiet
tonight. But I'll keep my ears pricked for you, just in case."

"Thanks, Brackenfur." Jaypaw was relieved he had at least
one Clanmate who didn't fuss over him as though he were a
newborn kit. "I'll be back as soon as I can," he called as he
padded away from the entrance.

As he climbed the slope, the leaves slippery with frost
beneath his paws, Jaypaw started to feel less eaten up with
anxious thoughts. The noisy buzz and flow of the Clan,

which invaded his senses like mosquitoes nipping at his ears, was gone. He followed the route he'd taken with Leafpool toward WindClan territory; the memory of it seemed burned into his paws as they retraced the path that grazed the WindClan border and led up into the hills.

His ears were sharp enough to hear the tumbling of the stream before his paws felt the ground turn to rock. His nose twitched, smelling for danger, but he scented nothing other than clean, fresh air rolling down from the mountains. He followed the stream steadily upward until he was scrambling up the rocks that led to the bushes circling the hollow. The whispering voices, the softly walking cats who weren't there, surrounded him again. Their presence was oddly reassuring, as if they had come to welcome him.

Jaypaw paused at the top of the spiraling path; though his eyes saw nothing, he could clearly picture the sloping walls of the hollow and the pool below cradling the moon. The whispering grew louder until it became a droning purr that echoed around the rocks. As he followed the path down to the Moonpool, his ears twitched, straining to make out words from the murmuring sigh.

"You are welcome, Jaypaw."

"Come, Jaypaw."

Scents flooded around him, the scents of cats he had no memory of, yet who seemed familiar.

"Dream with us, Jaypaw."

A pelt brushed his and then another as the cats guided him down to the pool. A faint memory stirred of a long, snowy journey, where his mother's voice had comforted him and two soft pelts had urged him on.

Jaypaw stopped at the edge of the pool and lay down on the smooth stone shore. Closing his eyes, he touched the water with his nose.

He opened his eyes and found himself in lush woodland. Trees soared into the blue sky above his head. Ferns unfurled their arching fronds above his back. Warm air, carrying the fresh scents of the forest, lapped at his fur. Everywhere thrummed with damp green life.

"Bluestar?" he called. "Lionheart? Cinderpelt?" Perhaps he could contact Leafpool's mentor where Leafpool had failed.

But there was no reply.

Frustrated, Jaypaw stood up and wandered into the trees. Why had all those voices welcomed him to the hollow and then not come to greet him? He felt a twinge of resentment. Why did StarClan have to make everything so difficult? He only wanted to know if he was meant to be a medicine cat.

At least he felt warm here, and safe. And he could *see*. He began to run and found his paws carrying him so swiftly through the trees that he felt as if he were flying. He raced beneath the ferns, listening to the slightest whisper of the leaves and smelling the forest scents that wafted on the very edges of his consciousness.

Suddenly he sensed emptiness ahead. No scent. No sound.

His fur prickled with unease, and he slowed his pace. Through the gaps in the trees he could see a wall of mist blocking his way. He padded forward, and as the mist began to swirl about his paws, he noticed that the undergrowth was becoming thinner. The trees around him grew stiff and lifeless, their branches too high for a cat to reach.

"Jaypaw?"

His pelt stood on end, and he scanned the murky forest up ahead. Gradually he made out a figure that seemed familiar. The broad shoulders and wide muzzle reminded him of his father, Brambleclaw.

"Jaypaw!" the voice called again.

A second figure loomed from the shadows and stood beside the first. Outlined against the fog, they shared the same strong shoulders and broad muzzle.

"Yes?" Jaypaw mewed, his voice sounding tiny among the trees.

The two cats approached him and stopped, their tabby pelts as dark as the shadows beyond the trees.

"Welcome. Don't be afraid. We are kin," the larger cat meowed. "I am Tigerstar, your father's father, and this is his brother, Hawkfrost."

Jaypaw stared at the cats in astonishment. He had heard nursery stories about Tigerstar and the terrible things he had done. What were they doing here, and why had they come to him?

"It is good to meet you at last," Tigerstar meowed, his eyes glittering.

"Brambleclaw is blessed to have three fine kits," Hawkfrost added.

"We watched you in battle earlier," Tigerstar purred. "I am

glad to see you have inherited your father's skill."

Hawkfrost glanced at his father. "And yours, Tigerstar," he meowed.

Jaypaw narrowed his eyes. Why were they complimenting him when they must know he couldn't fight as well as he wanted to?

As though reading his thoughts, Tigerstar went on, "We can teach you how to improve your skills if you like," he offered, his voice smooth as honey.

Jaypaw searched the massive tom's gaze, hunting out the sentiment that lay behind his words. To his surprise he found murky darkness where he would normally have sensed feeling and thoughts. He shifted his paws uneasily. "I-I'm not sure I want to become a warrior," he confessed.

"How can any kin of mine say such a thing?" Tigerstar snorted. "It is bad enough that I have to watch Mothwing wasting her talents as a medicine cat." His whiskers twitched. "At least Hollypaw is finally starting to realize that her destiny does not lie in pandering to the weak and the sick."

"Hollypaw?" Jaypaw echoed. What did Tigerstar know about his sister's destiny?

"Why don't you let us teach you some fighting moves?" Hawkfrost urged. "Once you see how easy they are for you, you'll realize that you were born to lead your Clanmates in battle, not spend all your time in the camp with herbs and poultices."

Jaypaw flicked his tail. Brightheart hadn't taught him anything about fighting. She obviously thought it was a waste of time training a blind cat. He might have done better in the battle against ShadowClan if she'd shown him some moves. Perhaps these two cats really could help him.

A swish in the ferns far behind him made Jaypaw glance over his shoulder.

"Who's there?" Tigerstar called.

"I have come to fetch Jaypaw back where he belongs."

Jaypaw recognized the mew at once and, as the cat emerged through the mist, he recognized the pretty tortoise-shell pelt as well. "Spottedleaf!" he mewed.

Spottedleaf nodded but did not take her eyes off Tigerstar and Hawkfrost.

"Do you know this cat?" Tigerstar asked Jaypaw.

"She helped me when I fell over the cliff," Jaypaw explained.

"You shouldn't have wandered this far, Jaypaw," Spottedleaf warned him.

"Nor should you." Tigerstar glared at the medicine cat. "How did you cross the border?"

"I come with the permission of StarClan," Spottedleaf replied, meeting his gaze with a challenging stare.

"Did they give Jaypaw permission too?" Tigerstar inquired, tipping his head to one side.

Spottedleaf did not answer. Instead she looked at Jaypaw. "Come back with me," she ordered.

"What about Tigerstar and Hawkfrost? Can they come too?"

"They have chosen their own path," Spottedleaf replied.

She turned back and waited for Jaypaw to follow.

But Jaypaw hesitated. Tigerstar and Hawkfrost had offered to give him what he wanted most.

"Jaypaw!" Spottedleaf called more urgently.

He had to choose between the cat he knew—the cat he instinctively trusted—and those he didn't. He turned and followed Spottedleaf.

As she led him back through the mist, he glanced over his shoulder. Tigerstar's eyes blazed like fire even after his pelt had been swallowed by the gloom.

Spottedleaf broke into a run, and Jaypaw raced after her. His paws carried him lightly through the shadowy forest until the trees became leafier, their branches dipping once more to brush the undergrowth. Fern tips caressed his spine, and a feeling of freedom and safety enfolded him once more.

Spottedleaf drew to a halt. "You must not go there again," she told him.

"Why not?" Jaypaw asked.

"Tell me why you came to share with StarClan," Spottedleaf prompted.

Resentment jabbed Jaypaw's belly. If she wasn't going to answer his questions, he wasn't going to answer hers. "I came because I could," he answered huffily.

Spottedleaf narrowed her eyes. "You came to find out where your true destiny lies, didn't you?"

Jaypaw blinked. "How did you know?"

"How did you find your way to the Moonpool when you are blind?" she countered.

"Are you going to answer all my questions with more questions?"

Spottedleaf sighed. "Sorry," she mewed. "But I cannot tell you more than you are ready to know."

"I'm ready to know everything!" Jaypaw insisted. "Why does StarClan make it so hard to get answers?"

"Because they fear for you," Spottedleaf answered, her eyes darkening.

Jaypaw snorted. Even StarClan were treating him like a helpless kit! "Tigerstar and Hawkfrost don't seem worried about me," he snapped. "They think I'm destined to be a warrior!"

"Do you trust them?"

Jaypaw remembered the impenetrable mist that had hidden the true feelings of the two warriors. "I guess not," he mewed hesitantly.

"Do you trust me?"

"Yes," he murmured. He could sense something else inside her, affection tinged with sorrow. Concentrating hard, he tracked the feeling, following it like a shimmering stream: a flame-colored cat, green eyes clouded with grief . . . it was Firestar! This StarClan cat was in love with the ThunderClan leader! But how could that be? Spottedleaf had left the forest long ago, and Firestar had another mate. Jaypaw searched further. There was more, he knew, some knowledge obscured by shadows, something he could not name. . . .

"You have a remarkable gift," she mewed. Her eyes were wary, as though she'd felt him probing her mind. "You can see what no other cat sees. You can go where even StarClan cannot. You must use this power for the good of your Clan."

"But how?" Jaypaw asked.

"You must become a medicine cat," Spottedleaf meowed.

No!

He didn't want to hear that. He wanted to believe Tigerstar and Hawkfrost.

"I want to be a warrior!"

"But you have a gift!"

"Seeing in dreams? That's not a gift. The rest of the Clan see all the time!"

"But they don't see what you do. They can't go where you go."

"So I can visit StarClan! Big deal!"

"It *is* a big deal!" Spottedleaf hissed.

"But where does it get me?" Jaypaw argued. "The rest of my Clan think I'm useless."

"They don't know the power that you have."

"Power?" Jaypaw echoed.

Spottedleaf was trembling now. "Jaypaw, you have power enough to shape the destiny of your entire Clan."

Jaypaw stared at her. "But I want to be a warrior!"

"Accept your destiny!"

"It's not fair!"

"I know." The medicine cat's voice suddenly grew soft. She brushed his muzzle with her tail, silencing him. Jaypaw felt weariness spread through his limbs, dragging him toward sleep. "Your gift is not a burden," she whispered. "But you must be brave, because it has more power than the sharpest claw. . . ."

Jaypaw tried to fight the sleepiness. There were still questions he wanted answered. "No," he complained weakly as his legs buckled beneath him.

Jaypaw opened his eyes. The world was black once more, and his body ached with cold. He was lying beside the Moonpool. Slowly he got to his paws and stretched. The image of StarClan's hunting grounds was still fresh in his mind as he followed the path out of the hollow.

More power than the sharpest claw . . .

When he reached the top, Jaypaw glanced over his shoulder.

The hollow was filled with starlight—he knew it as surely as if he could see it. The Moonpool was radiant beneath the brilliant light, and every rock and stone shone like crystal. The whispering that had followed him down to the Moonpool rose again until the voices swirled around him like a relentless wind.

Accept your destiny, Jaypaw.

And in that instant, he realized that however many moons he searched, and however far he ran, he would never escape what he had known all along.

CHAPTER 17

Hollypaw woke up long before dawn. The walls of the medicine den glistened with frost. She had tossed and turned for most of the night, and she knew she wouldn't be able to go back to sleep. All she could think of was how exciting the battle with ShadowClan had been, and how impossible her apprentice duties had seemed afterward, when she'd been faced with so many injured warriors. Why did healing seem to involve inflicting *more* suffering first?

She stretched and crept out of her nest. Her body ached, but the bruises and scratches had been worth it to see the ShadowClan warriors fleeing across the border like terrified rats. She glanced at Leafpool, who was still asleep. The medicine cat's breath billowed in the freezing air. Careful not to disturb her, Hollypaw slipped out of the den. The brambles at the entrance were stiff with ice, and crackled as she nosed her way out.

The clearing was empty. Even the forest was silent, as though the cold had frozen every leaf, and the dawn sky glowed pink behind the frost-whitened branches at the top of the hollow. She looked hopefully toward the fresh-kill pile.

It was empty. The sudden cold had already driven most of the prey deep into their burrows, and the cats would have to wait until hunger drew them out into the open once more. Perhaps she could find something outside the camp. Ferncloud and her kits would need food once the sun rose. She padded across the clearing and out through the thorn barrier.

Brook paced outside the entrance, her thick fur sparkling with frost. She jerked her head around when she heard Hollypaw's pawsteps.

"You're awake early."

"I couldn't sleep." Hollypaw yawned. "Has the dawn patrol left yet?"

"Not yet."

"I thought I could find some prey for Ferncloud," Hollypaw explained.

Brook gazed at her curiously. "That's kind, but won't Leafpool need you this morning?"

Hollypaw sighed.

"Such a troubled sigh for one so young," Brook meowed, her gray eyes softening with concern.

"Leafpool would probably get on better without me," Hollypaw muttered.

"Surely not," Brook meowed. "She couldn't have managed to treat everyone without your help yesterday."

"She almost had to," Hollypaw confessed. "I was so excited after the battle, I completely forgot that I was a medicine cat apprentice. And then when I tried to help, it was awful. I had to make my Clanmates swallow foul-tasting leaves. And the balms seemed only to make the wounds sting more. It didn't feel like I was helping at all." She sat down miserably. "I thought that I could serve my Clanmates best as a medicine cat. That's why I asked to be Leafpool's apprentice. She's so important to the Clan."

"You want to be important?" Brook queried.

Hollypaw thought for a moment. It was more complicated than that. "Everyone respects Leafpool and listens to what she says."

"But is being listened to and respected the same as serving your Clan?"

Hollypaw glanced up at the mountain cat. Brook's eyes were round with sympathy. "I guess not," she mewed. "I just thought it would be the best way to help the Clan."

"And now you think differently?"

"I don't think I can help the Clan at all as a medicine cat," Hollypaw mewed quietly. "I can't remember the names of the herbs. I feel more excited about fighting ShadowClan than fighting sickness. And I'd rather hunt for mice than borage or tansy." Frustration welled inside her. "It's all gone wrong! No cat will ever respect me now."

Brook ran her the tip of her tail down Hollypaw's back. "Cats win respect from their Clanmates by being loyal and brave, not holding important positions," she meowed. "Did you think Graystripe less important than Brambleclaw when you fought beside him yesterday? Or Lionpaw less important than Leafpool when he helped you drive off that ShadowClan tom?"

Hollypaw shook her head.

"It is hard for someone so young to make such big choices," the mountain cat went on. "When I was with the Tribe of Rushing Water, there were no such choices. All duties were divided into hunting or guarding. Prey-hunters like me were thin and lithe; guards were stocky and strong. The decision was made from birth which duty a cat would perform best."

Hollypaw was shocked. "You couldn't choose at all?"

"It wasn't impossible for a cave-guard to be a prey-hunter or a prey-hunter to be a cave-guard, but generally it was a good way to make sure each cat made the best use of the strengths they were born with."

"I wasn't born with a head for herbs." Hollypaw sighed.

"Think of your strengths, not your weaknesses," Brook urged her. "As a Clan cat, you have the freedom to shape your own destiny, which Tribe cats never have. Use that freedom wisely."

Hollypaw remembered her battle training with Cinder-paw. Every move had come so naturally. Even Cloudtail had been impressed. And in the battle she had known instinctively what she was doing when she had knocked that ShadowClan warrior's paws from under him. "I can fight," she mewed, flexing her claws.

"You have warrior strengths," Brook agreed. "What better way to serve your Clan than by being the best warrior you can?"

Hollypaw's heart felt lighter than it had for days.

"Don't forget, though, you will have to tell Leafpool."

Hollypaw sagged a little. "Of course." She looked down at her paws. "She'll think I'm letting her down."

"Leafpool is wise enough to see where your gifts lie," Brook meowed. "She will only think you courageous for speaking up now, rather than struggling on out of pride or stubbornness."

"Do you think so?"

"You will be doing what is best for your Clan. Leafpool will know that."

The sound of pawsteps inside the thorn barrier warned that the dawn patrol was preparing to leave. Hollypaw blinked gratefully at Brook. "Thank you," she whispered.

Brook dipped her head and turned back to watch the forest. Hollypaw ducked through the thorn barrier just in time to avoid being swept aside by Graystripe, Sandstorm, and Honeypaw as they raced out. She knew what she had to do. She would become a regular apprentice like Lionpaw and Jaypaw, and work hard to serve her Clan as a warrior.

But first she had to tell Leafpool.

Stiffening her shoulders, Hollypaw nosed her way into the medicine den.

Leafpool was smearing honey onto a leaf. "Let's hope this freezing weather breaks soon," she muttered. "Longtail and Icekit both have sore throats."

Hollypaw suddenly felt as if there were a thorn stuck in her chest. She was turning away from something she had set her heart on because she was not good enough. Sadness welled inside her. Should she be giving up so easily?

"What's wrong, Hollypaw?" Leafpool looked up. "You look as though you've just lost our entire supply of poppy seeds!" Then her face grew serious. "You haven't, have you?"

Hollypaw shook her head. "No. But I have something very important to tell you." She forced herself to look her mentor in the eyes. "I can't be a medicine cat apprentice anymore," she mewed.

Leafpool blinked. "Why not?"

"I have to choose my destiny based on my strengths," Hollypaw meowed. "I'm just no good at being a medicine cat. You must know that."

"You are clever and hardworking. You can learn."

"But it doesn't feel right," Hollypaw tried to explain. She tipped her head to one side. "Can you understand?"

"You feel like a fish swimming upstream?" Leafpool suggested.

"Exactly." Hollypaw nodded, her heart aching. "If I change direction and swim with the current, I will swim so much faster."

"So you want to train as a warrior instead."

"I think it will be better for the Clan if I do."

Leafpool's eyes clouded with sorrow. "I feel as though I've let you down."

"No!" Hollypaw felt a stab of guilt. "You've been patient and kind. It's just not right for me."

"You would have been a good medicine cat." Leafpool flicked her tail. "But I see that you want to be the *best* at whatever you do."

"I have to be, for the sake of my Clan."

Leafpool stepped forward and brushed Hollypaw's cheek with her muzzle. "You will make a wonderful warrior, Hollypaw," she purred. "You have a warrior's spirit—I have seen you being noble and loyal and brave, and now I see you sacrificing your ambition for the good of the Clan." Her eyes shone. "I couldn't be more proud of you."

Leafpool's words soothed the grief that pricked like a hedgehog at Hollypaw's heart. "I must go and tell Firestar so he can find me a new mentor."

"There's no rush," Leafpool cautioned. "You might want to think about it some more."

"I've thought about it lots," Hollypaw insisted. "I want to sort it out as soon as I can."

"I'll come with you," Leafpool offered.

"Thank you." The thought of facing Firestar made her paws itch. What if he thought she was being fickle?

Together they padded across the frosty clearing. Leafpool let Hollypaw climb the rockfall first and followed her up. Hollypaw announced her arrival at the den entrance with a nervous mew.

"Come in."

Hollypaw stepped into the cave. The dawn light seeped in behind her, lighting the gloom. Sandstorm was grooming Firestar's ears. She looked up as Hollypaw and Leafpool entered.

Firestar drew himself into a sitting position. "How is Longtail's throat?" he asked.

"It's not whitecough," Leafpool reported. "Mousefur insists it's just sore from his snoring."

Firestar turned to Hollypaw. "What is it?" His green eyes were round with concern. "You look worried."

Hollypaw shifted her weight from paw to paw. What if she was breaking the warrior code in some way? Surely Leafpool would have said something? She took a short, sharp breath. She *had* to follow her instinct. The Clan needed a medicine cat they could rely on, and she knew that wasn't her.

"I want to become a warrior apprentice," she blurted. "I don't think I'm cut out to be a medicine cat."

"And you think you'd make a better warrior," Firestar guessed, narrowing his eyes.

"I know I would!"

Firestar looked at Leafpool. "Do you think she's right?"

"I believe that this is what she really wants." Leafpool stroked Hollypaw's flank with her tail. "She's worked hard at her duties, and I've loved training her, but she feels her strengths lie elsewhere. And if this is what she believes, then she will make a better warrior."

"I'll remember everything Leafpool has taught me," Hollypaw promised. "It might be useful one day."

Firestar nodded. "Very well. Since Leafpool agrees, you can train as a warrior. I'll find you a mentor as soon as I can."

Hollypaw looked up at Firestar, wondering if he would say more, but he was gazing wordlessly at her. He must be trying to think of a suitable mentor. She turned and began to head past Leafpool out of the entrance.

"It must have taken a lot of courage to do this," Firestar called after her. "I'm very proud of you."

She glanced back at the ThunderClan leader. "Thank you," she mewed.

She leaped down into the clearing, her paws light with relief. Suddenly she remembered that she had intended to go hunting this morning. Perhaps Lionpaw would come with her. She glanced toward the apprentice den, wondering if he was awake yet, and then she saw Jaypaw slipping in through the thorn barrier. Brook followed him in, looking relieved. From the way he stumbled wearily into the clearing, Hollypaw guessed her brother had been out all night. She hurried over to him as Brook padded toward the warrior den to get some well-earned sleep.

"You look exhausted!" she mewed. "Where have you been?"

Jaypaw's eyes were bleary and his fur unkempt. "I'll explain later," he mewed. "I have to see Firestar."

"You should get some sleep first," Hollypaw advised. "Besides, Firestar is busy talking to Leafpool."

"I have to see her too."

What was he talking about? Had something happened? Alarm shot through Hollypaw's tail, making it twitch.

Jaypaw tripped as he tried to climb the tumble of rocks up to Firestar's cave.

"Let me help," Hollypaw offered. "You're too tired to manage alone."

For once Jaypaw didn't object. Hollypaw's anxiety grew

stronger, but she bit her tongue. He was obviously determined to speak to Firestar, and she wasn't going to waste time arguing. Instead she laid her tail over his shoulders and guided him up the rockfall.

At the ledge outside Firestar's den, Hollypaw announced her arrival once more.

"Back already?" Firestar called her inside.

He looked surprised to see Jaypaw with her, but before he could speak Jaypaw stumbled into the center of the den. He fixed his sightless gaze on Firestar, his stare so intense it seemed as though he could see the ThunderClan leader as clearly as the rest of them could.

"I need to train to be a medicine cat," he mewed.

CHAPTER 18

Hollypaw stared at her brother in astonishment. Jaypaw had always been so sure that he wanted to be a warrior, ever since he had been old enough to pounce on a scrap of moss.

Firestar looked at Hollypaw. "Did you know anything about this?"

"No!" Hollypaw gasped. Firestar sounded as if he suspected they had planned it together.

Jaypaw looked over his shoulder at her, his blue eyes round with anxiety. "Hollypaw, I'm sorry."

"It's all right." Leafpool padded over to Jaypaw and brushed his ear with her muzzle. "Hollypaw has already told Firestar that she wants to train as a warrior apprentice instead."

Jaypaw blinked. "Really?"

Hollypaw nodded. A tingle of hope pricked her paws. Perhaps this was the perfect solution! After all, Jaypaw had always known the herbs better than she did. But would Firestar agree?

Firestar looked at Leafpool. "Are you ready to take on

another apprentice so soon?"

Leafpool sat down and wrapped her tail over her paws. "I would be honored to be Jaypaw's mentor." She dipped her head. "I think the Clan would be lucky to have him as its medicine cat."

Hollypaw stared at Leafpool. *Why does she look like she's hiding something?*

"What about his blindness?" Firestar queried.

Hollypaw bristled. Surely Jaypaw wouldn't let Firestar get away with that? "He knows the herbs far better than me," she mewed quickly.

"His sense of smell is incredible," Leafpool agreed. "He can already tell an infected wound from a clean one a tail-length away."

Hollypaw waited for Jaypaw to point out that blindness had nothing to do with it, but he only murmured, "I will try as hard as I can. Leafpool will soon see whether I can manage or not."

"Very well." Firestar nodded, looking a little dazed. "Leafpool will be your new mentor."

Jaypaw dipped his head.

"But first," Firestar went on, "we must tell Brightheart."

Jaypaw's ears twitched. "She'll be hurt." Hollypaw could hear anxiety in his mew. Her brother had never gotten on particularly well with his mentor, but he was clearly worried about her feelings.

"Maybe Brightheart could be my mentor," she suggested.

Firestar shook his head. "Her skills were perfect for training Jaypaw, but not for you." He shifted his paws. "She will be a mentor again very soon; don't worry."

"What if she doesn't understand my decision?" Jaypaw mewed.

"It's up to you to *make* her understand," Firestar answered. "I may be able to tell the Clan what to do, but I can't tell them how to feel."

"I'll make sure that she knows my decision has nothing to do with her," Jaypaw promised. "This is something I *have* to do."

His mew was oddly flat. Hollypaw felt a ripple of unease stir her pelt. It was almost as if being Leafpool's apprentice wasn't Jaypaw's choice at all, but something that had been forced upon him.

Leafpool glanced at Firestar and Sandstorm, the sort of meaningful glance that told Hollypaw that they wanted to exchange words in private.

Taking the hint, she bowed her head. "Shall I fetch Brightheart?"

Firestar nodded. "Yes, please."

"She's in the warriors' den," Jaypaw told them.

Hollypaw's whiskers twitched. It was weird that Jaypaw was always totally aware of what was going on in the camp. She bounded down into the clearing and padded over to the warriors' den. Sticking her head through the entrance, she called Brightheart's name.

Brightheart was sitting up in her nest, washing, her warm

breath billowing in the gloom.

"Firestar would like to see you in his den," Hollypaw told her.

Brightheart stopped, her tongue still half out, and stared at Hollypaw. She looked as if she was about to ask why.

Hollypaw ducked out of the den. She did not want to give Brightheart time to speak. She knew she would not be able to hide the truth, but she also knew that it was Jaypaw's duty to break his news to his mentor. She slipped into the apprentice's den before Brightheart emerged. It seemed a good time to visit her new home. The scent of the yew was strange, and the nests were all empty. Jaypaw's nest would be hers now, she guessed. She sniffed it out and gazed around the shelter, happy at the thought of sleeping among her Clanmates. After the nursery, her nest in the medicine den had seemed cold and lonely. She wished some of the apprentices were here to welcome her. *Everyone must be out training.* The thought brought a prickle of excitement. Before long, she would be out with them.

When Hollypaw slipped out of the den, she saw Brightheart scrambling up the rockfall to Firestar's cave. Thornclaw lay by the halfrock, sharing tongues with Whitewing. Spiderleg was dozing in the early morning sunshine below Highledge.

Foxkit and Icekit burst from the nursery entrance in a flurry of fur and whiskers.

"Don't stray into the clearing," Ferncloud's voice called from inside the den. "I don't want you getting under anyone's paws!"

"We won't," Icekit replied.

Icekit flicked her brother's russet-colored muzzle with her tail. Foxkit retaliated with a lunge that sent her tumbling toward Hollypaw.

Hollypaw steadied the snow-white kit with her paw.

"Hi, Hollypaw!" Icekit glanced up at her, then spun and leaped at her brother. She tumbled him over, grasped him with a paw behind each cheek, and began to pummel him enthusiastically with her hind paws.

"Tuck your head in, Foxkit, and give her a good nip!" Hollypaw called.

Icekit squeaked and let go of her brother. "That's not fair," she wailed. "You're helping him."

"It doesn't look like you need any help!" Hollypaw mewed.

Foxkit hurled himself at his sister.

"Duck!" Hollypaw warned the snowy kit.

Icekit rolled out of the way just in time, and Foxkit skidded past her into the frosty grass outside the apprentice's den. He turned and, crouching low, prowled back toward Icekit.

"Not so fast," Hollypaw advised. Icekit was waiting with her chest pressed to the ground and her tail lashing excitedly. "Let her come to you."

Foxkit stared at his sister, his eyes defiant. "She won't dare come near me!"

Icekit wriggled closer, unable to resist her brother's challenge. Foxkit waited until she was so close that her breath billowed in his face.

"Get behind her now!" Hollypaw urged.

Foxkit darted out of the grass and shot behind Icekit. By the time she had spun around he had jumped onto her back and was rolling her onto her side.

"You two are going to make great warriors!" Hollypaw purred.

A flash of ginger-and-white fur caught her eye. Brightheart was leaping down the tumble of rocks. Hollypaw felt a pang of sympathy. Jaypaw had been Brightheart's first apprentice. She must have been eager to prove that she could make as good a mentor as any other warrior. Hollypaw hoped Jaypaw had persuaded her that his decision had nothing at all to do with the way she had been training him.

"Show us a fighting move!" Foxkit was reaching up to Hollypaw's shoulder with his forepaws, tugging at her pelt.

Hollypaw ducked down and, twisting like a snake, rolled over onto her back.

"Wow!" Icekit breathed. "You're really quick." The white kit's gaze flicked across the clearing, and she suddenly looked nervous. "Firestar's coming," she whispered.

"I've decided on your new mentor," Firestar announced, stopping in front of Hollypaw.

"You've got a new mentor?" Foxkit mewed in surprise.

Firestar gazed down at the little kit. "She's going to train as a warrior," he explained.

"I thought she was training to be a medicine cat," squeaked Icekit.

Hollypaw felt a prickle of unease. She still couldn't help worrying that she had broken the warrior code.

"Hollypaw knows best what lies in her heart," Firestar meowed.

I do, Hollypaw thought.

Cloudtail came hurrying through the camp entrance. "I've told him," he called to Firestar. "He's on his way."

"We'll have an apprentice ceremony later," Firestar told Hollypaw. "But I've called your new mentor back from the hunting patrol. If he agrees to take you on, you might as well start right away. You've got plenty of training to catch up on."

Hollypaw nodded, unable to speak because her throat seemed to have closed up with excitement.

The thorn barrier quivered.

"Firestar?" Brackenfur hurried toward the ThunderClan leader, panting. He must have run all the way back. "What is it?"

Hollypaw flicked her tail happily. Not only was Brackenfur a great fighter, but he was also clever and thoughtful; she trusted his judgment as much as his strength.

"Would you be willing to take on Hollypaw as an apprentice?" Firestar asked.

Brackenfur's gaze shot toward Hollypaw. "What happened?"

Hollypaw tensed. Was he going to say no? After all, she had already let one mentor down. "I-I don't think I'm cut out to be a medicine cat."

Brackenfur gazed at her a moment longer; then he turned back to Firestar. "I'd be pleased to train her."

Hollypaw felt a wave of relief.

"Good," Firestar meowed. "I'll leave her in your paws, then." He turned and padded away.

Brackenfur looked Hollypaw up and down. "You've got some catching up to do," he warned.

"I know, and I'm going to train extra hard."

"Good." Brackenfur flicked his tail. "We'll do battle training every day to begin with."

"Great!"

Brackenfur stared at her with his head to one side. "I'm not going to ask what made you change your mind. If you're going to be a warrior, I want you to concentrate on the present, not the past. You've made your decision, and I expect you to stick to it."

"I will!" Hollypaw vowed.

Brackenfur kneaded the ground with his front paws, his shoulders flexing. "Are you ready to start training right away?"

Hollypaw nodded.

"Good. You can join our hunting patrol." He headed back toward the thorn barrier and raced out of the entrance. Taken by surprise, Hollypaw pelted after him, her tail fluffed out. Her first real hunt!

Brackenfur didn't slow down to accommodate her shorter legs, and Hollypaw had to run twice as fast to keep up with him. He raced up the slope and headed through the forest. All the time Hollypaw had spent sorting herbs had exercised her mind more than her body. She realized with a jolt how much fitter the other warrior apprentices must be.

Brackenfur glanced over his shoulder as she struggled after him. "We're nearly there," he encouraged.

Hollypaw dug her claws into the frozen earth and tried even harder to catch up. A fallen tree blocked the path, but Brackenfur cleared it with ease. Hollypaw skidded to a halt in front of it and wriggled through the narrow gap underneath.

Brackenfur was waiting for her on the other side. Graystripe and Millie were pacing the small clearing in the undergrowth. Ashfur and Spiderleg talked quietly nearby, while their apprentices, Lionpaw and Mousepaw, competed to see who could skid farthest through the fallen leaves.

Lionpaw stared at Hollypaw in surprise. "What are you doing here?"

"Meet my new apprentice," Brackenfur meowed.

Lionpaw's tail flicked. "That's great!"

Graystripe padded forward and touched his muzzle to hers. "Congratulations."

"Did you catch anything while I was gone?" Brackenfur asked.

"The prey's hiding from the cold," Ashfur complained.

"There must be some way to tempt it out," Brackenfur meowed. "It'll be as hungry as we are."

"We could dig it out," Lionpaw suggested. "The shallow

burrows would be easy to scent."

"The ground's probably too frozen," Ashfur pointed out.

"What about that huge beech tree near the old Thunderpath?" Spiderleg suggested. "There are always beechnuts on the ground, even this late in leaf-bare."

"The prey's more likely to venture out there than any-where else," Brackenfur agreed.

He raced away again. The patrol took off after him. Taking a deep breath, Hollypaw followed. Did Brackenfur always give such little warning before he shot off? And how did the others know to follow him? Her muscles were screaming for her to stop, but there was no way she was going to show she was struggling to keep up.

Her paws lightened with relief when she recognized the leaves of the beech up ahead. They rustled in the wind, as golden as Brackenfur's pelt. The patrol skidded to a halt before they reached it and padded forward silently, weaving through the bracken toward the clear ground around the trunk. Hollypaw watched and copied them.

No one spoke as Brackenfur drew himself forward and peered from the edge of the bracken. While the others lined up alongside, Hollypaw slid into the space beside her mentor.

"Keep your tail still," he whispered.

Hollypaw realized that the tip of her tail was twitching with excitement. "Sorry," she breathed. When she held it still, the dry bracken fronds above her head stopped rattling.

The rest of the patrol lined up along the edge of the

bracken, their eyes all fixed on the leaf-strewn earth around the tree.

"I see something!" Lionpaw hissed.

Hollypaw searched the forest floor, but could see nothing. She looked at Lionpaw and followed his gaze. He was staring at a single leaf trembling beside an exposed root. Was that really prey? She sniffed the air. At first all she smelled was the pungent mustiness of dead leaves. And then she smelled mouse.

She thrashed her tail, setting the bracken rattling again. The leaf up ahead flipped over, and Lionpaw shot out of the bracken and hurled himself toward it.

"Too late!" he cursed as he slammed his paws down on empty ground. He glared at Hollypaw. "You scared it off!"

Hollypaw's ears grew hot. "I'm sorry," she apologized.

"Don't be hard on her," Ashfur chided Lionpaw. "It's her first hunt."

Lionpaw shrugged. "It's okay, Hollypaw. I was just annoyed because I wasn't fast enough."

"You looked fast enough to me!" Hollypaw told him.

"You're only fast enough if you catch the mouse," Mousepaw mewed pointedly.

"Keep quiet, or nothing is going to stir from its burrow for the rest of the day," Brackenfur ordered.

Lionpaw hurried back to the bracken, and the patrol took up their positions once more.

* * *

Hollypaw's back was beginning to ache from crouching in the same position so long. Lionpaw had caught his mouse at last, Ashfur had caught a vole, and Mousepaw had spotted a sparrow flitting from tree to tree and disappeared into the undergrowth to track it.

"Your turn," Brackenfur meowed in Hollypaw's ear.

Her shoulders stiffened. "Are you sure?" She thought she was more likely to scare the prey away than catch anything.

"You learn more by trying than by watching," Brackenfur replied.

Hollypaw focused on the beech tree up ahead. The clearing still smelled of blood. Surely no more prey would be foolish enough to stray out after Lionpaw and Ashfur's kill?

"Shouldn't we try somewhere else?" she suggested.

"There are beechnuts here," Brackenfur reminded her. "If a creature's hungry enough, it'll risk anything for food."

Hollypaw stared among the roots of the tree. Almost at once she noticed a leaf flickering on the ground. She dashed out of the bracken and threw herself on top of it. Her heart sank when she realized that the ground felt flat and lifeless beneath her paws. She had caught nothing more than a dead leaf, flapping in the breeze.

She glanced back at her Clanmates, her pelt prickling with embarrassment. Graystripe's whiskers were twitching.

Millie glanced sharply at her mate and his whiskers stopped moving. "It's the same for every cat to start with," the kittypet reassured Hollypaw. "Have another try."

Hollypaw closed her eyes and took a deep breath. Then she blinked them open and glanced around the clearing. *I'm not fast enough yet to hunt from the bracken,* she decided. She studied the tree. Its pale bark darkened at the roots, which snaked out from the base before disappearing into the earth. Her black pelt would blend in well. Climbing stealthily onto the largest root, she crouched and began to wait. She looked over at Brackenfur, wondering if she had done the right thing. He nodded.

Relieved, Hollypaw turned her attention back to the forest floor. She kept perfectly still, not letting even an itch make her ear twitch. Far away, a sparrow screeched an alarm before falling silent. Still she did not move.

Then, almost directly below the root where she crouched, a tiny movement in the leaves made her tense the muscles in her hind legs. She waited. Sure enough, the leaf stirred again, and a small pink nose came snuffling to the surface. A wood mouse! Hollypaw held her breath, waiting like an adder preparing to strike. The mouse nosed its way farther out into the open, heading for a beechnut. Hollypaw knew it had no idea she was there.

She pounced, catching the mouse squarely between her forepaws.

"Well done!" Brackenfur called.

Hollypaw looked up, the warm mouse dangling in her jaws. Her first kill! She closed her eyes, remembering how Lionpaw and Ashfur had given thanks to StarClan when they had made their kills.

"Thank you for the life of this prey, given to feed my Clan. I shall take no more than I want . . ." She paused. "I mean, *need*, and I shall give all that I can."

She was on her way to being a warrior at last!

CHAPTER 19

"Mousefur kept me awake half the night coughing," Longtail complained.

"It's a wonder you could hear me over your snoring!" Mousefur retorted.

Jaypaw sighed. He was in the elders' den, listening to the denmates bicker like kits. He didn't know why they argued so much. Even now, Longtail's complaint was only his way of telling Jaypaw that he was worried about Mousefur.

"I can't feel any swelling around her throat," Jaypaw told him. "Just make sure she eats the coltsfoot I brought. Leafpool says it will ease her breathing."

"I don't need herbs," Mousefur grumbled.

"Take them anyway," Longtail urged. "At least it means you'll eat *something*. You've not had anything since sunhigh yesterday."

"I don't like to take prey from the fresh-kill pile when food is so scarce," Mousefur meowed. "There are younger bellies to feed than mine."

"Well, eat the coltsfoot instead," Longtail meowed. "If only to give me some peace."

Muttering crossly, Mousefur used her tail to sweep the pile of shredded leaves toward her nest.

Jaypaw sighed. Listening to the elders fussing, he felt as though nothing had changed since his days with Brightheart. After hardly a quarter moon he was bored to the ends of his whiskers with doling out herbs. He was meant to visit Stormfur in the warriors' den next and apply a honey-and-horsetail poultice to his shoulder wound *yet again*. The warrior refused to rest, and the balm seemed to rub off as quickly as Jaypaw could apply it.

Leafpool appeared at the entrance of the honeysuckle bush, bringing with her the scents of the medicine den. "How's Mousefur's throat?" she asked.

"It feels fine," Jaypaw answered tersely. "Although it would be easier to tell if she stopped complaining long enough for me to feel it properly."

Leafpool's irritation spiked the air. "If you can't be polite to your Clanmates, you may as well come back to the medicine den and help me tear up the tansy that Hollypaw was kind enough to fetch for you yesterday!" she snapped.

Jaypaw rolled his eyes. Another moment in the medicine den and he would burst! So much for his great destiny as a medicine cat. Spottedleaf hadn't warned him that life would be one tedious chore after another.

Leafpool led the way back to the den, her shoulders tense. Jaypaw padded miserably after her. He felt a lecture brewing in her like a storm, and nosed his way reluctantly through the trailing brambles and sat down.

"You drift around the camp like a little dark cloud looking for someone to rain on," Leafpool snapped.

"I'm bored!" Jaypaw complained.

Exasperation flashed from his mentor. "Anyone would think I had forced you to become my apprentice!"

"You didn't force me," Jaypaw agreed. "But it's what you wanted all along, isn't it?" He lashed his tail. "Are you happy now?"

"Do I sound happy?" Leafpool hissed. Jaypaw could feel the fury seething beneath her pelt. Why did she have to be so mad at him? Couldn't she understand that he had expected more from his life than this?

"It's okay for you," he snapped. "You always wanted to be a medicine cat!"

"And you don't?"

"It's my destiny," he muttered. "Wanting doesn't seem to come into it."

"Then deal with it!" Leafpool growled unsympathetically.

Unhappily, Jaypaw padded to the heap of tansy Hollypaw had left and began to strip the leaves from the stems. He ripped at them carelessly, leaving long strings of stalk attached. Leafpool sighed and sat down beside him. Wordlessly, she began to nip off the trailing strips he had left. Her disappointment showed in every small, silent movement she made. Guilt pricked at Jaypaw like a bellyful of thorns. He wished he could find the words to explain his frustration, but he knew that whatever he said would only make it worse. What would she say if she knew just how miserable he was at giving up his dream of being a warrior? And for this! A life of sorting herbs and worrying about scratches and bellyaches.

"Leafpool?" Stormfur pushed his way into the den. Jaypaw could smell the sour odor of the scratches festering on his shoulder. He had forgotten to apply the new poultice. He jerked his head around, feeling guiltier than ever.

"Didn't you treat Stormfur's scratch?" Leafpool demanded.

"You told me to come back here," he pointed out.

"You're right." She sighed. "Never mind. I'll do it. You get some rest. It's half-moon tonight. We'll be traveling to the Moonpool with the other medicine cats."

Brightheart was lying next to Cloudtail by the halfrock, washing herself. Jaypaw felt her hurt like thorns in his pads as he waited for Leafpool by the camp entrance. Firestar had promised Brightheart that she could mentor Icekit or Foxkit when their turn came, but the warrior hadn't gotten over the pain of losing Jaypaw as her apprentice yet.

"Staring at her isn't going to make her forgive you." Leafpool's meow surprised Jaypaw; he had been too busy worrying about Brightheart to hear his mentor approach.

"But she won't listen to me when I try to talk to her," Jaypaw mewed. "She just changes the subject or finds an excuse to go somewhere else."

"She'll listen when she's ready to hear," Leafpool advised. "She's had to fight hard to prove to her Clanmates that she's as good as them, and this must feel like a battle she has lost."

"I never meant to hurt her," Jaypaw mewed.

"It takes some cats longer to see past their weaknesses clearly enough to appreciate their strengths," Leafpool meowed. "And until they do, they feel every hurt like a tongue on raw flesh."

Jaypaw felt that Leafpool was urging him to understand more than Brightheart's anger, but he didn't want to think about it now. He was eager to leave camp. He hadn't been farther than the Sky Oak in days, and his paws were itching to be on their way to the Moonpool.

Leafpool must have sensed his impatience. "Come on," she meowed, leading him through the thorn barrier.

The night felt brittle with cold. Frost had driven most creatures into hiding, and Jaypaw's and Leafpool's pawsteps were the only movement that disturbed the frozen earth. As they neared the WindClan border, Jaypaw felt anxiety flutter in his belly. What if the other medicine cats thought a blind kit wasn't fit to be one of them?

He sniffed the air. It was tinged with the scent of ShadowClan and RiverClan.

"The others must be waiting," Leafpool observed, picking up the same scents.

Jaypaw followed her out of the forest and padded onto open grass. Moorland lay ahead; he could smell the scent of gorse and heather mingling with cat scent. He recognized Willowpaw and Mothwing from their visit to the hollow a moon ago. But the reek of the ShadowClan cat with them brought back the raw memory of battle.

"Hi, Mothwing." Leafpool sounded pleased to see her RiverClan friend.

"Hello, Leafpool," Mothwing purred.

"Is the frost as bad in RiverClan territory as it is here?" Leafpool asked.

"We seem sheltered from the worst of it, but the cold has driven the elders into their den. They're complaining of aching bones."

"You've enough poppy seed?"

"Yes, thank you."

"Hello, Littlecloud," Leafpool greeted the ShadowClan medicine cat. "Is all well with you?"

Jaypaw bristled. It wasn't long since ShadowClan invaded ThunderClan territory. How could she be so polite to her Clan's enemy?

"It is," Littlecloud answered. "Are your Clanmates recovered?" He had to be referring to the injuries they had suffered at the paws of ShadowClan warriors. Suspiciously, Jaypaw searched the ShadowClan cat's tone for any hint of triumph, but he found only concern.

"One wound unhealed," Leafpool reported. "And yours?"

"Oakfur is still limping," he told her.

"Try wrapping his paw with comfrey each night when he sleeps," Leafpool advised.

"I've run out," Littlecloud confessed.

"You should have come to us!" Leafpool meowed.

"Blackstar wouldn't let me."

"I'll leave some at the border tomorrow morning," Leafpool promised.

Jaypaw couldn't believe what he was hearing. Did Firestar know that Leafpool was helping ThunderClan's enemies?

He felt a soft pelt brush his. Willowpaw from RiverClan. "Where's Hollypaw?" she asked quietly.

She sounds disappointed to get me instead. Jaypaw flicked his tail. "Didn't you know?" he hissed back. "Hollypaw found it so boring being a medicine cat that she let her poor, useless brother do it instead."

Willowpaw flinched.

"I see you're getting to know my new apprentice," Leafpool meowed.

Jaypaw felt the gaze of all four cats burn his pelt.

"This is Jaypaw," Leafpool announced.

Jaypaw stared back, ready to challenge any comment about his blindness.

"Hi, Jaypaw," Mothwing meowed.

"How are you enjoying being an apprentice?" Littlecloud asked.

Jaypaw felt anxiety pulse through his mentor. *She's afraid I'm going to say it's boring!* "It's great," he replied.

"Jaypaw's a fast learner." Leafpool sounded relieved. "He knows all the herbs already."

"Really?" Littlecloud was clearly impressed.

A new scent caught Jaypaw by surprise. Another cat was hurrying toward them over the WindClan border.

"Barkface!" Littlecloud called to the WindClan medicine

cat as he approached. "Where's Kestrelpaw?"

"He's come down with whitecough," Barkface panted.

"Not badly, I hope?" meowed Leafpool.

"He's young and strong," Barkface replied. "He'll fight it off. But I'm making sure he doesn't spread it around. With prey scarce and bellies empty, the Clans are vulnerable to sickness."

Mothwing mewed in agreement.

"The moon's rising," Littlecloud observed.

"We'd better hurry if we want to catch it in the Moonpool," Leafpool urged.

Jaypaw followed the cats as they began to climb the slope.

"Willowpaw!" Mothwing called to her apprentice. "Walk with Jaypaw. I'm sure he'll have plenty of questions about the Moonpool."

I've been there before, you know! Jaypaw bit back the words as Willowpaw fell in beside him. She kept a wary distance, making sure that her pelt did not touch his.

"Has Leafpool brought you here yet?" she mewed, sounding as if she didn't really want to talk to him.

Jaypaw was about to tell her that he'd traveled there alone when Willowpaw grabbed his scruff without warning and dragged him sideways. He struggled free from her grip and turned on her, lunging at her with unsheathed claws.

"Jaypaw! What are you doing?" Leafpool screeched.

"He almost fell down a rabbit hole!" Willowpaw wailed. "I was just trying to help him."

Jaypaw let go, shame burning his ears. "I didn't know!" he

snapped. Why had she tried to help him? He wasn't a kit!

"Apologize at once," Leafpool ordered.

"But I knew the hole was there!" Jaypaw retorted. It was true. He had smelled the strong scent of rabbit, and his paws had been well aware of the approaching dip. "I didn't need help!"

"That's no excuse," Leafpool hissed. "Apologize!"

"I'm sorry," Jaypaw muttered.

"That's okay," Willowpaw growled. "Next time I hope you fall in!" She padded ahead of him, flicking her tail past his nose.

"Keep up, Jaypaw!" He felt the flash of Leafpool's angry gaze as she glanced back at him. It wasn't his fault. Willowpaw had started it! He padded after Willowpaw, ignoring the trail of resentment she left in her wake, and concentrated on the older cats' conversation.

"This late frost has damaged a lot of new leaves," Barkface commented.

"I was looking forward to restocking," Littlecloud agreed. "But now it'll be another moon before the plants recover."

"There are a couple of sheltered spots in RiverClan territory where the herbs have escaped damage," Mothwing told them.

Jaypaw strained to hear more. He wanted to know the location of every plant that could be of use to his Clan, no matter where. He was listening so hard that he didn't hear the stream, or notice the ground turn from grass to rock beneath his paws as they approached it. The freezing air had turned the stone to ice, and suddenly his paws slipped from under him.

Willowpaw lunged toward him, then stopped as though claws had grabbed her tail. She watched Jaypaw slither ungracefully onto his side and waited without saying a word as, hot with embarrassment, he struggled to his paws. Then she padded on, not even slowing down as he limped after her. Jaypaw felt a flash of admiration at her stubborn refusal to help.

She offered him no help as he scrambled up the steep ridge either, though he could sense anxiety sparking from her as she watched him haul himself up the perilous rocks. He was relieved that he had made the climb before and knew the route well.

He paused at the top, listening for the voices that had guided him last time. But the only sound was the wind spiraling into the hollow and the trickling of water as it echoed around the rocks. He padded down the paw-dimpled stone to the Moonpool, stopping when he felt cold water lap the tips of his paws.

The breath of the other cats warmed the air as they ringed the pool.

"StarClan!" Leafpool called up to the sky. "I bring you Jaypaw, my apprentice, and pray you accept him as you once accepted me."

Jaypaw heard the soft chafing of fur on stone as the cats settled down at the water's edge, and he lay down beside Leafpool, tucking his paws under his chest. He did not touch his nose to the water immediately. Instead he listened until the other cats' breathing fell into the deep rhythm of sleep. Only then did he close his eyes and lower his head until the icy water stung his nose.

In an instant he was in StarClan's hunting grounds, the undergrowth pricking his pelt. He blinked, adjusting to the shock of sight, letting his eyes get used to the chaotic colors until they fell into shapes he could recognize. Trees soared around him, their green leaves trembling against a bright blue sky.

Does it look like this to Willowpaw? he wondered. He pricked his ears, listening for her. *Do we share the same forest when we dream?* Sniffing, he searched for her scent and it appeared on the breeze, almost as if he had drawn it to him. He padded quietly toward her, keeping low, somehow aware that he was trespassing.

"Mudfur?" her soft voice was calling.

Jaypaw peered over the root of an oak and saw her gazing around a clearing. She was smaller than he had imagined. Her body was sleek and lithe, and her tabby markings were hardly more than delicate stripes along her pelt.

"Yes, little one?" A mottled tom padded out from the ferns and greeted her, touching his muzzle to hers.

Jaypaw ducked down.

"It is good to see you, Mudfur," Willowpaw mewed.

"You dealt well with Dapplepaw's stomachache."

"Was I right to give her reassurance rather than herbs?" Willowpaw sounded anxious.

"Yes. She got better on her own, and the herbs can be saved for a cat with greater need," Mudfur praised her.

Jaypaw peeped over the root again. Willowpaw was flicking her tail happily. "Have you news to share with River-Clan?" she asked.

"Beware the Twolegs upstream. Their kits are trying to block the water that feeds the Clan."

"I'll warn Mothwing," Willowpaw promised.

Jaypaw's whiskers tingled. Why didn't Mudfur tell Mothwing himself? Had the two cats argued? Would he share tongues only with Willowpaw?

He backed away from the oak tree. If Willowpaw was dreaming of Mudfur, what was Mothwing dreaming of? He opened his mouth to taste the air, searching out Mothwing's scent.

He smelled nothing. Willowpaw's scent had disappeared, as though her dream had slipped from his paws. He tried to draw Mothwing's scent to him, as he had done with Willowpaw, but nothing came. He closed his eyes and allowed the forest to slide from his consciousness, letting himself fall back to the hollow. When he opened his eyes, the Moonpool was shining far below him. He could see the other cats still sleeping around the pool—including him. Mothwing was breathing more heavily than the others, her body twitching while the others lay motionless.

Closing his eyes, Jaypaw focused on her mind, willing himself into her thoughts. He smelled prey, and then water, and opened his eyes to find himself among reeds at the edge of a lake. Mothwing was a few tails ahead of him, stalking a frog. She pounced on it as it hopped, then let it go and watched it hop again, her whiskers twitching with amusement as it struggled clumsily among the reeds. A butterfly fluttered above her head, and she sprang up and grabbed it from the air, holding it close so that its wings tickled her nose.

With a jolt, Jaypaw realized this was not StarClan's hunting grounds. This was the shore of the lake that stretched between ThunderClan and RiverClan. The RiverClan medicine cat was dreaming the ordinary dreams of any Clan cat.

CHAPTER 20

❧

Were any more of the medicine cats dreaming ordinary dreams? Jaypaw let his vision flit back to StarClan's hunting grounds. He wanted to see the other cats, find out which ones truly shared with StarClan. Sunlight flickered once again through the trembling canopy of leaves and warmed his pelt.

He was back.

"Spottedleaf was right." A rasping purr sounded from the long grass beside him. The grass quivered as a disheveled she-cat padded out. Her long, pale fur was matted in places, and her pawsteps were heavy. Jaypaw recognized her broad, flat face at once. It was the face that had stared directly at him from the ranks of StarClan when he had first seen them at the hollow.

"What did Spottedleaf say?" he asked.

"She warned me not to leave you to your own devices too long."

"I wasn't doing anything," he mewed defensively.

"I've lived long enough to learn the look of mischief on a kit's face," she grunted.

"I'm not a kit!" Jaypaw retorted.

"At my age, you all appear like kits." The old cat's mew croaked with amusement.

"Who are you?" he meowed.

"Yellowfang. I was ThunderClan's medicine cat before Cinderpelt. You've heard of Cinderpelt, I assume?"

"Of course," Jaypaw mewed, lifting his chin. "Leafpool keeps looking for her among StarClan, but she can't find her." He narrowed his eyes. "Have you seen her?"

"Yes, I've *seen* her," Yellowfang answered. "But I didn't come here to talk about Cinderpelt." She cleared her throat. "You're trying to walk in other cats' dreams, aren't you?"

"So what if I am?"

"You should be careful," she warned. "A cat with big ears sometimes hears more than he should."

"And who decides what I should and should not hear?" Jaypaw countered.

"You do." Yellowfang's gaze burned into his. "But you are young, and curiosity can be dangerous. Be careful where you tread."

Jaypaw bristled. Why was this old fleabag telling him what to do? "Leafpool knows I can walk in other cats' dreams," he snapped. "She told me it was a special gift."

"It is," Yellowfang agreed.

"Then why shouldn't I use it?"

"You have claws?" Yellowfang's eyes glinted as she asked him the question.

"Of course!"

"Then why don't you silence me by shredding me with them?"

What a stupid question. "You're a member of StarClan!" he retorted. "I wouldn't attack you."

"Why not?"

"It would be wrong!" What did she think he was? A weasel? "You're my ancestor and my elder—"

"And I'm three times your size." Amusement rumbled once more in Yellowfang's mew.

Jaypaw stared at her. What was she trying to say?

"There are many reasons why we don't use every power we have. Sometimes the warrior code guides us, sometimes instinct, sometimes common sense." She leaned closer toward Jaypaw, and he tried not to shrink away from her stale breath. "You have a remarkable gift, Jaypaw, but you must think before you use it."

Was she calling him stupid? Jaypaw lashed his tail mutinously.

Yellowfang narrowed her eyes and sighed. "Kits!" she muttered. "I'm wasting my breath." She turned, ready to leave.

"Wait!" Jaypaw wasn't going to lose a chance to speak with StarClan. He wanted to solve the puzzle of Mothwing. "Do you often share things with the medicine cats?"

Yellowfang glanced back at him, her eyes glittering with suspicion. "Sometimes. Why?"

"Have you spoken with Mothwing?"

Yellowfang's ears twitched. "You want me to waste more

words on answers you won't understand?"

"I just want to know if you've spoken to her."

"You are driven only by curiosity," Yellowfang hissed. "That is not a good enough reason."

Jaypaw plucked at the ground with annoyance. "Why won't you tell me?"

"Because," Yellowfang growled, "if the answers are there, you will find them anyway."

Before he could say anything else, the old cat stalked away into the grass. It quivered, then fell still, and her scent disappeared like mist in the wind.

Jaypaw itched with crossness. There was so much he wanted to know; why couldn't StarClan just be open with him? *Well*, he decided, *if the answers are there to be discovered, I'll discover them!*

He padded through the trees, trying to draw the scent of another medicine cat to him. A WindClan odor, earthy as moorland air, hit him.

Barkface.

Eagerly, Jaypaw followed his scent. He ducked low and crept through a clump of ferns, weaving carefully between the stems so as not to set them rustling. Peeking out the other side, he spied Barkface. The medicine cat's eyes were shadowed with worry. Another tom stood with him—WindClan by his scent, his pelt black and white.

"How many dogs will come, Tallstar?" Barkface asked fearfully.

"I don't know," Tallstar replied.

"When will they reach us?"

"The Twolegs will bring them when they bring the sheep to eat the newleaf grass," Tallstar told him. "You must be ready."

"I will warn Onestar."

As Jaypaw watched Barkface dip his head to the Clan leader, he felt soft fur brush his pelt. Startled, he jerked his head around.

Spottedleaf was beside him. "This is not your dream," she mewed sharply.

Jaypaw bristled. Everywhere he went, there were cats telling him what to do! "I'm only watching," he objected.

"You were not given this gift so you could spy on other Clans," Spottedleaf scolded.

"Then tell me why I was given this gift at all," Jaypaw demanded.

Before Spottedleaf could answer, another voice called his name.

"Jaypaw?"

He felt a muzzle nudging his shoulder.

"It's time to wake up." Leafpool's warm breath ruffled his fur.

He opened his eyes to darkness. The forest was gone and the Moonpool lapped at his paws. He could hear the other cats stirring. Littlecloud and Barkface were padding around the Moonpool, while Leafpool stood quietly at his side.

"Did you dream?" he asked her.

"Yes."

Jaypaw's whiskers twitched with curiosity. Shadows were clouding Leafpool's thoughts. "What did you dream about?"

"A medicine cat does not discuss what StarClan shares with her unless there is good reason to," she told him.

Did that mean he couldn't tell her about Onestar's warning to Barkface? Then he'd tell Firestar as soon as he reached camp. It was his duty. His tail trembled with anticipation. Firestar would be impressed.

Mothwing was yawning on the other side of the Moonpool, as though she had enjoyed her sleep. Jaypaw leaned forward, focusing on her thoughts, but he could perceive only a careful blankness in her mind.

Willowpaw's excitement suddenly flitted across the Moonpool, breaking his concentration like a warm breeze disturbing fallen leaves. *I bet she's dying to pass on Mudfur's message.* He felt her curious stare graze his pelt, and wondered if she had noticed him eavesdropping in her dream. He turned away from her quickly.

"Come on, Willowpaw!" Mothwing called. "It's too cold to hang around."

"We should get home," Leafpool meowed.

"Have you got something important to tell Firestar?" Mothwing asked.

"I want to be back in camp before the dawn patrol leaves," she replied. "Or they'll waste time searching for us before they check the borders." She turned and followed Barkface and Littlecloud to the top of the ridge. Jaypaw padded after her. At the top he glanced backward, finding only stillness and silence.

"You go first," Mothwing meowed. She waited for him to scramble down after the others and caught up with him as he followed them down the narrow valley.

"How's your training going?" she asked.

"Okay, I suppose," Jaypaw replied. He thought for a moment. "The best bit is sharing with StarClan." He held his breath, waiting to see how she would react.

"Of course," came the unsatisfying reply. "Any tough cases?" Jaypaw noticed she changed the subject immediately.

He thought of Stormfur. "One warrior has a scratch that won't heal."

"What are you treating it with?"

"Honey-and-horsetail poultices," he replied. "But he rubs them off as quickly as I put them on. His nest is sticky with honey, and there's a trail of it over half the camp."

"Have you tried covering the scratch with catchweed after you've put on the poultice?"

Jaypaw recalled the feel of the fuzzy green balls on long, clinging stems. The tiny catchweed burrs would stick to Stormfur's thick pelt without hurting and stop the poultice from being rubbed. "Thanks," he mewed. "I'll try it."

"It helps to share ideas," Mothwing commented.

"Does StarClan give you good advice, too?" he asked innocently, but Mothwing appeared not to hear. She was already hurrying to catch up with Willowpaw.

Jaypaw's mind buzzed with curiosity as they trekked to the WindClan border. Mothwing kept a few pawsteps ahead of him, until the cats paused at their meeting place.

"Good-bye," Littlecloud meowed as he turned toward the lake.

"See you at the Gathering," Mothwing added, dipping her head to Leafpool.

"Travel carefully," Leafpool called as Littlecloud, Mothwing, and Willowpaw headed lakeward together. "I'll remember to leave those herbs for you, Littlecloud."

"Thanks, Leafpool," the ShadowClan cat called over his shoulder.

Barkface crossed the border into his own territory. "Take care," he meowed.

And you. Jaypaw heard the heather rattle as the WindClan cat hurried home.

Left alone with Leafpool, Jaypaw was aware that the air had grown colder. He fluffed out his pelt. Frost was forming, stiffening the grass beneath his paws. Dawn must be coming.

He padded beside Leafpool into the forest. "Do you ever know what other cats dream about?" he asked, trying to sound as if he weren't really bothered.

"I told you," she answered, "we don't discuss it."

"But all medicine cats have dreams, don't they?" he pressed. Did she know about Mothwing?

"Each medicine cat's relationship with StarClan is different." Leafpool spoke carefully, like a cat picking its way through a briar patch.

"But sharing tongues with StarClan is the most important part of being a medicine cat, isn't it? Any cat could learn to heal his Clanmates, but a true medicine cat has to be able to pass on messages from StarClan."

"There is more to being a good medicine cat than interpreting signs," Leafpool told him firmly. "Come on." She broke into a run. "The dawn patrol will be heading off soon." She ran the rest of the way through the forest, checking to make sure Jaypaw was keeping up, but moving fast enough to keep him too busy to talk.

She knows more than she's telling me, he thought as he followed her scent through the undergrowth.

They arrived at the camp just as the dawn patrol was preparing to leave. Brambleclaw was pacing restlessly. Ashfur kneaded the ground, and Brackenfur sat washing his paws, his eagerness to be off showing in every urgent lick. Brambleclaw halted as Leafpool and Jaypaw padded through the thorn barrier; Jaypaw sensed his father's relief at their safe return. "All well?" he called to Leafpool.

"Everything's fine," she replied as she padded away to her den.

Now was Jaypaw's chance to share what he'd learned. He scrambled up the tumble of rocks to Highledge. "Firestar!" he called, rushing into the leader's den.

Firestar twitched in surprise. "Jaypaw?" he meowed.

Sandstorm woke up on the other side of the cave. "What is it?"

"I had a dream about StarClan," Jaypaw began. "WindClan is going be attacked by dogs." He sensed Firestar's tail bristling and went on. "This would be a great chance to take some of WindClan's territory! They'll be distracted at the other end of the ridge, and there won't be any patrols around to stop us. We can take the strip of trees, the stream. . . . We could become stronger than the other Clans. ShadowClan would never dare invade us again."

"Did StarClan tell you this?"

Why did Firestar sound so wary?

Jaypaw nodded eagerly. "About the dog attack, yes."

Sandstorm fixed Jaypaw with her steady green gaze. "Are you sure that this is what StarClan meant? That we should use the dog attack against our neighboring Clans?"

"Why else would they let me hear Tallstar's warning?"

Then Firestar spoke. "We will not take advantage of WindClan's troubles," he meowed.

"But surely StarClan let me share this so we *could* take advantage of it!" Jaypaw argued.

"Are you sure they didn't just want to warn us that dogs were loose nearby?"

Jaypaw's tail twitched with indignation. "You weren't there!" he snapped. "How do you know what StarClan meant?"

He marched out of the den and bounded down the rocks back to the medicine den. *Why don't they believe me?* he thought furiously. *I'm the one who shared with StarClan! What's the point of being a medicine cat if they don't listen to me?*

CHAPTER 21

"Dog attack! Dog attack!"

Whitewing's yowl jerked Lionpaw from his nest. Instantly awake, he scrambled to the entrance of the den. Berrypaw and Mousepaw had already shot outside. Hollypaw pressed behind him—her tail was bushed out, her ears flattened—ready to defend her Clan.

"Can you see them?" she gasped.

"Are they near the nursery?" Hazelpaw called.

Lionpaw blinked against the rain. A steady drizzle drenched the camp, and the morning sky was gray with clouds. There was no sign of dogs.

Only cats filled the clearing, staring wildly around, their claws unsheathed. Spiderleg and Birchfall came streaking from the warriors' den. Graystripe and Millie skidded after them as Whitewing paced urgently below Highledge.

"Where are they?" Ferncloud's terrified mew sounded from the nursery. She crouched at the entrance, shielding Foxkit and Icekit, her eyes round with terror.

"It's just like the badger attack!" wailed Daisy, cowering beside her.

Firestar leaped down from Highledge in one bound, Sandstorm on his heels. "Where are the dogs?"

Whitewing's words came in gasps as she fought to get her breath back. "They're not on ThunderClan territory," she panted.

"Where are they, then?" Firestar demanded.

"On WindClan territory," Whitewing reported. "I was patrolling with Thornclaw and Cloudtail near the border, and we heard dogs barking and cats shrieking from the moor."

"Where are Thornclaw and Cloudtail now?"

"They went to investigate."

"StarClan protect them!" Ferncloud whimpered.

Lionpaw's heart was still pounding like a woodpecker on oak. "I hope Heatherpaw's okay!"

Hazelpaw's whiskers grazed his cheek. "Is Firestar going to send a patrol?"

"He *must*!" Hollypaw's eyes were round. "WindClan could be wiped out."

Leafpool rushed out of the medicine den. "Any injuries?"

Whitewing shook her head. "We didn't see WindClan; w-we just heard them screeching, and the dogs . . ." Her ears twitched. "They were howling for blood."

Jaypaw flashed a look of triumph at Firestar. "Do you believe me now?" he mewed, flicking his tail.

Lionpaw stared at his brother in surprise. *Did he know this was going to happen?*

Firestar glared at the blind apprentice. "This is not about you proving a point. Cats might *die* today!"

Lionpaw glanced questioningly at Hollypaw, but she looked as puzzled as he was.

"We must send a patrol to help WindClan," Firestar decided.

Spiderleg blinked. "Have you forgotten the last time we fought dogs?"

"We lost warriors that day," Sandstorm remembered grimly.

"It's up to WindClan to look after themselves," Jaypaw growled.

Firestar glanced at Brightheart. She had lost half her face when she'd confronted a pack of vicious dogs many moons ago. "What do you think?" he asked gently.

"We nearly lost everything when the dogs attacked us." She held her head high, but Lionpaw could see she was trembling. "We can't let the same thing happen to WindClan."

"But if we go, we risk leading them here," Dustpelt pointed out.

"They might find their way here anyway," Firestar meowed.

Brambleclaw nodded. "WindClan territory is too close to our own to ignore this," he agreed.

"Exactly." Firestar gazed at each of his warriors. "You will be risking your lives to save WindClan, but you will also be defending ThunderClan from a deadly enemy."

"We must help them!" Birchfall called.

Spiderleg paced in an agitated circle. "We have to drive the dogs away!"

Lionpaw clawed at the ground. *I hope I get to go!*

"Ashfur! Graystripe!" Brambleclaw called. "You've fought dogs before. I'll need your experience. Birchfall and Spiderleg! You come too."

Lionpaw lifted his muzzle. "What about me?"

Brambleclaw glanced at Ashfur. "Is he ready?"

Ashfur gave a quick nod.

"Okay," Brambleclaw meowed. "Millie!" He swung his head toward the kittypet. "You know about dogs from when you lived in the Twolegplace, don't you?"

Millie nodded. "They don't scare me," she meowed. "And I know how easy they are to trick."

"Good." Brambleclaw nodded. "Come with us, then." He turned to his apprentice. "You too, Berrypaw."

Berrypaw unsheathed his claws, his eyes shining.

"Shall I come too?" Whitewing meowed.

"Yes. We'll need you to show us which way Thornclaw and Cloudtail went," the deputy told her.

"What about me?" Hollypaw was staring hopefully up at her father.

He shook his head, and Lionpaw saw disappointment cloud his sister's gaze. "I need you to stay here and help Brackenfur guard the camp," Brambleclaw explained. "Someone will have to patrol the entrance and make sure no dogs get in if we can't stop them at the border."

Hollypaw flicked her tail. "Yes, Brambleclaw."

The deputy glanced at Firestar. "Will Onestar accept our help?"

"I think so. Onestar's proud, but he's no fool," Firestar meowed.

"Ashfur?" Ferncloud had left the nursery and was padding toward her brother. Lionpaw knew that their mother, Brindleface, had been killed by Tigerstar to give the other dog pack a taste for cats' blood. Ferncloud would have only the worst memories of dogs. "Be careful." The she-cat rubbed her cheek along Ashfur's.

"Don't forget I've outrun a dog pack before," he meowed.

"You had me at your side then," she reminded him.

"And now I have you and your kits to protect." He licked her between the ears. "I won't let you down."

Brambleclaw was racing toward the entrance. Ashfur spun and pelted after him, falling in behind Graystripe and Millie. Birchfall and Spiderleg dashed after them, and Lionpaw followed, Berrypaw's pelt brushing his as they raced side by side.

The patrol pounded out of the camp, picking up speed as it headed up the slope toward the WindClan border. Would they get there in time? What if the dogs were already at the border? Images of vicious fangs flashed in Lionpaw's mind, making his tail tremble. He unsheathed his claws and pushed harder against the sodden earth.

His pelt was plastered against his skin by the time they reached the border. He scanned the moorland as the patrol streamed up into WindClan's territory, but the wind drove the rain into his eyes.

A distant howl ripped the air.

A panicked meow shrieked from over the heather. "We

have to lead them away from the camp!"

"This way!" Whitewing called, taking the lead. Lionpaw could smell Thornclaw's scent on the heather as they charged up the moor.

Berrypaw pulled ahead of him, his drenched cream fur bristling into spines. Lionpaw lengthened his stride. The springy grass beneath his paws made it easy to speed along between the gorse thickets. Ahead he could see Bramble-claw's powerful shoulders rise and fall as the warrior bounded through the dripping heather.

A shaggy-haired black-and-white shape streaked across the grass ahead. It sped swiftly over the rough moorland, yelping and snarling. Two cats fled only tail-lengths ahead of its snapping jaws. Lionpaw recognized the black pelt of Crowfeather and, with a jolt of panic, he saw Heatherpaw beside him, her brown pelt pale against the grass.

"They're leading it away from the camp," Brambleclaw realized. He skidded to a halt and the patrol pulled up beside him. Lionpaw dug his claws into the earth and slammed to a stop.

A second dog was pelting in the other direction, its shoulders pumping as it sped across the grass. Two more WindClan warriors—one black, one light brown—swerved out from the heather ahead of it. The dog spotted them and chased them down a rock-strewn slope. Its eyes flashed with triumph, and its yelps grew higher pitched as it began to catch up.

Suddenly Thornclaw and Dustpelt darted out from the

rocks at the foot of the slope. They raced side by side up the hillside, past the two WindClan cats. Lionpaw stared in shock. They were heading straight for the dog!

The dog's eyes gleamed as they drew nearer. Then they parted, like a stream breaking around a rock. The dog twisted and lunged toward Thornclaw. Lionpaw heard Whitewing gasp in terror as its jaws closed only an inch from Thornclaw's flank. The ThunderClan warrior ducked into a narrow crack between the rocks and left the dog spinning in confusion as the WindClan cats and Cloudtail raced away from it.

"I told you dogs were dumb," Millie growled. "They can think of only one thing at a time."

"Then let's give them as much to think about as we can!" Brambleclaw decided. He flicked his tail toward a long dip in the earth, lined with craggy boulders. "Ashfur, you and Lionpaw lead one of the dogs down there, and we'll ambush it from above."

Lionpaw's heart twisted with fear and excitement.

"No." Ashfur's mew was firm. "It'll be safer to face them on open land."

Brambleclaw narrowed his eyes and stared at the gray warrior. His shoulders tensed, but Ashfur met his gaze unflinchingly.

"I won't lead Lionpaw into a trap," Ashfur insisted. "We need room to dodge out of the way. The dogs are bigger and faster, but we're more agile."

Lionpaw heard a low growl in Brambleclaw's throat. Then

the ThunderClan deputy nodded. "Okay. Take Birchfall and Lionpaw; catch up to Crowfeather and Heatherpaw. Together you may be able to put up a fight. I'll take Spiderleg and Berrypaw and help Nightcloud and Owlwhisker." Lionpaw guessed he was referring to the black and light brown cats he had seen near the rocks. "Graystripe, Millie! Look for more dogs. Find the camp and help any cat who needs it."

Graystripe nodded and hared away across the grass with Millie.

Lionpaw pelted after Ashfur as the warrior headed toward Crowfeather and Heatherpaw. The two WindClan cats were still keeping the dog away from the camp, their paws sending up clumps of moss as they skimmed over the wet grass. The dog pounded after them, but they swerved one way and then the other, sending it skidding off course long enough to pull ahead for a while.

They must be exhausted, Lionpaw thought, pushing himself on as fast as he could. He could not take his eyes off Heatherpaw. She raced bravely beside her mentor, her pelt slick with rain, following his movements step for step.

"Crowfeather!" Ashfur yowled to the WindClan warrior as he cut across their path.

Crowfeather stared in surprise.

"We've come to help!" Lionpaw called to Heatherpaw. She jerked her head to look at him and stumbled. A rabbit hole had caught her paw, and she crashed to the ground. Lionpaw gasped in horror as the dog swung toward her. Without thinking, he turned and raced for the dog. Crowfeather had already swerved to a halt and was heading back to help his apprentice. Birchfall sped after Lionpaw. Ashfur yowled a battle cry and joined the chase.

Heatherpaw struggled to her paws and began to run, but the dog was nearly on top of her. Screeching in fury, Lionpaw launched himself at the dog's flank and gripped its coarse pelt. The dog yelped and spun, snapping at Lionpaw but unable to reach him. Lionpaw hauled his way onto the dog's back and dug in his claws. The dog tried to shake him off, but Lionpaw would not let go. Crowfeather leaped at the dog's face, raking its muzzle before swerving away from it. Ashfur darted underneath the dog's paws, nipping its foreleg so viciously that blood spurted from the wound. Lionpaw felt the dog stumble beneath him and dug his claws in harder.

The dog, yowling in pain, tried to shake Lionpaw off again. Lionpaw held on, looking for Heatherpaw, desperate to see if she was safe. His heart plummeted when he saw her pale brown pelt flash toward the dog.

"What are you doing?" he screeched.

"Helping you!" she yowled back. She darted behind the dog and raked its hind legs with her claws. The dog yelped and fell. It rolled onto Lionpaw, and he shrieked in surprise. The wet, mossy earth cushioned him as the dog scrambled off him and turned. Its jaws dripped with blood and foam as it lunged toward him with a snarl. Lionpaw flipped onto his paws and darted out of the way. He heard jaws snap behind him and then another agonized yelp. He turned to see Ashfur rearing at the dog, slashing its muzzle with his forepaws.

Crowfeather and Birchfall joined him while Heatherpaw dashed behind the dog and snapped at its hind legs. Lionpaw raced to help her, and together they slashed and nipped and clawed until the dog turned tail and fled.

Lionpaw began to give chase, but Ashfur called him back. "I think it's had enough!"

Lionpaw skidded to a halt and watched as the massive dog howled away from its attackers. Where was the other dog? He glanced around and saw with a thrill that it was already racing away into the heather. It spattered the bushes with blood as it hurried to catch up to its companion.

Graystripe padded out from the gorse, his fur hanging out in clumps and one ear stained with blood, but his eyes shining. Millie emerged beside him, followed by Tornear and Harepaw.

"Where's Brambleclaw?" Ashfur called.

"Here!" Brambleclaw's deep mew sounded from the heather on the slope above them. He bounded out from the springy bushes, Spiderleg, Nightcloud, and Owlwhisker following.

"WindClan owe you a debt of thanks," Crowfeather meowed formally.

Brambleclaw dipped his head. "May we accompany you back to the camp? I want to be sure that all's well there."

Crowfeather narrowed his eyes, then nodded. "Follow us," he meowed, turning and heading away over the grass.

Lionpaw fell in beside Heatherpaw as they followed their mentors back to the WindClan camp. The rain was beginning to ease, but Lionpaw could still feel water running along his whiskers.

"Are you okay?" he whispered.

She glanced at him with her soft gaze. "I'm fine."

Lionpaw's pelt was stinging from being scratched by the gorse, and his body ached where the dog had fallen on him. He was thankful for the mossy earth that had softened the fall. But he was also proud of his scars. This time he had won them defending another Clan.

"You were very brave, leaping on the dog like that," Heatherpaw mewed. She pointed ahead with her muzzle. "We're here," she told him.

Gorse and heather interlaced with pricking brambles formed a barrier around a dip in the earth. Lionpaw followed Heatherpaw as she wove her way through a complicated tunnel. Suddenly they emerged in a clearing open to the gray sky; around its edge, Lionpaw saw tunnels leading into the thick hedge, and he guessed that was where the dens were hidden.

As the patrol entered the camp, faces peered from the dens, and cats began to creep out into the open. A kit was squealing, its tiny cry filled with fear.

"Hush, Buzzardkit," a queen soothed from somewhere deep inside the brambles.

Onestar slid out from a tunnel near to where the kit was still mewling.

"We chased them off," Tornear reported.

"Good," Onestar meowed.

"How are the kits?" Crowfeather asked.

"Frightened, but they'll recover," Onestar answered.

More WindClan cats began to emerge. Lionpaw recognized some from the Gathering. They stared warily at the ThunderClan cats.

"Firestar sent a patrol to help," Crowfeather told Onestar. The WindClan leader let his gaze slide over the ThunderClan cats. "WindClan thank you," he meowed, dipping his head.

"We heard the dogs from the border," Brambleclaw explained. "I hope you will forgive our crossing the markers, but we were not sure how many dogs threatened you."

"Fortunately we knew they were coming, thanks to Barkface." Onestar nodded to the brown medicine cat. "StarClan warned him, and we had a plan ready to draw them away from the camp."

Lionpaw looked at Barkface in surprise. So Jaypaw had not been the only cat whom StarClan had warned about the dogs.

"Your plan was working," Brambleclaw meowed.

"But we could never have chased off the dogs without you," Heatherpaw put in. "The dogs were faster than I ever imagined." She glanced sideways at Lionpaw. "Lionpaw saved me from one of them."

Crowfeather instantly weaved between the two apprentices, blocking their view. "That was brave, Lionpaw, but WindClan is perfectly capable of taking care of its own cats."

Lionpaw felt anger flare inside him. No other cat had been near enough to the dog to reach it before it had harmed Heatherpaw. "But—"

Ashfur silenced him with a warning twitch of his tail, and Lionpaw looked down at his paws.

The brambles shivered as Breezepaw raced into the camp. "No damage to the barrier," he called.

"Have you checked it all the way around?" Crowfeather asked.

Breezepaw glared at his father. "Of course! That's what Whitetail ordered me to do."

Nightcloud stepped forward. "You should have more faith in our son, Crowfeather," she chided.

"Whitetail's my mentor, not you," Breezepaw added.

"Is that the kittypet?" A brown kit had crept out of the tunnel behind Onestar.

She was staring at Millie with round eyes. The other Clan cats turned to look at Millie, their expressions mistrustful.

"I'm training to be a warrior now," Millie told the little cat.

"But you can't ever be a real w—"

A mottled tabby queen hurried out of the tunnel. "Sedge-kit, come away," she called. "You'll get wet out here."

Sedgekit glared at her mother and stomped back inside.

"We should go," Brambleclaw meowed. He dipped his head to Onestar. "Those dogs won't dare come near this part of your territory again."

"If they do, we can manage them by ourselves," Breezepaw muttered.

"Breezepaw!" Nightcloud snapped. "Heatherpaw might have been hurt without this brave apprentice." She blinked gratefully at Lionpaw.

Lionpaw glanced away, conscious that Heatherpaw wouldn't have stumbled if he hadn't distracted her.

"Do you need some herbs for your wounds?" Heatherpaw asked him.

Lionpaw shook his head. "Leafpool will treat them when we get home."

Brambleclaw turned and headed out of the camp. The rest of the patrol filed after him. As they followed the twisting tunnel back up to the moorland, Lionpaw thought about what Jaypaw had said to Firestar. He had known that the dogs would come too; had Firestar really refused to believe his brother's warning? Surely he would believe him next time— Jaypaw had been right. But thoughts of his brother quickly slid away, to be replaced with the memory of heather-colored eyes and a soft voice asking if he needed herbs.

CHAPTER 22

The quarter moon had passed. Gray clouds hung heavy over the forest.

Jaypaw shivered, his pelt damp from the rain. "I'm going to my nest," he mewed, nodding good night to Hollypaw and Lionpaw as they finished their evening meal beside the halfrock.

Hollypaw looked up. "Already?"

"I'm tired."

"You want to get out of the rain, more like," Lionpaw joked.

Jaypaw growled. It wasn't the dampness that made him want to leave; Lionpaw had been going on about the battle against the dogs for days, and Jaypaw didn't want to hear it all again tonight. He already guessed that Lionpaw had taken off his cobweb dressings early so he'd have some scars to show his Clanmates.

Jaypaw thrust his way crossly through the bramble entrance to the medicine den. The only scars he'd ever get to show his Clanmates would be from falling down rabbit holes. Why couldn't he do something *real* to help his Clan, like

Lionpaw? He had patched up his Clanmates after they'd driven the dogs away, but that wasn't the same as fighting on behalf of his Clan.

"It sounds like it's still raining," Leafpool commented as he padded into the den.

"It's not as heavy now," Jaypaw told her.

"Well, at least there may be new herbs to gather by full moon," she mewed hopefully.

Jaypaw wasn't so sure. The air had been tinged all day with the raw scents of the mountains; he had a feeling that ice would claw the forest once more before newleaf brought fresh life. "Perhaps we should look for the first leaves tomorrow," he suggested as he curled into his nest. *Before frost has a chance to destroy them.*

"Perhaps," Leafpool murmured, already half-asleep. "But let's not gather them too early, before they've had time to grow."

Jaypaw wanted to argue, to point out the change in the wind. But since Firestar had dismissed his warning about the dogs, he had burned with resentment. *What's the point in warning them if they only ignore my advice?*

Jaypaw did not dream, and when he lifted his nose from his nest at dawn, the sharp tang of ice in the air stung his nose. He knew without doubt that a heavy frost lay thick over the forest. He stretched and realized that Leafpool was already awake, raking through her herb supply.

"We should have gathered herbs yesterday," she fretted.

"Are we running low?" Jaypaw padded sleepily to her side.

He could tell that some scents were missing from the pungent mixture of smells.

"This is the worst time of year." Leafpool sighed. "There are precious few fresh herbs, and the Clan is at its weakest after a long leaf-bare."

"At least there's been more prey since the last frost," Jaypaw pointed out.

"It'll have all bolted back into its burrows now," Leafpool warned. "Some of the warriors will go to their nests hungry tonight."

The frozen brambles at the entrance to the den crackled, and Jaypaw scented Longtail pushing his way through.

His anxiety turned to irritation. No wonder supplies were running low. He had been doing nothing but padding back and forth to the elders' den with herbs for Mousefur. The elderly warrior claimed she was fine, but Longtail kept worrying over her like a fretful queen fussing over her kit.

"Mousefur's wheezing," Longtail announced.

Of course she's wheezing, Jaypaw thought irritably. *She's older than the Sky Oak, and it's freezing!*

He turned to the pale tabby elder. "We've tried just about every herb already."

"Let's try juniper berries this time," Leafpool suggested.

Or a pawful of poppy seeds, Jaypaw muttered to himself. *She might sleep long enough to give me a break.*

"Here." Leafpool rolled a pawful of small berries toward Jaypaw. "Take these to her." Their aromatic flavor filled his nose. He bent and picked them up carefully between his jaws.

Then he turned and followed Longtail back to the elders' den.

The twining honeysuckle was stripped of its greenleaf foliage, and drafts whipped around the den like swirling water.

"Jaypaw," Mousefur greeted him. "You're not back *again*!" Her voice seemed to scour her throat like dried thistles. "You should be with cats your own age instead of spending every waking moment in here."

Jaypaw's tail twitched with frustration. *If only!*

"He's here so often only because he's worried about you," Longtail meowed.

"Because *you're* worried about me," Mousefur corrected. "You really shouldn't fuss so much. A cat my age is bound to feel the cold more easily."

"But your eyes and nose are streaming," Longtail pointed out.

"That's just the cold air," Mousefur croaked.

"I can get Brambleclaw to organize some warriors to pad your den walls, if you like," Jaypaw suggested.

"That would be kind," Mousefur admitted. "The chill does seem to have reached right to my bones this morning."

Jaypaw nosed the berries toward her. He could tell she was shivering, and yet heat flooded from her. It seemed strange, but he had been to check on her so many times, he still thought Longtail was fussing over nothing.

"I'll speak to Brambleclaw," he promised. Perhaps if he got their den fixed, the two elders could manage without him for a while.

He turned and padded out of the den, lifting his nose to scent for Brambleclaw. As he scanned the camp, he stopped dead. A tiny prick of doubt, which had been smothered by irritation with the two elders, broke through. Mousefur had accepted his help too easily. And her breathing was irregular.

He swung his muzzle back toward the den. The pungent juniper berries had masked another smell—the smell of illness.

Mousefur really was sick.

He pelted toward the medicine den, his paws skimming over the icy ground. Crashing through the patch of brambles, he skidded to a halt.

Leafpool's pelt bristled in alarm. "Jaypaw!"

"Mousefur has greencough!"

"Are you sure?"

Jaypaw listed the symptoms. "Irregular breathing, streaming eyes and nose, wheezing, fever . . ." *Fever!* That explained the heat he had felt coming off her in waves.

"We need catmint," Leafpool meowed, rushing out of the medicine den.

Jaypaw knew that catmint was one of the missing scents when Leafpool had raked through the herbs earlier. He followed his mentor out and paced anxiously as she called to Cloudtail.

"You must fetch catmint," Leafpool explained as the warrior came racing to the medicine cat's side. "At once!"

Surprise sparked from the warrior. "Catmint? Why?"

Leafpool's pelt ruffled with uncertainty. She obviously

didn't want to spread panic through the Clan. She lowered her voice. "Mousefur is ill."

Cloudtail kneaded the ground anxiously. "Where do I get it from?"

"By the old Twoleg nest," Leafpool told him.

"I know what it smells like," Jaypaw mewed. "I'll be able to find it."

He sensed Cloudtail's doubt at once. "Medicine cats can run, you know! And I'll be able to spot it quicker than you."

"He's right," Leafpool agreed.

"Okay," Cloudtail mewed. "We'll take Cinderpaw with us. She can help carry it back." He called across the clearing to his apprentice. She was sharing tongues with Poppypaw, but at Cloudtail's call, her small steps came pattering toward them over the frosty ground.

"What is it?" she mewed.

"We have to find catmint," Jaypaw told her. "Mousefur is ill."

Cinderpaw gasped. "Catmint's for greencough, isn't it?"

"Come on," Cloudtail ordered. "There's no time to waste." He raced toward the thorn barrier, and Jaypaw hurried after him. Once out of the camp they headed straight for the disused Thunderpath.

Jaypaw could feel Cloudtail's eyes flashing back at him as the warrior checked that their blind companion was keeping up. But Jaypaw's paws were swift with fear, and he easily kept pace with Cinderpaw. He could feel her warm pelt rippling beside his, and matched her step for step.

"Tree!" she warned him. But he had already scented its bark and swerved to avoid it.

He couldn't stop thinking about Mousefur. Why hadn't he realized that she was so unwell? Longtail had been trying to tell him for days. Guilt gnawed at his belly. Once they had the catmint he would feed it to her himself until she was fully recovered. The sharp little stones on the abandoned Thunderpath grazed Jaypaw's pads, but he quickened his pace, pulling ahead of Cinderpaw.

Cloudtail halted by the crumbling stone wall around the nest. Jaypaw felt a twinge of nerves. Although he knew the place was empty, it felt dangerous to be going onto Twoleg territory.

Cloudtail jumped up onto the wall first.

"It's not high," Cinderpaw mewed.

Jaypaw reached up with his forepaws, and Cloudtail flicked his tail down to give him some sense of how far to jump. He sprang, and as he scrabbled to get a grip, Cloudtail grabbed him by his scruff and swung him over the wall into the long, frost-stiffened grass on the other side.

As soon as he landed, Jaypaw sniffed the air, searching for the catmint. He found a trace of it and began picking his way through the grass.

"Wait for me!" Cinderpaw called, jumping down after him. She hurried to catch up. "Cloudtail's keeping guard on the wall," she panted.

"It's over there," he told her.

Cinderpaw sped ahead, and Jaypaw could hear her rooting

about in the vegetation along the wall. "There's nothing here but dead leaves!" she called back to him. "The frost has killed it all."

Jaypaw's belly heaved, and the ground seemed to drop away from beneath his paws. There had to be catmint here! "Let me look!" he mewed.

He rushed over to Cinderpaw and sniffed at the plants around her paws. He could smell catmint, but it was sour, scorched by the frost.

"It's all black." Cinderpaw sighed.

Jaypaw touched it with the tip of his tongue. The leaves felt pulpy and wet. But a delicious flavor seeped from deeper within the plant. He dug down, fearful of damaging roots that might yet recover but desperate to find something that would help Mousefur. Around the base, just beneath the soil, he smelled fresh leaves. Feeling carefully with the tips of his paws, he touched the soft furriness of new growth. Not much, but it was better than nothing. He scraped away the earth and delicately nipped off the new stalks with his teeth. Then, holding them gently on his tongue, trying not to absorb any of the precious flavor, he nodded to Cinderpaw.

"Will that be enough?" she asked.

Unable to speak, he shrugged.

She seemed to understand, for she turned away and began to hurry back to where Cloudtail waited on the wall. Together they scrambled over and set off back to the camp.

* * *

"This is all that was left undamaged," he explained to Leafpool as he dropped the mouthful of stalks on the floor of the medicine den. He could feel disappointment turning her paws to stone.

"It's better than nothing," she meowed. She picked up the stalks with her teeth and hurried out of the den.

Jaypaw followed her. Would Mousefur be worse?

The old she-cat's labored breathing echoed around the honeysuckle bush. The air smelled bitter, and it prickled with Longtail's anxiety.

"Is that catmint?" he asked hopefully.

Leafpool dropped it beside Mousefur. "Yes."

"There's not much," Longtail observed.

"It'll have to do," Leafpool told him. "Frost has damaged the rest." She crouched down and whispered to Mousefur, "I want you to chew this and swallow as much as you can."

Mousefur groaned. Jaypaw slid around beside the old she-cat and pressed his cheek to her flank. She was burning with fever and trembling. Then she coughed and he heard her breath bubbling beneath his ear. He jerked up his head and stared desperately at Leafpool.

"She may be old, but she's strong," the medicine cat reassured him. Then she urged Mousefur, "Come on, eat a little."

The old cat took a few stalks in her mouth and began to chew. Jaypaw felt her pain like thorns in his pelt as she swallowed. She must have seen him flinch, for she lifted her muzzle toward him so that her sour breath ruffled his fur. "What a fuss you're making over me," she rasped. "Anyone would think I was about to join StarClan." She forced a purr, and Jaypaw felt the pain of it shake her body. "I don't think they're ready for me yet. And besides, if I go, who will make sure Longtail remembers to check his pelt for fleas?"

"You'll be better in no time," Jaypaw told her, willing it to be true.

Pawsteps padded quickly outside the den, and the honeysuckle rustled. Jaypaw smelled Daisy's scent at the entrance.

"Leafpool?" The kittypet sounded worried.

Leafpool lifted her head. "Yes?"

"Ferncloud is unwell."

Alarm shot through Jaypaw.

"What's wrong?" Leafpool asked.

"She's wheezing, and her eyes and nose are streaming."

Mousefur let out an agonized groan. "I went to the nursery yesterday to see the kits," she croaked.

"Foxkit and Icekit seem fine," Daisy mewed at once.

"I'll come and check on Ferncloud," Leafpool meowed.

"Shall I stay with Mousefur?" Jaypaw offered.

"No." Mousefur began to cough. "Check on the kits!" She pushed the rest of the catmint away from her. "Don't waste your time fussing over an old warrior like me."

"You must take these herbs," Leafpool insisted, pawing them back under Mousefur's nose. "You're not as strong as Ferncloud."

"Check on the kits first," Mousefur answered stubbornly.

"Okay, I will." Leafpool slipped out of the elders' den.

Jaypaw followed her as she raced across the clearing. He squeezed into the nursery behind her. The familiar smell of his old home was tainted by the smell of sickness. Ferncloud was struggling for breath, and even without touching her, Jaypaw could feel the heat pulsing from her body.

"It's definitely greencough," Leafpool announced. "But the kits are not infected."

"We should get Ferncloud away from them," Jaypaw suggested.

"I can look after them instead." Daisy had followed them into the nursery. "They're close enough to weaning now."

"Thank you," Leafpool meowed, nudging Ferncloud to her paws.

Grief flashed from Ferncloud as Foxkit and Icekit began mewling. "I'll be back soon," she promised weakly.

Daisy's fur brushed their tiny pelts as she curled around them. "We'll have fun with all this space to ourselves," she told them. "Ferncloud will just be across the clearing. She's not leaving the camp."

"Why can't she stay here?" Foxkit wailed.

"Because we don't want you getting sick too," Daisy explained.

"Be good," Ferncloud mewed, her breath coming in gasps as Leafpool began to guide her from the den.

"Don't worry, we'll be fine," Icekit called.

Jaypaw could sense the anxiety behind Icekit's brave

words. He flicked his tail over her back. "I'll ask Hollypaw to come and teach you all the new fighting moves she's been learning," he offered.

"Really?" Icekit squeaked, brightening.

"Fetch Mousefur," Leafpool called to him from outside. "We'll settle both cats in the medicine den, where we can keep an eye on them."

Jaypaw's heart began pounding again as he scrabbled out of the nursery. He had wanted a chance to protect his Clanmates, but a warrior could do it with teeth and claws, while all he had to offer was a pawful of pulpy roots. How could this be his destiny?

Dawn brought another victim. Jaypaw was woken by Whitewing as she limped into the medicine den, tail down and wheezing. He had learned the deadly scent of green-cough by now and sprang from his nest. But Leafpool was already beside the white warrior, listening to her breathing.

"Make a nest for her beside Ferncloud and Mousefur," she ordered Jaypaw.

He hurried to fetch some of the spare moss they kept at the side of the den. At least they had plenty of that, he thought bitterly. He quickly shaped a nest beside Mousefur, who was sleeping at last, her breathing short and irregular. And Ferncloud seemed to be comfortable, though her fever was rising as she battled the illness.

Whitewing collapsed gratefully into the nest.

"We need more catmint," Leafpool hissed so that only

Jaypaw's sharp ears could hear.

Jaypaw sensed terror in her voice. What did she expect him to do? Grow some?

"Check all the other warriors and apprentices," Leafpool ordered more loudly.

He nodded, then turned and headed out of the den. Why hadn't StarClan warned them this was going to happen? Instead of lecturing him, Spottedleaf or Yellowfang could have told him that greencough was coming. He could have gathered catmint before the frost had come.

Dustpelt was pacing outside the nursery. Jaypaw recognized the warrior's heavy pawsteps on the frozen earth and sensed the turmoil of fear that gripped his thoughts.

"How's Ferncloud?" he demanded as soon as he saw Jaypaw.

"No worse," Jaypaw assured him.

"Should I visit her?"

"It's probably better if you stay away," Jaypaw advised. "We want to stop the illness from spreading."

Daisy wriggled out of the nursery. "Your kits are fine," she told Dustpelt. "But if you keep hanging around here you're going to worry them." Jaypaw had never heard her sound so stern. "You should be out in the forest hunting; that's the best way you can help them."

Jaypaw felt surprise flash from Dustpelt.

"I want to know if Ferncloud gets worse," the warrior meowed. Then he padded toward the barrier of thorns and headed out into the forest.

As Jaypaw turned toward the apprentice's den, the dawn patrol pounded into the clearing, led by Graystripe. Hollypaw was among them, her scent laced with the fresh smells of the forest.

"How are the sick cats?" she called to Jaypaw.

"Sleeping," Jaypaw mewed back. "How's the prey running?" Perhaps if the rest of the Clan could fill their bellies, they might be able to resist the sickness.

"There's hardly anything aboveground," Hollypaw reported. "Even the squirrels are staying in their dens."

Jaypaw closed his eyes. *Where are you, StarClan? I've hardly had a dream without you sticking your whiskers in! Why don't you help me now?* But he heard nothing except Leafpool's voice as she padded to his side.

"Check the apprentices, Jaypaw," she reminded him grimly. "StarClan are watching us already. But there are some battles we have to fight alone."

CHAPTER 23

"Dawn's coming," Leafpool whispered to Jaypaw. "You should get some rest."

Jaypaw shook his head. "Not while we have so many sick cats to look after."

He sniffed Poppypaw. The apprentice had developed a fever during the night and come to the medicine den. She lay now in a nest beside Ferncloud, her eyes sticky with pus, her breathing labored. The heat flooding from her frightened Jaypaw.

He listened, his pelt pricking with panic. The medicine den was crowded, the sound of wheezing and coughing jarred his ears, and the smell of sickness made his paws tremble with frustration. He had done everything he could to help his Clanmates, but no one was any better.

"Should we move them to the elders' den?" he suggested to Leafpool, who was massaging Mousefur's flank to try to help clear her breathing. "There's more room there."

"Mousefur and Ferncloud are too sick to move," Leafpool pointed out. "Besides, there is water here."

The pool of fresh water that trickled down the rock wall

and gathered in a dip made it easy to soak moss for the thirsty cats. Jaypaw fetched a dripping ball of it for Poppypaw. He nudged her in an attempt to make her drink, but the tortoiseshell's eyes were half closed, and she only groaned and pushed him away.

"If you won't rest, at least get some fresh air," Leafpool urged.

Jaypaw nodded. Wearily he padded out of the den. The air outside was clean and cold after the stuffy stench of the den. Even though it was barely dawn, Firestar was already below Highledge with Brambleclaw. They were organizing the patrols. Ashfur and Birchfall paced restlessly around them.

"We need to keep the patrols short," Brambleclaw meowed to the ThunderClan leader.

"But we must make sure the ShadowClan border remains well guarded," Ashfur pointed out. "We don't want them to take advantage of our weakness."

"Lots of small patrols would be more efficient," Birchfall suggested.

"Yes," Firestar agreed. "I don't want our warriors to wear themselves out when there's so much sickness around. We need them fit."

"I can do two patrols a day." Millie's mew rang around the frozen hollow. The gray kittypet padded out from behind the warriors' den, Graystripe at her side.

"Are you sure?" Firestar checked.

"I was given medicine by the vet to stop me from getting sick," Millie explained. "Whenever other cats fell ill in

Twolegplace, I always stayed well."

Brambleclaw looked confused. "Vet?"

"The Cutter," Graystripe explained.

"Well, it seems the Cutter has done me a favor," Firestar meowed. "He has given me a healthy warrior."

Firestar had called Millie a warrior.

Pleasure glowed from the she-cat, and Jaypaw heard Graystripe's proud purr as his fur swished against hers.

"But," Firestar went on, "I don't want Graystripe to go with you."

Graystripe's purr died in his throat. "Why not?"

"You're still weak from your journey," Firestar replied. "And I can't afford to lose you again. There are plenty of ways you can help in camp." The ThunderClan leader's voice was firm, and though Jaypaw felt Graystripe bristle with indignation, he did not challenge his old friend.

The yew bush quivered as Hollypaw and Lionpaw slid out of their den. Anxiously Jaypaw lifted his muzzle to taste their scent. He relaxed when it was clean and healthy.

"We want to go on the first patrol," Lionpaw mewed.

"Unless the Clan needs us in camp," Hollypaw added.

"Firestar?" Brambleclaw looked to the ThunderClan leader to decide.

Firestar swept his tail thoughtfully over the ground. "Lionpaw, you can patrol the border with Ashfur and Millie," he meowed. "Hollypaw can hunt with Birchfall."

"I'll do my best," Hollypaw promised.

Jaypaw padded over to her. "Make sure you stay away from

the sick cats," he warned. "Don't share fresh-kill with any cat." He glanced at Lionpaw. "And drink water as far from the camp as you can." How would he cope if he had to watch them suffer along with his other patients? If only they had more catmint!

"Come on, Hollypaw!" Birchfall's call was edgy with impatience, and she shot away to join him.

"We'll join the hunt as soon as we've checked the border!" Ashfur called after them as they raced out of the camp.

"Don't tire yourselves out," Firestar warned.

"We won't." Lionpaw raced away from Jaypaw and pounded out of the camp behind his mentor.

A dark sense of dread pulsed across the clearing and swept Jaypaw like an icy wind. He jerked his head around and stared at Firestar. *He's terrified for us.*

Paws hammered outside the thorn barrier. Squirrelflight and Sandstorm were returning to camp. Jaypaw smelled fresh-kill. They had been hunting.

"Is that all you could find?" Firestar's greeting was sharp with shock.

A mouse and a sparrow. Jaypaw heard the two small bodies drop onto the empty space where the fresh-kill pile used to be.

"Shall we go out again?" Squirrelflight offered.

"Rest first," Firestar meowed. "Birchfall and Hollypaw are hunting, too."

His pelt swished as he wove around Sandstorm. Jaypaw sensed that her touch soothed some of the anxiety pounding through his body. The smell of fresh-kill made his belly rumble; he hadn't eaten since yesterday. But Icekit and Foxkit needed food more than he did.

"Shall I take the mouse to the nursery?" he called to Firestar.

"Yes, please—" Firestar's answer was cut short by a rustling on the slope outside the thorn barrier. Jaypaw tensed. He smelled WindClan.

Firestar padded to the entrance and sniffed the air.

"There's only two of them," Jaypaw called. He did not recognize the scents of the two WindClan cats who were padding toward the entrance of the hollow, but he sensed their anxiety as they padded into the camp.

The older of the two cats spoke first. "Forgive us for trespassing on ThunderClan territory."

"Weaselfur!" Firestar sounded surprised. "What are you doing here?"

Jaypaw padded closer. The younger cat smelled of herbs.

"I've brought Kestrelpaw to speak with Leafpool," Weaselfur meowed.

Kestrelpaw! Jaypaw remembered Barkface mentioning his apprentice when they had traveled to the Moonpool.

"Hi, there," he called.

Kestrelpaw was fidgeting nervously, kneading the ground. "Are you Jaypaw?" he asked. "I need to speak to your mentor."

Leafpool was already out of her den and padding toward Kestrelpaw. "What is it?"

"There's greencough in WindClan," Kestrelpaw mewed.

"Barkface was hoping you could share your catmint."

Leafpool sighed. "We have none. The frost killed it. We have sick cats too, and there's nothing we can do to help them."

Squirrelflight padded to join her sister. "RiverClan have catmint," she meowed. "They would share it with us, wouldn't they?"

"I've wondered about that," Leafpool meowed.

Jaypaw's tail bristled. Why hadn't she mentioned it before?

"Let's go and ask them," Kestrelpaw suggested.

"Mothwing might need all her supplies for her own Clan," Leafpool fretted.

"She wouldn't let our Clanmates die if she knew how sick they were," Squirrelflight argued.

"She might already know," Kestrelpaw pointed out. "StarClan might have told her."

Yeah, right, thought Jaypaw.

Leafpool shuffled her paws. "But what if there's green-cough in RiverClan too? She couldn't risk giving away her supplies."

Jaypaw didn't understand why Leafpool was hesitating. "We've got to try!" he mewed. This was their chance to save the Clan.

Squirrelflight's fur was pricking with frustration too. "The Clans have helped one another before when it's been life or death."

"*I'll* go and ask RiverClan, if you're too scared!" Jaypaw put in.

"I'm not scared!" Leafpool growled. "I just don't want to put Mothwing in a difficult position."

Jaypaw clawed the ground. "What would she say if she found out cats died and you never asked for help?" He felt Leafpool's mind recoil with alarm—and something else, the horror of a long-buried memory. "She'd be devastated!" he pressed.

"Very well," Leafpool agreed. "I'll go and ask her."

Jaypaw knew she'd travel faster without him. "I'll stay here and look after the sick cats," he offered.

Leafpool leaned down and touched her muzzle to his. "Thanks, Jaypaw."

"I'll do my best," he mewed briskly. Then he realized that he would be responsible for every one of his Clanmates while Leafpool was away. The thought struck him like a kick to the belly.

Leafpool entwined his tail with hers. "Rely on your instincts, Jaypaw. They are sharper than any cat's."

He nodded, taking a deep breath. *I know all the herbs*, he reminded himself. *And this is a chance to prove that I can help my Clan.*

"Brightheart will help you if necessary," Leafpool went on. "She's worked with me before."

Jaypaw's tail pricked. Brightheart was the last cat he wanted watching him struggle to help his Clanmates. But he wasn't going to let Leafpool know that.

"We'd better get going," Leafpool meowed to the two WindClan cats.

Firestar padded over to block the entrance before Leaf-pool could head out. "I want Thornclaw and Brambleclaw to go with you," he meowed.

"But we're medicine cats," Leafpool pointed out. "No cat will dare stop us."

"You're going to have to skirt the lake around ShadowClan territory," Firestar pointed out. "I don't trust ShadowClan right now."

"Very well," Leafpool meowed. She waited impatiently while Firestar called Thornclaw from the warriors' den, and then the patrol raced out of the camp like rabbits.

Sandstorm came up to Jaypaw. "Can I help with anything?"

He didn't know where to start. The medicine den was full, feverfew was running short, and he was so hungry he could hardly think straight.

"The mouse!" He suddenly remembered. "I was going to take it to the nursery for the kits."

"I can do that," Sandstorm meowed. "You go back to the medicine den."

Her steady mew calmed him. "Thanks," he murmured.

He returned to the den to find that Poppypaw's fever had risen even more. Mousefur's breathing was so shallow he had to press his muzzle to her flank to feel it. Ferncloud was begging for water, and the bedding stank.

StarClan, help me! Jaypaw closed his eyes for a moment. Summoning all his strength, he went to fetch a wad of soaked moss for Ferncloud.

"Sandstorm told me you need some help." Brightheart's voice sounded from the den entrance.

"Yes." Jaypaw's ears twitched nervously, but for the first time in days he felt no anger flash from the one-eyed warrior. "Can you help me clear out the old bedding?" he asked.

"I can do the bedding by myself," Brightheart told him. "You see to your patients." Something small and sweet-smelling thudded at his paws. "Sandstorm said you should eat this." Brightheart had tossed him a piece of the mouse.

He shook his head.

"You have to keep your strength up," Brightheart insisted. "While Leafpool's gone, you are responsible for the whole Clan."

Which meant that until Leafpool returned with catmint, there was nothing he could do except watch his Clanmates die. Jaypaw felt the same hopelessness as when he flailed his claws at Owlpaw in the battle against ShadowClan, never sure where his enemy would lunge from next.

"Eat the mouse," Brightheart prompted.

"Okay." He wasn't going to act like a mewling kit. Did he want every cat to know he couldn't cope? They already thought he was useless; they didn't have to think he was weak and scared too!

Jaypaw gulped down the morsel, and then, while Brightheart started tugging out the foul bedding, he chewed up mouthfuls of feverfew and tried to persuade Poppypaw to swallow some. "Come on," he urged her. "Just taste a little."

Poppypaw pushed him away with a burning paw. "I can't swallow," she rasped.

"You must try."

Jaypaw suddenly felt another pelt against his. He smelled Sorreltail, Poppypaw's mother.

"She's worse, isn't she?" the she-cat mewed.

"Leafpool's gone to WindClan to ask for catmint," Jaypaw told her.

"But will Poppypaw survive until she returns?" Sorreltail's mew cracked with grief.

"I'll make sure she does," Jaypaw growled. He tried to stop his paws from trembling as he pushed the feverfew under Poppypaw's nose yet again. He had been a medicine cat apprentice for less than a moon. Could he really keep a promise like that?

"Come on." Brightheart nudged Sorreltail. "Jaypaw will do what he can. You should go hunting with Brackenfur. The more fresh-kill we have, the stronger the Clan will be."

As the one-eyed warrior guided her Clanmate out of the medicine den, Jaypaw rubbed the feverfew pulp onto Poppypaw's lips, hoping that some of it would find its way into her fever-racked body. *For StarClan's sake, eat this and get better!*

Jaypaw woke with a start. He had dozed off without meaning to. The silence of night lay heavily on the forest. An owl hooted far away as Jaypaw struggled to his paws. He felt light-headed with hunger and exhaustion, but he had to check on the sick cats.

Brightheart was sleeping at the entrance to the den. Her steady breathing comforted him as he picked his way around the sick cats. Mousefur was shivering, and he pulled fresh moss over her to keep her warm, though heat pulsed from her body. Ferncloud murmured the names of her kits, and Whitewing fidgeted uncomfortably in her sleep. Jaypaw sat and listened. Something was not right. He ducked down beside Poppypaw. Her breathing had slowed.

Jaypaw's heart began to race. He slid into the nest beside her and pressed his body against hers. She was unnaturally still. Fear gripped him; he had promised Sorreltail that he wouldn't let her die. He focused on Poppypaw's breathing and let his body relax. Then he steadied his breath until it fell into the same slow rhythm as hers. He closed his eyes, and the world opened up before him in shades of black, white, and silver, washed with moonlight. He could see the pale shape of Poppypaw padding through a forest. He recognized the trees and the undergrowth and the feel of the leaf-strewn earth underneath his paws at once. Poppypaw mustn't come here!

"Poppypaw!" He hurried to catch up to the apprentice, and she turned to gaze at him.

"I've never been to this part of the forest before." She sniffed the air. "It doesn't smell like home. Do you know where we are?"

"Yes," Jaypaw whispered.

"It's strange," Poppypaw mewed. "Whatever herbs you gave me must have worked, because I don't feel sick anymore."

Jaypaw didn't reply. How was he going to bring Poppypaw back from this place? He padded wordlessly beside her, terrified of losing sight of her.

"The trees are so tall and leafy, and the undergrowth is thicker than anything." Poppypaw obviously didn't realize that Jaypaw could see it for himself. "Can you smell all the scents of prey? It's like greenleaf here!"

"We've got to go back!" Jaypaw told her.

"But it's so beautiful."

"You shouldn't be here!" *I promised Sorreltail!*

The trees opened before them.

"Stop!" Poppypaw gasped. "There's a drop in front of us."

Jaypaw could clearly see the hollow below them, the Moonpool cradled at the bottom like liquid starlight. In this place everything was connected, and the forest led all the way into the mountains. Jaypaw's heart sank when he saw the shining pelts of StarClan gathered around the slopes.

"There's a pool at the bottom," Poppypaw breathed. "There are cats all around it. . . ." Her mew trailed away. "It's StarClan, isn't it? Does that mean I'm *dead*?"

Jaypaw's throat went dry.

"Am I dead?" she repeated more urgently.

"Not yet."

Jaypaw spun around when he heard Spottedleaf's voice.

"Coming here with her was very brave," murmured the tortoiseshell cat.

"I promised her mother I'd keep her safe," Jaypaw told her.

Poppypaw's eyes clouded with confusion as she stared at Spottedleaf. "Who are you? Have you come to guide me to StarClan?"

"No!" Jaypaw growled. "Come back to the Clan with me, Poppypaw. I'll take you home."

"It's okay, little one," Spottedleaf meowed. "You can go with Jaypaw. There is a place here for you, but not yet." Stretching forward, she touched her muzzle first to Poppypaw's and then to Jaypaw's. "Take her home," she whispered.

Thank you! "Follow me," he told Poppypaw, and, turning away from the glittering hollow, he led her back into the forest.

Brightheart's voice cut through the air. "Jaypaw!"

He blinked open his eyes into darkness. "Brightheart?"

"I thought you were ill too," Brightheart whispered. "Your breathing was so slow."

Poppypaw!

He leaped to his paws and pressed his ear against her flank. She was still sleeping, but her breathing was deeper, steady and strong.

"How is she?" Brightheart asked.

"Better than she was." Jaypaw sighed, closing his eyes with relief.

"I woke up and found the two of you hardly breathing." Jaypaw could feel Brightheart's gaze burning his pelt. "I'm glad you're all right." She brushed her tail briskly over the den floor. "Dawn's nearly here. I'll go and find Sorreltail. She'll be relieved to hear the news."

As Brightheart padded out of the den, Jaypaw felt fresh energy tingling through his paws. He leaned down and whispered in the apprentice's ear, "I promised I would save you."

Poppypaw stirred. "Jaypaw? Is that you?" Her voice was weak and whispery. "I had the strangest dream!"

Jaypaw tensed. He couldn't let the other cats know what he had done to bring Poppypaw back from StarClan. "I expect it was because of the fever," he soothed her.

"Maybe." Poppypaw sounded uncertain. "I was in a forest I'd never seen before, but it felt like home. There were other cats there—and you, Jaypaw! You said I didn't have to stay. . . ."

Jaypaw turned away. "It was just a dream. You're better now. That's all that matters."

"Leafpool's here!" Brackenfur's cry filled the hollow, and Jaypaw raced from the den. He could smell the catmint already, and knew that Leafpool had brought plenty.

She was hurrying toward him, fragrant leaves bunched in her jaws. Thornclaw and Brambleclaw followed, carrying more. They dropped them at the den entrance while Jaypaw followed Leafpool inside.

"We left Weaselfur and Kestrelpaw at the lake," she told him when she had put down the catmint. "Mothwing had plenty. She gave us enough to cure all our sick Clanmates. She said she'd have sent some earlier if she'd known."

And who would have told her? thought Jaypaw. *Not StarClan.* He began to help Leafpool dose the sick cats.

Sorreltail nosed her way into the den, relief and gratitude flooding the air around her. "I don't know how you did it, but I know you helped Poppypaw survive the night." Her voice was thick with emotion. "Thank you."

Jaypaw felt Leafpool's tail gently flick his flank. "I knew you'd be fine without me," she meowed.

As Jaypaw pressed another pawful of catmint beneath Whitewing's nose, he heard Leafpool slip out of the den. The medicine cat had been quiet since she returned. Not just because she was busy tending to the sick cats—Jaypaw could sense that something was troubling her. He lifted his muzzle, intrigued, as the brambles swept back into place after her.

"Eat these slowly," he advised Whitewing. "I'll be back in a moment."

He nosed his way out of the den and sniffed. Leafpool was sitting below Highledge with Firestar. Quietly, he hurried into the clearing and ducked down behind the halfrock. The two cats were sharing words in hushed whispers.

"There's sickness in all the Clans," Leafpool told Firestar. "Greencough and whitecough. The frosts have taken their toll on prey in every territory, and all the Clans are weakened by hunger."

"Even ShadowClan?"

"Littlecloud joined us to fetch catmint," she answered. "He told me that they had lost an elder."

Sadness pulsed from Firestar. "It's been a hard leaf-bare for every Clan."

Jaypaw pricked his ears. He could tell that Leafpool had not said all that she meant to. Then Leafpool whispered so quietly that Jaypaw had to stretch forward to hear.

"There's a lot of bad feeling in the Clans," she murmured. "A feeling that this run of cold weather and sickness and poor prey is more than just bad luck."

Jaypaw's blood pounded, and Leafpool's mew was suddenly swamped by the murmuring of distant voices that rang in his ears, voices from all four Clans around the lake. . . . *StarClan doesn't want us to stay here! The new territories can't support us all. What if the sickness spreads?*

The whispers of doubt crowded his mind. He pressed himself to the earth and closed his eyes. Was StarClan punishing the Clans, and if so, why?

CHAPTER 24

Hollypaw twitched her nose. Something was different. The air smelled damp and warm.

Happily, she stretched in her nest, pushing against Hazelpaw's back with her hind paws.

"Get off!" Hazelpaw complained.

"Can't you smell it?"

Hazelpaw yawned. "Smell what?"

"It's warmer!" Hollypaw jumped out of her nest.

She ducked out of the den and screwed up her eyes against the light. The frost had gone. The clearing was damp where the ice had melted, the bushes dripping, and sunshine was already filling the camp with pale yellow. At the top of the cliffs, the trees seemed wrapped in a green haze. Newleaf had arrived at last.

Firestorm was grooming Sandstorm below Highledge. His bones looked sharp beneath his pelt as he crouched to lick Sandstorm's ears, but his tail flicked happily. Icekit and Foxkit squealed with delight as Birchfall and Berrypaw chased them in circles outside the nursery. Ferncloud rested beside Daisy at the den entrance, clearly enjoying the morning's warmth.

Her eyes were clear, and only a little crust around her nose betrayed that she had been so ill. Poppypaw was on the mend too, recovering in the elders' nest with Mousefur, though she wouldn't be well enough to go to the Gathering tonight.

Hollypaw heard paws pounding through the thorn barrier, and Thornclaw charged into camp at the head of a patrol. A mouse dangled from his jaws. Whitewing followed him, carrying a small chaffinch, and Ashfur and Lionpaw came in last, each carrying a vole.

Hollypaw's eyes grew round. She hadn't seen so much fresh-kill in ages.

As Thornclaw dropped his catch onto the patch of earth that had been empty for too long, Firestar got to his paws to greet the returning patrol. "It looks like the prey's running richer already!"

Lionpaw padded excitedly around Ashfur. "There were primroses on the ShadowClan border and buds on the Sky Oak!"

"And prey seemed to be moving in every burrow," Whitewing added.

Firestar scanned the clearing. "Brambleclaw?"

The deputy came hurrying out of the warriors' den, Squirrelflight behind him.

"The prey's running again." Firestar flicked his tail toward the fresh-kill pile. "Lead another patrol out toward the WindClan border and see what you can catch."

Brambleclaw's eyes lit up with excitement. "Berrypaw!" he called to his apprentice. "We're going hunting."

Berrypaw stopped chasing the kits.

"Can we come too?" Foxkit begged.

Icekit swiped her brother playfully around the ears. "We're only kits," she mewed. "They'll never let us go with them."

"But watch this hunting move!" Foxkit crouched down, sticking his tail in the air and wiggling his haunches. He lunged forward and landed on a leaf, pinning it to the ground.

Icekit's short whiskers quivered with amusement. "Next time we need leaves, I'm sure Brambleclaw will ask you to help!"

"You'll make a great warrior," Berrypaw told him. "And I promise to bring something tasty back for you."

Hollypaw darted forward. "Can I go with them?" she asked Brambleclaw.

"You're going to the Gathering tonight," he meowed. "I want you to save your energy for that."

"But I've been asleep half the morning," she protested.

"You're half-starved, like the rest of the Clan," Brambleclaw told her. "Rest and eat today. You can hunt tomorrow."

"But Lionpaw's been hunting!" Hollypaw answered hotly. "It's not fair."

"Life isn't fair. Stay in camp." He nodded to Squirrelflight and together they led Berrypaw out into the forest.

Furious, Hollypaw turned and stomped across the clearing. Her Clan was starving and they wouldn't let her hunt!

For a moment she wondered whether to sneak out of camp and hunt by herself. But if she got caught Firestar probably wouldn't let her go to the Gathering *or* hunting tomorrow. It wasn't worth it.

Overhead, the great white moon made the hollow glow with silver light.

Hollypaw sniffed the air. *Clear skies. A good sign.*

Graystripe and Millie waited in the clearing with Ashfur and Stormfur. Brackenfur sat beside them, tugging with his teeth at the fur between his claws. Squirrelflight washed her ears as Brambleclaw stood next to her and glanced up at Highledge. They would leave for the Gathering as soon as Firestar appeared.

The apprentices were fidgeting beside the thorn barrier.

"Do you think Blackstar will mention the battle?" Cinderpaw mewed.

Honeypaw paced in front of the camp entrance. "I bet ShadowClan never talks about its defeats."

"What do you think, Hollypaw?" Lionpaw asked. But Hollypaw hardly heard. Jaypaw was staring at the patrol as it prepared to leave camp. His clear blue gaze gave nothing away, but she knew how disappointed he must be.

She padded over to him. "I'll tell you about it as soon as I get back," she promised.

Jaypaw didn't reply.

She pressed her flank against his. "You'll go to the next

Gathering, I'm sure," she comforted him. "Poppypaw and Mousefur will be better by then."

"I know." Only the smallest twitch of his tail betrayed his frustration.

"Hollypaw!" Brackenfur's call made her jump. Firestar had leaped down from Highledge, Sandstorm behind him.

"I've got to go," she mewed.

"Hurry up!" Lionpaw called as she hurried to join the others.

Hollypaw glanced over her shoulder at Jaypaw. He had gotten to his paws and was padding slowly toward the elders' den.

"Jaypaw will be fine," Cinderpaw reassured her.

Hollypaw stiffened her shoulders. Jaypaw was taking care of his Clan. Besides, she didn't want to worry about her brother right now. This was her first Gathering as a warrior apprentice, and her paws tingled with anticipation.

Firestar signaled with a flick of his tail, then dived out through the thorn tunnel. Brambleclaw and the other warriors sped after him. The apprentices bunched together as they raced to be first out of camp. Lionpaw's pelt brushed against Hollypaw's. His fur was bristling as they burst from the tunnel.

"Do you think the other Clans know I'm a warrior apprentice now?" Hollypaw panted, ducking through the bracken.

"If they don't, I'm sure you'll tell them," Lionpaw teased.

Hollypaw nudged him with her shoulder and sent him veering against a bramble bush.

"Hey!" he protested. Hollypaw sped ahead and Lionpaw pelted after her.

She raced past Ashfur and Stormfur and swerved to shelter behind Brackenfur. "Help!" she squealed. "Lionpaw's trying to get me!"

A purr rumbled in Brackenfur's throat. "Don't hide behind me!" He lengthened his stride and shot forward, leaving Hollypaw undefended. Lionpaw caught up with her and nudged her, making her stumble.

"Now we're even!" he called.

"I'll get you later!" she threatened.

The patrol pounded down the slope toward the lakeshore. Graystripe pulled ahead, clearly excited to be going to a Gathering with his Clan once more. He glanced, eyes shining, at Millie, as she caught up with him. "Do you still think you made the right decision, coming with me to the Clan?"

"Wherever you are is the right place for me to be," Millie replied quietly.

Leaves turned to grass and then marsh beneath their paws, and the cats slowed as they skirted the lake. They had to travel slowly over the boggy earth, which gave way under every pawstep.

Before long Hollypaw could see the silhouette of the fallen tree bridging the gap between shore and island. Her paws tingled, and she quickened her step. Firestar and Squirrelflight were already crossing, with Sandstorm and Honeypaw right behind them, while Brambleclaw and Berrypaw waited their turn next to Leafpool.

"Are you ready?" Brackenfur asked as he caught up to her by the tree-bridge.

"Totally!" she mewed.

"Up you go, then." Brackenfur waited while Hollypaw scrambled up among the tangled roots. She unsheathed her claws, ready for the slippery bark. Gripping on tightly, she wove her way among the twigs and knotholes, relieved when she had crossed the black, lapping water and could jump down onto the shore.

While the other cats crossed behind her, Hollypaw watched for Firestar's signal. Moonlight glittered on the lake beyond the trees, and she could smell the scents of the other Clans already on the island. Her heart thumped as hard as rabbits' paws when Firestar nodded and headed into the undergrowth.

Hollypaw couldn't wait to talk to her fellow apprentices. She was one of them now, and she realized how much she had felt like an outsider when she had been a medicine cat apprentice.

"I hope—" she began.

But Lionpaw had halted. He was staring into the clearing. "Something's wrong," he whispered.

"What?" Hollypaw glanced around, suddenly apprehensive.

It seemed different from last time. The other cats were huddled with their Clanmates, not milling around or sharing tongues with different Clans. They looked thinner and angrier, their eyes gleaming like foxes'.

"What's wrong with everyone?" Hollypaw mewed.

"It's been a tough leaf-bare," Firestar reassured his Clan-mates. "Everyone's weaker and hungrier. They'll be warier. So be cautious."

Hollypaw stayed by her brother. She didn't like the angry glances that flashed from warrior to warrior.

"Don't worry," Lionpaw murmured. "Everyone will settle down soon."

A hiss and a yowl made Hollypaw jerk her head around. Fur and claws flew as Berrypaw leaped onto Owlpaw. The ShadowClan apprentice wrestled him over and pinned him to the ground, but Berrypaw slid sideways with a quick, clean jerk and unbalanced him.

"Stop it!" Brambleclaw's fierce mew echoed around the trees. He raced to his apprentice and plucked him away from Owlpaw by his scruff. Berrypaw's legs still churned in the air, his claws gleaming in the moonlight.

"There's a truce!" Brambleclaw reminded him sternly.

Hollypaw glanced up at the moon. Thin wisps of cloud were drifting in front of it. Her heart lurched. Had Berrypaw and Owlpaw upset StarClan?

Berrypaw shook out his pelt as Brambleclaw dropped him unceremoniously to the ground. "Owlpaw started it," he growled. "He called me a kittypet!"

Hollypaw felt her pelt bristle. Berrypaw had been training for moons to be a ThunderClan warrior. And yet he wasn't truly Clanborn. He had been born in horseplace with

Hazelpaw and Mousepaw, not in the hollow. Daisy had brought them to ThunderClan only to stop the Twolegs from taking them away.

A yowl sounded from the Great Oak. "Let the Gathering begin!" Firestar called.

Hollypaw wove her way through her Clanmates to sit between Leafpool and Brambleclaw. Lionpaw squeezed in beside her.

"Look at the way Blackstar is glaring at us!" she gulped. The ShadowClan leader was staring down at the Thunder-Clan cats through slitted eyes, his lips twitching as though he only just suppressed a snarl.

Leopardstar spoke first. "RiverClan has suffered this past moon." The golden-spotted tabby gazed solemnly around the Clans. "Just when we hoped newleaf would bring an end to the hard season, new frosts brought more hunger, and with it, sickness."

Cats from all four Clans murmured in agreement.

Leopardstar narrowed her eyes. "Who knows what the next seasons will bring? Twolegs invaded our territories last greenleaf. Will they come in greater numbers this time and destroy our land, just as they did in the forest?"

"Why should they?" Ashfoot called from among Wind-Clan.

"Why should leaf-bare have brought so much tragedy?" Leopardstar shot back. "Is StarClan trying to send us a message? Could it be that we do not belong here?"

"I've had no signs from StarClan to suggest anything like

that!" Leafpool put in quickly.

"Nor I!" Barkface agreed.

"We've always had to endure times of hunger and sickness," Squirrelflight pointed out. "Even back in the forest!"

"Squirrelflight's right!" Onestar agreed.

Leopardstar glanced sideways to Blackstar, and Hollypaw noticed her flick her tail, as though she was prompting the ShadowClan leader to do something.

Blackstar's eyes grew thin and hostile. "Littlecloud has had a sign!" he announced.

All eyes turned to Littlecloud. The ShadowClan medicine cat's pelt was ruffled, and his eyes were clouded with anxiety. "I dreamed that a warrior brought strange new prey into the camp, a bird I had never seen before. I bit into it and found its belly writhing with maggots."

Anxious whispers rippled around the Clans. They were silenced by Blackstar. "StarClan is warning us that strangers are poisoning the Clans!"

"They might be warning us to be wary of unfamiliar prey!" Leafpool objected.

A shadow fell over the clearing, and Hollypaw saw with dread that more thin clouds were passing in front of the moon. StarClan was definitely unhappy.

Blackstar glared at Firestar. "You have given a home to so many cats born outside the forest that you are weakening Clan blood," he accused. "Why else would StarClan let us suffer?" He stared accusingly at the ThunderClan leader, then let his gaze sweep over Stormfur, Brook, Berrypaw, and Millie.

Outrage churned in Hollypaw's belly. *They are all warriors!* Even she had distant kittypet blood, but she was Clanborn through and through.

"Kittypets and outsiders!" Oakfur sneered.

"You are destroying the warrior code!" Owlpaw yowled.

Brambleclaw's pelt bristled, and Stormfur got to his paws, curling his lip in a snarl. But Firestar's fierce gaze flashed across the Clans, silencing them.

"We will not be blamed for bad weather!" he hissed. "We suffered worse things in our old home. StarClan led us here. Did any cat expect that they would lead us to an easy life?" The Clans listened in silence at first; then some cats began to murmur in agreement as he went on. "Surely it is our struggle against hardship that makes us true warriors." He glared at Blackstar. "You think fresh blood in the Clans will weaken us? A life without hardship would weaken us more."

Onestar nodded. "Blackstar talks as though StarClan should grant us nothing but blessings. Does he want us to live the spoiled life of kittypets?"

Blackstar shot him a look of cold fury.

Ashfur got to his paws. "Pure blood is no guarantee of virtue!"

"May I have permission to speak?" Hollypaw turned and saw Squirrelflight padding her way to the front of the Clan. Firestar nodded.

Squirrelflight gazed calmly around the Clans. Hollypaw felt pride warming her pelt. *Go on, Squirrelflight!*

"We have all suffered," Squirrelflight acknowledged. "But

we must look forward, not back. Newleaf has come. Our territories are warming up and filling with prey. Thanks to Mothwing, we all have a good supply of catmint."

As she spoke, a warm breeze swept across the island. The clearing brightened as the clouds started to drift away from the moon.

"StarClan agrees with her!"

"It's a sign!"

Pelts smoothed and tails fell still as the cats began to calm down.

Squirrelflight went on. "This is the start of our second newleaf by the lake. We should mark its return with a special Gathering."

Hollypaw leaned forward, puzzled.

"While the moon is still full, we could meet in daylight."

"Why should we do that?" Blackstar snapped. "The truce comes only with the full moon."

"The moon is as full during the day as it is at night," Crowfeather pointed out.

"We should meet," Squirrelflight pressed, "to share skills and training methods. To show that we have not forgotten the Great Journey that brought us here, when the warrior code protected us as one."

"We could have contests!" For the first time Pebblepaw spoke. The RiverClan apprentice's eyes were shining with enthusiasm.

"The apprentices from each Clan could compete against

one another to see who has the best skills!" Heatherpaw called out.

Even Owlpaw looked interested. "I bet I could beat any ThunderClan cat at hunting!" he boasted.

"No cat could beat Pouncepaw at catching fish!" called Mistyfoot.

"That's cheating!" Lionpaw mewed. "Every cat knows only RiverClan enjoy getting their paws wet!"

Hollypaw realized that the Clans' fear and anger had turned to excitement and friendly challenge. Her mother had distracted them from accusations of impure blood by reminding them of the time they had united to make the Great Journey, and of how much they could still offer to one another. Hollypaw glanced up at Firestar. The ThunderClan leader sat in silence, his eyes gleaming with pride as he looked down at Squirrelflight.

Even Onestar seemed keen. "Where should we hold this competition?"

"What about on the land where we first sheltered when we arrived at the lake?" Ashfur answered.

Leopardstar shook her head. "It's too marshy."

"The land between the forest and the lake on our territory would be great for a Gathering," Firestar offered. "It's grassy, so all cats will be used to the terrain. And it drains well even in the wettest weather. There's enough space, and no cat will get his paws wet. So long as each Clan brings its own fresh-kill, we could meet there."

"The moon will still be almost full in two sunrises," Leopardstar meowed. "Shall we meet then?" She gazed around the Clans. Heads were nodding and tails flicking with excitement.

"Very well," Leopardstar concluded. She turned to Firestar. "If it's all right with you, we will meet at sunhigh."

Firestar nodded.

Hollypaw shifted her paws, suddenly uneasy. The Gathering would be fun, but it wouldn't stop the other Clans from blaming ThunderClan's mixed blood the next time something went wrong.

"Then it's settled," Onestar agreed. He leaped down from the tree, followed by Firestar and Leopardstar. Only Blackstar lingered, his eyes burning with anger.

But the Gathering was breaking up, the cats padding away from the clearing, chattering like starlings.

"Can you believe that?" Lionpaw asked.

Hollypaw glanced back at her mother, who was padding toward the trees beside Brambleclaw and Firestar. "Squirrel-flight smoothed things over." *But for how long?*

"I can't wait to tell Jaypaw!" Lionpaw mewed. "Do you think he'll like the idea?"

A knot of unease twisted in Hollypaw's belly. How could a blind cat join in with the contests? "Perhaps medicine cats won't take part," she mewed. "After all, they're not like warriors. They're more used to helping one another than competing."

Cinderpaw came hurtling up beside them as they neared

the fallen tree. "I bet Lionpaw wins the hunting," she panted.

Lionpaw purred self-consciously. "Well, Hollypaw will win the fighting," he mewed.

Brook's quiet voice sounded behind them. "As long as you all try your best, your Clan will be proud of you."

Hollypaw couldn't imagine *not* trying her best. Her pelt tingled. Perhaps this kind of Gathering might resolve something after all. It would be a chance for ThunderClan to prove to the other Clans—especially ShadowClan—that they were *all* worthy warriors, and that being Clanborn had nothing to do with it.

CHAPTER 25

Sunhigh was approaching—Jaypaw could feel the warmth on his back. He padded into the camp with a wad of dock leaves clasped in his jaws. The sour flavor had sucked all the moisture from his mouth. It disguised every other scent, and he had to rely on the memory of his paws to find the path back to the medicine den.

As he crossed the clearing, he could hear the pawsteps of his Clanmates hurrying around him. The whole Clan had been busy since before dawn preparing for the daylight Gathering. *They're only going to spend the day hunting and fighting,* Jaypaw thought irritably. *Why are they acting like it's something special? They get to do that anyway.*

"Squirrelflight!" Firestar called down from Highledge.

"Yes?" She sounded out of breath.

"Did you find a good route for the squirrel hunt?"

"I sent Brambleclaw out with a patrol," she replied. "He's checking it now. The ShadowClan border might be best. The squirrels are still busy there, digging up their nut stores."

"What about the tree-climbing contest?" Firestar prompted.

"Spiderleg told me that the Sky Oak is in full bud, but he doesn't think it'll be damaged by having so many apprentices climbing it at once."

"Good," Firestar meowed. "Are there hunting patrols out? We don't want our visitors to think we are prey-poor."

"Two. Birchfall and Thornclaw are leading them."

"Jaypaw!" Firestar scrambled down from Highledge and caught up to him. "Leafpool will need your help today in case of any accidents. You won't be able to join in any of the contests, I'm afraid."

The whole Clan had been tiptoeing around him like mice since the daylight Gathering had been announced, too scared to say out loud what he knew they'd all been thinking—that he would be useless in any apprentice contest. He had noticed right away how they never mentioned his name as they speculated about which apprentices would win. Jaypaw didn't reply to Firestar and scraped angrily through the bramble entrance to the medicine den.

"Oh, good!" Leafpool was waiting for him. "You found lots. Now we'll be ready for any scratches."

Jaypaw dropped the dock leaves on the ground. He flicked his tongue, trying to wet it again. "I don't see why we have to be responsible for all the other Clans," he complained. "If their apprentices want to show off on our territory, their own medicine cats should look after them."

"All the medicine cats will be working together to make sure every cat is cared for properly," Leafpool reminded him.

"I bet Willowpaw and Kestrelpaw haven't spent the

morning looking for herbs," Jaypaw muttered. "Even *they* will have been practicing their hunting skills for the contests."

He sensed frustration in Leafpool's quick movements as she stored the dock with the other herbs, but her mew was calm. "I know how much you want to take part, Jaypaw, but I need you to help me."

The fury that had been simmering in Jaypaw's belly suddenly bubbled over. "Don't lie!" he fumed. "I'm not allowed to take part because there's no way I can compete against real apprentices! Firestar doesn't want me embarrassing the Clan."

"You know that isn't true!" Leafpool told him, shocked.

"Then why doesn't he let me try one of the contests?"

"Maybe if you'd had more battle training or hunting experience, he would!" Leafpool's mew was brittle as she tried to keep her temper. "But you started your medicine training late, and the outbreak of greencough has stopped us from working on your other skills."

Jaypaw didn't reply. Hollypaw had been a medicine cat apprentice for only the blink of an eye, and *she'd* had battle training from Leafpool. He was beginning to wonder if his mentor had decided it was a waste of time to teach him any warrior skills at all.

Leafpool changed the subject. "Squirrelflight must be getting tired. She's been busy all morning. Will you take her some herbs?"

Jaypaw padded sulkily to the herb store and mixed the leaves Squirrelflight would need, then folded them in a wrap, which he picked up delicately between his teeth. He nosed his way out of the den and listened for his mother's voice. He found her beneath Highledge talking to Brambleclaw.

Jaypaw dropped the herbs at Squirrelflight's paws. "Leafpool wants you to eat these."

"That's kind of her." Squirrelflight sniffed at the herbs. "Did you mix these yourself? They smell sweeter than usual."

"I put in some heather nectar to help with the taste," Jaypaw mumbled.

Squirrelflight thanked him with a brisk lick between his ears. "That was thoughtful."

"It's nothing," he muttered. He turned away before she could do anything else embarrassing, though he couldn't ignore the small glimmer of happiness that flickered in his chest.

Suddenly pawsteps drummed through the entrance and skidded to a halt. It was Lionpaw and Hollypaw; their excitement howled into the camp like a rush of wind, rippling Jaypaw's fur.

"They're here!" Lionpaw panted.

Hollypaw trotted in circles, unable to keep still. "WindClan are heading down toward the lake!"

Foxkit's and Icekit's tiny paws pattered from the nursery.

"Are they really here?" Foxkit demanded.

"Any sign of ShadowClan?" Icekit's mew was tinged with nervousness.

"Not yet," Lionpaw told him. "But it looks like just about the whole of WindClan have come."

"I wish we were going!" Foxkit mewed.

"We'll have fun here," Ferncloud called from the nursery entrance.

"Why do we have to stay in camp?" Icekit wailed. "It's not fair."

"Life isn't fair," Jaypaw growled, and padded mutinously back to the medicine den. *That's why I'm going to be stuck in camp like a kit!*

Birchfall and Thornclaw pounded through the thorn tunnel, their patrols crowding after them. Jaypaw smelled the delicious flavors of fresh-kill. Every cat must have caught a piece of prey.

"Well done!" Firestar told them. "No cat will go hungry today."

A yowl rang through the forest above the hollow.

"That's Leopardstar!" Lionpaw mewed. "RiverClan have arrived!"

"It must be time to go," Hollypaw put in. "The Gathering starts at sunhigh."

Hollypaw was taking part in one of the first contests, a match to see which apprentice had the best fighting skills. At the same time, Lionpaw would be set against a WindClan apprentice in a hunting contest. Jealousy seared Jaypaw's fur.

Rocks clattered from Highledge as Firestar bounded down into the clearing, but Jaypaw nosed his way into the medicine den, away from the eager mews of the warriors and apprentices as they paced impatiently around the entrance. He tried to block his ears as Firestar called "Good luck!" to the Clan.

But he still heard the drumming of paws as ThunderClan raced away through the thorn tunnel.

An eerie silence gripped the camp.

"Jaypaw." Leafpool's mew sounded from the herb store. "Will you help me make up some poultices?"

Jaypaw forced away his black thoughts and padded to Leafpool's side to begin chewing up some of the dock he had brought back earlier. As they worked, Icekit and Foxkit charged noisily around the clearing.

"Don't forget," Ferncloud was calling, "you each have to bring me a beetle, some moss, and a fly."

"I'm going to win!" Icekit mewed.

"No, you won't," Foxkit replied. "I'll find them first and I'll be champion!"

Their mews echoed around the deserted camp, and Jaypaw was aware of the emptiness like hunger in the pit of his belly.

Am I always going to be left behind?

"That's enough for now." Leafpool's mew took him by surprise. "There's enough there for scratches on every cat in all four Clans."

Jaypaw spat out the last mouthful of dock and sat back on his haunches, licking his paws to clear the taste from his tongue.

"I should be at the Gathering, in case there are injuries," the medicine cat announced. "Besides, I want to go and watch Hollypaw fight. Why don't you come with me?"

Jaypaw shook his head. There was no way he was going if

he wasn't allowed to take part.

"Very well." Leafpool didn't try to persuade him. Instead she padded quietly out of the den.

Left alone, Jaypaw suddenly felt lost. Far in the distance he could hear the excited cries of warriors and their apprentices drifting through the trees. He wanted to wail to StarClan that it wasn't fair. But he would not behave like a kit, however much he was treated like one. Instead, he began to tidy up the herbs, pushing all the leaves into neat piles and lining up the poultices, ready for any cats who might return injured.

Suddenly a strange sensation began to prick his tail. It crawled along his spine, setting his pelt tingling. Images flooded his mind, swelling behind his eyes.

He was buried, unable to breathe, choking on dry earth soaked in the stench of fox and badger. His mind swirled in terror. Where was the fox? The badger? He expected to feel their teeth rip his flesh at any moment. He stared wildly around, but all he could see was crumbling brown soil. Above him light flickered, then dimmed as more soil tumbled down on him, stinging his eyes, filling his ears and nostrils. He was drowning—not in water this time, but *earth*.

"Help!" Dirt filled his mouth as he tried to scream.

He scrabbled desperately, trying to fight his way out. Was StarClan so disappointed that they had ordered the earth to swallow him up? He kicked out with his hind legs, trying to fight his way up. His lungs were screaming for air. He could see his paws churning in front of his muzzle. But they were not his own mottled paws; they were pale and wide, their fur thick and bunched at the claws.

He was seeing through Lionpaw's eyes!

Jaypaw drove the images out of his head and knew he was back in the medicine den, surrounded by the scent of leaves and with the hollow empty and silent outside.

Where was Lionpaw right now?

The hunting contest!

He would be scouring the ShadowClan border for prey.

Like lightning, Jaypaw shot out of the medicine den and pelted into the forest, every sense alive as he wove through the undergrowth like a snake. He had to get to Lionpaw before this *thing*—whatever it was—happened.

Hollypaw watched as Lionpaw and Breezepaw scampered up the slope and disappeared among the trees to hunt. The fur along Lionpaw's spine was spiked with excitement.

Good luck!

"Hollypaw, are you ready?" Onestar called.

Hollypaw spun around. Heatherpaw was already waiting on the patch of smooth grass, circled by warriors and apprentices, her shoulders squared, ready for the match.

"Come on, Hollypaw," Brambleclaw urged. He stood beside Brackenfur, his eyes shining.

Hollypaw could hear the excited murmuring of the Clan cats. She felt as though fish were wriggling in her belly, but she wasn't going to show any cat she was nervous. She crouched opposite Heatherpaw, narrowing her eyes.

"Keep your claws sheathed," Onestar ordered. He swept

his tail over the grass, and Hollypaw tensed. The WindClan apprentice was small, but Hollypaw knew that Heatherpaw had two moons' more experience than she did, and that her sleek pelt hid hard muscle.

"Begin!" Onestar called.

Heatherpaw leaped. She crashed into Hollypaw, bowling her over. Hollypaw felt teeth grip her scruff, not hard enough to break the skin, but firm enough to make her freeze with alarm. She couldn't be beaten this easily! Heatherpaw had caught her like a rabbit.

Thinking quickly, Hollypaw tucked her head and kicked out with her hind legs. She somersaulted forward, taking Heatherpaw with her and sending the WindClan apprentice sprawling onto her back. Free of her grip, Hollypaw leaped up, spun around, and flew at Heatherpaw. But her rival had rolled out of the way. Seething, Hollypaw landed on bare grass.

She glanced sideways. Heatherpaw was darting toward her. Energy flashed in her paws, and she leaped high into the air. As Heatherpaw skidded wildly beneath her, Hollypaw crashed down onto the confused WindClan cat's back. Wrapping her paws around her opponent, she rolled Heatherpaw over and began pummeling her with her hind paws.

Heatherpaw, slippery as a snake, wriggled free of her grasp. She reared onto her hind legs and faced Hollypaw with flailing forepaws. Hollypaw rose to meet her, and the two apprentices battled like dancing hares.

"Finish her, Heatherpaw!" Crowfeather called.

"Knock her off her paws!" Brackenfur yowled.

What do you think I'm trying to do?

Hollypaw's muzzle was beginning to sting. Heatherpaw's blows were strong and well aimed, and Hollypaw didn't want this to go on for much longer. Taking a deep breath, she ducked, leaving Heatherpaw flapping her paws at thin air. She scooted between Heatherpaw's hind legs, unbalancing the WindClan apprentice. Then she twisted and sank her teeth—careful not to draw blood—into Heatherpaw's scruff, pressing her chin into the ground. Heatherpaw let out an angry wail, struggling furiously, but Hollypaw had dug her claws into the earth on either side of the WindClan apprentice. Heatherpaw could not get free.

"It's all over!" Onestar meowed. "Hollypaw is the winner!"

The ThunderClan cats cheered, and Hollypaw let go.

Heatherpaw jumped up. "Well done," she panted. "That was a great move at the end!"

"Thanks," mewed Hollypaw. "You fought well, too."

"Good work, Hollypaw!" Brambleclaw rushed over and swept his tail over his daughter's flank.

"She wouldn't have beaten *me* so easily," hissed a voice close by.

Heatherpaw narrowed her eyes at Ivypaw, a ShadowClan apprentice.

Hollypaw spun around. "Want to bet on that?"

She felt a paw cuff her ear. "One win is enough." Brackenfur was staring at her proudly.

Suddenly Hollypaw saw a distinctive gray shape flash across the top of the slope. "Jaypaw! You just missed me winning the contest!" But her brother didn't seem to hear. He pelted away into the trees, heading for ShadowClan territory. What in the name of StarClan was he up to now?

Jaypaw dashed along the slope toward the ShadowClan border, remembering the stench of fox and badger from his vision. There was an old badger set near the border, dug out of a fox den. His mother had described it to him. She had helped chase a badger from it long ago, soon after the four Clans came to the lake.

He dug his claws harder into the grass and pushed himself on. Fresh scents rolled in from the lake, but he focused on the smell of badger, searching it out as he raced into the woods. His instincts and senses were not enough to guide him quickly through this strange territory. He skidded to a halt, sniffing desperately, and began to feel his way with his whiskers. *StarClan, let me see now! Please! I have to find Lionpaw!*

Suddenly he tasted the rank stench of badger. It was old and laced with the smell of fox. He gazed around blindly, wondering where Lionpaw was. Then he heard pawsteps speeding over the leaf-strewn forest floor ahead.

He could smell Lionpaw.

Then Breezepaw.

Then squirrel.

Their excitement singed his pelt. With a jolt of terror, Jaypaw realized that the two apprentices were chasing the squirrel straight toward the badger stench. The place where the ground was not safe, where the earth would swallow them up . . .

"No!" His wail rang through the trees. He pelted forward, breathless with fear. Then shock pierced him and he skidded to a halt.

There was no sound of pawsteps. Only the squirrel's claws skittering away up a tree. The forest was deadly silent.

"Lionpaw!" Jaypaw shot forward. He stumbled as the earth became rock beneath his paws. The sun was suddenly hot on his back. A clearing, ringed with trees. Boulders reared up before him.

His fur stood on end as muffled mews sounded from above.

"Help!"

"StarClan, save me!"

Feeling his way frantically, Jaypaw clambered up the rocks. Where had they fallen in? Was he near? The ground was still rock beneath his paws. It flattened, then sloped smoothly away in front of him. He began to slide forward. Blood roared in his ears. *What if I fall in too?* The vision played in his mind again—earth choking his ears, his eyes, his lungs screaming for air. He unsheathed his claws. They scraped over the stone as he half crept, half slithered downward.

Suddenly his front paws touched sand and sank. Jaypaw sprang backward, clinging to the rock with his hind paws. Then the sand moved; he felt it quivering beneath his forepaws as though something squirmed beneath it.

They're down there!

Gripping with his hind claws, he squatted down and began to dig, scooping out earth as fast as he could.

"Help!" he wailed, hoping some cat would hear. "Over here!"

His hind claws lost their grip and he slid forward, his forepaws sinking into the sand. "StarClan help me!"

He reared backward, his muscles screaming with the effort. He couldn't give up now. He slithered forward again and kept digging, his hind paws trembling with the effort of keeping him out of the sinking ground. Soil pressed up against his chest and chin. Terror gripped his whole body. The vision was so strong in his mind he could feel soil in his throat and see nothing but earth.

Suddenly his paws brushed against fur. With a rush of hope, he hooked his claws into it and heaved with all his strength. The fur wriggled and fought in his grip, struggling to push upward until Jaypaw could scrabble far enough back to drag the body out of the soil.

Spluttering and gasping, Lionpaw slithered away from the patch of soft earth and collapsed on the rock. Jaypaw plunged his paws back into the soil. Breezepaw was still down there.

"What's going on?" Crowfeather's shocked cry sounded behind him.

Without stopping Jaypaw screeched at the WindClan warrior, "The den collapsed. Lionpaw and Breezepaw fell in!"

Crowfeather was at his side in an instant, sending sandy soil flying in his desperation to save his son.

Claws scrabbled up the boulders behind them. "Crowfeather?" Heatherpaw's mew sounded breathless.

"Breezepaw's still buried!" Crowfeather panted.

"Breezepaw?" Nightcloud's horrified gasp sounded close by. The WindClan she-cat must have leaped up the boulders with Heatherpaw. She pressed in beside Jaypaw and began digging. "Oh, my precious kit!"

Then Jaypaw felt another movement in the earth beneath his claws. "I can feel him!"

Crowfeather burrowed his paws toward Jaypaw's and lunged down. A growl of effort rose in his throat as he heaved his son out from the suffocating earth. Jaypaw felt soil spray his face and sting his eyes as Breezepaw's body was dragged free. He listened closely for the apprentice's breathing. It had stopped.

"Fetch Leafpool!" he shrieked.

"I'm here!" Leafpool's voice came as a rush of warm air to Jaypaw's ears.

"Can you save them?" he begged. "I came here as fast as I could, but—"

"Lionpaw is breathing," Leafpool told him. "I've cleared the soil from his throat."

Jaypaw felt Breezepaw stir, and for a moment he thought the WindClan apprentice had recovered. Then he realized that Leafpool was wrenching open his jaws.

"Your paws are smallest," she told Jaypaw. "Reach into his mouth and clear as much dirt as you can."

Jaypaw sheathed his claws. Then, forcing himself to stop

trembling, he reached delicately into Breezepaw's mouth. He could hear Crowfeather's heart pounding. Nightcloud was quivering in terror behind him. Leafpool's concentration was the only calmness he felt around him, and he clung to it as he scooped the earth from the back of Breezepaw's throat.

Suddenly Breezepaw coughed and his body writhed as he spat up earth from his stomach and lungs.

"Will he be all right?" Nightcloud whispered.

"Yes, he will," Leafpool promised.

"Thank you, Leafpool," Crowfeather murmured.

"I would give my last drop of blood to save your kit," Leafpool meowed softly to Crowfeather. "You know that."

Jaypaw flinched at the tension between them, pricking the air like rain.

"*Our* kit was lucky that Jaypaw was here." Nightcloud's comment was edged with sharpness.

"Jaypaw?" Lionpaw croaked.

Jaypaw spun around and crouched beside his brother. "That was close, even for you," he mewed.

Lionpaw's breathing was labored but steady. "I thought I was going to join StarClan."

Leafpool's whiskers brushed Jaypaw's cheek. "They were lucky you were here."

"I nearly wasn't fast enough," he replied.

"But you made it to them in time," she pointed out. "You were brave to try to get them out on your own." She flicked his shoulder with her tail. "Come on, let's get them back to the hollow."

* * *

Jaypaw held out his paw so that Lionpaw could lick the poppy seeds from his pad. Lionpaw lapped them up gratefully. He was still trembling, even though he was safely in Jaypaw's nest, curled beside Breezepaw.

Lionpaw had managed to stagger back to the ThunderClan camp on his own paws. Hollypaw and Squirrelflight had pressed against either side of him to take some of his weight, while Brambleclaw had rushed to fetch Firestar.

Nightcloud had carried Breezepaw like a kit. His hind legs had dragged over the forest floor, but he was too exhausted by shock to complain. Crowfeather had padded beside his mate the whole way, offering to help, but Nightcloud kept hold of her kit as though she might lose him again at any moment. Now she lay curled around him, warming his quivering body, her breath falling and rising in time with his.

"Try to persuade them to sleep," Leafpool told Jaypaw. "I'll go and tell the others they're all right." Firestar, Crowfeather, Heatherpaw, Brambleclaw, and Squirrelflight were waiting anxiously outside. The brambles swished as the medicine cat padded out of the den.

"I'll make sure they sleep," Nightcloud meowed. Jaypaw heard the swish of her tail as she swept it rhythmically over the earth-powdered pelts of the two apprentices.

"You were so brilliant." Hollypaw's breath tickled his ear.

Her comment made his ears hot with embarrassment. Why did she have to treat him like a hero? Crowfeather had acted the same way as they'd padded home through the forest.

"You behaved like a warrior," the WindClan cat had told him.

But Jaypaw did not feel like a warrior. If he had run faster he would have been able to warn Lionpaw. If only his blindness had not slowed him down.

"Lionpaw and Breezepaw wouldn't have been hurt if I'd gotten there sooner," he mewed to Hollypaw.

"But how did you find them at all?" He felt her stare burning his pelt. "They were chasing a squirrel—it could have run anywhere."

Jaypaw hesitated. "I had a vision," he confessed. "I saw what was going to happen." Panic swept through him as he remembered the sensation of choking, the taste of soil in his mouth, and the sight of paws churning desperately in front of his muzzle. "When I saw the color of the paws, I realized they weren't mine, but Lionpaw's."

"Saw?" Hollypaw's gasp made Jaypaw jump. "You *saw* his paws?"

"Shhh!" Suddenly he wished he hadn't told her anything. If StarClan thought he was trying to show off, they might take his one chance at sight away. Jaypaw tried to make his sister understand. "Sometimes I can see in dreams and visions," he whispered. "It's hard to explain how. It's . . ." He paused, groping for words. "It's just different."

He felt her mind teeming with questions. Then it cleared and a purr rumbled in her throat. "StarClan must have given you this gift for a reason. I knew you'd make a great medicine cat." She brushed her cheek along his, then padded out through the brambles.

Jaypaw sighed. He was glad Hollypaw hadn't asked any difficult questions, but was this how it was going to be from now on? A separate life, beyond the understanding of his Clanmates? With their every heartbeat depending on him?

"Jaypaw!" Brambleclaw called through the brambles. "Come down to the lake for the end of the Gathering."

"Firestar's going to be announcing the winners!" Heatherpaw added excitedly.

Jaypaw curled his lip. The last thing he wanted to do was to watch the other apprentices celebrate their warrior skills. He pricked his ears toward Lionpaw and Breezepaw. Nightcloud had done as she promised, and both apprentices were sleeping deeply. He pushed his way out of the den. "Who's going to watch Lionpaw and Breezepaw?" he asked, looking for an excuse to stay in the camp.

"I will," Leafpool told him.

"Come on, Jaypaw," Hollypaw begged. "It'll be fun."

"You should meet some of the apprentices from the other Clans," Firestar meowed. "You haven't had the chance yet."

Reluctantly, Jaypaw followed his Clanmates as they trekked down to the slopes beside the lake. Crowfeather and Heatherpaw went to join WindClan, and Firestar headed off to speak with the other leaders by the lakeshore. Brambleclaw sat down to wait on the hillside, and Jaypaw sat beside him with Squirrelflight and Hollypaw.

"I've not seen the Clans so relaxed since the Great Journey," Brambleclaw observed.

Squirrelflight's happiness warmed the air around her. "Even ShadowClan seem content."

"But Blackstar is staring at everyone, proud as a black-bird, as if his apprentices won every contest," Hollypaw chipped in.

"Clans of trees, hills, and streams!"

Jaypaw heard his leader's call. The cats fell silent, and Jaypaw sensed their gazes turn toward the ThunderClan leader like the sun shifting in the sky.

"All our apprentices did well today," Firestar declared. "They hunted and fought like true warriors!"

Jubilant mews rose from all the Clans.

"I have talked with Leopardstar, Blackstar, and Onestar, and we have decided that the contest is a draw," Firestar went on. "Every Clan showed itself to be worthy of StarClan's approval."

"That's not fair!" Owlpaw snarled, the ShadowClan apprentices bunched around him muttering in agreement. "I was the best hunter! Lionpaw and Breezepaw didn't even come back!"

"Hush!" A ShadowClan she-cat silenced him. "They almost died!"

Blackstar told Owlpaw, "It's all right; we all know who really won, even if we have to share the victory. You shall have first pick of the prey when we get home."

Leopardstar lifted her voice. "Out of RiverClan's apprentices, Pouncepaw will eat the best fish tonight as a reward for her excellent hunting skills."

"Heatherpaw shall have the fattest rabbit," Onestar called. "She climbed to the top of the Sky Oak!"

Jaypaw's muzzle sank to his chest. He didn't want to hear how well every other apprentice had done.

"And from ThunderClan," Firestar announced, "Hollypaw may choose first prey from the pile. She fought excellently for such a new apprentice."

Jaypaw felt pride surge in his sister's pelt, and hated the jealousy that throbbed in his paws. "Well done," he mumbled. "I'd better get back and see if Leafpool needs help."

"Please stay," Hollypaw mewed.

Jaypaw shook his head and turned away. He began to climb the slope toward the tree line. Then Onestar's voice sounded from below.

"There is one apprentice who deserves a special mention above all the others today."

Jaypaw kept on walking.

"Jaypaw."

Jaypaw stopped.

"This young ThunderClan apprentice has earned the gratitude of every cat for his courage and quick thinking today."

Jaypaw felt the curious gaze of all the Clans ruffle his pelt. He turned self-consciously to face them.

Firestar joined in. "He saved two apprentices. They nearly suffocated when an old badger set collapsed beneath them. Jaypaw found them in time and dug them out."

Shocked mews turned into cheers. They were cheering for him! Hollypaw's and Squirrelflight's pelts suddenly brushed against his flanks.

Hollypaw pressed her nose against his cheek. "You're a hero."

Could blind cats be heroes? Jaypaw wondered. *Perhaps . . .*

"This has been a good Gathering," Firestar meowed as the cheering died down. "It has reminded me of the Great Journey, and I think it marks a successful start to the second newleaf in our new home. A lot has changed, but we are still true warriors!"

True warriors! Like plunging into freezing water, Jaypaw remembered how lost he had felt in the fight against ShadowClan—how desperately he had longed to see, how he knew he would never be able to defend himself properly, let alone his Clanmates. StarClan had seen this too, which was why they'd decided he should be a medicine cat.

But Jaypaw didn't want consoling. He wanted things to be *different*. He turned back toward the forest and began to pad home to the camp. It didn't matter if all the Clan leaders called him a hero. He would never be a true warrior.

Nightcloud was sleeping beside Breezepaw and Lionpaw when Jaypaw returned. Leafpool was dozing in her nest.

"Is the Gathering over?" she mewed sleepily as Jaypaw padded into the den.

"Nearly," Jaypaw replied. "The others will be back soon, I expect." He listened to the apprentices' breathing, relieved to find it deep and slow. The weight of the day suddenly dragged at his paws. He longed to curl up in his own familiar nest, but Lionpaw and Breezepaw needed it more than he did.

Instead, he padded out of the den and clawed up a few clumps of grass. Pressing them among the old brambles piled beside the medicine den, he shaped himself a makeshift nest. He spiraled down into it, his claws aching from the digging. There was still dirt trapped between them, but he was too tired to clean them. Instead, he rested his nose on them and closed his eyes.

"Jaypaw." Leafpool's mew made him jump. The medicine cat was leaning over him.

"Is everything okay?" he asked anxiously, beginning to scramble out of his nest.

Leafpool pressed him gently back with a paw. "Don't get up," she mewed. Something warm and soft touched his paws, and he smelled fresh mouse. "I thought you'd be hungry."

"Thank you," Jaypaw murmured.

"You did well today." As she turned and padded away, a strange sensation prickled through Jaypaw's pelt. There had been something wrong with the way Leafpool spoke to him just then. It was as if she were *wary* of him.

No. He must have imagined it.

He realized how hungry he was. His Clanmates were not yet back from the Gathering, and Jaypaw welcomed the peace in the hollow. With no other thoughts to crowd his mind, he ate his mouse and settled back down to sleep.

* * *

Jaypaw blinked open his eyes. He had not intended to dream. But here he was, in an unfamiliar place, standing on a dry, sandy bank in a narrow, high-sided gully. Above him, the night sky stretched like a black river, speckled with stars. There were no bushes to shelter him, no soft ferns thick with the smell of prey, just a few prickly shrubs and smooth boulders casting round shadows like puddles on the ground. A familiar scent pricked his nose.

Firestar.

Jaypaw gazed around, looking for the ThunderClan leader. But Firestar was nowhere to be seen.

Suddenly a low mew echoed from the roots of a tree on the far side of the gully.

Pelt pricking with curiosity, Jaypaw padded toward the sound and saw, among the great black arching roots, the shadow of an opening. Firestar's moonlit form was silhouetted against the dark entrance. Jaypaw ducked down behind a thick root.

"I will not fail!" Firestar was meowing.

What was he doing here? Who was he talking to? Jaypaw peered over the root. He could just make out the shape of an aged tomcat sitting in the shadows beneath the tree.

"Sometimes the destiny of one cat is not the destiny of the whole Clan," the old cat rasped.

Firestar's mind clouded with confusion; Jaypaw felt it like mist. The ThunderClan leader's breathing quickened as the tom spoke again, his voice suddenly smooth.

"There will be three, kin of your kin, who hold the power of the stars in their paws."

Blood pounded in Jaypaw's ears. An image scorched his mind: he saw himself beside Lionpaw and Hollypaw, eyes gleaming and pelts rippling with strength. With a dreadful, ominous certainty, he knew what the old cat was trying to tell Firestar.

He, Hollypaw, and Lionpaw were the three cats in the prophecy.

Coldness reached through his pelt, setting his fur on end as it drove into his flesh. And at the same time, excitement surged through his paws. *This* was his destiny—and Firestar had known all along, but had chosen not to reveal it. Why? Because he was afraid of having three such powerful cats in his Clan?

Jaypaw stifled the purr that rose inside him, knowing he must not be seen by the other cats. Suddenly it didn't matter that he was blind, or that he couldn't take part in the contest. None of that mattered in the face of this prophecy, that promised a greater destiny for him and his littermates than anything a cat had dreamed of before. Leafpool was right to be wary of him. *All* his Clanmates should be. And not just of him, but of Lionpaw and Hollypaw as well.

One day we will be so powerful that we shall command even StarClan!

KEEP WATCH FOR

POWER OF THREE

WARRIORS

BOOK 2:

DARK RIVER

Paw steps sounded behind her.

Hollypaw froze and glanced over her shoulder.

"It's just me." Cinderpaw's mew sounded from the darkness, and the gray tabby stepped out of the shadows. "I thought you might want company."

"Thanks." If Lionpaw was really making dirt, there was no harm in Cinderpaw's knowing, but if he wasn't and, as Hollypaw feared, he was out in the forest, she would be pleased to have a friend with her.

One after the other, they squeezed through the small tunnel to the dirtplace.

"He's not here," Cinderpaw whispered.

Hollypaw sighed, her heart heavy. "No."

"What do you think he's up to?"

Hollypaw didn't dare reply. She could guess why he might

have left the camp under cover of night, but she didn't want to believe it.

"His trail leads this way," Cinderpaw announced, pointing with her nose up the lakeward slope.

Hollypaw's belly tightened. The trail led up over the ridge and then around onto the moorland: WindClan territory. *Perhaps he's just exploring.* Hope stirred in her chest, but beneath it, like a rock, lay the dark suspicion that he was meeting Heatherpaw.

"We're going to follow him, aren't we?" Cinderpaw was staring at Hollypaw, her eyes clouded with worry. Had she guessed, too? Surely not. How could she know?

"Perhaps it's none of our business," Hollypaw suggested feebly.

"Of course it's our business! Our denmate is out there alone. What if something happened to him?"

"Is that the only reason you want to follow him—because he might be in danger?"

"No." Cinderpaw sat down. "I think he may be doing something he will live to regret."

Hollypaw was taken aback by her friend's serious tone. "Do you know something I don't?" she asked.

Cinderpaw shook her head. "It's just a feeling I have. I can't explain it. A feeling that Lionpaw is making a mistake that's been made before, that should never be made, that only leads to trouble. . . . " Her mew died away but her eyes were shining with emotion.

"Okay." Hollypaw could not ignore the strength of her friend's feeling. Nor could she ignore her own. All her instincts told her that Lionpaw was breaking the warrior code, and it was her duty as a Clan cat to stop him. She charged up the slope, sniffing the twigs and brambles for Lionpaw's scent, following the path he had taken to the top of the ridge. Cinderpaw bounded after her and they quickly reached the edge of the trees. The ground sloped away in front of them, down to the shore where the lake sparkled in the moonlight. Hollypaw scanned the distant moorland, half hoping to see Lionpaw, half hoping she wouldn't. If Lionpaw was roaming around at night, she wanted it to be on ThunderClan territory.

There was no sign of movement in the shadowy heather. Hollypaw plunged down the slope, following an old rabbit track through the coarsening grass. Underpaw the ground grew more peaty as they neared the WindClan border. Heather bushes sprouted on either side of the track as the slope flattened and the sound of water lapping the shore grew louder.

"Did you hear that?" Cinderpaw's hiss startled Hollypaw.

She pricked her ears. A small hollow, ringed by heather, lay in shadow ahead of them. From it came the sound of voices. Hollypaw's tail bristled as she recognized Lionpaw's mew. He sounded happy; happier than she had heard him in days. She crept forward, keeping low, and ducked into the swath of heather that shielded the hollow. Setting the bushes rustling, she wriggled between the bare stems and peered over the top of the slope.

Her brother was charging after a ball of moss like an excited kit. He dived at it as it landed and, with a tremendous swipe, sent it flying back in the other direction. A lithe shape leaped up from the grass to catch it. Its tabby pelt glowed in the moonlight. Hollypaw's heart sank like a rock. Heatherpaw!

"You don't seem surprised." Cinderpaw had slid in beside her and was peering down into the grassy dip.

Hollypaw shook her head. "I'm not." Reluctantly she wriggled out from the heather. "Lionpaw!" she called.

Lionpaw and Heatherpaw froze, staring at each other in alarm. The moss ball fell to the ground.

"What are you doing here?" Hollypaw demanded.

Slowly Lionpaw tore his gaze from Heatherpaw's and turned to face his sister. His eyes sparked with defiance. "What are *you* doing here?"

"Looking for you!"

"*Spying* on me!"

Hollypaw flinched. "You shouldn't be here, playing with her!" She glared at Heatherpaw.

"Why not? She's just a friend."

"A friend from another Clan!"

"*You're* friends with Willowpaw!"

"I don't sneak off every night to see her."

Lionpaw opened his mouth to object, but no words came out. Hollypaw knew she had won the argument. But her brother's eyes did not concede anything. They shone with rage. He turned to Heatherpaw. "I'd better go."

Heatherpaw dipped her head. "I know," she sighed.

Hollypaw clenched her teeth as Lionpaw brushed muzzles with the WindClan apprentice. Did he really believe it was just friendship that brought him here?

Lionpaw padded up the slope and glared at Cinderpaw. "Did you have to tell the whole Clan?" he hissed at Hollypaw.

Cinderpaw flicked her tail. "I just came to make sure Hollypaw was safe," she explained. "No one else knows."

"And they won't know," Hollypaw added, "so long as you stay away from Heatherpaw."

Lionpaw glared at her. "Is that a threat?"

Hollypaw backed away. She had never seen Lionpaw this angry. Even when they had quarreled as kits, there had always been a lighthearted twinkle in his eyes. But not now. His eyes were cold as stars.

"If you continue meeting Heatherpaw, I will have to tell Brambleclaw," she insisted, trying not to let her voice tremble.

Lionpaw bristled.

"There's a good reason why the warrior code forbids mixing with cats from other Clans," Hollypaw went on. "How can you be loyal to your own Clan when your heart lies in another?"

"Are you accusing me of disloyalty?" Lionpaw flattened his ears.

"I know you'd never be disloyal," Hollypaw mewed. "But you're making it difficult for yourself. That's why you must stop this." It was hard enough having kin in another Clan without deliberately making friends outside the forest. Weren't Lionpaw's Clanmates enough for him?

A low growl sounded in Lionpaw's throat. He barged past Hollypaw and padded toward the trees. Hollypaw felt Cinderpaw's tail run along her flank, smoothing her ruffled fur.

"He'll get over it," Cinderpaw promised.

"I hope so," Hollypaw sighed. She knew she'd done the right thing, but she hadn't expected Lionpaw to react so angrily, as if he believed that he'd done nothing wrong. Would he ever forgive her?

SEEKERS

THE QUEST BEGINS

"*A long, long time ago, long* before bears walked the earth, a frozen sea shattered into pieces, scattering tiny bits of ice across the darkness of the sky. Each of those pieces of ice contains the spirit of a bear, and if you are good, and brave, and strong, one day your spirit will join them."

Kallik leaned against her mother's hind leg, listening to the story she had heard so many times before. Beside her, her brother, Taqqiq, stretched, batting at the snowy walls of the den with his paws. He was always restless when the weather trapped them inside.

"When you look carefully at the sky," Kallik's mother continued, "you can see a pattern of stars in the shape of the Great Bear, Silaluk. She is running around and around the Pathway Star."

"Why is she running?" Kallik chipped in. She knew the

answer, but this was the part of the story where she always asked.

"Because she is being chased," Nisa said in a hushed voice. "Three hunters pursue her: Robin, Chickadee, and Moose Bird. They chase her for many moons, all through the warm days, until the end of burn-sky. Then, as the warmth begins to leave the earth, they finally catch up to her.

"They gather around her and strike the fatal blow with their spears. The heart's blood of the Great Bear falls to the ground, and everywhere it falls the leaves on the trees turn red and yellow. Some of the blood falls on Robin's chest, and that is why the bird has a red breast."

"Does the Great Bear die?" breathed Taqqiq.

"She does," Nisa replied. Kallik shivered. Every time she heard this story it frightened her all over again. Her mother went on.

"All through the long, cold months of snow-sky, Silaluk's skeleton lies buried under the ice. But then burn-sky returns, and the Great Bear is reborn as the ice melts and the bear spirits are freed into the sky. And then the three hunters gather, and the hunt begins all over again, season after season."

Kallik snuggled into her mother's soft white fur. The walls of the den curved up and around them, making a sheltering cave of snow that Kallik could barely glimpse in the dark, although it was only a few pawlengths from her nose. Outside a fierce wind howled across the ice, sending tendrils of freezing air through the entrance tunnel into their den. Kallik was glad they didn't have to be out there tonight.

Inside the den, she and her brother were warm and safe. Kallik wondered if Silaluk had ever had a mother and brother, or a den where she could hide from the storms. If the Great Bear had a family to keep her safe, maybe she wouldn't have to run from the hunters. Kallik knew her mother would protect her from anything scary until she was big enough and strong enough and smart enough to protect herself.

Taqqiq batted at Kallik's nose with his large furry paw. "Kallik's scared," he teased. She could make out his eyes gleaming in the darkness.

"Am not!" Kallik protested.

"She thinks robins and chickadees are going to come after her," Taqqiq said with an amused rumble.

"No, I don't!" Kallik growled, digging her claws into the snow. "That's not why I'm scared!"

"Ha! You *are* scared! I knew it!"

Nisa nudged Kallik gently with her muzzle. "Why are you frightened, little one? You've heard the legend of the Great Bear many times before."

"I know," Kallik said. "It's just . . . it reminds me that soon snow-sky will be over, and the snow and ice will all melt away. And then we won't be able to hunt anymore, and we'll be hungry all the time. Right? Isn't that what happens during burn-sky?"

Kallik's mother sighed, her massive shoulders shifting under her snow-white pelt. "Oh, my little star," she murmured. "I didn't mean to worry you." She touched her black nose to Kallik's. "You haven't lived through a burn-sky yet, Kallik. It's not as terrible as it sounds. We'll find a way to survive, even if it means eating berries and grass for a little while."

"What is berries and grass?" Kallik asked.

Taqqiq wrinkled his muzzle. "Does it taste as good as seals?"

"No," Nisa said, "but berries and grass will keep you alive, which is the important thing. I'll show them to you when we reach land." She fell silent. For a few heartbeats, all Kallik could hear was the thin wail of the wind battering at the snowy walls.

She pressed closer to her mother, feeling the warmth radiating from her skin. "Are you sad?" she whispered.

Nisa touched Kallik with her muzzle again. "Don't be afraid," she said, a note of determination in her voice. "Remember the story of the Great Bear. No matter what happens, the ice will always return, and Silaluk will always get back on her paws. She's a survivor, and so are we."

"I can survive anything!" Taqqiq boasted, puffing up his fur. "I'll fight a walrus! I'll swim across an ocean! I'll battle all the white bears we meet!"

"I'm sure you will, dear. But why don't you start by going to sleep?" Nisa suggested.

As Taqqiq circled and scuffled in the snow beside her, making himself comfortable, Kallik rested her chin on her mother's back and closed her eyes. Her mother was right; she didn't need to be afraid. As long as she was with her family, she'd always be safe and warm, like she was right now in their den.

Kallik woke to an eerie silence. Faint light filtered through the walls, casting pale blue and pink shadows on her mother and brother as they slept. At first she thought her ears must be full of snow, but when she shook her head, Nisa grunted in her sleep, and Kallik realized that it was quiet because the storm had finally passed.

"Hey," she said, poking her brother with her nose. "Hey, Taqqiq, wake up. The storm has stopped."

Taqqiq lifted his head with a bleary expression. The fur on one side of his muzzle was flattened, making him look lopsided.

Kallik barked with laughter. "Come on, you big, lazy seal," she said. "Let's go play outside."

"All right!" Taqqiq said, scrambling to his paws.

"Not without me watching you," their mother muttered with her eyes still closed. Kallik jumped. She'd thought Nisa was asleep.

"We won't go far," Kallik promised. "We'll stay right next to the den. Please can we go outside?"

Nisa huffed and the fur on her back quivered like a breeze was passing over it. "Let's all go out," she said. She pushed herself to her massive paws and turned around carefully in the small space, bundling her cubs to one side.

Sniffing cautiously, she nosed her way down the entrance tunnel, brushing away snow that the storm had piled up.

Kallik could see tension in her mother's hindquarters. "I don't know why she's so careful," she whispered to her brother. "Aren't white bears the biggest, scariest animals on the ice? Nothing would dare attack us!"

"Except maybe a bigger white bear, seal-brain!" Taqqiq retorted. "Maybe you haven't noticed how little you are."

Kallik bristled. "I may not be as big as you," she growled, "but I'm just as fierce!"

"Let's find out!" Taqqiq challenged as their mother finally padded out of the tunnel. He sprinted after her, sliding down the slope of the tunnel and scrambling out into the snow.

Kallik leaped to her paws and chased him. A clump of snow fell on her muzzle on her way out of the tunnel and she shook her head vigorously to get it off. The fresh, cold air tingled in her nostrils, full of the scent of fish and ice and faraway clouds. Kallik felt the last of her sleepiness melt away. The ice was where she belonged, not underground, buried alive. She batted a chunk of snow at Taqqiq, who dodged away with a yelp.

He chased her in a circle until she dove into the fresh snow, digging up clumps with her long claws and breathing in the sparkling whiteness. Nisa sat watching them, chuffing occasionally and sniffing the air with a wary expression.

"I'm coming for you," Taqqiq growled at Kallik, crouching low to the ground. "I'm a ferocious walrus, swimming through the water to get you." He pushed himself through the snow with his paws. Kallik braced herself to jump away, but before she could move, he leaped forward and bowled her over. They rolled through the snow, squalling excitedly, until Kallik managed to wriggle out free.

"Ha!" she cried.

"Roar!" Taqqiq bellowed. "The walrus is really angry now!" He dug his paws into the snow, kicking a spray of white ice into their mother's face.

"Hey," Nisa growled. She cuffed Taqqiq lightly with her massive paw, knocking him to the ground. "That's enough snowballing around. It's time to find something to eat."

"Hooray, hooray!" Kallik yipped, jumping around her mother's legs. They hadn't eaten since before the storm, two sunrises ago, and her tummy was rumbling louder than Taqqiq's walrus roar.

The sun was hidden by trails of gray clouds that grew thicker as they walked across the ice, turning into rolls of fog that shrouded the world around them. The only sound Kallik could hear was the snow crunching under their paws. Once she thought she heard a bird calling from up in the sky, but when she looked up she couldn't see anything but drifting fog.

"Why is it so cloudy?" Taqqiq complained, stopping to rub his eyes with his paws.

"The fog is good for us," Nisa said, touching her nose to the ice. "It hides us as we hunt, so our prey won't see us coming."

"I like to see where I'm going," Taqqiq insisted. "I don't like walking in clouds. Everything's all blurry and wet."

"I don't mind the fog," Kallik said, breathing in the heavy, misty air.

"You can ride on my back," Nisa said to her son, nudging him with her muzzle. Taqqiq rumbled happily and scrambled up, clutching at tufts of her snow-white fur to give himself a boost. He stretched out on her back, high above Kallik, and they started walking again.

Kallik liked finding the sharp, cool scent of the ice under the dense, watery smell of the fog. She liked the hint of oceans and fish and salt and faraway sand that drifted through the scents, reminding her of what was below the ice and what it connected to. She glanced up at her mother, who had her nose lifted and was sniffing the air, too. Kallik knew that her mother wasn't just drawing in the crisp, icy smells. Nisa was studying them, searching for a clue that would lead them to food.

"You should both do this, too," Nisa said. "Try to find any smell that stands out from the ice and snow."

Taqqiq just snuggled farther into her fur, but Kallik tried to imitate her mother, swinging her head back and forth as she sniffed. She had to learn everything she could from Nisa so she could take care of herself. At least she still had a long time before that day came—all of burn-sky and the next snow-sky as well.

"Some bears can follow scents for skylengths," Nisa said. "All the way to the edge of the sky and then the next edge and the next."

Kallik wished her nose were that powerful. Maybe it would be one day.

Nisa lifted her head and started trotting faster. Taqqiq dug his claws in to stay on her back. Soon Kallik saw what her mother was heading for—a hole in the ice. She knew what that meant. *Seals!*

Nisa put her nose close to the ice and sniffed all around the edge of the hole. Kallik followed closely, sniffing everywhere her mother sniffed. She was sure she could smell a faint trace of seal. This must be one of the breathing holes where a seal would surface to take a breath before hiding down in the freezing water again.

"Seals are so dumb," Taqqiq observed from his perch on Nisa's back. "If they can't breathe in the water, why do they live in it? Why don't they live on land, like white bears?"

"Perhaps because then it'd be much easier for bears like us to catch them and eat them!" Kallik guessed.

"*Shhhh.* Concentrate," Nisa said. "Can you smell the seal?"

"I think so," Kallik said. It was a furry, blubbery smell, thicker than the smell of fish. It made her mouth water.

"All right," Nisa said, crouching by the hole. "Taqqiq, come down and lie next to your sister." Taqqiq obeyed, sliding off her back and padding over to Kallik. "Be very quiet," Nisa instructed them. "Don't move, and don't make a sound."

Kallik and Taqqiq did as she said. They had done this several times before, so they knew what to do. The first time, Taqqiq had gotten bored and started yawning and fidgeting. Nisa had cuffed him and scolded him, explaining that his noise would scare away the only food they'd seen in days. By now the cubs were both nearly as good at staying quiet as their mother was.

Kallik watched the breathing hole, her ears pricked and her nose keenly aware of every change in the air. A small wind blew drifts of snow across the ice, and the fog continued to roll around all three bears, making Kallik's fur feel wet and heavy.

After a while she began to get restless. She didn't know how her mother could stand to do nothing for such a long time, watching and watching in case the seal broke through the water. The chill of the ice below her was beginning to seep through Kallik's thick fur. She had to force herself not to shiver and send vibrations through the ice that might warn the seal they were there.

She stared past the tip of her nose at the ice around the breathing hole. The dark water below the surface lapped at the jagged edge. It was strange to think that that same dark water was only a muzzlelength below her, on the other side of the thick ice. The ice seemed so strong and solid, as if it went down forever. . . .

Strange shadows and shapes seemed to dance inside the ice, forming bubbles and whorls. It was odd—ice was white from far away but nearly clear up close and full of patterns. It almost seemed like things were living inside the ice. Right below her front paws, for instance, there was a large, dark bubble slowly moving from one side to the other. Kallik stared at it, wondering if it was the spirit of a white bear trapped in the ice. One that hadn't made it as far as the stars in the sky.